A Sense of Rage

Richard D. Thielmann

Copyright © 2007 by Richard D. Thielmann

All rights reserved. No part of this book shall be reproduced or transmitted in any form or by any means, electronic, mechanical, magnetic, photographic including photocopying, recording or by any information storage and retrieval system, without prior written permission of the publisher. No patent liability is assumed with respect to the use of the information contained herein. Although every precaution has been taken in the preparation of this book, the publisher and author assume no responsibility for errors or omissions. Neither is any liability assumed for damages resulting from the use of the information contained herein.

This is a work of fiction. Names, characters, places, and incidents either are the product of the author's imagination or are used fictitiously. Any resemblance to actual events or locales or persons, living or dead, is entirely coincidental.

ISBN 0-7414-4353-8

Published by:

INFINITY
PUBLISHING.COM

1094 New DeHaven Street, Suite 100
West Conshohocken, PA 19428-2713
Info@buybooksontheweb.com
www.buybooksontheweb.com
Toll-free (877) BUY BOOK
Local Phone (610) 941-9999
Fax (610) 941-9959

Printed in the United States of America

Printed on Recycled Paper

Published February 2008

Also by the Author

A Matter of Revenge

The Price of Redemption

Prolog

Kyle Dixon stood alone on a hill above Murietta, California, the warm wind pouring over him with a rush. He ignored the few stars visible in the moonless night sky as he focused on the scene below. The lights of civilization spread in all directions. His frustration was as immense and dominating as the powerful view that confronted him. Here was the ugly vision of suburban sprawl, a glowing, pulsating symbol of a modern world he hated. They called it progress, he called it destruction and desecration. Raping the land, defiling nature, absolutely ruining his memories of how it once looked. He could also see the seemingly endless snake of lights on I-10 and its convergence with I-215 and his mouth drew tight, his throat constricted. He sipped from the water bottle he had carried loosely in his left hand, but it did not help his throat; he was too angry. He spit and it blew away to oblivion. It was an act of conviction as much as defiance. He made up his mind it was time for action. Time for drastic measures, time to put his plan into effect. It was time for the awakening of society he felt was so absolutely necessary.

"They shall suffer," he said out loud, "and the suffering shall serve notice of what is required."

Was this the declaration of a madman? Perhaps; maybe not. However, it was at the very least a declaration of a man who could no longer contain his frustration. It was his anguish over a litany of grievances that had festered for a long time. Grievances that meant the ruin of the environment and spoiled his world. It was an environment diminished for everyone. It was a merciless progression of change touted as society advancing. For him it was poisoning our very future.

The land was being violated, polluted, and misused. Houses, apartments, shopping malls, restaurants, car dealers, golf courses, and much more spilled across the land like a giant Monopoly set splattered everywhere you looked. There were acres and acres of parking lots that drained rain water away instead of soaking into the ground, that consumed more energy by being lighted, and that formed adverse microclimates from absorbed and radiated heat. These hateful parking lots were paved in order to accommodate the thousands upon thousands of cars and trucks and SUVs that sucked up way too much gasoline and spewed way too much pollution. All of this growth, all of this progress, contributed to the tremendously wanton waste of resources. Flaunting and wallowing in the excessive use of electrical power and of water followed the endless construction. This was a frightening reality he rejected; he did not want this so-called progress. He would not have it. There was a solution.

And what had Dr. Simmons told him?

"You cannot change the world to suit you," the good therapist had softly reminded him.

Kyle had no answer for that concept. He merely sat stoically, silently refusing to accept that possibility. He had his own perceptions of how society should behave. A skewed reality to be sure, but nevertheless, a belief he defiantly clung to with the tenacity of a pit bull. He worked tirelessly to combat the progress he hated.

Kyle would not accept his place in the broader scheme of things in which he was powerless to change what was happening, nor face the fact he had little control over much of anything. Even with Dr. Simmons' help, he did not understand how alienated he was. After all, he was successful in recruiting other powerless-feeling folks who believed progress was ruining just about everything. So he wasn't alone with his beliefs, right?

He thought he could change things, that he could control the future. It would be the end result of his crusade, a plan of action he had considered for a long time. He saw himself as the modern-day Don Quixote battling for environmental and social justice without considering what justice and whose justice it was.

He had disconnected himself from the reality Dr. Simmons had so diligently tried to help him recognize. Now the time had come to appease his sense of rage.

1.

A mangy, stray dog loped across the parking lot of the Cloverfield convenience store just ahead of a Cadillac Escalade that had swiftly entered the lot. The Escalade braked slightly to avoid clipping the nondescript mutt before parking in a slot away from the store entrance. There were three other cars and a pickup truck also parked in front of the store and no cars at the gas pumps. It was almost ten thirty in the morning, a searing hot midweek day in Parris, California, light traffic going by the place. Four men in the Escalade sat surveying the store. Kyle Dixon was in the right front passenger seat.

"This shouldn't take too long," the man behind the wheel said, as he pulled a ski mask over his face.

"Not long at all," Kyle responded, pulling on his mask.

The other two men also slipped on their masks.

Kyle and the three others moved quickly out of the Escalade and entered the store. They wore gloves and each carried a black automatic pistol. The young Hispanic woman behind the counter knew right away what was happening.

"Please don't shoot me," she yelled.

Her manager, a short, older Hispanic woman raised her hands and appeared ready to burst into tears. She said nothing.

"Get the money out of the registers," Lippert ordered, "and you'll be okay." Mark Lippert was the Escalade driver.

Kyle said nothing, but pointed the other two men towards the customers.

"Everybody git over here and put yer money in this bag."

The speaker was Ellis Wilson and he had pulled a plastic grocery bag from his pocket and hung it on a snack rack. He sounded menacing and jabbed the gun for emphasis. The five customers dutifully deposited their wallets in the bag.

"Now move on back there by the cooler."

They quickly headed for the rear of the store.

Lippert had also produced a plastic bag and the two women employees emptied the cash drawers.

"Get on back there with the others...and stay there. We'll shoot anyone that tries to follow us."

"Thanks for the donation," Kyle yelled as they left the store.

The four men were back in the Escalade and gone before a license plate number could be noted or the vehicle determined. This had been a well-practiced maneuver, the location well scouted.

"What was the time?" Lippert asked as he drove.

"Four minutes and thirty-three seconds," Kyle answered. "Very reasonable for our purposes. Better not to rush things, but on the other hand, we don't want to dally."

"Dally?" Wilson laughed.

"Yes, dally. Means to waste time or loiter...hang around."

"Oh...yeah." Wilson shook his head.

Kyle was annoyed the man had questioned him like that, but made no more comment. He needed this man's help even if he were a dullard. He laid his head back on the headrest to forget about the stupid question and surveyed the leather interior of the plush SUV.

The silver Escalade had been an easy lift for Ellis Wilson, a practiced car thief. He was, in fact, a formidable thief no matter what it was to be stolen. Ted had dropped him off at a shopping center parking lot on the outskirts of Riverside where the SUV was stolen, then drove to a mall in Temecula where he met Kyle and Lippert. There the three men waited for Ellis to pick them up and move on to the work at hand.

The choice of the Escalade was deliberate, the SUV a symbol of the decadence and waste Kyle hated. The brand was an American icon of self-indulgence and conspicuous consumption. Kyle made a mental note to himself to have Ellis steal a Lexus for their next excursion.

As Lippert drove, the cash was removed from the wallets and all the money emptied into a green nylon athletic bag. The wallets were put in a small tote bag and the plastic bags used for the robbery were pocketed.

"I'll take those wallets," Kyle directed and Wilson handed the bag to him. "There might be something here that is helpful."

It took less than fifteen minutes to get to the next Cloverfield store on the other side of Parris where the whole process was repeated. This time the store had ten customers and two cars at the pumps. Only one of the pump customers came inside the store where she was immediately stripped of her wallet and sent to the rear of the place. Kyle and the others were gone before the victims could check out their vehicle. Again, Kyle had called out, "Thanks for the donation," as they exited.

"Next stop...Valley Citizens Bank." Kyle chuckled after he said the name. "This is a bigger challenge."

"Just stay calm, guys, and it'll work the way we figured." Lippert sounded assured when he gave this advice that was intended for the two men behind him.

Lippert parked the Escalade in a spot that could not be seen from inside the bank and also allowed the four to get to the entrance without their approach being noticed. This way, at the last moment, they could slip on their masks and enter without showing their faces.

Ted Sloan was over the counter and behind the three young, female cashiers before a word was spoken, before an alarm could be sounded, and before the other two female employees working at desks across from the counter could react defensively. It was a stunning, blunt surprise and none of the women were expecting to be robbed. The five women were ordered to lie on the floor in the middle of the bank.

"Where do ya keep yer purses?" Wilson demanded.

"Take the bank's money," one of the prone young women yelled, "don't take mine."

"There's a loyal employee," Wilson sneered. "Where?" He pointed his automatic at the woman. "Keep your face down. Where?"

"In the room back there," one of them muttered.

Kyle stood over the women as Wilson found the purses and emptied them of wallets and, in two instances, loose cash and change.

"We want to thank you ladies for the donation," Kyle chirped, obviously quite pleased with himself.

"Donation for what?" one of the women asked.

"To help wake up the masses," Kyle yelled, "to make everyone aware."

None of the women responded to his seemingly incomprehensible answer.

Lippert and Sloan took all the bills from the cash drawers and the men were gone. The women never saw the Escalade and never were able to describe the men. The robbery took slightly less than eight minutes.

Lippert drove casually, carefully back to the large shopping mall on the east side of Temecula where he dropped Kyle off at his car with the money and all of the wallets. He took Ellis and Ted to Ted's truck and then found a spot to park the stolen Escalade. He walked away from the SUV, over three rows, down another fifty yards, and was picked up by Kyle. They all headed for the ranch.

It had been a busy morning.

2.

"Well, this kind of thing is not quite a science and I wouldn't want to keep doing it on a regular basis, but it sure seems easy if you plan, prepare, and execute."

Kyle made this declaration to Lippert knowing the man would understand what he meant. Mark would know that he was not being flip or boastful with the remark. He was merely stating the obvious simplicity of seemingly anonymous random theft.

"We've created a pattern," Lippert sighed, "the cops will figure it out. The MO, our MO is now an imprint. We can't do it this way again."

"Right, right. But I'm not sure…" Kyle hesitated. "I don't think we need to do this again. We'll have to check our numbers. It takes money to buy what we need and support our friends out in the desert. We have a few purchases to make yet. And two significant jobs to do. At night…that could involve…" He stopped to think about what he wanted to say. "It might involve some resistance. We have to be prepared for that."

"We'll do what we need to do," Lippert assured him. "Ellis and Ted know what's at stake."

"Post did a nice job of covering those Cloverfield stores for us didn't he?" Kyle asked the question with real admiration for the information they had received.

"You bet. Big help, big help. No doubt about it"

Larry Post was a recruited sympathizer, ready to help the crusade in any way he could. He was one of dozens who had been influenced by Kyle's zeal and intensity about protecting the environment. Post was a Frito-Lay driver who delivered snacks to Cloverfield stores and other locations in the area which made it simple for him to detail which places should be hit. He was invaluable help.

"And Em gave us the bank," Lippert added. He was referring to Emery Whitten, friend and fellow believer in their cause. Whitten, a smooth-talking salesman who sold irrigation equipment, was another perfect candidate to provide needed information from his travels around Riverside County.

Kyle and Lippert were seated in well-worn, overstuffed chairs on the side porch of the ranch house. They faced west towards the rows and rows of full-grown avocado trees. The sun was high and two hours away from moving out beyond the porch roof overhang. A cool breeze wafted over them that had wandered in from the ocean through the backdrop of hills. They were seated in their own world of contentment. These were two friends who had known each other for over thirty years and had roiled together in the anguish each felt about what was happening in the world. They were emotional when it came to their sense of doing combat against unwanted change and their desire to make the world, their world, a better place.

The ranch pushed out over rolling hills a few miles northwest of Fallbrook. The eastern perimeter of Camp Pendleton was not far away. It was a picturesque rural setting of lush, green foliage, a tranquil escape from Southern California's population crush. The eighty acres of land comprising the ranch had been purchased years before by Ramsey Dixon, Kyle's father, who used the place for just such a getaway. Ramsey, an aeronautical engineer for Lockheed, owned the property for several years before seriously getting into the business of avocado harvesting. And in the early years, the whole family came here from Santa Monica for the pleasant weekends: Ramsey, wife Doris, Kyle, and daughter Kelli. But as Ramsey became more involved with making the ranch a real avocado producer, Doris stopped coming on the weekend jaunts. Kyle and Kelli continued to accompany their father, however, and their recollections of good times there with Ramsey were fondly retained. Eventually, those memories were aggrandized to almost mystical proportions for both of them.

As adults, they could not understand how it had all changed and their father had changed and the ranch stopped being fun and their father stopped being the nice man he once was.

Later on, after Ramsey and Doris had divorced and after he retired, he lived at the ranch most of the time while still maintaining a small apartment in Santa Monica. Four years ago, in somewhat fragile health, he deeded the property to Kyle so there would be no inheritance problems when he died. Two years later, he was found by one of the hired hands lying among the avocado trees a hundred yards or so from the house. The emergency medical team got him to the hospital barely alive and he died the next day without regaining consciousness. Coronary arrest was the official cause. Kyle no longer shared the ranch with Ramsey.

"That's right, Em knows his stuff," Kyle affirmed.

"What's next?" Lippert asked. It was a soft question meant to extend the conversation. What they wanted to accomplish was no secret, but the details still floated in Kyle's head. It was a master plan that only was revealed as they went along.

"Mark…," Kyle paused. He tapped the long-neck beer to his chin. "I think we have enough kerosene and ammonium nitrate. Enough for three serious strikes. We have enough weapons and ammo to cover ourselves. But we need to get plastic explosives. I know where to get that…you know where I mean. Then we can execute Fire and Brimstone."

"What?" Lippert sat up.

"I'm calling our action plan Fire and Brimstone. Very Biblical, very appropriate, I think."

"Kinda corny if you ask me."

"I suppose it is, but what we are about is just that. Fire and Brimstone."

"Okay, if you say so."

"You knew I meant Gladstone. About the plastic."

"Of course."

"We go onto their facility and get the stuff. I know where it is, I know how we can get it."

"We can do it," Lippert moaned, "but as a former employee, you'll be on the suspect list. They'll get to you eventually. They would figure it would have to be an inside job. Only an employee or former employee would know they have plastic and know where it was kept."

"You give the authorities too much credit for smarts. They stumble into most of their successes..."

"Gladstone has its own security, you know that."

"True," Kyle agreed, "they do. Very good security. So we have to work quickly...make the other parts of the plan come together very soon. Our friends up at Chiriaco are ready to move. They know what they have to accomplish. All we have to do is get them some plastic. Enough to make a big boom. Hayfield is the start, then we roll from there. We get the Perris Dam the same night and it all begins. We begin to raise the awareness of what society needs, what is necessary."

"Have you written the letter?

"I'm two-thirds done. I'll finish it in the next few days."

"We use snail mail?"

"Yes. E-mailing is too dangerous even from a library. They could still trace you there."

"When do we go into Gladstone's?" Lippert took a long draw on his beer after he spoke.

"Soon. We need a little more rehearsal time with Ellis and Ted first before we hit. Soon...soon. Early next week. Tuesday or Wednesday. We can be ready by then."

3.

The idea of being a modern-day sort of Robin Hood appealed to Kyle. He was stealing to help a worthwhile cause that would benefit everyone. But it was not lost on him that he considered himself a mixture of historical analogies: Don Quixote and the bandit of Sherwood Forest. He preferred the later after some deliberation about it. The sheer bombastic nature, pure pomposity, and downright foolishness of such thoughts never occurred to him. He took himself very seriously. The results of his self-assessment, however, were very serious to the victims, some of whom came very close to being shot by one or more of the three men who accompanied Kyle on each of the robberies. Also very serious for the Riverside County Sheriff's department which was responsible for the territory in which each of the crimes had been committed.

Henry Gonzales, lieutenant in the Special Investigations section, had given the robberies very serious attention. He already had a prodigious file and had begun to chart each of the hits on a map in his office. He was frustrated. Over a several month period, fifteen convenience stores and three banks had been targeted. The take was estimated to be in the neighborhood of $65,000.00. There was scant information and only sketchy descriptions of the robbers. There were no witness to the vehicles of escape, and of course, no license plate numbers.

There was, on the other hand, a thread of similarity that linked each of the hits in question. A signal of continuity, a mark that it was the same guys just by the way each went down. And at most of the crime scenes, witnesses remembered hearing one of the gang of four men thanking them "for their donation."

"What the hell does that mean?" Gonzales asked his assistant, Don Borders.

Borders shook his head and shrugged his shoulders; he did not know what to say.

"Almost every place they hit one of those guys said that. Thanks for your donation."

Borders stayed silent.

"Donation for what? Probably the same guy saying it, don't you think? I think so. A ritual, maybe a declaration, maybe a joke like he was giving everybody the finger for his own personal reasons. But suppose the guy was serious. What are the donations for?"

"One of the bank witnesses said she asked that and the guy answered 'to help wake up the masses and make everybody aware,'" Borders said.

"Yeah, this may be some self-righteous bastard who is doing this for…" He paused and stared out the window at the city buildings that crowded into his view.

"For a cause?" Borders offered quietly.

"For a cause. Exactly," Gonzales confirmed. He looked at the map again. "For a cause. Right. This is some kind of goddamn trouble maker, not some small time perps hitting just for the money. For these guys the money means something else."

"Gotta have the money to buy something they want," Borders said, with a matter-of-fact air. "Something for their cause."

"Yes, Don, I think you may be right. Now, what is their cause? Wake up the masses to what?"

"Beats me."

"Yeah, me too, for right now."

Borders waited, shoulders sagged, his mouth slightly agape, waiting to hear what needed to be done.

Gonzales stood staring at the map, analyzing the relationship of the pins he placed there to mark the crimes. He stepped closer and moved his index finger from one to another in an offhand way.

"All eighteen pins were in an area that was outlined by the cities of Perris, Sun City, Menifee, Murrieta Hot Springs, and Lake Elsinore. Most of the C-stores were Cloverfield brand with the rest independents. The banks were Moreno National, Murietta First National, and Valley Citizens. No big name stores, no big name banks. They picked their targets very carefully. Made it easy for themselves. Each location had ease of access, low traffic area, and away from most other businesses. In most of the cases, stand-alone buildings. That cut down on the chances for witnesses."

"What do you think," Borders asked, "we re-interview the witnesses?"

"Yes. And we talk to the FBI."

4.

Kyle Dixon was good-looking in an almost feminine way. He was blonde, blue-eyed, and six feet two inches of muscular athletic build that had not been put to much use other than tramping around the ranch and carrying protest signs. He was well-spoken, articulate and could spout the facts and figures of environmental devastation with great facility. He always dressed well, although casually, and was particularly conscious of his appearance and its affect on the donors to his causes. He was fond of smoking dope and drinking beer and, unbeknownst to his father had a prodigious sexual appetite. He was intelligent, complex, and energetic.

He has been counseled on and off for several years by Dr. Alan Simmons, whose third ex-wife, Gloria, age fifty, is a close friend of Kyle's sister Kelli. Kyle sometimes paid attention to Simmons' counsel, although generally he merely listened and went his own way. He continued the contact with Simmons because he felt that the relationship provided him with an outlet for his conflicting views of the world. No one else fit the role. Not his father surely, nor Mark nor his sister nor even his mother. There were many feelings about which he could confide in his mother, but not everything. With Simmons, everything was fair game. He wanted Simmons' counsel, he wanted his time when he wanted it.

The relationship Kyle had with his father was deceptive to each of them and to most who knew them. On his part, Ramsey had convinced himself that he was an attentive, caring parent who loved his son. In his mind they had a great relationship. Kyle, on the other hand, created a fantasy relationship about his father. He convinced himself there was some special bond that did not account for the man's austere nature, his preoccupation with airplane design and his own pleasures, and simply, the utter lack of time father and son spent together. Kyle overlooked all of that and instead enjoyed a different, more satisfying perspective. Others assumed all was well between father and son. This was because Kyle continued to spend weekends with Ramsey at the ranch long after Doris quit going and beyond the time Kelli had decided ranch weekends were a waste of time. "I don't want to be an avocado rancher," she asserted.

Ramsey was disappointed in how Kyle's life floundered; his expectations for his bright and clever son had been so high. He never gained a sense of how his son "lost his way," as he expressed it, he only knew that Kyle was "promise unfulfilled." He also grew concerned that at age thirty Kyle had yet to find a wife and, in fact, rarely dated. At least as far as he knew his son rarely dated. Kyle kept that part of his life hidden from him. His son had grown to be a mystery he could not solve.

Kyle had been an excellent student, readily accepted to Cal Tech where he attended for several years, with plans to be an engineer like his father. But he lost direction somehow, never really focused on a program that suited him, and did not graduate. He drifted from one low-level technical job to another before joining Gladstone International as a technician. He left that job soon after Ramsey had deeded the ranch to him. It was his chance to fulfill his destiny as a leader in the environmental movement.

Mark Lippert got him pointed toward environmental activism. Mark and Kyle had been friends all through high school, and it was Mark who first was interested in pollution of all kinds. He talked incessantly about the evils of pollution. Pollution was his cause, his hobby, and his total preoccupation. It was sort of like someone caught up in and completely immersed in sports or antique car restoration. Not enough was being done about pollution and he was determined to change all of that. Eventually, he got Kyle interested. Little by little, bit by bit, Kyle took on pollution and waste and all of the other key environmental issues and would eventually surpass Mark with his zeal and intensity for saving planet earth. Another incident solidified his feelings and generated his angst for protecting society. He met Laurie Hart. It was at a demonstration organized to protest the demolition of houses to make way for a parking lot. He went with Mark to the protest, each carrying a homemade sign that screamed for the salvation of the neighborhood. No parking lot here, bellowed their mantra.

Laurie was there with her homemade sign, indignantly angry and loudly vocal. She spotted Kyle and was attracted, realizing she had not seen him at a protest before this one. She pushed her way over to him, between Kyle and Mark, and introduced herself.

"Haven't seen you before," she said, "I'm Laurie…"

She waited for him to respond, but he looked away and said something to Mark. "What's this" or something like that.

Mark shrugged.

"Laurie. What's your name?" She stood her ground and stayed after him. She was not easily offended. She should have been, but was not.

He looked down at her with a bland expression of little interest. He was currently involved with two young women romantically, simultaneously, who did not know each other, who were gorgeous-looking beauties, sexually giving, and who demanded little from him. A third attractive woman was a part-time dalliance. There next to him, this creature, demanding his name, was a short, plump young woman with long, shining brunette hair and beautifully pursed lips. Luscious, untinted red lips that were full and poised for action. She was a sharp contrast to the three other women who occupied his time. He wondered what the hell the deal was with this unappealing woman who he instinctively knew would not be compliant to his sexual demands.

And yet...and yet there was something that happened within him which he could not understand. He knew he liked her aggression, her confidence, and her energy. Those were appealing, those attracted him, and he knew it right there. But she was dumpy and she dressed like a frump without context to style or convention. Still, her face was very attractive with violet eyes that burned into him, Superman's x-ray eyes that penetrated his soul, that took him apart and pieced him together again in her vision of an attractive man. She was satisfied with him. He wondered what the hell was happening.

"Kyle," he said, stupefied by the sound of his own voice. "This is my first...my first event...my first protest. My buddy got me to come here..."

Mark smiled and bowed his head in acknowledgement.

"Let's go over there," she pointed, "I've got some stuff in my bag."

She had indicated an open space between two houses and the three of them walked over there and sat down among the weeds and discarded trash that had accumulated over the years. She pulled out a plastic bag that contained several already-rolled joints.

"Jesus," Mark hissed, "put that stuff away."

"Okay," she said calmly, "don't get in a knot."

"I thought you might have some hot tea or something," Kyle said. "We don't do drugs. And we like a beer now and then. Caught with drugs, you get bad problems."

"I know," she said, sadly, "I know."

"Well..."

"I like to smoke, like the take, like the pause, like the lift...you know, the jam...the smooth feeling in my head."

"See you," Kyle said.

The truth was, both Kyle and Mark were already heavily into drugs and booze, but they assumed that this person who called herself Laurie was a cop or DEA plant to get someone on a drug charge and discredit their cause. They were wary of the authorities.

"Take it easy," she said as she dropped the plastic bag into her backpack. "There, it's gone."

"Thanks," Mark said, "We don't want any trouble."

"You a cop?" Kyle asked quickly.

"What?" The girl looked stunned.

"We thought you might be a narc," Mark said.

"God, no," she laughed. "Here look at this."

She pulled her wallet from her backpack and showed them her drivers license and student ID card from UCLA.

"It pays to be careful," she said, "I hate getting busted. I've been busted a couple of times and it stinks."

They talked, she showed her intensity about environmental stuff and they were impressed. Kyle wanted more from her and over time there would be more.

5.

A slash of light cut across Jim Fuller's office as the morning sun brought the day hard onto his world. Bank robbery was a continuing problem, but in the last few weeks there had been three hits that had gotten his attention. There was a similarity of MO that included the slick in and out of the robbers and the fact that one of the perps had thanked the staff for "the donation." Strange. A signature, most likely inadvertent, but nonetheless a way to tag the same guys with those crimes.

Fuller was the Special Agent in Charge of the FBI Riverside office. His case load had been increased by these robberies and that was an annoyance. He had bigger fish to fry, he thought, so this diversion was crap. The focus now for his office was on anti-terrorism efforts; that was more important. Chasing bank robbers was mundane and outside the charter with which he was operating, which he knew could get him promoted. But the responsibility of going after bank robbers was with the FBI and he could not shrug off that duty as much as he would like to forget them.

"What do we know?" he snarled at Andy Tobin, the agent who assisted him most of the time. "What the hell are these guys doing? They're not getting big bucks."

"Hoping for more I suppose…maybe they don't care"

"What do you mean?"

"Maybe they're just looking to get what they can and move on. Maybe they are not…"

"What?"

Maybe they're something else. Just looking to get small stakes to pay…to pay their bills.

"I don't follow you."

"Supposing they don't expect to make a bit hit, supposing they just want to get a series of smaller hits to reach a target number."

"Come on, guys don't rob banks to get small amounts, they rob banks to score big."

"Maybe not. All I'm saying is that maybe these guys know the take is not going to be big, but the risk is small at each location, and if they do enough of them the total take is what they want. These guys are very accomplished, very smooth, you've got to admit that. All three went down with minimum time and no hassle from the staff. Our boys were in and out in a snap."

"What's going on?"

"They're…they're just accumulating the takes."

"That's stupid."

"Perhaps. Perhaps not."

"What do we know for sure," Fuller demanded. "Any ethnicity? Mexicans, blacks?"

"No, these are white guys. They take the bank by surprise, grab the open cash and money from the employees, and are gone. They're masked, so there are no personal identifications, and no one ID's the getaway car. Same all three times. No prints, no IDs, no witnesses outside the banks…nothing. Mighty slick."

"What do you make of what the one says?"

"You mean about thanking for the donation?"

"Yeah."

"It sort of ties in with what I was saying."

"How so?" Fuller's brow wrinkled when he asked.

"Well, it's like they're collecting. They need a certain amount and are content to get smaller takes until they get what they need. My guess is that when they reach what they need, they're done. Bingo, they stop. I think they're robbing banks for a reason."

"Maybe more than just banks," Fuller conjectured, "maybe they're hitting other businesses. They're all over that outlying area away from the city of Riverside. Why don't you touch base with that guy Gonzales over at the county Sheriff's office and see if he has anything going on."

"Roger, that's probably a good idea," Tobin replied.

6.

"She's in your office," Christy said with a hushed voice as if she were announcing some secret that needed to be kept secret.

"Who?" Kyle whispered in return.

"That girl Carrie. The one who shows up at all the rallies."

He nodded with a frown. He knew the circumstance did not require such hush-hush treatment, but knew also she was fiercely protective of him. She felt he needed to be warned. After all, Christy had no idea that Carrie Barnes was living with him in the small apartment he had rented just blocks from the office. Certainly, Carrie had no idea that he was having sex with Christy before they had met. Bedding both of these women without either knowing or suspecting was testimony to Kyle's ability to compartmentalize. In that, he was a master.

Kyle moved by her desk which stood to one side of the cluttered reception area. Magazines, stacks of pamphlets and brochures, video tapes, boxes of envelopes and stationary, envelopes stuffed and ready to be mailed, correspondence to be filed, and an assortment of odds and ends contributed to the mess. There was barely room on her desk for the computer terminal and keyboard. The printer on the table behind her was not visible underneath several three-ring binders. His own office matched this one for messiness.

He closed his office door behind him to find Carrie looking out the window. She appeared to be unhappy and he expected that. Whenever he disappeared for a few days, she sulked.

"Where have you been," she demanded in a quiet, but firmly measured voice.

"At the ranch...getting more donations..."

It would be nice if you would let me know when you're going to be gone like that. I worry. Something could happen to you. Something could be wrong. How would I know?"

"Things happened quickly...you were at work. It's how it happened...sort of rolled out."

She flopped down into the chair in front of his desk. There was no point in belaboring it; she had said what she wanted to say and he wouldn't apologize nor give any recognition he had done anything wrong. Why waste more time?

"We're getting close to having the plan put in motion," he explained, "I might be away a lot from now on."

She sat staring at him with brown-gray watery eyes, head cocked to one side, frowning. Tall and thin, her body was at all angles with the chair. She was flat-chested with inordinately large nipples constantly on display no matter what she wore. Her dirty straw-blonde hair was pulled back to a pony tail. A recovering alcoholic with a chronic cough, she was still trying to quit smoking.

"I want to help. Its time I got involved for real, 'cause I'm tired of being on the sidelines."

"I think that...," he started.

"You're going to need all the help you can get. I know how to use a gun, you know that."

He had met Carrie Barnes at a small diner where she was a waitress. She was an ex-con who had done time for shooting her boyfriend. She was upset she did not kill him and believed her time in prison was worth the effort. She was passionate about the environment when he struck up a conversation with her. When she found out he was the Executive Director of the Alliance For A Better Environment she became a diligent follower. Diligent enough to move in with him a few weeks later. She was also a committed vegen and to anything natural or organic. Uneducated, but bright, she was described by her parole officer as "quietly dangerous."

"Maybe you're right. Maybe you're right." His mind was whirling.

Perhaps it would be best if she was at the ranch, he thought. Maybe the time is right to quit the apartment and stay fulltime in Fallbrook. He could leave the office to Christy on a day-to-day basis and come in here once a week or so. After the plan gets rolling he wasn't sure he wanted to spend time in this office; in fact, he knew he did not. He would only come by to pick up the contribution checks and get those cashed.

"Let's look at this," he said angrily as he picked up an envelope from a small pile on his desk that Christy had ready for him, "see how much this amounts to."

He slit the envelope open and pulled out the letter and check enclosed. The check was made out to The Committee To Stop Urban Sprawl.

"Ten goddamn dollars. This is what I have had to contend with since we began operating to work on the people's behalf four years ago. Four years of dribs and drabs coming in for the most part. Oh yeah, there were those fund raisers in Santa Monica, but that was chump change compared to what we needed. A pamphlet here, a brochure there, a few public service ads on TV…it's not been enough for the people of paradise to get the picture. Well, they'll get the picture once we show them the future, what happens when they try to live their paradise lives without electricity and water…"

"Shhh, keep your voice down," Carrie cautioned, "you don't know who might hear."

"The money has never come in fast enough, mostly small amounts" he continued. "Citizens For Reasonable Change, that was the only action group that brought in any real money. All those rich, arrogant friends of my sister. Their philosophy is pay money to some charity to handle things for them. Then they won't have to worry about the environment anymore because the charity will take care of it. Damn stupid. It takes everyone to be on board, it takes laws, zoning code changes, cutting out the special privileges to contractors. Damn, it takes a whole society and it takes politicians. It takes everybody to get the picture of what we are up against. That's why we have to act, that's why we have to put Fire and Brimstone into full motion. It's why we have to take draconian measures to turn this thing around."

"Fire and Brimstone?" she asked, shrugging her shoulders.

"Is that all you got out of what I said. Yes, Fire and Brimstone...Biblical, in Genesis, like Sodom and Gomorrah. You've heard of Sodom and Gomorrah?"

"No," she said blankly.

"Forget it...take my word for it, it's Biblical."

"That makes it the thing to do...?"

"Forget it, we have a mission to carry out and that is all that is important."

"Someone could get hurt. You're going to bomb some stuff, people could get killed."

"That's not our worry when we have a cause as important as ours. Results are important, getting results. If we can get people to be aware of what is at stake then everything is justified."

"How can you do what you want to do...build bombs and shut stuff off?"

"Building a placement is a simple matter," he said smugly as he folded his arms, "if you have the technical skills. I have those skills. Getting the placement to the target is the real challenge."

He picked up the phone and punched speed-dial to the ranch.

"Ted, yeah, let me talk to Mark." He opened another envelope as he waited. "Hah, fifteen bucks and a nice note. Quote: All of us in our family are concerned with the environment. We wanted the Alliance to know that it has our support. Keep up the good work. Sincerely…Hey, Mark, everything okay? Good, good. Listen, something I hadn't thought of has come up. Yeah. Carrie…she can help us big time. But not from Riverside. She's got to be at the ranch. Yeah. She's coming down this afternoon. She's going to live with us…yeah, I'm going to bail, too. I don't know when I'll see you, but get her settled. Oh, yeah, she'll be sleeping with me. You bet. Talk to you later."

"Thanks," she whispered and came to him and kissed him.

"Go to the diner, tell Benny you're moving back east to be with family and you reluctantly have to quit, get your stuff, and get up to the ranch. Mark will take care of you."

"I know that bedroom," she laughed.

"I know you do, now get going."

She grabbed her purse and headed for the door, then stopped, and came back to his desk and leaned over to him.

"What's your plan after this?"

"What do you mean?"

"What do I mean? I mean, where do we go, what do we do after mission accomplished?"

"I have that all worked out. We'll talk about that at the ranch. Don't worry about it."

"Don't worry? You bet I worry, I grew up worrying. Things aren't all nice and easy like you want them to be."

"Everything has gone to plan so far. There is no reason to think that won't continue. Good planning and smart execution trumps all. You watch. It will all unfold just as I want."

She didn't argue, she smiled, and she left.

Christy came into Kyle's office and hovered over his desk, her large, loosely suspended breasts dangling in from of him as lure to fish. He was eager for the bait and enjoyed the temptation.

"Are you okay?" she sputtered, "I know she puts a lot of pressure on you. All of the radicals do that. They demand to get things done. Are you okay?"

"Christy, we must keep our constituents satisfied. It's how we keep the donations coming in. Each supporter has a right to establish his or her agenda. We need to be able to respond to those agendas."

"Yeah, I guess so," she said, her voice taut and excited.

"Things are going to change, Christy," he intoned, "we need…I need…to be in the field more. Do more grass roots work. Get more support for our causes."

"I know…"

"So the point is…the point is, I won't be around as much as I have been. There are things that need to be accomplished and I can't get those things done here in the office. You know what I mean?"

She did not know what he meant and she stood there stunned, her breasts now pulled up to attention.

"Wow…wow…you've got me…"

"Here is what I want. I want you to come to work and do your job every day even if I don't show up. There's plenty to do. Make sure the office runs smoothly just like it always has, just like you've made it run since you got here. Doesn't matter whether I'm here. I'll check in with you all the time. Once in a while I'll come by and pick up the donation checks. You can let me know when there are enough checks to make my time worthwhile."

"What are you going to be doing?" she asked shyly. "Are you sure everything is okay?"

"Everything is fine. But there are some things that need to be done. I would not kid you about that. But don't worry...this will all work out for us. You'll be part of history and change and our mission for society will get fulfilled."

"Sounds...sounds really exciting."

"It is, sweetheart, very exciting. I've got to get back to work, but we'll...I'll see you at your place tonight. We need to reaffirm our...friendship. Good friends need to stay bonded."

"We can bond tonight," she giggled, "bonding is good."

When she left his office, he punched in the number of Alan Simmons. A machine answered.

"Alan...Kyle. Don't screen me out, I need to talk to you. Today. Get back to me, I'm in my office, you have the number. Call me back...today. I need...to talk. Things are at the brink. I...I...give me a call, damn it."

7.

Alan Simmons' office was designed for seduction. No matter who came into its presence, he wanted them to be seduced into thinking he was erudite, masterful, and the plain, simple savior to solve their problems, salve their frustrations, cure their fears, and calm the waters of their life anxieties.

Kyle knew better. He knew that the calculated warmth and comfort of this office was not sufficient to solve his problems. He had been coming here long enough to know that, and to Simmons' previous office where the ambiance was much the same. But he still came, still wanted to talk to Simmons, still wanted to confide in him, and still wanted this safe outlet for his frustrations, confusions, and pitiable anger.

The furnishings were exquisite, selected in New York by Simmons' interior design consultant. There were muted, sensuous colors and patterns which fostered relaxation and revelation. A broad expanse of window-wall exposed a breathtaking view of Newport Bay with its yachts and waterside condos. The rich were nearby; Kyle liked that. The rich didn't know him or care about what he stood for; Kyle hated that.

This office, in its physicality, its representation, and in its décor was an illusion intended to hide the personal turmoil of Simmons himself. It presented a calm oasis that he desired, and believed his patients desired and needed. He showcased an environment of working surroundings which were a falsehood of contentment. This was his world of healing troubled souls, including his own.

Alan Simmons, Ph.D. licensed therapist, is Kyle's confidante and his father substitute. He knows about the rage within Kyle, knows what this means for Kyle – the why. In some measure, he understands how this rage will be manifested on society. Simmons first met Kyle at his office on San Vicente

Boulevard in West Los Angeles. This was before Simmons' divorce motivated his move to Newport Beach.

Simmons was married and divorced three times and now lived alone in a bayside condo. He was currently hustling women in a series of Newport Beach night spots, all the while courting a very rich widow, Ellie Lewis, who was his client, and ten years his senior. She was crazy about him, wanted to marry him, and in turn, make him a very rich man. He would then become another of those undesirables that Kyle would instinctively hate. He also was involved with Nadia Jenski, the wife of a neighbor. Simmons knew that what he was doing with Ellie and Nadia was wrong and wrong to continue casual dalliances with lonely young women hanging out at his favorite bars. But he couldn't help himself; it was so easy.

Simmons had four children with his three wives; two with wife number two, one each with wives one and three. All four children adored him and, figuratively, he seduced them with the same charm and energy and excitement with which he had charmed and seduced their mothers. He was, indeed, a true man of seduction.

Simmons brought Kyle into this lair with graciousness and aplomb, and Kyle proceeded to flop onto a couch and stare out and away at the beautiful blue-green Pacific Ocean. He thought that Kyle was a colossal pain in the butt. But he was steady income and reliable pay. Kyle's file was substantial. Simmons held two inches of that file in his left hand.

"You sounded distraught on your phone message."

"We're down to the wire," Kyle snapped. "You took long enough to get back to me, Al…"

"Forty minutes to be exact." Simmons hated being called Al, but tolerated Kyle's lack of respect. "In this profession, that is nano-seconds, Kyle, a blip on the counselor's radar screen, not worthy of criticism. Others have problems which need…"

"Spare me. I know your sad story about helping all those other people…rich people…those rich people who worry about nothing more than…"

"How can I help you right now?"

"I'm ready to put the plan into play. I've had enough of society's reluctance to listen and act properly. Things keep going on with no changes. There is a constant of nothing happening, a constant of complacency. It's time to act, to get everyone's attention. Then, maybe, we can get something done."

"Folks in society are leading their lives. Few are social activists, Kyle, few have much time for activism."

"It's important enough to take the time," Kyle said loudly, "we wouldn't even be a country if our founding fathers had not taken the time. You take the time to get active when the cause is critical. Like this is…changing how society proceeds, how we protect the land and our environment."

"Our founding fathers were a small minority and not everyone in the country agreed with them," Simmons responded reflexively.

"Yeah, right. Well, let me tell you that most people agree that something has to be done to protect the environment, but they're too lazy to do anything about it. I'm not too lazy. I know we have to shakeup society so they are fully aware and become part of the revolution. Our founding fathers jolted people by taking a stand. I'm taking a stand. It's time."

"When do you…?"

"In a few days. We have to get some things…further donations. My old company is going to provide some of what we need. A big part of what we need, as a matter of fact. Then we cut off water and power to the Southland. Attention will be paid."

"Why are you telling me this again…today?"

"Someone needs to know the truth. You know what I stand for. You know what I'm trying to do…"

"Haven't we discussed many times how there are different realities? How we must respect other beliefs, other perspectives? Those realities are linked, but they don't necessarily coincide. I thought we had come to an understanding about that concept. What are you trying to do?"

"What do you mean, "trying to do?" You know, you know…"

"Know what?"

"Know that minds have to be changed. We can't wait. This has all gone on too long…"

"What has? What has gone on too long?"

"Goddamnit, why are you asking that? You know what I'm talking about; you know what our mission is…"

"Our mission? Our mission? You are going to destroy things and disrupt people's lives to try to accomplish something? That's very negative and negativity rarely accomplishes much. We've gone over that many times."

"That's your concept. I'm supposed to accept your concept."

"I'm trying to help you understand and cope with the world around you. Help you understand that you can have your ideas, but you can't expect to mold other folks to suit what you want."

"That has to be done. It has to be changed, molded as you say, for our own salvation. And it's often necessary to…to destroy, to take away from people so they understand what they have had and to realize what they are doing to our world."

"What does Carrie say?"

"She's moving to the ranch to be part of what we are going to do. She wants to be in the forefront. She wants to help. What do you think of that?"

"She's obviously caught up in what you are about, just as obviously Laurie isn't."

"She...she," Kyle fumbled for an answer, "she doesn't understand anymore."

"Laurie believed in you once."

"She doesn't understand what this is all about."

"You have a very complicated life?"

Simmons dropped Kyle's folder on his desk and looked carefully at Kyle who stared at the floor.

"You mean," Kyle laughed, sitting upright, "juggling Carrie and Christy..."

"Yes, partly. And Laurie." Simmons could not, would not counsel him about the women; his own situation was much the same. His probing was intended for something other than the women.

"It's easy. Christy is dumb and Carrie doesn't think I might be doing another woman because I'm so busy, so dedicated, and so sincere about the cause. The way it has gone...and you know this, my first cause was women and my second cause was the environment. The line blurred, then things got clarified, and I am committed to getting change. If I'm screwing women in the process, secondarily, that's just the way it works."

"And what about Laurie?"

"I don't want to talk about her." He slumped down in the chair.

"All right. However, the business with the women in your life is not exactly what I meant."

"So?"

"So, are you still robbing…stealing?"

Kyle sat up again quickly and looked at Simmons.

"Yeah, we need the money…"

"Let's hope no one gets hurt…"

"They won't."

"Why did you want to see me today? You sounded frantic on your voicemail message. You have second thoughts?"

"I just needed you to listen to me. No," Kyle screamed, "I didn't have…don't have second thoughts."

Simmons turned his back on Kyle and walked to the window. He had lost track of the number of years he had been working with this young man. He only remembered the continuing frustration of trying to help him reach some sort of life equilibrium so Kyle could function with a better state of mind. Counseling him through his various crises of life meaning and life direction, the angst of a father-son relationship, his rejection by friends, the pointed criticism from coworkers, the anxiety of job changes, and the deterioration of his marriage to Laurie were some of the bits of continuity that filled Kyle's record.

He wondered what he possibly could have done for this young man to avert this showdown with society. He felt as if he had been trying to flag a runaway truck, to stop it from careening to destruction and death and injury of others. The crash had merely been postponed, sidetracked as it were. And now, here he was, still trying to keep Kyle from destroying himself and a portion of society. The impossible was truly impossible.

"What else?" Simmons asked, as he turned to face Kyle and then came and sat in the chair next to the young man before there was a reply.

Kyle watched him intently as he came near and seated himself. He felt the closeness of the man and it bothered him.

He wanted to get up and move, but steeled himself and remained seated.

"Ours should not be an adversarial one," Simmons said softly. "I'm trying to help you think things through."

"You want me to change my mind. Try to stop me."

"I would like you to consider other options and also not get so upset. I believe there are reasonable approaches to take using the strength of your action groups. With your Alliance For A Better Environment you could begin to exert political pressure to accomplish some of your goals, for instance. I'm not sure you have given enough time, enough campaigning for that to work."

"You just don't get it, do you," Kyle scoffed.

"I guess not. Tell me what I don't get."

"The money has the clout. Everywhere you look…about anything, the big money calls the shots. Developers, big corporations, big-box retailers, mass merchandisers, the oil companies…they have the money to skew the system their way. They get done what they want done. The politicians, city commissioners, mayors, planning commissions…they smile and agree with me and others who talk to them about protecting the environment and then they turn their back to us. They have their hand out to take the payoffs that pave the way for the big boys. And I mean pave the way. There is probably more concrete and asphalt paving per square mile in southern California than any other place in the world."

Kyle quickly rose and headed for the door. He was finished with the attempted seduction.

"You can't stand the truth, can you? The truth can be enlightening or it can be very debilitating. That's what you've danced around all these years. The truth; magic or mayhem. You don't want it, you've never wanted it. You've spent a lot of time and money with me to avoid it. I haven't yet quite figured out why...other than the obvious psychological stuff that we haven't really indulged in."

Kyle stopped short of the door and turned. He did not look at Simmons, but instead looked out the window.

"It's a beautiful view, Al, you're a lucky man with this nice office facing the ocean. Life really is simple for you isn't it? It's your truth. Get laid, listen to people bitch. Get laid, listen to people bitch. Over and over again with the repetition being the goal. What a nice racket you've got. Wow. On the other hand, my life is more complex...you know that. My goals are...well, different. My goals are righteous and meaningful. I will pursue them...vigorously. I have my truth and you've helped me get to it. The truth is...life is a lot of bullshit that is coated with social niceties, hidden in ritual, tucked away in the rules, and manipulated by the power brokers. The little guy doesn't stand a chance. That's what truth is."

"Kyle, we have more time to talk..."

"Thanks, Al, for listening to me."

"I'm just concerned that you haven't thoroughly thought about what your planned actions can really mean...for you, for your family, including your wife and children and sister and your mother. All of their lives will be changed forever if you go ahead with your plan.

"It's got to happen, Al, it's got to happen. Thanks. And don't worry, no matter what happens you're going to get paid."

Kyle was out the door and gone before Simmons could reply.

Simmons sat down at his desk and flipped open Kyle's folder. He then swiveled his chair around to his credenza, pulled open one of the doors, and reached in to press the OFF switch on the control panel of a tape recorder. Turning back to the open folder, he began to make notes on the yellow pad on top of the file. He wrote ten or twelve lines of notes before he closed the file and leaned back. Kyle was right on two counts, he said to himself as he savored the view, I'm a lucky man and life is quite simple for me. He wondered if he would ever see Kyle in person again.

8.

Hardly a cloud spoiled the sharp blue sky, the noon sun an oven of comfort for the long rows of avocado trees that spread a shiny green cloak across Kyle's ranch. There was no discernable air movement and the trees drooped as if the weight of the brilliant sunlight was too much for them. In reality, they were basking in their near-perfect environment. There was the sound of crows in the distance and a mockingbird trying to sound like a robin, but otherwise it seemed as if little were happening in the world. This was the quiet serenity that Ramsey Dixon had lived for and that Kyle had come to appreciate.

In the ranch house kitchen, Kyle and the three men who worked closely with him sat around the large table. They were eating the sandwiches and soup Carrie had prepared for them. She stood by the sink watching them eat, sensing the nervousness in all but Kyle and thought it was curious. Why would they be upset? She assumed the morning's robbery had gone well. She had driven them all to a large parking lot in Murietta where she watched in fascination as Ellis stole an almost new Buick Lucerne. She watched as Kyle, Ted, and Mark got in the Buick with Ellis and drove away to Lake Elsinore where they would rob the targeted Cloverfield store. Later, she picked them up at a small mall parking lot in Murietta Hot Springs. Little was said on the drive back to the ranch. She was now officially part of the operation.

Ted finally revealed the concern as he munched on his sandwich. "Do you think she died?" he asked softly.

"Naw, I just shot her in the leg," Ellis said

"She could bleed to death if you hit her just right."

"No way. Just nicked her. Kept her from being trouble and kept the others in line, too."

"That's the last one," Kyle said firmly, his voice taut, belying his outward manner. "It's a wonder something like that hasn't happened before."

"What?" Carrie asked.

"Someone resisting," Kyle explained. "No one has balked before today. This woman was pissed because she was in a hurry. She didn't seem to realize or care that a gun was pointed at her."

"Pain in the ass," Ellis barked, "that kind always causes trouble no matter what the situation. They think they're the only ones that count."

"We've been lucky until now. It doesn't matter. She'll be okay. But we all need to be prepared at Gladstone's tonight. They have armed guards...well trained. They're not rent-a-cop types, they know how to use their weapons and they're not afraid."

"What's the chance they'll spot us...we have to shoot our way out?" Mark asked carefully.

"Slim," Kyle sniffed. "They're good, but they spend most of their attention at the ad min building and the buildings adjacent to it. We just follow my plan and we'll be okay...no shooting. We'll go over it again this afternoon."

"I gotta get a van yet," Ellis reminded.

"Yes," Kyle nodded, "Carrie will take you to...to a good location. There's that mall in Temecula, the one we saw the other day. Use that one; get a Honda or Toyota."

"Easy," Ellis smiled. "They'll be there...one of them."

Kyle motioned to Carrie and she moved toward the door to the porch.

"You guys relax, get some rest. We're going to take a walk."

They kicked through the red-brown dried leaves which were the lingering residue of seasons of change the trees registered. Dust scuffed ahead into the air and fell back on their hiking boots. The calm hot air was oppressive even within the shade. The avocado trees were soaking up the energy, but in no way lessening the sun's impact. Only at sunset would there be temperature relief. Carrie and Kyle relished the heat.

"Hear anything?" he asked.

Carrie stopped and stood very still.

"Only the leaves we're kicking," she replied.

"The birds are at siesta, waiting it out until evening. They talk then. This quiet world everyone should experience. Maybe if they did, if they could feel this tranquility, maybe things would be different."

"Won't happen. Never will. Folks too set in their ways, too spoiled with their conveniences, their pleasures, too zoned out to get this picture. Folks need to be deprived of the soft cushion, feel some hard reality. Maybe that would help. That's what we're going to do, isn't it; to give the people a dose of reality? See what will happen if things don't change? That's what this selfish society needs. Kyle you're going to provide a dose of medicine. There's a sickness and you've got the right prescription. Better than the drug companies, those bastards."

"Not bad," Kyle laughed, "not bad at all. You can help me finish writing the first letter to the LA Times."

"Oh, yeah?"

"You bet. The voice of the people will speak through you...and me, of course."

"You know...we have lots of time," she grinned at him, "maybe we should go back to the house. We could get undressed...take a nap or something."

"Or something? What did you have in mind?

She took his hand and kissed it and sucked on his index finger.

"I could touch you in a certain place. You might like it."

"I would."

They walked back to the house hand in hand and went upstairs to the master bedroom suite that Kyle used when he was there. The rooms had been his parents' and then his father's until his death. Kyle truly felt heir to this suite. Her things were already piled around the large sitting area and bedroom, in the closet, and crowded the bathroom. This suite would be his and Carrie's.

She was naked and standing on the bed before he could remove his clothes. He marveled at her long skinny body with the outrageous nipples. She was ripe, sensuous, ready for their encounter, and hungry to show him passion.

"Come on, get those things off," she said in a stage whisper, "I'm ready."

She bounced on the bed just enough to make it seem as if she were on a trampoline and then flopped onto her back with her legs straight into the air.

"Come on," she screamed.

"Hey, keep it down. I don't want the guys to hear what's…"

"I don't give a damn. Come on, climb aboard."

She had never acted like this. The other times before when they had sex she had been more reserved, cautious, as if she were pacing herself for a long race, almost tentative and wary. This was a new Carrie. He was wondering if this spectacle was too overt for him, but he decided he was willing to give it a try. He peeled off the rest of his clothes.

"Shhh," he whispered as he got on top of her. "This is no one else's business. Just us. Just us."

He was lost inside of her, lost in the whirl and power of her emotion more than of his own, and he was carried to an ecstasy that almost frightened him. He least understood what was happening other than he had lost control and he never wanted to lose control. Control was everything he had fought for, what he had spent his life trying to grasp and retain. He nearly passed out, consumed by her passion, by her dominance, and the surety which was hers. She tightened the grip of her legs wrapped around his body, a death-like grip, the black widow after fertilization, the ultimate clutch of desperation. She coughed the hacking smokers cough and he could feel it throughout her body and into him in an odd sensation of muscular contraction that gripped his penis. She wanted the feeling as long as possible. She knew that once he rolled off of her she was out of control and he again was dominant. She resisted her fate for an eternity of lust, a bloom of mingled sweat, and the panting rejoice of their naked bodies welded together in exhaustion.

Consumed by the aftershock of their love making, he laid there on the bed for a long time before he dared look at his watch. When he did, it was almost two in the afternoon. The need to begin preparations for tonight was the thought that ran through his half-paralyzed brain.

"You have to take Ellis to lift a van," he said slowly, his mouth cottony as he slurred the words. "Time to get going."

She didn't move. Her eyes were wide open, staring at the ceiling. She was not ready to move.

He ignored her inaction and got himself dressed. He went to the bathroom, washed his face, and slowly, deliberately combed his hair.

"Now," he said, as he stood over the bed, "that was then, now is now."

The spell was over, the feeling gone, the emotion drained, just as she had thought it would be.

"Okay," she replied, and got dressed.

Carrie drove Ellis to a large mall parking lot in Temecula where they were able to locate an almost new Honda Odyssey van. He was inside and on his way before she could even exit the lot. Both of them were certain no one had witnessed the theft.

Later that afternoon, after the stolen van had been loaded with the equipment they would need, the five of them sat around the kitchen table. Kyle unfolded a topographical map which he had edited to include the key elements of the Gladstone installation east of Temecula.

"We've studied this several times before, but we should take another look to make sure of what we're doing." Kyle was almost professorial as he spoke to them. "Here is the farthest point from the ad min building. It's wild country. This is where we go through the fence."

The other men nodded with rapt attention. Carrie, arms folded, watched Kyle's face intently. She wondered if they might all die tonight. This would not be the last time she had such a feeling.

"We move cross country with the two wagons until we get to this building here." He pointed to a red X on the map. "Get it open, get the plastic out and loaded, and slug back to the van. It won't be easy. The two wagons full of plastic will be heavy and difficult to move, but we have time to do it. As I've said, the guards concentrate on the ad min buildings. They don't expect someone to come overland to steal anything. Besides, they're mainly interested in snoopers during the day, at night, they don't think much will happen because they're so remote. Hell, this place used to be remote, but the population is surrounding them and pushing in on them all the time."

"Kyle, how long will this take?"

"I estimate that we will take at least an hour to get to the plastics bunker, opening and loading will take about a half hour, then at least two hours to get back to the van. If we start at ten that should get us out of there by about two o'clock in the morning."

"And I meet you at the McDonald's in Hemet," Carrie confirmed. "The one on Florida Avenue."

"Right. We'll make the transfer to our truck and follow Ellis to Perris where we dump the van."

"Will we stay in contact?" Carrie asked.

"On the hour as we talked about. Well, look…it's almost four. Better get some rest. We roll out of here at nine."

Kyle was too keyed up to rest. He was not nervous in the sense that he had fear, but nervous with anticipation and excitement at the prospect of getting one of the important elements he wanted. The plastic explosives. He knew they were there on the Gladstone site and that they would be the factor which gave his plan power. The plastic explosives would help create the damage he wanted, produce the destruction he wished to create. Plastics were the edge. The fertilizer placements could be effective, but combining them with the plastic was crucial for getting the powerful blasts he wanted.

Carrie went upstairs to lie down and Mark disappeared to his room on the first floor. Ellis and Ted lounged on the sofas in the great room off the kitchen. They eventually fell away to snoring sleep.

Kyle went outside and walked to the large out-building that served as a processing facility during the picking season. The main door was unlocked, but inside was a locked workshop and several locked storage areas. He unlocked the workshop and went inside. This was were he had been building timing and detonating devices for the placements he was building and that were stored in various stages of assembly in the other locked rooms. He did not want to work on any of the devices right now, he was too preoccupied with tonight's project to do that, he merely wanted to examine and review what he had already assembled. He compared assemblies to his own drawings and compared them to other resource material he had accumulated over the years. He was satisfied with his work and knew that final assembly could be ready when he had enough plastic. They would get what they could tonight and then in a few days they would go to the other Gladstone site and get the rest of the plastic he wanted.

He checked on the stolen Honda van waiting just inside one of the closed overhead doors that allowed trucks access to haul away boxes of selected, inspected, and sized avocados. It was an unassuming silver shade that appeared to be just another suburban housewife's van. He carried a used paint can half full of muddy sludge he had mixed for use in obscuring license plates. Carefully, with a sense of the artist, he brushed the mixture across the rear bumper and the plate. Just doing the plate would be too obvious, he thought, so it was necessary to make the entire rear end look as if it had been splattered with mud. He also covered the lower front end including the lens of the daytime running lights. Satisfied with his work, he replaced the can's cover and washed the brush in the nearby utility sink.

By eight o'clock the others were rested and ready to head for the job ahead. But Kyle held them off, asking them to be patient, to recheck their gear, and to review the action plan one more time. They did as he asked, but they were nervous. And scared.

"Let's get going," he finally called out from the porch just as his watch registered nine o'clock.

He could tell they were relieved to be on the move, to get into action, to lessen the tension they continued to feel.

"We take our time…no need to rush. We are going to do this very deliberately. We move carefully, thoroughly…then everything will be fine."

Carrie stood nearby watching as the men got into the van. She wanted to kiss Kyle good-bye, but she knew he did not want that, not in front of the others. He turned and looked at her. It was a strange look, she thought, and she wondered what was going on in that high-powered brain of his. It did not matter right now because he was in the van without saying another word. She punched the button that activated the door opener and the huge metal door lumbered upwards with a rattling noise that jarred her.

Ellis drove the van over the narrow road from Fallbrook to I-15, took the northbound ramp, eased in behind a Wal-Mart semi, and kept pace with the truck. They went north to the exit for state road 79 and headed east on 79 coming off the exit ramp.

"Hold your speed down," Kyle directed, "I'm going to have to spot where we turn off."

"Fifty?" Ellis asked.

"Forty-five would be better. Not much traffic along here this time of night so going slow shouldn't be a problem."

"Hey look," Mark pointed, "isn't that the road that runs in to Gladstone's?"

"Yes, it is," Kyle said grimly, "but we're going to go around to the back door...so to speak. A back door we create."

After another five or six minutes, Kyle reacted.

"Slow down, slow down...we're just about there."

Another minute passed.

"There it is...there by that olive tree just ahead on the right. Take it easy pulling off, there's a kind of depression that could give us a bad time. Go very slowly...very slowly."

"Don't you worry," Ellis snapped, "I don't turn no vans over...or get 'em stuck."

He steered the van at an angle across the shallow dip that passed for a ditch with little difficulty and rolled on to the underbrush in front of them. He braked twenty feet or so shy of the bushes.

"Turn the lights off," Kyle directed and jumped out of the van to determine where it was they could get through.

It did not take long for him to find the spot he knew was there. He motioned for Ellis to where he was pulling at some branches.

"It doesn't look like it, but you can slip right through here. Just beyond is a clearing...stop there, we'll unload."

Ellis got the van through the brush where it seemed impossible for a vehicle to pass, drove slowly a few more yards to the clearing, stopped, and turned off the engine. All this, guided only by Kyle's flashlight.

"Maybe I should turn this baby around," Ellis suggested, "just in case we have to leave in a hurry."

"Probably a good idea, Ellis," Kyle agreed.

Ellis started the engine and positioned the van so that it pointed back at the spot in the brush where they had just entered.

"Ted, take this fir branch we brought along and cover our tracks from the road. No sense in having anyone see tracks off the road. Someone might think there's been an accident or a deputy sheriff going by might be suspicious if he saw the tracks."

Ted nodded and headed off through the brush.

Although the sun had already set there was still a considerable amount of twilight that allowed the men to go about their tasks without the aid of flashlights. However, it would not be long until the lights would be needed to get to their target. Two dark green, heavy plastic four-wheeled yard haulers were taken out of the van and the tools and equipment they needed were dropped into them. Purchased at Home Depot, they were really like oversized wagons that kids would use. Ted and Mark would each pull one.

"What's that?" Ellis asked as he saw Kyle holding a small flashlight at some kind of instrument.

Kyle had squatted with his back against a small tree while he programmed the hand-held GPS device that Ellis noticed.

"This is a GPS receiver and it's what will get us out of here efficiently so we can backtrack without stumbling around trying to find our way. It uses satellites for tracking and positioning."

They moved cautiously at first, but with their eyes more accustomed to the low light level they were able to maintain a steady pace, even pulling the wagons. There were minor obstacles to be sure, a random stick or small branch, an unsuspected rut, the miserable stray rock; each of these threw them off-stride as the wagons were yanked forward and the men stumbled to keep their balance. At one point, Mark fell to his knees when his wagon hit a rock and the jolt pulled him down. For the most part, however, it was relatively easy to follow Kyle as he made his way to the destination only he knew. The others were satisfied he was well in control of the situation.

Kyle regularly checked his watch and at ten o'clock he stopped to call Carrie.

"We're doing okay," he reported to Carrie. "Not moving as fast as I thought, but doing okay. Roger."

They continued the slog for another half hour with flashlights used periodically to help navigate. Then Kyle stopped abruptly.

"Here it is," he whispered.

The "it" was a four-strand barbed wire fence of a kind they had never before seen. It looked menacing.

Kyle carefully checked the strands and the steel fence posts.

"I knew there didn't used to be electronic security way out here and they haven't added any since I last checked. Just as I figured."

He motioned to Mark with a nod and slight wave of his hand.

Without a word, Mark pulled long-handled wire cutters from Ted's wagon and proceeded to snip each of the four strands. The strands fell away leaving a large opening for them to move ahead.

They were now on Gladstone property and the terrain changed little. After a hundred yards or so, a bit more sandy, but otherwise, the same obstacles, the same steady, deliberate pace.

"God, look at that sky. All them stars." Ellis was awed by the canopy above them.

"Some people," Ted said, "think God's up there."

"Whose God?" Mark asked. "Not mine."

Kyle stopped and looked.

"This," he groused, "is the way the sky would look in lots of places if there wasn't so much light pollution. See that glow over there? That's our so-called civilization…polluting the night sky."

They moved on, hauling the wagons, silent except for heavy breathing. They had been walking slightly uphill for more than a mile and were now sweating profusely.

"You can see the lights of the compound," Kyle announced. "Hold down the talk."

"How far?" Mark asked quietly.

"Half mile. Maybe a little less. I haven't heard the dogs, but we need to be alert. Use the pepper spray if they come to us. They patrol the perimeter in this area, but not back where we came in. No one in security thinks it's necessary."

"How do you know?" Mark asked.

"I asked once. I was told the head of security, Marwood, didn't think it was required. He didn't figure anyone would come at this place overland from the wilderness area."

"Wilderness?" Ellis muttered.

"Yeah, the Agua Tibia Wilderness area...part of Cleveland National Forest. Federal land. That's what we crossed to get to the fence."

He moved ahead and the men followed. They were cautious and quiet moving to within fifty yards of a strange looking mound at the edge of the compound. This was the explosives bunker. It was lighted by a single sodium vapor light suspended from a pole that was twenty feet in front of the bunker. They hunkered down behind a large clump of Manzanita bushes.

"Now, we wait," Kyle said softly, "we wait to see what the guard timing is."

Fifteen minutes went by. Twenty.

"Let's work our way through those trees to the back and stay out of the light," Kyle directed.

"No one is around," Ellis said.

"They're around someplace, even if they're screwing off. Let's go."

It was a strange procession, an improbable sort of parade. Four men hunched over, mincing on their toes as if they were sneaking up on Santa, two of them pulling oversized wagons, the noise of the wheels and their boots in the sand a dry squishing sound, and all casting weird angulated shadows into the stand of trees behind them. It still seemed that no one was aware of their trespassing presence. They stopped behind the bunker.

"There is no electronic security on the door of this thing," Kyle said, "just a padlock. Get it snipped."

Mark again took the long-handled cutters from the wagon. He walked around the bunker into full light and stepped quickly to the front door and in one strong motion clamped onto the lock. He furiously pulled the handles together and the lock snapped. He took the lock and moved quickly around to the back of the bunker.

"Open."

"Ellis, you stay here. Cover us. We take the wagons in, get them loaded, and get out. Keep the door closed once we get in. We work fast, we work efficient, and we're gone. Ellis, if it's necessary, shoot anyone that comes and discovers us inside. If we have to shoot our way out, so be it. That's how it happens. They only have six guys out here tonight, so the odds aren't too bad. Come on."

As the three men worked furiously inside the bunker, Ellis crawled around the mound until he had a clear view of the administration building and some of the other buildings in the compound. Beyond, he could see the main gate and guard house. There seemed to be no one else around. As he scanned the scene, one of the guards came out of the guard house. The man looked around the area and then began to circle the grouping of buildings which comprised a campus of sorts.

Ellis could tell he was engaged in a cursory inspection, with no expectation of anything amiss. Wherever he walked it was well lighted, wherever he went he seemed unconcerned with the situation. Once he checked out the compound buildings, he headed for the bunker.

Ellis circled around the bunker away from the oncoming guard and waited out of sight, but close to the door that had been breeched. He was only steps away from the entrance. The guard approached in a lackadaisical manner, without anticipation, to discover the lock missing. His reaction was to pull open the door. He did so without preparation, in other words without drawing his weapon, and without realizing or considering the potential situation.

With three strides Ellis was to the man and struck him with the butt of his M4 rifle on the side of his head. The guard fell sideways without making a sound and Ellis rolled him against the front wall of the bunker. Kyle's head appeared at the door. He took one look at what had occurred and closed the door. Ellis grabbed the man's boots and pulled him around the bunker into the shadows before dropping his legs. There was no point in telling Kyle to hurry, the urgency was already known.

Several minutes later the men emerged from the bunker pulling the wagons loaded with plastic explosives. In short order they had the wagons around the bunker and into the shadows and cover of the trees and underbrush. They were panting and sweating and swearing under their breath, but able to keep moving toward the back fence.

"Hold it," Kyle ordered. "Get the guard and put him on top of one of the wagons."

Ted and Ellis went back behind the bunker, picked up the unconscious man, brought him back to where they had stopped, and flopped him on top of a wagon.

"Did you kill him?" Kyle asked.

"Naw, just knocked him cuckoo. He's out for awhile..."

"Someone will eventually check for him, but we'll be well on our way."

Kyle pulled the GPS unit from his pocket, consulted it, and pointed the way.

"No need to tell you to move fast as possible," he said.

They plunged ahead at a half trot, the light of the compound aiding them, the wagons a formidable restriction to greater speed. After twenty minutes or so at that pace, Mark stopped, leaned to his left, and threw up violently.

"Sorry," he said, as he reeled against a tree.

"Take a drink." Kyle handed him a canteen from his backpack.

"Okay."

"Eat this energy bar. Drink more water." Kyle was solicitous, yet unemotional in the way he offered the water and food to Mark. He was simply the leader and all of them had to get out of there fast.

"Thanks." Mark said as he stood up away from the tree and began walking.

The guard was beginning to regain consciousness and Kyle pulled him off the wagon. He took a roll of gray tape from his backpack and wrapped the man's mouth so he could not speak or shout. He then wrapped the legs at the ankles and knees and pulled his arms behind his back and taped the wrists. When he finished, he took an aerosol can from his pack and sprayed around the entire area.

"That should give us enough time," Kyle said.

"What's that?" Ted asked.

"Dog and cat repellent. Keeps animals from peeing on your bushes. I thought it might help us here."

The pull back to the fence was an ordeal. The men took turns tugging the wagons over the same terrain that was easy when they were light with a few pieces of equipment, but which were now difficult to keep moving at a good pace. Plus, there was the constant fear of being chased.

"Think they'll let the dogs loose?" Mark asked.

"Probably. Eventually." The idea did not seem to concern Kyle. "By the time they do, if they do, it won't really matter."

The men were relieved to reach the fence at the opening where they had entered.

"Thank you, Garmin," Kyle said out loud, more to himself than to the others.

"Who?"

"The name of the GPS unit," Kyle laughed. "Come on, let's keep moving."

When they reached the van, all but Kyle could hardly walk. They were completely exhausted. They had hardly stopped other than the two times Kyle checked in with Carrie. They had done the majority of the hard work as he had been the leader, although he did most of the load transfer from the wagons to the van. The others sat on the ground agonizing from aching muscles and joints, only occasionally lifting and carrying a few blocks of the plastic explosives and detonator boxes. The material loaded, the wagons and gear inside, he motioned them into the van.

"Give me the keys Ellis, I'll drive. You're too tired...you're all too tired. Get in...let's get out of here."

Kyle drove through the channel in the underbrush with lights off, made sure there was no traffic approaching, and pulled onto Highway 79 heading east before turning on the headlights. Using narrow back roads, he left 79 and headed north to Hemet. Except for the guard, they had been successful and lucky. The men had been prepared for a shootout. It was difficult dragging the wagons back to the van, but the operation had been simple enough. Again, things went exactly the way Kyle told them it would happen, just like the robberies. It could have gotten out of hand, but it didn't and they were thankful, silent in their appreciation for what they had just accomplished.

The McDonald's in Hemet was closed and dark when Kyle pulled into the parking lot and drove to the back. Carrie was already parked and waiting with the ranch truck. Quickly, the men moved the plastic explosives and detonators to the back of the truck and the slabs and boxes were covered with a tarp that was tied down by Mark.

Once the transfer had been made, Ellis got in the van. They would follow him to Perris, with Carrie driving, leave it on a residential side street, and head back to the ranch. When they arrived at the ranch, the truck was pulled into the avocado processing building and the explosives unloaded into one of the work rooms that Kyle locked when they were finished. It was after three in the morning. All of them were strung out and almost giddy with what had happened that night. No one wanted to go to bed. They all went to the ranch kitchen and opened beers. At one point during the prior evening, Carrie had gone to a pizza joint in Fallbrook and bought four large pizzas that she warmed in the oven. The men devoured them. And cold Mexican beer.

Kyle walked outside with his beer and a huge slice of pizza and, facing the east, he hunched his rump onto the railing. It was cool and a light breeze flitted in from the coast and the sky was still clear and filled with stars. Carrie came to join him, glad to be apart from the other crude men. She brushed his hair back from his forehead and kissed his cheek lightly. She took a long pull from her beer and pushed herself close in to him. It was sort of like a snuggle, but much less tender. Kyle barely reacted to her contact with him. He was deep and away in thought. She sensed his detachment and sat down in one of the porch chairs.

"Where are you?" she asked.

He did not respond at first, but then slowly turned toward her, still caught up, off somewhere.

"What?"

"Are you all right?"

He focused on her, his eyes narrowed, his mouth a thin line.

"We were lucky...it could have been a fiasco."

"It wasn't"

"It could have been."

"Now what?"

"Now?" He didn't look at her.

"You make a bomb?"

"Placements, yes. We need big ones and small ones. I build placements, the guys take care of the ranch, and you..."

He stopped. His thoughts were whirling in all directions and he wondered what he should say to her. How valuable would she be over the long haul? To get the job done.

"You will be able to do some things for me."

"Like what? I can't just sit around here. I can...can...I can help you with the bombs. Making the bombs."

"Maybe so."

"I think so."

He turned to her and smiled. It was that disarming smile he used when he wanted to control a situation, a smile that signified something positive even when he had no such intention or thought. It was wonderful aspect of his compartmentalizing that allowed him to function with no qualms about deceit or deception. Results were his elixir, methods be damned.

"I can be very helpful," she giggled out of relief and lack of sleep.

"Tomorrow, I have to drive to Santa Monica. There's a big fund raiser my sister has arranged and I can't miss it. Too much money involved. Good timing and bad timing, I guess. Too little, too late. Anyway, they expect me there."

"I'll go with you."

"No, you stay here."

"But..."

"Learn about the avocado business. Help the guys, read, take a walk, but stay here. Don't leave the ranch."

"But I…"

"Look, there are enough things going on right now. I don't want to get into the introduction routine with my mother, my sister, or anyone else. Not right now. We'll be going back to Santa Monica…west LA later. Be patient. You'll go with me then. We'll all go. It will be our LA party. It's all part of the plan. Stick with me and be patient. Find out how we grow avocados. It's a good business."

"What business are we going to be in when this is over?"

The question stunned him and he wished she had not asked. He had an answer, but now was not the time to talk about what he had in mind.

"The avocado business," he lied.

She came to him and kissed him and pulled his head to her chest and flattened her cheek against the top of his head. They went upstairs and crept onto the bed, both too tired to take off their clothes let alone make love. Ted and Ellis and Mark were still drinking beer, the pizza long devoured, and the faint sounds of their voices drifted into the night.

9.

Kyle had to be in Santa Monica. His sister, Kelli, had arranged for an important fundraiser to benefit the Alliance For A Better Environment. Dozens of important people would be there; power couples from the entertainment and music businesses were expected. Dozens more would be those enlightened, passionate hard-core environmental activists. The rest of the invitees would be the casually supportive crowd who were either acquaintances or associates of Kelli and husband Kevin.

Driving from Fallbrook to Santa Monica was a nerve-wracking drag for Kyle and for awhile he contented himself by reviewing the previous evening's escapade at the Gladstone site. They had been fortunate. No confrontation. For whatever reason, he did not think the guard Ellis knocked unconscious counted in that regard. In any case, it had been a relatively easy time of it. Just the way he had figured.

The drive was a drag because it was tedious and frustrating to be locked in traffic. It was a time-consuming test of his patience. From his way of thinking, it was also quite dangerous. An accident could happen at any time and you could be killed without warning. Your death would be out of your control, randomly caused by some stranger. You would be a victim of circumstance, and an inconsequential casualty in the traffic death toll statistics of southern California. He hated the idea.

He remembered when this drive was relatively easy. Oh, sure, there were still lots of cars then, but not like now when hordes upon hordes of vehicles crawled over the concrete landscape like ants on a mission. Back then, traffic moved along, you got where you were going quicker, and without so much fuss. It had been a different time, a time in his memory that he liked better.

He alternately gripped the steering wheel with a vicious clamp, both hands white from the pressure, and then eased back into his seat, relaxing to use just his fingers for control. Grip, relax; grip, relax. Steering became an isometric exercise and a method of maintaining composure. He wanted to arrive in Santa Monica at ease and in control of himself. After all, he was meeting his mother.

She was a formidable woman, considered tough by many, thought of as wily by others, and certainly regarded as very successful in her art and antiques business. At seventy-three she was still quite attractive, her gray hair colored away to a perpetual ash blonde. She led a very active life with multitudes of friends and a lover three years her junior. She was spry, energetic, and assertive, sometimes aggressive. A robust woman, she was once almost six feet tall, about the same as Ramsey, but age had shaved a couple of inches. She liked to dominate, she could dominate, she would dominate; she was a formidable woman.

Kyle was relieved when he pulled into the parking garage on Fourth Street. He was ten minutes early. He had agreed to meet his mother at eleven-thirty. He walked up Fourth to the corner and into P. F. Chang's. The lunch crowd had yet to surge and he could see she was not there yet.

"Welcome to P. F. Chang's. Just one for lunch?"

"Ah, no, there's going to be two of us. A lady…"

"Would you like to be seated now, sir? We can direct the…"

"Yes, a booth. Where it's quiet. We have business to discuss."

"Certainly, sir. Follow me please."

Once in the booth, Kyle ordered a beer and watched for his mother to enter. He checked his watch. Still not eleven-thirty. Almost twenty more minutes and working on his second beer, he saw her enter the restaurant. She pushed through the group of business yuppie success stories waiting to be seated. The hostess started to engage her, but she already had spotted Kyle and headed for his booth.

She knelt on the cushion of the booth and pulled his head to her so she could kiss him furiously on the cheek. Then she sat down across from him.

"I might have known," she sighed. "I told you eleven-thirty thinking you would get here late. So I timed it for eleven-forty five. So much for anticipation and planning."

"I'm rarely late," he offered lamely.

"I know dear, but I operate with contingencies to keep things moving."

She would overwhelm the most secure in their own persona, overwhelm Solomon, tyrannize any who doubted her power, and she could totally demoralize anyone she wished. She would not have wanted it that way; she was, if revealed, a sweet, caring woman. However, she was strong and grounded in her own vision of herself. In her view, she was working against a harsh, judgmental society that made little accommodation for a woman of her caliber.

"Don't apologize, Kyle, the misappropriated logistics are my own...my own...part of my own obsession. You are blameless, sweet boy."

"I am not a boy."

"Oh, really, that is just a manner of recognizing the generational difference. You will always be my baby boy. Don't fight it, its endearment, it's caring, it's loving consideration."

"It's bullshit," Kyle said slowly, waiting for her reaction.

"The fund raiser is tonight," she said, ignoring his comment. "How is your campaign going?"

"Ridiculous. No one cares. People give money, they have good intentions, but after they donate they think somehow the situation is taken care of. They don't realize the problems. We send out newsletters, brochures...it doesn't matter. People just go on thinking it's going to be all right. It's not...it's not. Things are..."

"There comes a crisis time."

"Yes," Kyle said and he reached for her hand, "there comes a crisis time."

"People must become aware and emotionally attached to the cause before they can fully get on board with what is happening to our environment."

"Yes."

"They must be made aware. Am I right?"

"Yes, mother, you are so right. And I have a plan in place to do that. A plan that is already set in motion. It...it will shock people. But it is necessary to get people to understand where we are and what has to be done."

"Can I help, sweet boy, can I help? Tell me what I can do."

He hated what she asked, what she said. There was the assumed need, the suggested vulnerability, the implied lack of something, whatever it was, to accomplish his plan. He needed her to be on his side and he swallowed what he would have liked to say in rebuttal. He wanted to substantiate his ability to get the job done, but he choked his thoughts back and squeezed them into a small nook of his mind. He smiled and squeezed her hand slightly, an almost loving gesture. He needed her. For awhile, at least.

"Of course you can, Mom, you are a key ingredient in what we want to accomplish. Frankly, I need your space behind the gallery, I need you to understand and put up with some strange things that may happen in the next week or so, and I need you to...to...."

He paused, not because he did not know what to say, but rather to suck her in to the scheme he had prepared. It was seemingly an act of submission to her dominance, when in reality it was a way of controlling her overriding compulsion to be in the forefront. He knew it was a way to have his own way. She would be his champion, his defender, his accomplice.

"…be supportive," he finished.

"Of course I'm supportive, dear boy. I know how important this is to you."

The efficient waitress came and they ordered. They had learned the menu long ago and could rattle off their choices to her with ease. There had been numerous lunches at P. F. Chang's, a many-times ritual of their meeting and talking. Each was an attempt to relate as adults, something Doris made very difficult to happen. He was her baby boy and would be forever. She recognized his brilliant mind, but was not sure how well he used it. She only trusted her own ability and made scant accommodation for others, even her son.

There was that silly vacant silence after they ordered and Doris took that opportunity to jump to her crusade of righteousness on behalf of her daughter-in-law, now suffering at the hands of this sweet boy across from her, the estranged husband.

"Laurie needs money," Doris stated flatly.

"Mother, I am pressed to the wall…"

"Stop. Please, just stop…right there. Tonight, you will, thanks to your hard-working sister, take in a goodly sum of money. Take some of that for Laurie. Write her a check this afternoon. Take it over to the hospital and give it to her…in person. Thank her for her indulgence in not suing your ass for divorce and ask her to come to the fund raiser with you."

"I will not ask her to the fund raiser."

"Why not?"

"Not appropriate. A great deal would...would have to be decided...circumstances resolved before I would do something like that."

"Take her a check."

"I...I will do that."

"Eight thousand dollars...at least"

"I'll give her a check."

"Good. Eight grand. She's worth more and you can afford it."

"That's just it...I can't. I can't afford it."

Their food was served and neither said a word as hunger took over and they began to devour what they had ordered.

"I want to come back to the gallery after we finish. I want to check out a few things."

Doris never mentioned Laurie again through the meal, but he knew there would be a follow-up exam. He could count on that. As he drove to her gallery on Olympic Boulevard, he wondered how much he should reveal to her of the plan he had made. He decided that, as is the case with all successful plans of insurrection, the fewer folks there were who knew the details the better off things would be. Right now, he alone knew all of the details.

Taylor Gallery was an art, antique, and artifacts business Doris had conducted for almost fifteen years in a renovated manufacturing plant in Santa Monica. The large building was unimposing from the outside, but inside was another story. Inside, it had been gloriously designed, decorated, and detailed for visual sumptuousness, almost breathtaking in beauty of presentation. What Kyle wanted was the use of the rear storage area where large overhead doors made it possible to drive in and hold several vehicles.

He marveled at his mother; she was a masterpiece of assertion and success. She was a poster girl for a certain way of life. It was a life he secretly envied, but could not adapt, a way of life he felt would eventually kill the society to which he had tried to reconcile himself. Doris the queen, as he referred to her in his inner most thoughts, divorced his father Ramsey ten years earlier and had married Nathan Krause the following year. She had moved into Nathan's home, leaving the Dixon residence to daughter Kelli and her husband Kevin. Each of these homes was really palatial in scope from the perspective of most folks, each in a well-respected and substantial neighborhood in Santa Monica. When Ramsey had died, Kelli was awarded the house officially, Kyle got the avocado ranch, and Doris was given most of the cash and stocks. The arrangement suited each of them and Kyle had moved in with his mother and Nathan after he left Laurie. In her mind, he was still living with her, although he rarely spent time in the house any more.

Nathan's death was not exactly a shock since he was fifteen years older than Doris and his health was never that great. There was no pre-nuptial agreement, no children, and Doris graciously accepted his multi-million dollar estate as her inheritance.

Kyle got back to the gallery before his mother, parked at the rear, and waited. She pulled in beside him and quickly went inside. She had been away from the business for less than an hour, but was nervous about the time. She waved at him. There was some weird sort of comfort for him with that wave. It was a signal of recognition, but also of acceptance and approval. He knew that it probably did not mean those things, but he liked to think it did. In any case, he knew he could count on his mother.

The rear storage area of the gallery was perfect. Plenty of room for the roach coach he wanted to hide here, plenty of room to store the materials he would stash for the placements. This would work very nicely.

She watched him standing there surveying the building.

"I've got a roach coach in storage in Riverside," he said, "don't be surprised, Mother, when I bring it in here in the next week or so."

"A what?"

"A catering truck. You've seen them around…serving snacks and drinks and lunches to the laborers…then driving on to another job site. They're called roach coaches…for obvious reasons."

"Why would you need one of those?" she grimaced.

"Part of the plan, Mother, part of the plan. It will all become clear to you eventually. Letting me keep it back here is a tremendous help, believe me."

She shook her head and hunched up her shoulders as if to express her lack of understanding in what he had in store. Then she quickly put it out of her mind and returned to the agenda of Laurie.

"Get her the money. She needs it. Go over to Saint John's and write a check and be done with it and know you have done the right thing."

"I want to see the kids."

"Why? Do you care?"

He stared at her.

"What I am asking is not cruel. You pay them little attention. I assume you don't care about them. Why do you want to see them now?"

"They are my children. I care about them, I always have. But I have a mission and that supercedes everything."

"They're with Hanna, of course. She would not deny you. She could not. You can see them if you wish. But only Sadie if you go there now. Justin and Carol are in school. They'll be home later."

She looked at him waiting for a response, but he simply stared at the ceiling. He left his mother without saying a word, but gave her a quick, perfunctory hug.

He stood at the counter of the nurse's station and watched as Laurie typed at her computer keyboard. She still had a lovely face. Her calm demeanor and easy manner as she worked filled him with desire and frustration. She sensed someone was there and she turned to face him. She quickly rose and came to the counter.

"Kyle…"

"Hi. I…I've got some money for you." He pulled a check book and pen from his jacket pocket and proceeded to write.

"Justin wants to see you…"

"Later." He continued writing.

"…and Carol and Sadie. Do you remember their names?"

He looked up at her.

"I remember their names."

"Good, because memory isn't forever. They will forget you if you don't see them, don't maintain contact."

"I will see them later." He continued writing.

"I'll call Hanna and tell her you're coming."

"Good." He tore the check from the pad.

"We should talk."

"It doesn't matter any more," he said. "You probably will never ever see me again except on TV. I will send you one more check and that will be the last check you ever get from me. It will be…good…a substantial amount. And it will be the last."

"Kyle…"

"I'm only here because my mother nagged me. I know she talks to you all the time and if I didn't do this she would nag me more. Thank my mother for this. He slid the check on the counter toward her.

She picked it up and read the amount.

"Five thousand dollars. Thank you. Thanks a lot. Fifty would be appropriate, but thanks at least for this."

"I love gratitude, it's so great."

"Gratitude? You moved out three years ago and in all that time you have barely supported us...barely. Done your share? Let's see now...ahem. Five thousand added to the generous amount you've already given and we total almost nine thousand dollars. How generous you are Mister Idealist, Mister Moralist, Mister Environmentalist. Nine thousand dollars in three years. Yea, for you. If it weren't for the money your mother and sister have given us we would be in deep trouble."

"I have a mission..."

"I have a mission...raising our children."

"I know, I know. It's important. There was a time you knew how important my mission was..."

"A long time ago. I focused on it, but I've grown up, grown away from that focus. The environment is important, but it's not my life. My kids are my life right now."

"Well, any way, you'll get more, believe me."

"Before something happens?"

"Yes."

"Your remark before had an ominous sound to it. What is going to happen?"

"You are going to..." He pulled back from the counter and put the pen and checkbook back in his pocket. "You will receive a just amount. Soon."

Laurie picked up the check, folded it, and put it in the pocket of her uniform. She watched him as he rushed away down the hall. A chill came over her. She assumed she would never see him again alive. She knew how determined he was and accepted what he had said to her. She called home and alerted Hanna that he would be coming by to see the children.

Kelli Rothstein, thanks to her husband Kevin, was well-connected, socially dynamic when entertaining friends and acquaintances, politically active, and certainly a desirable neighbor. She taught political science at Santa Monica City College and was self-righteously politically correct. With undergraduate and Masters degrees with honors from UCLA, she reveled in the world of academia. She now is ambivalent about her father, adores her brother, tolerates her husband, and cannot fathom her entrepreneurial mother.

She was studiously pouring over a cookbook in the kitchen when Kyle came in the back door without knocking or ringing the bell. She was okay with his unannounced entry. She jumped up and gave him a big hug and kissed his cheek with all the hammy demonstration she could muster.

"God, it's good to see you. I am so excited about tonight. You will love who's coming…John Walker, Ted Ligmon, Shania Hammond…"

"You planning to cook for the guests?" He pointed at the cookbook in front of her.

"Oh, hell no, you know better. It's all catered. They should be here any minute to get started. Tent is all set up in back. You noticed, of course. Tables, chairs, flowers all arranged…we're pretty much ready."

He considered telling her about seeing Laurie, but decided that would lead to a conversation he did not want. However his decision, it did not matter.

"Bringing Laurie?"

"Why do you ask?" He realized it would be difficult to fend off Kelli, but he would try.

"Might be nice. She still is your wife. She needs your support."

"I just saw her. Gave her a check."

"I don't mean money. I can give her more money than you can, I would guess. Money isn't the issue. Support means something else."

"Right, I know, I didn't mean..."

"Look, I don't want to nag. I know mother does that about Laurie, but I can't help but feel sorry for her. She is raising three kids...without your help."

"She has no feeling for what I am doing..."

"Stop, stop, don't say anything else. I should not have even said a thing. So she..."

"She would not attend. She doesn't see the importance of this cause anymore."

"You're right, you're right..."

"I just wanted to swing by and see if everything was okay. I had lunch with Mom at Chang's, so I was nearby. Checking in with you, I guess. We haven't really talked for a couple of weeks."

The doorbell rang.

"There's the caterers...you get going. Remember, dress for success tonight. Don't look like..."

"What?" he laughed.

"Please don't look like an avocado farmer. Look like an environmental activist. Look important."

"Don't worry, I have plenty of success clothes in my closet."

"Get out of here."

When Kyle got to his house, the house he had shared with Laurie, Justin and Carol were not yet home from school.

Little Sadie, three years old, was with Aunt Hanna. Sadie cried when she saw her daddy.

Hanna Hart was Laurie's sister. She was thirty-five, five years younger than Laurie, looked older than her years, and had never married. Her features were plain and she did little to her hair or with makeup which would have enhanced her appearance. Today she had yet to comb her hair, but it had been pulled back and held in place with clips. Kyle thought her hair looked dirty and wondered about the young woman's cleanliness. It bothered him that she might not be clean.

She had suffered from Multiple Sclerosis for many years and struggled to walk with pronounced difficulty. Her dedication to her sister and the children was unquestioned, and she had lived in the house since Justin was born.

Hanna scowled at Kyle.

"I gave Laurie a check…"

"She told me."

"There will be more…a lot more."

"And then no more."

He stared at her.

"She told me what you said."

Sadie was clinging to his legs and he picked her up and hugged her and kissed her neck.

"How soon before Justin and Carol get home?"

She shifted her body in the chair where she was sitting and looked at him without answering right away. He ignored her delayed response and continued to nuzzle Sadie.

"Half hour," she snapped, finally.

"I'll wait," he said, turning, carrying Sadie to the porch. "We'll wait for brother and sister right here," he almost cooed to the toddler. The response was a giggle.

Hanna remained in her chair and the interminable wait began. The time passage for each of them was miserable. She was the protective, angry, indignant sister-in-law; he the impassioned, driven, defiant father. Each was fortified by their own justification for point and position.

Justin and Carol arrived home from school thrilled to see their dad. They tossed and tumbled with dad and baby sister, and had a snack Hanna fixed for them. They played a game, then another, listened as dad read a book, and chattered some about school. They cried when he said he had to go, and then he was gone. Hanna was relieved when he left and the three children sulked for the rest of the day.

Kyle went to the house he had shared with his mother before moving to Riverside. It was a lovely home in Santa Monica that looked quite unpretentious from the street because of its low profile and foliage coverage. In reality, however, it was a five thousand square feet wonder of design, detail, and distinction. His bedroom-bathroom suite was always ready for his return and the staff knew accordingly.

Raymond Estancia answered the door. Raymond was the all-doer. He took care of the yard and garden, supervised the pool man, did minor repairs and hired needed contractors, and made sure the property was secure. He also acted as butler when required. He lived over the garage in his own elegantly furnished apartment. Supe Meroz was the cook. She came at ten in the morning seven days a week and left at ten in the evening. She prepared lunch and dinner, did the grocery shopping, and helped with the substantial entertaining. Josey Sela came Monday through Friday at nine and cleaned the house, non-stop as she claimed, until five, and was gone. Kyle loved the luxury of this, but knew that somehow it was in contradiction to a kind of life he believed was more important.

Kyle stripped off his clothes, shaved, showered, and stood naked drying himself in front of the closet. He was considering what to wear to the fundraiser. Dress for success,

Kelli directed. He decided on the tried and true. It would be a blue blazer with his embroidered initials on the handkerchief pocket. He laid that on the bed. It would be gray slacks that he put beside the blazer. Then there was a custom-tailored silk shirt that he dropped on the blazer. It had been a gift from Nathan, the considerate, but short-term stepfather. He selected tastefully coordinated blue knee-length stockings which he flipped over the shirt, and exquisitely hand-made loafers that he kicked out of the closet toward the bed. He considered this ensemble a costume. In his case, perhaps he was right.

There was a knock at the bedroom door and Raymond entered without waiting for Kyle to respond. He carried a tray with a bottle of Dewar's, a cocktail glass filled with ice, a cold Heineken, several chunks of some kind of white cheese, and a half-dozen Ritz crackers.

"Supe wanted you to have this," Raymond explained with an air of indifference that Kyle did not notice. "A tide-me-over. A decent snack, she says, to keep you going. She says your work is important and you must keep going."

"I don't know if the Scotch would keep me going or make me pass out," Kyle laughed. "I'll take the beer, though. Too full from lunch with Mother for cheese and crackers."

"Would you need a glass?" Raymond asked. "Supe forgot to put one on the tray."

"Naw, she knows I don't need a glass."

Raymond placed the silver tray on a table by the window.

"Can I get you anything else?"

"No thanks, Raymond. But you can tell me something."

Raymond looked down at the carpet as he waited for the question.

"You helped Kelli get this shindig ready for tonight, right?"

"Yes, I did. Your mother volunteered my services."

"What do you think? Will we be successful?"

"Depends how you define success."

"We need money."

"We...?" Raymond cocked his head to one side when he said it and then smiled.

"The Alliance For A Better Environment."

"Oh...yes...your..." Raymond paused for several beats before he said, "...cause. I forgot the name. Well, if your sister's planning and preparations are any indication for success, then I think you will be. But you can't always tell with the entertainment glitterati. They sometimes clutch their wallets and checkbooks very tightly. In their eyes, even with the connections of your sister and her husband, you are a nobody. Sorry. I would not have high expectations...just to be realistic."

"Thanks a lot."

"As I say, you have to be realistic."

"Pick a number," Kyle demanded.

"Hard to figure."

"Give me a number, give me your best estimate."

Raymond stared into space, his eyes glazing, as if he were actually calculating a well-thought out dollar amount.

"You'll be lucky to net twenty-five thou after Kelli pulls out her expenses."

"Her expenses?"

"Yes. You did plan, that is to say the Alliance did plan to pay her costs, didn't they? Tent, tables and chairs, flowers, catering, musicians, waiters and waitresses, parking attendants, security, and so forth. It all adds up. Cuts into the take."

"Damn."

"I know. Let's hope it's worth the effort."

Raymond closed the door behind him before Kyle could engage him any further. He already had enough of Kyle for one burst of time, about as much as he could tolerate.

When Kyle arrived at Kelli's, which was the primary and last house in which they were raised, he could not readily find her. She was busy somewhere and the guests had begun to arrive in full force. His search for her was interrupted as Kevin grabbed his arm.

"Hey, buddy, come on in the den. Let's chat finances for a minute."

Kevin Rothstein was three years younger than Kelli, tall, lean, and had the look of a man in great physical condition, which he was. An excellent athlete, he started at second base his senior year for the UCLA baseball team. Undergraduate degree in economics, law degree from Berkeley, he is an attorney for a large LA law firm and personally handles several very high-profile clients in sports and entertainment. He has four Dodgers box seat season tickets and prides himself on this possession. He passed on Lakers and Kings tickets, neither sport he appreciated. Also a CPA, he handles the financials for Kyle's non-profit organizations. In his personal life he keeps a low profile and stays out of Kelli's way. He is very fond of his mother-in-law and sometimes hangs out at her store when Kelli is involved with some project. Tonight, however, was a command performance. Besides, all of his clients were to be here.

Kyle allowed himself to be half pushed, half eased into the study that he remembered as both a foreboding and yet, in contrast, a calm and luminous space of revelation and inspiration.

"There is no money in any of the accounts." Kevin announced this as if his saying the words could and would inspire some revelation.

"Really," Kyle mustered. He knew it was so because of the draws that he had made against these accounts, but played it as if it were a surprise.

"Where did the money go?" Kevin asked.

"We spent it...it was needed." Kyle was unapologetic. "It takes a lot to get the job done."

"But...there are no receipts, no invoices...nothing to justify or validate expenditures."

What money was in the accounts, Kyle had used to finance the initial phase of the robberies. He had not bothered to return any of it once they had begun to accumulate cash. That cash he had kept at the ranch to pay for what he needed to get materiel and supplies to build his placements. He had not bothered to deposit any of the small contributions that had continued to come in to the office.

"That's easy to fix," Kyle excused. He did not want Kevin to know what he was doing, to be a part of the plan of "making them suffer." We've had donations that have not been deposited, checks still in the office."

"Things don't look very good for your organizations," Kevin offered.

"Well, I have the ranch. I'll be all right and I think I can keep going on with the cause, especially if we can raise some money tonight."

He was consciously disingenuous and he could feel the heat of his own lie burning within him, a hot poker that seared in his chest, a feeling to be disregarded, to be compartmentalized, to be secluded, and away from other thoughts. His denial of the truth was part of his amoral personality that covered his morally superior attitude about society's need for environmental protection. The end result mattered most.

"Would you want me to handle those financials...the ones for the ranch?"

"No," Kyle said slowly, "I've got a guy in Fallbrook...CPA, very conscientious, and knows the avocado business. He's fine. He'll take care of the ranch."

"Okay," Kevin retreated, "it has its ins and outs that are very specific. If he knows the avocado business, its better you stick with him."

Kelli charged into the room like a low-grade earthquake and grabbed her brother's arm.

"Time to work the crowd," she exhorted, "the big donors are here. I'll introduce you around and then I want you to give your speech...the sad one, the one that makes me cry, the one that will energize and really solicit the wonderful people here who are behind your cause."

Kyle met almost everyone in attendance, his hand aching from all of the hands shaken, his throat parched from the large quantities of banalities he exchanged, his heart beating from the perceived potential of all the money this crowd represented. He kissed the last hand which was that of a fat, outspoken woman from Beverly Hills who had no previous idea the environment was being brutalized. He stepped to the dais which the bandleader gladly relinquished for his presentation. He spoke for fifteen minutes, without notes, strictly from the soul of his commitment, and mesmerized the crowd with statistics and facts and details and emotion. His performance was impressive in a world where the listeners were used to impressive emoting and attempts at persuasion. Kyle met their standard and more and was the critical salvation for what would have otherwise been another wonderful, well-orchestrated, yet meaningless function to raise money.

As he spoke, he looked skyward as if he were invoking the aide of some supreme being, some powerful force, some undefined spirit he felt loathe to submit to as deity, yet powerful as a source of inspiration, righteousness, and divine intervention. The white, cloud-like spread of the tent roof was his sky, a restriction to contain this event. A circus tent, the big top, with all of the energy and excitement buzzing within, he in the center ring, drawing full attention as the waiters and waitresses continued to serve drinks and hors d'oeuvres as the crowd nodded and murmured agreement with his evocation. Only the amount of the take was in question, not the sentiment of the assembled.

After his speech, Kyle submitted to more hand shaking and bantering with the ones Kelli selected and directed. He finally was able to free himself and retreat to a chair by the pool, alone for a brief time, suffering the hangover of rabble-crush, of ignorance in the guise of concern. A moment later, Kevin was beside him.

"It's going to be good, very good," Kevin whispered into his ear, "I'll get it into the bank account as soon as I can get it collected, but it looks like about fifty grand net...after expenses. That should help."

That should help. The phrase haunted him. He needed that amount months ago, it would have meant that many fewer robberies they would have needed to commit, that much more equipment he could have gotten on hand. Now, with tonight's money an indefinite amount to be collected and deposited some unknown time in the future, he could only shrug in response to Kevin.

"Good," he said, "that's good."

It wasn't late, but he knew he had to get out of there, and he knew the party would go on for several more hours, the last straggler staggering away after midnight. He found Kelli, kissed her cheek and said good-bye and that he would talk to her soon and walked away to his car. She had smiled and nodded and patted his cheek and never stopped talking to this hunk producer with the chiseled granite face.

The lights were on in Raymond's apartment over the garage and the front door was unlocked. Supe was just finishing in the kitchen.

"About done...another day complete?" He asked her.

"Si. Eso es," she said with a smile. "Your party go well?"

"Real good, Supe, real good."

"I am going now. Will I see you soon?"

"Maybe, I don't know."

"Buenas noches, Señor Kyle."

"Yes...buenas noches."

He went upstairs and could see the lights still on in his mother's room through the open door. She was asleep on the bed, fully dressed, the television alive with the sound turned way down. There was an open book collapsed on her chest. He turned off the TV, removed the book, placed it on the dresser, and turned off the lights. He went to his sometime room and removed his clothes. He carefully hung the pants and jacket in the closet and kicked the loafers in underneath. He threw the shirt and socks in a corner where he knew Josey would find them and take care of them. He crawled into bed and before he passed into some unknown dark abyss, he wondered how soon he would be in this room again.

Kyle awoke with a start just after four in the morning. Some kind of internal alarm clock brought him to consciousness and he rose on one elbow to survey the dark room. For an instant he was disoriented, not knowing where he was, but quickly realized he was in his mother's house. Without turning on a light, he dressed as quickly as he could in the surreal dimness where the glow of clock numbers was sufficient light by which to see. He carefully made his way through the house and saw the bright red warning light on the security system control panel. Raymond must have armed it after he had gone upstairs to bed. He disarmed the system with his own code. Once outside, he stopped on the front porch, and took a deep breath. It was damp and cool without a hint of wind. The scent of night-blooming jasmine cut through the stagnant city air that still had the remnants of the previous day's smog clinging relentlessly. He was sorry he had bothered to take that deep breath. He was starting the day angry; he was convinced that it was impossible not to be angry with such miserable conditions. For him, the cup was indeed half empty.

He drove along deserted side streets and soon was on the Santa Monica Freeway headed for the long, monotonous, and, for him, somewhat torturous drive to Fallbrook. At this hour, the traffic trenches of LA should hardly have been used if this were a normal city. But LA is not a normal city and the volume of vehicles was astonishing even to him. Who are all of these people traveling through the city at this time that was still considered night? Where are they going, what will they be doing when they get there? Did they want it to be like this, that they be subjected to this? He thought not, he thought they were part of a population symbolizing depersonalization. It resulted from the capitalist decadence. They characterized a society he knew had to be brought to realization. His alienation made him squirm, stretch his head back, and flex his shoulders to reduce the tension *This* was the tension that motivated him and one of the reasons he saw Dr. Simmons. He thought about Dr. Simmons with some degree of respect and a portion of disdain. Dr. Simmons was a caregiver of the establishment, helping those who needed and wanted help, reaping the rewards in generous terms. Dr. Simmons listened to him and made suggestions, tried to help eliminate the alienation or at least minimize its impact on him, and could not have cared less about his cause. Dr. Simmons would have been shocked if he knew the full extent of his plan for creating the suffering to bring awareness. He would not have been able to understand the necessity of it nor condone its execution.

A kind of despair came over him as he thought about the previous evening's fundraiser. It was not what he had wanted, but Kelli insisted. So it was over, there would never be another. Despite the need to do so, he felt tainted by putting in his appearance with the hypocrites. He had been soiled by them, diminished in some sense, and caught in his own self-assessed hypocrisy. No point now in worrying about it, he considered, it was more important to think about the second Gladstone operation. That was really more important, the last maneuver before his plan went into full gear. He needed more plastic than they had gotten from the first Gladstone theft and he knew he could get what he wanted at the second Gladstone facility.

10.

The sky broke open in front of Kyle with a band of dull orange that widened and intensified as he drove east. It was becoming a fiery precursor to daylight. Slowly the sun emerged with a shot of light that stabbed at his eyes, inched upward, and spread its power. Now shut out behind a line of buildings, it reappeared and disappeared as if it were some kind of tease. This alternating condition was like some kind of game until the sun was high enough to dominate everything. Kyle flipped down the visor and slipped sun glasses to his eyes. I am the real McCoy, he reckoned, a true Californian with shades to the face and driving a car somewhere. Such was the penalty of being a Californian, the punishment of driving so much, of driving long distances out of need. He hated the concept as much as he hated doing it and as much as it was his need.

The hot day was already in place when he arrived at the ranch. All of the boys and Carrie were nearly finished with breakfast. It had been sparse: cereal for those who wanted it, fruit, toast and jam, and boiled eggs. There was hot coffee remaining and Kyle poured himself a cup. He leaned against the sink and watched the others finish eating. Their greetings, other than Carrie, had been minimal and they waited for what he had to say. Carrie eased to his side and rubbed his chest with the flat of her hand. She still had a piece of toast in her other hand and was chewing. She brushed her face against his upper arm almost like a cat would do and she probably would have purred if not for the food in her mouth.

She coughed and grabbed her cup to slurp some coffee to ease the sensation, but it did not help. She went out onto the porch and continued the hacking. She had smoked since she was ten. She wanted desperately to quit, but had not been able to manage it. The persistent chronic cough was a continuing affliction that plagued her. Carrie rarely smoked around Kyle, so while he had been gone she indulged heavily, her pacifier for staying off the booze. Her lanky frame was angled against the railing, her large protruding nipples showed through her cheesecloth-thin white tee shirt. Those men there who ogled her in the morning light as she balanced on one foot with crossed ankles, nipples so obvious, had no idea how dangerous she was. She was fiercely loyal to Kyle. She didn't really know what love was, only loyalty. Loyalty she valued, loyalty she understood. She would do anything he asked, she would kill for him. She had killed before when she was a teenager, well before she met Kyle. She fully understood death and killing and would surely kill for him and his cause. If any of them had dared make a move on her, she would reject them severely. To the extreme; she would kill, if necessary. She was indeed dangerous.

Carrie finally got control of the coughing and heard Kyle explaining something to the others. She was torn. She craved a cigarette and wanted to walk away from the house, into the trees, and have a smoke. She also wanted to know what Kyle was saying, what he was telling the men. She choked away the urge and went back inside.

"…has to be done…today. There isn't time for a lot of planning, so we do the easiest thing, we make a frontal assault. We go right to the front gate."

"Is this the location near the Cahuilla Indian Reservation?" Mark asked.

"That's it. North from Highway 371. Remote and lightly guarded. But I imagine after our hit on the main facility, they've probably beefed up security. How much? Hard telling."

"I suppose we need another van," Ellis said, making it more of a statement than question.

"Not just a van," Kyle said, "but the right kind of van. We want one without windows, a delivery version, if possible."

"Might be hard to find right away, Kyle, are you sure it matters?" Ellis asked.

"We'll use a regular van if we have to, but that's the kind of vehicle I want. When we get to the gate I want it to look like a delivery van. You guys will be in back to overpower the guard. And the guard might have help we need to deal with. I'd rather they didn't see two of you in back before we could surprise them."

"This is a muscle operation then," Ted Sloan offered.

"It is…not much finesse about this one. We have to be tough and fast and it will work. We can get in and out quickly and be on our way."

"Ellis…Ted," Mark directed, "get your guns and gear. We're going to leave right away."

The two men moved out to Ellis Wilson's beat-up truck to get what they needed. Kyle watched them with a sort of wonder and a bit of admiration at their uncomplicated, unsophisticated, uneducated approach to life. They neither seemed to think much about the future nor got caught up in their past. Each day was an adventure and the days just rolled along. Working the avocado ranch was easy, they got paid enough, and there was always plenty of beer to drink. Ellis, older by six years at thirty-six, was divorced with an ex-wife and 14-year old son living in Wilmington, North Carolina. He hasn't seen them in eight years. He had come to California to get away and to start over with a new life. He was the kind of person one would call a confirmed loser. He was dedicated to a confounding kind of life, complicating it in ways others might find unimaginable. One might also call him a risk taker, but he seemed always to stumble into poor risks and rotten luck that kept his life a shambles. Ellis was in the Army ten years before being booted out for a variety of crimes and indiscretions. He has, surprisingly, avoided a civilian criminal record. Before working at the ranch, his longest job stint was six months. He had been at Kyle's avocado ranch for two years and believes in whatever Kyle says. He firmly believes these have been the best two years of his life. He shares a rented house in Fallbrook with the younger Ted Sloan. Ted attended the University of California Riverside on and off for several years taking various agriculture and horticulture classes without knowing how he wanted to focus his program. He had studied hard, got poor grades, and never graduated. He was, however, fully attuned to plants and animals with a natural sense about both and had been an asset at Kyle's ranch. He had worked for various citrus growers before arriving at Kyle's avocado operation. He believes in Kyle with blind adoration. He, too, has no criminal record.

"This it?" Mark directed at Kyle after the other two men had exited.

"Yeah…we're ready to put the plan into motion."

There was silence as Kyle sipped his coffee.

"Well…?"

"Well what?" Kyle put down his cup.

"Can you share the plan? For Christ's sake, we've known each other a long time and I still don't know what the details are. Only that we're going to "make the fools suffer" and "awareness has to come" and "pain will bring belief." Those are all goddamn generalities. I need to know the details if I am going to be a part of this…if I am going to help you."

"Me, too," Carrie chimed in, holding back a cough, wishing she could have a cigarette.

"Okay, okay…tonight…after we get this done. I'll give you the complete lowdown. Until now, if something went wrong and the law got involved, you would not have been able to reveal much. When I tell you all that is going to happen you will be up to your eyeballs in the whole thing. There will be no turning back and the plan will unfold."

"I understand," Mark said quietly.

"I do what you ask," croaked Carrie, her throat still dry and raspy, still longing to smoke.

Finding the right van that Kyle had in mind was not easy. They tried the Promenade Mall in Temecula and the Murrieta Town Center without success. Finally, driving through the parking lot in Sun City Shopping Center, they found what Kyle wanted. There was a brand new white Chevy Express 3500 passenger van with tinted windows that did not allow you to see inside.

"There it is," Kyle yelled, "perfect…perfect."

Carrie pulled into a nearby parking spot and did not turn off the engine.

"Someone might be inside," she warned, "you can't see."

"We have to take that chance." Kyle was calm when he spoke. "Give it a whirl, El."

It did not take Ellis long before he was backing the Chevy out of the slot and driving by them on the way to the far end of the lot. Carrie carefully followed. Ted and Mark jumped out and got into the back of the van with their gear and Ellis' backpack. Kyle hesitated in order to direct Carrie.

"We're going to drive the stuff we take from Gladstone back to the ranch and unload. You go back to the ranch and wait. When we have the stuff unloaded, you follow me to Hemet and we dump the van."

"Be careful."

"Yes, I know…this will not be easy."

"Be careful."

He nodded and got into the van.

Ellis followed Kyle's directions and they drove to the second Gladstone facility. This site was not used as much as the first they had robbed and contained no developed compound as the other had. There was a guard house, a couple of other buildings, and the explosives bunker. In a remote section of the site was a landing area for combat-style helicopters. Kyle had already determined that no training sessions were planned for this week. Along the way, Kyle primed them on what to expect and how to react. He was confident they could handle it. They had worked successfully for several weeks robbing and stealing and the men reacted and performed well in stressful situations. He knew, however, those jobs had been planned and this one was extemporaneous, but he trusted their ability to get it done.

The last several miles were dirt road and the dust kicked up behind them rooster-tail fashion that fanned out in a gray-brown plume. The trail of dust would give the guard plenty of advance notice someone was coming. It could not be helped; this was the frontal attack.

A large sign with the name GLADSTONE INTERNATIONAL in bold blue letters let them know they were close and then they were confronted by gated, high chain link fencing, and a uniformed guard. Their dust had indeed notified the guard that they were coming and he stood waiting next to the road in front of the gate. He carried a holstered 9mm automatic. Behind him, at the door of the guard house, stood another man in khakis and tee shirt. He was holding an M4 assault rifle loosely in front of him, but ready to use it if the need arose. Ellis stopped the van right next to the guard. The cloud of dust settled slowly behind them through the still air, as if a brown curtain were slowly falling.

"Usually only the guard here," Kyle said, "must have added that other guy since we hit the main location. Let me do the talking. Buzz down the window."

The guard stepped to the van as the window lowered.

"Morning. Makin' lots of dust this morning."

"Good morning. Sorry about that. Ah...," Kyle eyed the man's name badge so he could be more personal, "...Larry. Kept our speed down, too."

"That's okay...can't be helped, dry as hell around here. What's your business?" The guard was polite, but seemed very serious.

"We've got a delivery." Kyle said

"No one's here..."

"I know. The stuff we've got is hush-hush and we know where..."

"Let's see your papers." The guard placed his hands on his hips. He was wary and ready to be suspicious.

"No papers. Elliott Hoover gave us our assignment directly...said no paperwork was needed."

Kyle dropped Hoover's name knowing the man was one of the top officials at Gladstone and one who often worked outside the system.

"Aw, shit, he's always pulling something."

"Hey, listen, why don't you have your guy over there check us out in back while you call headquarters and verify this. Save some time."

The guard wheeled and headed for the guard house where the man in khakis had become alert to something out of the ordinary.

"Check out the back of the van," he ordered, as he jabbed his thumb over his shoulder.

"Grab him when he opens the door," Kyle hissed to Ted and Mark. To Ellis he said "Once they grab him we have to get the guard."

"Right." Ellis stared straight ahead.

The man in khakis came to the back of the van with the M4 hanging over his shoulder on the rifle sling. He pulled open the rear door and was immediately yanked forward and knocked senseless before he could react. Ellis and Kyle were out of the truck to get the guard, but he sensed something wrong and started to run. He was intent on sounding an alarm. He almost got to the door of the guard house and decided to pull his weapon.

As he drew the pistol and turned, Ted, now out of the back of the van, fired his own semi-automatic and hit him in the upper right side of his chest. Ted had not taken time to carefully aim, but had jerked a shot cowboy fashion. It was a lucky hit, not a lethal one, but painful and disabling. The guard fell to one knee and could not raise his arm. He fired into the ground. Ted ran to the guard before Kyle or Ellis could reach him and kicked the gun out of his hand. He smacked the guard on the side of his head and man rolled onto his right side. Ted picked up the guard's pistol as the man groaned word sounds without meaning.

"Sorry, Kyle, but he'd a shot ya if he could have." Ted held his pistol at his side.

"I know," Kyle said, "I know."

"Come on," Mark directed, "let's get that gate open and get our stuff. Ted, use the gray tape and get these guys taped up. Keep the rifle. And watch out for anybody else."

Ted taped both men's hands behind their backs then taped ankles and at the knees. By this time khakis man was awake and groggy, yelling profanities. Ted taped his mouth shut and pulled him inside the guard house. He then pulled the guard inside and flopped him next to khakis man.

Ellis pushed the button for the gate and it rolled aside to let them enter. Kyle was already behind the wheel and drove them to the bunker where he knew the plastic was held. The bolt cutter made short work getting the lock off and the men began loading the van.

"Look at this," Ellis yelled.

The others came to where he stood.

"Yeah, hand grenades. I didn't know if they would be here," Kyle said. "We'll take some of those, too. Never know when you might need them. Could come in handy."

It took less than twenty minutes to get all of the plastic explosives, detonators, and hand grenades that Kyle wanted into the van. There was a bonus and Kyle smiled when he saw the box. Timers. Simple gadgets which would make his job easier.

When they finished loading, they drove outside the fence and Ted activated the switch that closed the gate. Ellis was driving.

"Guys, that was easier than I thought it might be." Kyle was pleased with them and himself.

"Are we ready?" Mark asked.

"We are, yes, we are."

"Lay it on me."

"When we get back...I'll draw it out for you."

"Okay."

It was several minutes before Kyle broke the silence.

"You know, Mark, the truth of the matter is that some guys like us, can rob and steal without difficulty, without detection, until a mistake is made and a connection is developed. It will be awhile before the authorities can do that...the sheriff...the FBI. By then we will be long gone, in hibernation, adjusting for a continuing effort. This will be a long, ongoing battle to gain the hearts and minds of society, but we will do it."

No one else said a word for several minutes, each of the other men contemplating what Kyle had said from their perspective. Each debating in his own mind whether what was unfolding and what could happen was a terrible negative or a positive they could be comfortable with and embrace. Each in his own way decided more needed to be known about what Kyle expected and planned to accomplish. That they could escape Scott-free and stay out of the hands of the law was not a serious issue in their minds. It was the level of confidence they had in him. But what would they get out of all of this? None of them wanted to pose that question to Kyle. It would all have to play out the way he wanted. In the excitement of their raids and robberies, no one had yet factored that they would be wanted by the authorities and hunted for these crimes.

The drive back to the ranch was otherwise uneventful and they could not see that anyone witnessed them pull onto the ranch property. So far so good in terms of the stolen van. Who knew if an APB had been ordered for it; probably, but not necessarily. Carrie ran out to meet them as they pulled up to the barn. The barn doors were opened and the van driven inside.

"How'd it go," she yelled.

"Real good," Mark announced, "real good. We got what Kyle wanted."

"We had to shoot a guard," Kyle said solemnly.

"Had to?" Carrie whispered.

"Had to…or he'd have shot one of us. Ellis was closest to him; he'd have gotten it first. Ted covered us and…and kept him from killing Ellis and me."

"Damn fella reacted fast, damn fast," Ted offered. "Sensed something wrong right away. We didn't make a fuss when we grabbed and cold-cocked the other guy, but he musta heard something…or maybe just intuition or something. I saw the guard stop and I knew we was in for trouble."

"You got that shot off just like Clint Eastwood," Mark laughed, "just like in the spaghetti westerns, only you didn't shoot the gun out of his hand."

"That stuff in those movies is so much bullshit. I was lucky to hit him."

"Let's take care of this stuff," Kyle said, stopping the banter. "You saved us Ted, that's all that matters. Thanks."

"Nothin' to it, Kyle." Ted Sloan was pleased with the thanks.

They unloaded the boxes into Kyle's workroom. When they finished, everyone went up to the house to have a beer. The men settled around the kitchen table as Carrie fetched the beer bottles from the refrigerator. Anchor Steam this time; Kyle loved Anchor Steam as well as Mexican beer. It was expensive, but it was what he wanted.

After a long draw on his bottle, Kyle spoke of its quality.

"You can't get a better beer in this country," he said definitively. "Look at the color, smell the flavor. It tastes the way beer should. Better than the Mexican beer. Mexican beer is good, but this is better"

The others nodded agreement as they slugged down large gulps of the brew.

"Costs a lot for a beer," Mark offered.

"Nothing is too good for you guys," Kyle laughed.

They all chuckled and then it was quiet for awhile.

"Right now is as good a time as any to tell us what we are going to do…what your plan is. What we might be up against. What your plan is to…to get folks attention." Mark had already sucked down his Anchor Steam when he spoke.

"Our modern society," Kyle began, stepping into his pontification mode, "doesn't get it when it comes to environmental issues. They only give lip service to what needs to get done. They figure someone else will take care of things, the government, and big business if we nudge them…someone else. The real nudge has to be given to society itself. To make them aware…to make them fully understand, we need to remove two basics: water and electric power. No air conditioning, no drinking water, no flushing of toilets, no water for cooking, no electricity for stoves or lights or TVs or video games or the operation of stores and restaurants and gas stations…nothing powered by electricity. Hospitals struggle, fire departments can't fight fires, traffic gets snarled beyond imagination and chaos takes over Southern California. Chaos pits citizens against the state and neighbor. All in the name of survival. Looting and criminal activity will go wild…"

"How?" Mark interrupted.

"We blow up pumping stations and we blow up transmission towers. We stop water and electricity from moving into and across Southern California. We already have a team in place to take care of the Hayfield Pumping Station. All we need to do is get them the placement they will use. We'll build it here and deliver it to them next week. The same night we make a placement at the Perris Dam pumping station and pick off three different transmission lines. I have a map with the locations noted so that we can coordinate our efforts. We are all going to be moving at once, each of us with an assignment. This is a basic, first-line attack on the two major points of infrastructure that are important. Then we move to west LA. LA proper needs to feel the full brunt of this. The water disruption around here won't immediately affect them, but in time it will. We will speed up the process by obliterating the water pumping station on San Vicente Boulevard and knocking down several key transmission towers in LA, Brentwood, and Santa Monica. This will all happen in a very short time frame…two, three days and the die will be cast for getting the attention of the rich, the elite, the decision-makers, the media moguls, and all the folks who can yell and scream and whose noise makes things happen. In the meantime, I will be sending…submitting articles of transgression to the LA Times and other newspapers and television stations and radio for what this all means and what society in this part of the world has to do to make things change."

"God damn, you think we can do all of that?" Mark asked.

"I don't know why not. The authorities don't know who we are or where we are or what we have in mind. We hit, hit, hit, and are out of the way for the time being as adjustments are made."

"You think this will change things?"

"Of course it will. People will see what is needed. They will demand changes from their city governments and state government in order to preserve lifestyle in a better way. All doable, readily attainable on our part."

"How do we get this done and get out of here without getting killed or arrested?" Mark was opening another Anchor Steam when he asked the question.

"I have a nice boat for us at Newport Beach. The boat is just another part of the cost of operations we have been getting money for. It is programmed to leave harbor when I say so. We will be on it, we will be on our way to a spot I have arranged in Ecuador and we will function there to fight the environmental fight that needs to be waged in this country. This society in the USA is way behind the curve dealing with environmental issues and we can promote and propose from there. We will succeed and we will be very comfortable in Ecuador. That's why we needed to conduct the operations we did and with the help of donated money we will be just fine and get done what we need to accomplish. My first order of business is to get a good night's sleep and then tomorrow build the placement that we will use at Hayfield. Tomorrow, you guys, with master lifter Ellis, need to pick off three vehicles we need while I am busy in my work room. Two trucks and a van will do nicely for a start. We will have them in the barn until we need them next week."

"Placement?" Ellis asked.

"Yes. We will be making placements around southern California to deliver our message. A placement will speak for our cause."

Kyle's dissertation stunned the men at first, but the truth was they knew something like this was in the works. They each had another Anchor Steam while Carrie heated two large pizzas in the oven. She was interested in her own agenda and she was not really sure how she fit into all of what Kyle had planned..

"You guys have all got guns...except me. I want my own weapon; I don't want to go into this thing without having some protection.

All of the men except Kyle stared at her. She might as well have slapped each of them.

Kyle did not look at her. "You think it's necessary? "You won't be..."

"I will be...I will be a part of what you guys do. You'll need all the help from me that I can give you. This isn't going to be easy. I know how to get things done and I know how to protect myself. But I need a gun to do that. I don't want to go into this thing naked. I'm naked without a gun."

Kyle sat quietly, looking ahead not wanting to recognize what she was saying, but knowing full well what she said was fact. They could use her, they would need her. He nodded and then got up and went to the small office off the living room that had once been a den and pulled a pistol from one of the desk drawers. It had been purchased at a gun show the year before. He made sure it was loaded, the safety on, and with an extra clip. He brought it back to the kitchen and handed it to Carrie.

She held the Beretta automatic in her left hand and slipped the clip in her pocket.

"That's a Beretta Model 84. It holds ten shots," Kyle instructed, "get familiar with it, do some shooting before we get into action. It shoots a three-eighty, so it's potent."

"Thanks," she said quietly, "now I'm a full member of the operation."

She fingered the gun delicately and turned it over in her hands as if she were savoring a piece of jewelry. She held it in her right hand and sighted it out the window.

"Put it away," Kyle said slowly, "it's not a toy."

"I know," she said, "I know what it is."

And the others did not know how well she knew.

The men ate slowly and discussed the details with Kyle to assure themselves it would all work the way he said it would. After awhile, after two more Anchor Steams, Kyle's plan became a sure thing and the getaway boat and the travel to Ecuador a new adventure. Shortly after dark, Carrie followed Ellis to the Hemet Valley Mall where the white Chevy van was deposited in the middle of the lot. She drove and did not speak to Ellis on the return to the ranch and he laid his head back and went to sleep in an easy, relaxed way she envied. She wished she could go to sleep that easily. She could not; sleep was a struggle of restlessness and anxiety. Sleep, satisfying sleep, was a luxury she rarely enjoyed. On the other hand, she felt good about having the pistol in her pocket; it was a comfort. For her it was a solid plus. She believed at some point she would have to use it to protect herself. And perhaps, Kyle, too.

11.

"I was wrong...big time. They actually have stolen more than three hundred thousand dollars." Andy Tobin said this as if he were a schoolboy giving the correct answer to the teacher, proud that he knew it, proud that he had the answer.

"What?" Jim Fuller did not comprehend at first.

"That's what it looks like."

"You're kidding."

"No." Tobin continued. "The last bank job they did had an open vault with a payroll sitting there waiting. They took most of it. A hundred and fifty grand."

"Inside job?"

"No, just at the right place at the right time. Lucky."

Jim Fuller's office of the Riverside section of the FBI was sparse and gray and cluttered. The afternoon sunlight bounced in from the glass wall of the building across the street, the best part of a nothing view to the outside.

"We're after the same guys...the same guys Gonzales and his boys are after?"

"Yes," Tobin said firmly.

"And you think they went after the Gladstone facilities to get the plastic explosives for some reason?"

"Yes, it fits. It fits with the donation comment of one of the perps. "Thanks for the donation." That's what was said. We have, in combination with the witnesses Gonzales' boys interviewed, ten persons to confirm that thank you."

"And?" Fuller wrinkled his brow.

"We talked about it...a cause. They are going to use plastic explosives to do something for their cause. The "thanks for the donation" comment gives it away.

"To do what?

"Well, hell, to blow up something."

"Damn, no kidding. And what would that be?" There was a sarcastic edge to the question. Fuller sensed that he was being outrun in the analysis department by his assistant and he did not like it.

"I don't think..." Tobin hesitated.

"Well...?"

"I don't think we'll know until they do it. Then they'll get out some kind of manifesto to the press and we'll know. We'll learn what their cause is."

"We got nothing at either Gladstone site," Fuller lamented, "no trace evidence except the one shell casing and slug that we checked out. The tire tracks in the sand mean nothing. Even if they could be ID'd the vehicles were probably stolen. The lab boys called this morning...bullet that hit the guard doesn't make a match in the database. Nine millimeter handgun is all they know...probably a Glock. Not surprising there is no match with all the guns out there not in the database."

"A man almost died with the second Gladstone job," Tobin said, "we've got to be in motion pretty good on this or the press will be on our ass."

"They don't know yet."

"Yes, well...sorry, they do. Riverside paper is all over it. Story out today. Family upset, wife wants something done."

"How..." Fuller hesitated. "It doesn't matter, we need to be active, you're right. Appearances are everything. Even if we have nothing in the way of leads to pursue."

"I told Margo to hold off the press until tomorrow. Said to tell them we're working on things and we'll have more for them then."

"Good, good. I don't know what it is, but we'll have to think of something. You know, both so-called guards are still in Valley Medical Center over in Hemet," Fuller said. "Why don't we get down there and see what they have to say? We've got to try to do something to close the gap with these guys. Let's see what they know, if they saw or remember anything. That guy from the first Gladstone job didn't have a clue about a thing."

On the drive to the hospital in Hemet, Fuller was constantly on his cell phone starting with Henry Gonzales. It took several minutes, but finally Gonzales answered.

"Gonzales here."

"Yeah, Henry, Jim Fuller."

"I heard about Gladstone. How's it going?"

"Slow, real slow, but don't tell anybody."

"I know what you mean," Gonzales laughed.

"Yeah, listen, I wanted to touch base with you see what was new on the robberies you're working on. Andy thinks we're after the same crew. Guys that did the banks did the C-store holdups. You thinking that way?"

"Yes, from what we know and what Andy knows, it's the same for me. And we've got a shooting victim to deal with, also."

"How's she doing?" Fuller asked. His question of concern was merely perfunctory, he didn't really care about the woman, but felt he should ask.

"She's going to be okay," Gonzales answered. "Lost quite a bit of blood, but she'll make it."

"Let's keep each other posted on this Henry. I think we've got some real problems ahead with these boys. And the press. The press is going to be all over us if we don't get somewhere with an investigation. They'll put things together real soon and then we need to be able to deal with it. We need to know something. And just remember...the boys we're after didn't steal those explosives for nothing."

Gonzales agreed, knowing full well that what Fuller said about keeping each other posted was code for "you tell all you know and maybe, just maybe, I'll tell you something if it suits my purpose." Recognizing what things really meant made it easier for him to stay on an even keel and not get frustrated. Otherwise, he knew Fuller could frustrate him.

"Should call Sylvester," Fuller said as he punched the phone off, "let him know what's going on."

"At ATF?" Tobin asked, sure of the answer.

"Yes, yes indeed, the guy with the backward name. Hicks Sylvester. Doesn't sound right. But anyway, I think we'll wait on that until we hear back from this guy Marwood. He's security at Gladstone. Don't want those ATF boys getting riled up and charging in too soon. Might muddy the waters don't you think?"

"Usually does," Tobin said with a sigh.

"Give him a call tomorrow, will you?" Fuller laughed.

"Right," Tobin said.

Fuller continued making phone calls all the way to the hospital. He made appointments with his barber and his dentist, the former being more important than the latter. Spoke with his girlfriend for a considerable length of time, returned a call to an LA Times reporter who had gotten wind of the Gladstone robberies even though those had not been widely reported on the news as yet, checked with several of his field agents about other cases, and left a message for his wife that he would not be home for dinner.

Tobin marveled at the ability his boss had for juggling the very important business stuff, with the tricky personal stuff, and the mundane in his life without missing a beat. Fuller's voice remained constantly modulated and in control. No doubt the man could beat a lie detector test hands down, Tobin figured.

"Park right there," Fuller directed. It was a No Parking zone. "What are the names of these guards, by the way?"

"Larry Harris and John Hanson."

Fuller flashed his badge to hospital security and to the small gray-haired woman at the information desk. She recited the room numbers very carefully. They were on the same floor several rooms apart.

When Fuller and Tobin got to the Harris' room, a pretty young woman was sitting in a chair close to the bed where he was recovering.

"Good afternoon, Mr. Harris, I'm Special Agent in Charge Fuller, FBI, Riverside office, this is Agent Tobin." He flashed his badge again. "We'd like to ask you a few questions. Looks like you might be up to it."

"I'll wait outside," the young woman said.

"Stay there," Harris snapped, "these guys won't be here long because there isn't anything I know or can tell them."

"May we ask you a few questions anyway?" Tobin asked politely.

"Sure...that's what you do, but don't expect anything."

"Are you from an outside security firm or are you on the payroll?" Tobin started quickly.

"No, I'm an employee, full security clearance."

"Can you describe the vehicle the...the attackers used."

"White van...longer than a usual van. It had windows, but you couldn't see in. A Chevy, I think...I didn't get the model or anything."

"Did you happen to see the plate?" Tobin wasn't optimistic with the question.

"Yeah, well...sort of. The last three numbers were six...ah...six nine five."

"How many guys were there?" Fuller interjected.

"Four, I guess. Two in front and two in back that grabbed me."

"What was said?" Fuller continued. "Anything unusual or notable?"

"It didn't get to me at the time, but laying here, reflecting on what happened, I do think now it was strange the way they invited John to have me check out the back of the van. Of course it makes sense. They had to get me back there to overpower me. I should have been more alert, but they...they didn't look suspicious."

"Average guys? Tobin asked.

"Yes."

"Young, white...?"

"White guys...not exactly young. Seemed older. At least the ones in front. I didn't see the guys that clocked me. Happened too fast. I should have been wary, but I wasn't."

"Think you'll lose your job?" Tobin asked cautiously.

"Marwood said no, could have happened to anybody. Who knows? Management might have other ideas."

"Marwood," Fuller said slowly, deliberately. "Got a message from a guy named Marwood. Who is this guy Marwood?"

Fuller knew who Marwood was, but he was testing Harris.

"My boss," Harris croaked through a drink of water. "He was in to see me. Head of security. He had been out of town for both of the hits. Good man. I think I can trust him."

"Really? Fuller said. "That's refreshing. How did you learn of the job at the other facility?"

Harris hesitated at first before he answered. "I...I got a call at home from Cathy Simon. She works for Marwood. I usually work at number one, but wasn't on duty when that shift got hit. She sent me over to number two. Number two is so off the beaten path and not much going on there recently so only John handled the gate."

"John Hanson," Tobin asked, "the guard that was shot."

"Yeah, he's alone there on the day shift when we don't have training there. In fact, there's only one guard for each of the three shifts when there's no training. We go round-the-clock at both locations."

"Training, what training?" Fuller asked.

"That's what we do. We train people."

"What kind?"

"All kinds. Security, counter insurgency, guerilla tactics, munitions, explosives; everything required for non-military, clandestine operations. That sort of thing."

"For whom?

"For any company or country that pays and sends students."

"You didn't set a good example for your students," Fuller sniped.

"Tell me about it, that's what Marwood said at first."

"You'll get fired," Fuller said firmly, "you can count on it. I don't care what Marwood said to you, you're toast."

"That's what I figure."

"Anything else you can think of?" Tobin asked.

"Naw, it all went down too fast and I was too stupid. Oh, yeah...they took my M4."

"Interesting," Fuller said, "our field agents tell us they also took Hanson's pistol."

"I heard Johnny was hit pretty bad," Harris said. "Down the hall. Not doing too well, I hear." He gave the words without much emotion, but anguish and frustration were in his eyes and he looked away at the girl and then out the window.

"Thanks for your help, Larry," Tobin offered, "if you think of anything else let us know. We're going to be working on this heavily. We need to get these guys."

"I guess I'm lucky to be alive," Harris said.

"I guess so," Fuller answered quietly.

They went on to Hanson's room, but he was sedated and in no condition to talk to them. He would be of no help.

As they drove back to their office in Riverside, Fuller thumbed through his notes until he came to the reference for Chet Marwood and his phone number. He punched the numbers into his cell phone.

After a few moments the voice of a young woman answered.

"Gladstone security, may I help you?"

"This is Jim Fuller, Special Agent in Charge, FBI…in Riverside. Who's this?"

"This is Cathy Simon…I work for Mr. Marwood."

"Well, I'm returning Mr. Marwood's call. He in?"

"Not at the moment. Can I take a message?"

"Yeah, have him call me again."

Fuller closed the cell phone and slipped it into the inside pocket of his suit coat and then checked his watch.

"This was an inside job," Fuller said, his pronouncement a shock to Tobin.

Tobin's amazement was that he assessed Fuller as only partially paying attention to the crimes at hand and the fact he considered his boss to have limited skills of figuring out much of anything beyond when he was going to get laid next.

"Why do you say that?"

"Who knew the stuff was there? This is an obscure company operating in the stratosphere of business. Only someone working there or who did work there would know exactly what and where. Our boys knew what and they knew where. It was inside, pure and simple. Okay? Speed it up will you?"

"You okay...time wise?" Tobin asked, leery of the answer.

"Yeah, I think so if you move it along. We should be back in time to make my appointment with Jacque."

Jacque owned a precious little salon not more than four blocks from the FBI office. He usually cut Fuller's hair every other week. His manicure was monthly.

12.

Chet Marwood looked at the telephone receiver as if it were a living thing, as if it would respond if he said something to it, as if its sensibilities would be affected if Marwood raised his voice. This was a plaintive look, one that cried out for relief from what he had just heard. It was not the phone, he knew that, it was the voice, the man on the other end of the line. That man was a fool, Marwood realized, that man was Jim Fuller, Special Agent in Charge of the Riverside FBI office.

"He wants to conduct an internal investigation of Gladstone. Says it's an inside job."

"It is," Cathy Simon, his assistant, answered quickly.

"Don't jump to conclusions. That's always dangerous."

She was silent.

"I held him off temporarily, but I've got to get some help with this."

The remark stung, but still she did not say anything. In her mind she was the help he should use. That was her first reaction. It did not take long, a few seconds, half a minute possibly, before she silently admitted to herself what he really meant by the remark. It wasn't a slight because she had little experience, and she knew she was a novice when it came to these kinds of situations. She would be a good assistant and listen and watch and learn and do what she was told.

Chet Marwood was the vice president of security for Gladstone International and the impact of the two thefts which Kyle and his men had pulled off fell directly on him. Top management stayed aloof with only two quick phone calls of encouragement and "go get 'em" remarks from the CEO and the COO. They expressed their support and "knew he could handle this thing." They were not concerned with what "handling" this really meant. It was Chet's job, not theirs; that's why they hired him, that's what they expected. They operated in another universe of contact with Congressional staffers, Pentagon lackeys from lieutenant colonels on up, and numerous foreign government operatives. Day-to-day Gladstone was in the hands of others like Chet.

He assumed his responsibility with a dedication and seriousness that he had once devoted to his job as a covert officer in the CIA and as a captain in the Army Special Forces before that. He managed eighty-five guards and special security specialists, and a small clerical staff. He had kept Gladstone's operation clean and neat and below media radar for almost eight years, including background checks of prospective employees, buttoned-down facilities, protection of information, and the protection of client executives and key operatives while they were in the U.S. There had been few problems until this business of the thefts. Not just one bold maneuver, but a second as daring and brash. It was embarrassing. His jaw clenched.

Security Specialist was a name that Chet had given to those in his security division who performed tasks outside the routine of being a guard. This designation was what he had given Cathy Simon, a 28-year old graduate of Long Beach State in criminal technology, but he knew he should have called her something else. She had more going for her than anyone else in his department and he should have made the distinction when he made her his assistant. It was a mistake and he needed to correct it. She had quickly become his alter ego and performed well beyond an entry-level, first-job-out-of-college staffer. She learned rapidly and her assertive, more mature style matched his iconoclastic approach to the corporate structure and its periodic nonsense.

Cathy was a magician with a computer in her ability at data mining and knowledge acquisition. A crack shot with her Beretta, thanks to Chet, and a quick study of the security industry, also thanks to Chet's careful tutelage, she was an extremely valuable addition to the Gladstone security division.

"This is all part of something else," she said firmly.

She was determined not to let his comment hold her back. She knew some things, had already done significant investigation about the Gladstone thefts, and was in a position to do more. She did not like the idea of being superceded, but that's how it was. She was reconciled to her inexperience, but wanted the challenge of dealing with the issue. She recognized Chet had something else in mind.

"What do you mean?" Chet asked.

"I think our thefts are connected with a group that has been pulling jobs all around that part of Riverside County. I'm sure of it. After our first hit I called the Riverside police and the county sheriff's office. Nothing clicked right then, but after the second hit I realized that what the sheriff's office told me made sense. I think…I'm sure it's the same four guys who have been robbing C-stores and a few banks in the area. They have something planned and it requires plastic explosives to get it done. No big hits with the other robberies, just a lot of small jobs. Why?"

"Why?" Chet stared at her and admired her remarkable way of accumulating information so quickly.

"Get cash to pay for something. Some ultimate…ah, project. They have something planned. I think it's the same four guys. They have a goal and we were just one part of it. But one of them, probably the leader, the planner, the mastermind, he worked for us at some point not too far back. He knew we had plastic, where it was, and how to get it. Only an insider would have the knowledge to make those hits. That's where we start. I think Fuller is right."

"That's…that's a lot of conjecture. A big stretch to make conclusions."

"I know, but the sheriff's people told me these guys were really slick. Everything planned and timed to the last detail. Nothing went wrong. There were no witnesses, no evidence, no trace of anything. Nothing to connect them to any crime and they know it was the same guys every time. Just like with our hits. In and out like magic. Quicksilver. Stolen vans for all the jobs. Sheriff's office has pretty well identified all of the vans used in the robberies or at least they think they've matched them up. Vans reported stolen on the same days from shopping center parking lots, all recovered later at other shopping centers in the region. No prints, no witnesses, nothing. Quicksilver…slipping away.

"Mercury," Chet said vacantly.

"Yes, Mercury," she concurred. "It's poisonous."

They both had been standing, talking face-to-face across his desk, she rigid with emotion about what might take place, he frustrated with the whole situation. He motioned her to sit and then slumped back into the overstuffed chair that ill-suited his energetic nature. She did not respond immediately, but when she saw that he was seated and had flopped his right leg up on his desk, she fell back into one of the uncomfortable chairs opposite. She pulled her note pad to her face and hid behind it waiting to hear what bullshit he would give her. She hoped she would have a major part in dealing with the situation.

"Fuller wants the FBI in here, but I've put him off temporarily with the excuse we needed to get a handle on classified stuff, that we would be right on it, and that we would feed them everything we can turn up. It is an inside job, he says."

"It is."

"Right. Well, my problem is that I have to be in…," he hesitated, looked away from her, and then down at his desk. "I am out of the country for a few days…starting tomorrow. That's why I said we needed some help. You're good, very good, but not experienced. I need experience here while I'm gone. The kind of experience you don't have yet. But you work with my guy and you'll get it, believe me. I already have top-level approval for bringing in an experienced hand at this sort of thing. He's someone I know who can help us...can help you. I really am sorry to have to leave and have this fall on you and...and our outside help."

"I'm sorry you can't trust me."

"Back off. You graduated from college two years ago. It isn't a matter of trust it's a matter of experience. Spook experience, terrorist experience, guerilla experience...the kinds of experience you don't have. On the other hand, you can be a big help to our man."

"You think this means something? These guys...the theft from us?"

"They didn't steal it for yucks. They have a plan, they mean to use it."

"Who is the guy?"

"An old friend. But he doesn't know about this yet. I've got to give him a call."

"Will he do it?"

"He'll do it and you'll like working with him."

She did not respond.

"Trust me, you'll like him. Now, get going with the computer records and see if you can come up with a prospect.

"Okay," she said softly and rushed out of his office.

Chet punched a number into his phone, pushed the speaker button, and walked over to the window that looked out onto the sunlit courtyard below. As the electronic sounds of making the phone connection beeped from the speaker, he stared at the courtyard. The view was green and well-groomed, and bright, but sterile in a way that a manicured urban landscape often is.

The sleepy voice of Butch Greiner caught his attention.

"Yeah..."

"Why aren't you up, a man of your energy?" Chet demanded jokingly.

"Well, shit, let' see..." There was silence for a moment. "It's nine here, Chet, I didn't think you got to the office that early. What, six o'clock out there? I thought with that cushy security job you had you rolled in about ten, ten thirty, let the underlings handle things."

"No way, I'm here at the crack of nine every day unless something unusual comes up. Today is one of those days...I got here a half hour ago."

I ran a 10K yesterday, so at nine in the morning I'm not up. Not at my age anyway."

"Still doing that competitive stuff?"

"Yeah, as long as the body lasts. Hey, what's up, you didn't call to chit-chat?"

"I need your help...today."

"That bad?"

"That bad. I'm leaving the country this afternoon and there is a...a situation that needs expert attention. I have an able assistant, but she's too inexperienced to run this thing. I need your experience."

"She?"

"Yes, indeed, she'll be a big help. She's good."

"What is it?"

"Four guys got onto two of our training properties and made off with plastic explosives and some other items. FBI wants in here which is no good. I've held them off temporarily, but I need you to shepherd this baby."

"With your security I didn't think something like that could happen."

"Neither did I," Chet answered. "It was an inside job, no doubt, and my girl is already working on that. Taking a run at the personnel database. Cathy Simon. She'll have something for you by the time you get here. She's good."

"You said. But who says I'm coming out there. I hate LA, you know that." Distress tinged Butch's voice, the anguish of a man who despises a place with specific certainty.

"I wouldn't call if it weren't important. I need your help...right away."

"Damn, I don't want to come out there."

"I know and I don't want to leave LA right now, but some things have to be done. I felt I could count on you. You're the only one I could call, the only one I could depend on."

"Okay," Butch sighed. "Damn, though, I hate LA."

"There is nothing here in this sun-drenched paradise to hate. Everything a man would want to enjoy is right here. You'll love it. Besides, you'll make a lot of money."

"Yeah, right. Money is no object. I've heard that before."

"It's true. Submit an invoice and it shall be paid."

"Anything else I need to know?" Butch asked quickly.

"Not right now. Cathy can help you. I'll stay in touch. All right?"

"Sure, sure, fine and dandy."

There was no denying this old friend.

13.

The airline jet was making its long slide into LAX, slowly descending, slowly moving over the endless carpet of lights that went every which way to the black horizon. Below was the waiting megalopolis ready to envelop Butch, to get him in its clutches, and squeeze the sensibility and energy from him. Or so he thought.

A deep, abiding friendship transcends time and place and circumstance, Butch thought. He stared out the window at the glowing panorama that moved by. He didn't want this in his life right now. This trip, this interruption, this aggravation, was a nuisance he could do without. But Chet would not have called if the need weren't real.

"I hate LA." Butch said the words softly, talking to himself.

The attractive young woman next to him smiled wryly, amused with his comment, herself dreading the arrival.

"It can eat you alive," she said.

He did not look at her. He had not looked at her or engaged her through the entire flight even though she had tried to make the connection. And he really did not want to talk to anyone right now. He leaned forward with his elbows on his knees

"I heard what you said," she continued. "You are so correct. I know, I come here every other week on business and it nearly kills me."

Now he looked at her, but he did not say anything. He leaned back into his seat.

"It's toxic and it's full of foreigners," she said, quite ready with comment. "What did the song say? LA's a great big city…"

"Ah huh," Butch muttered.

"From the San Fernando Valley to the Coachella Valley," she went on, knowing she had his attention and that she had made the connection with him that she wanted to achieve. "That's what we call LA, the whole mass and mess of people and places, one continuous crush of strip malls, fast food outlets, gas stations, and humanity with creeping cars edging along in a slow progression of wasted time and mounting frustration. It can get you down if you let it. On the other hand, it's just a damn great place to be alive. Where are you staying while you're here?"

"I thought you said it nearly kills you." Butch said the words as if he were poking her with a finger.

"So hectic, so fabulous. That's LA." She had not flinched at what he said nor how he said it. "You're here on business?"

"I guess."

She looked at him quizzically. He was good-looking, rugged, athletic, maybe a tad short, but certainly attractive. She thought he was probably a little weird, but it didn't matter. Everyone in LA was weird.

"Where are you staying? Maybe we could get together while we're here."

"I don't know," Butch offered quietly.

"Don't know which?"

"Where I'm staying," Butch said slowly.

"Really? You're arriving in LA and don't know where you'll be staying. That's a bit strange…if it's true. Are you married?"

"No."

"And you don't know where you're staying."

"A young woman is meeting me…she's made the arrangements."

"Oh," she said sharply, "I see."

She shut up, although she continued to look at him. He was glad she was contained. The remark about Cathy Simon meeting him did the trick and he slipped into his own thoughts about what lay ahead.

The plane landed, slowly trooped to the terminal, and stopped at its gate. The passengers grabbed and fumbled for luggage and other carry-on bags from the overhead bins and underneath seats. The attractive woman who wanted the connection was standing pressed tightly against Butch as they waited for the forward exit door to be opened. She presented him with her business card.

"I'm Barbara Quinn. The number where I'll be staying is on the back," she said breathlessly, "call me when you get to wherever it is you'll be staying. We can have dinner. I can show you around if you don't know LA."

"I know LA," Butch said. "Quite well, in fact. Thanks anyway, it's a very nice offer."

She pressed the card to him and he took it. He could feel her body against his and there was a flush of excitement from the contact and he wondered what would happen if he were to take her up on her offer. Nothing good, he assumed. He slid the card into his shirt pocket and smiled. Her return smile was very inviting.

Butch moved off the plane quickly, ahead of Barbara Quinn, and speed-walked out to the terminal reception area, along the corridor, and down to Baggage Pickup. At the baggage carrousel he realized he had lost her. He pulled her card from his pocket. It showed Barbara Quinn, vice president, sales and marketing, Dorman Commercial Properties, and a Farmington Hills, Michigan, address. Good-bye, Barbara, Butch thought, and good luck. What was it, what happened with this woman? Until a few hours ago when he got on the plane she had been a complete stranger to him. He wondered how a woman could get so focused on him when they had not spoken to each other on the flight, knew nothing about him, and yet, in a sense, had offered herself to him. There was, he figured, some kind of disconnect between himself and that kind of world. Was that the modern world with which he was out of touch? In any case, he was too old for that sort of thing, the fling, the easy sexual access, and the gymnastics of non-intimate intimacy. He put Ms. Quinn's card back in his pocket.

"God, I hate LA," he said once again, as if to confirm his feelings.

"You must be Mr. Greiner," the petite young woman said. She was standing nearby and heard his words.

"I guess I gave it away with that comment, huh?"

"Yes, you did."

She held a sign in front of her chest with thumb and forefinger at each lower corner. It was what he had agreed on with Chet - **CS for BG**- the letters big and bold and bright red.

"I guess we didn't need the sign," Butch said with a smile.

She laughed. She was short and compact and athletic looking and he liked that, and she was very attractive to him. She was, in fact, gorgeous. He hoped this would not be a problem.

"I really appreciate your picking me up. Didn't want you in the flunky position, but I couldn't resist the offer. Maybe we can get started working while you take me wherever it is you're taking me."

"A Gladstone apartment...one of the best ones. In Brentwood. Nice neighborhood. You'll like it, I think."

She stood by as he scrambled to get his bag off the carrousel and led the way to the waiting limousine.

The driver was in place, but another man, burly and rough looking, dressed in a warm-up suit and athletic shoes, took his bag, and reached for his briefcase.

"No, I'll hang on to this," Butch said as he turned slightly to shield the case a bit from the burly guy.

Cathy was already inside the stretch BMW. It was then, as he looked in at the back seat where she was perched, that he really noticed her, really looked at her, and fully assessed her beyond that previous first full blush of recognizing she was very attractive. First of all, her hair was copper red. That aspect should have clicked with him before, but it did now. And her facial features were well-defined, as if they had been sculpted by a clever artist, each highlight, each dimension, each angle conscripted for the best effect. Her coloration was exquisitely formulated by Mother Nature in a way that absolutely killed cosmetics companies trying to emulate the result.

"I appreciate your help with this situation Gladstone has," Butch said as he sat down beside her.

She looked down and did not respond.

The burly guy was in the car and they headed out of the airport.

"Look, let's not get off to a bad start. I've known Chet a long time…we worked together…with some tough assignments. He's known me a lot longer than he's known you. As good as you might be…"

"It's okay," she said softly, "it's really okay. I understand. I'd like it to be me running the show, but I know I'm not experienced enough. I'll help you all I can."

She turned and looked directly at him without blinking, not smiling, trying her damnedest to not show any emotion. He returned the look and she turned away first. Her recovery from averting his penetrating appraisal was to snatch the black planner from her case on the floor. She became all business.

"Thanks," Butch said, "I'll need it."

He unzipped a section of his briefcase and pulled out his own planner.

"The driver is Reverend Morris," she said as a way to begin their business. "Your bodyguard is Arnold Cramer. He is on assignment to you by Chet and so is Reverend Morris. Chet thought you might want to have a car of your own, so he has a Lexus sedan at your disposal if you want. Otherwise, Reverend Morris can do your driving for you."

Butch nodded and waited for her to continue as the limo cruised away from airport property and headed north on Sepulveda.

"We'll drop you off at your Gladstone apartment. It's used by visitors and stocked with everything you would need."

"Interesting," Butch said.

"In the morning, eight o'clock, Reverend Morris will pick you up and bring you to the Gladstone offices. The Lexus is there or you can use the limo, as I said. Arnold is supposed to go wherever you go."

"Is he sleeping at the apartment with me?" Butch asked.

"Ah, no…he's not. But he will be in the limo in the morning when you get picked up."

"Chet worried about me?"

"He thinks it's a good precaution. We don't know what else our thieves have in mind. They may have more in store for us."

"I doubt it. But when I get to Gladstone tomorrow morning, I want you to get me a nine millimeter Glock and waist holster. There's no way I'm going to screw around with this thing without being armed, Arnold or no Arnold."

"All right," she said.

"Arnold can you do anything beside look tough?" Butch had leaned forward when he asked the question of the burly bodyguard.

Arnold's neck was so thick he could not turn his head around towards Butch without turning his entire upper body. He scowled with tightly furrowed brow.

"Waddaya mean?"

"What I mean is that you are not going to be in my hip pocket while I'm investigating, it's a waste of manpower. On the other hand, you could be useful doing some legwork for Miz Simon and me. Think you could handle that?"

"Sure, but Mr. Marwood…"

"Mr. Marwood…Chet, insisted that Arnold…" Cathy started to explain

"Stop, let's regroup and get our organization straight right from the git go," Butch said, abruptly stopping them both. "I'm in charge of this operation, which is what Mr. Marwood told me I would be. Arnold, you are going to help us cover a lot of bases in a short amount of time and you won't be in the limo tomorrow morning. Get a good night's sleep, you'll need it. You will use your brain tomorrow, not your brawn. And you'll be meeting us at the office at seven thirty. Cathy, will you make sure we can get in then?"

"I'll be there'" she said firmly. "Security is biometric…thumb print and eye scan. No problem getting started earlier."

"Good. And Reverend, you pick me up at six. We'll hit a breakfast joint before the office."

"Yessir," Reverend said, "glad to do it, sir."

"Now, Cathy, tell me what you know so far."

As Cathy described the robberies, Reverend directed the limo through a maze of surface streets, judiciously avoiding the freeways. Soon they were on San Vicente Boulevard with its parade of imposing trees dominating the median strip. A quick turn and they were on a quiet side street lined with luxury condos and apartment buildings. He pulled to the curb in front of a four-story, creamy white stucco building with a gated drive to the left. The complex looked fairly new, somewhat faux Spanish in style with red tiled roof, and with abundant landscaping that was carefully designed. A large wooden door was the centerpiece of a lavish portico and required a key. To the right of the door was an intercom to each of the units. There were no names listed; you had to know the apartment number of the person you were visiting when you came here. Mail was delivered by special arrangement with the manager who gave the postman access to the individual boxes inside in the lobby.

Arnold was out of the limo, had gotten Butch's suitcase, and was waiting on the sidewalk.

"Here's the key," Cathy said. "Apartment four twenty four. Elevator is on the right when you get into the lobby. There's an electronic opener for the gate that lets you into the parking garage. That's in the Lexus if that's your choice." She chuckled.

"You know that's my choice."

"I figured," she smiled.

"Anything else I should know?"

"I've done some data mining of the personnel files and, assuming it's an inside job, we have some prospects. We can start with those in the morning."

"Very good. You get a good night's sleep, too. Tomorrow is liable to be a long day…and so is the next day and maybe the one after that and…"

"I get it…I will. Here's my card…it's got my home number. Call me if you think of anything else you need. Good night."

He took the card and stuffed it in his pocket with the one he got from Barbara Quinn. He eyed her carefully again and wanted to say something. Something that was…what? Wonderful? Encouraging? He had no clue. Instead, he merely nodded, got out of the limo and took his bag from Arnold as he walked to the fabulously carved wooden door. He did not look back, but slipped the key into the lock and let himself into Bedford Gardens. If he had looked back he would have seen Arnold still standing there waiting until he was inside.

The Bedford Gardens lobby floor was laid with dark green imported Italian ceramic tile. It was in a rustic style, but still looked cold and unwelcoming to him. Now fighting fatigue, Butch did not notice much else as he walked to the archway at the rear of the lobby, his footsteps echoing slightly. He stopped in the archway and surveyed the spacious courtyard. Here too the landscaping was imaginative and immaculately maintained. A large oval pool was the centerpiece and he caught a faint whiff of chlorine. After a moment, he went back to the elevator, and rode to the fourth floor. What was the room number Cathy had said? His hesitation in remembering was a sure sign of how weary he had become.

Four…four twenty four; that was it. A brass plate indicated the direction of the apartment numbers. At the end of the hall was four twenty four. He slid the key into the lock and it turned.

The apartment could not have been more luxuriously appointed. A polished wooden floor in the living room, mahogany he speculated, with well-preserved Persian rugs of several sizes in critical areas; a dazzling array of leather and chrome and glass in furniture and fixtures, and a complement of art and artifacts which would make any museum envious. The full kitchen had a prep island, granite counter tops, and professional chef quality appliances and cooking gear. The three bedrooms had wall-to-wall carpeting and each its own bathroom. The largest bedroom was at the corner of the building with views facing north and east. Butch chose this bedroom.

He tossed his bag and briefcase towards the dresser, pulled off his jacket and dropped it on a chair, and slumped onto the bed. He really felt whipped as he tugged at his shoes and began the undressing process. He remembered the business cards in his shirt pocket and pulled them out for inspection. He had not looked at Cathy's before stuffing it there.

Cathy Simon, Security Specialist, Gladstone International. Barbara Quinn, good-looking hustler. He flipped the cards onto the dresser, got down to his shorts, and wondered what the view was like. He checked both windows and saw little of interest. Wait for daylight, he said to himself.

He thought of Cindy, the painful emotion of the past, and wondered if he could ever get beyond the pain of the past. Cindy the wonderful wife was gone, her memory growing dimmer and dimmer despite his diligent efforts to kept the flame alive, the memory bright. This was a lingering frustration for him. He wondered how long he would be able to call up her picture in his mind. He certainly had enough photographs of her around his house and in his office. He wondered if clinging to her memory was really an obsession. He had been told it was by friends and a counselor. Move on with your life, they said, Cindy is gone and you are living and you have a responsibility to yourself to live your life, continue your life. Stop the obsession, they said. He wondered if it were an obsession or the persistence of a memory he wanted to keep. He wondered if he could let go if it were an obsession. He closed his eyes and could see Cindy's lovely face so clearly. He loved that image.

Eyes still closed, he wondered about the two beautiful young women who had come into his life today and how they fit in with anything about him and he wondered how Cathy would help him and who the hell was this guy he was supposed to find, and then he pitched headlong into a cascade of dull gray silliness as he fell sound asleep.

14.

Reverend Morris was leaning against the side of the BMW limo when Butch exited the Bedford Gardens front door. It was nine minutes to six.

"Good morning, Mr. Greiner. Have yourself a good sleep?"

"Dead to the world, Reverend. I went to the land of zees very fast."

Reverend opened the rear passenger side door for Butch. Butch extended his hand and they shook in a casual, yet respectful manner.

"How about I sit in front?"

"Sure enough, Mr. Greiner." He closed the rear door as Butch opened the front door and got into the limo.

"This is better," Butch said as he clicked in the seat belt.

"I knew you'd be early," Reverend laughed. "Sure enough, bang out the door before six like I figured."

"It's the last time you have to perform this service for me, Reverend. I'll be doing my own driving when I leave Gladstone's today. Where are you taking me? We're doing breakfast, right?"

"We're going to a nice place, you bet. Best breakfast I know. It's Minnie's place. She calls it Lucky's after her late husband. Course he wasn't so lucky, got hisself shot. Now, I wanna warn you we gotta take a slight detour to get to Minnie's. Gladstone's is less than ten minutes from here, Minnie's is twenty at least. And oh yeah, you the only white man in the place."

Butch's smile and nod were his only response.

Lucky's was on Pico Boulevard east of the San Diego Freeway in a nondescript block of stores that pretended to be doing well, but mainly struggled to survive until the next day. Minnie yelled when she saw Reverend and grabbed his arm to haul them to a booth away from the front door.

"You be good here," she said. "Tell me 'bout your friend."

"This here is an important man for Gladstone. Important work to do. Hush, hush, like always."

"Hush, hush, my ass, honey. You just coverin' up for screwin' around. Get a job, honey, this man will destroy you..."

"Minnie," Reverend said harshly, "this man is important, has important work to do and needs a good breakfast like you got."

"Sure 'nough, Tanya take care of these here two important men. Secret men do secret stuff nobody s'posed to know 'bout. We can handle it. We know you sneakin' 'round to protect us all. Snoop, snoop, thas all. Snoop, snoop..."

"Shhhh, Reverend admonished, "cool it or we outa here to another place give us the right service."

"Sorry, Reverend, so sorry. Tanya be right over."

The short, rotund black waitress came to the table at Minnie's bidding and stood waiting for their order. They told her what they wanted, but not without teasing her a bit, god knows why, taking longer than she wanted the interchange to last.

Minnie sauntered back to their table, unable to resist poking at Reverend and Gladstone.

"What are you goin' to do to keep this country safe," she demanded.

"Minnie," Butch said directly, "if we told you we'd have to kill you. So don't worry about it, just know everything is okay."

She walked away from them with that, but not without throwing the word *bullshit* over her shoulder as part of her editorial retort to Butch.

They ate quickly, Reverend taking his cue from Butch who seemed to wolf his sausage and eggs and grits. They barely spoke in the hurried process. Butch paid the laconic stub of a girl who didn't seem to care much about anything and they were back in the limo on their way to Gladstone.

"Like your breakfast?" Reverend asked.

"Yeah, very good. I'm partial to grits. If I didn't know better I'd think we had been in a restaurant in the South."

"In a way you were. Minnie's from Alabama…Georgia originally…most of her life in Bama. She's a survivor."

"Civil rights?" Butch asked cautiously.

"Yep. Brother disappeared…never was found…eighteen or so. He was a protester, a real pain in the ass for whites. Minnie was older…had a job…stayed off the streets. She stuck it out for awhile, but then came out here to LA. Has had some kind of restaurant or coffee shop or somethin' for a long time."

"Thanks, Reverend, I'll need to do that again while I'm here."

"You're welcome…ah, Mister…"

"Call me Butch, it's easier. Is this all you do for Gladstone, handle the limo?"

"Pretty much. But I don't work for Gladstone, I work for Mr. Merzak personally. He's the big man…CEO. Arnold, he works for the company. I was on loan to Mr. Marwood to take care of you while Mr. Merzak was in…out of the country. I'm available for anything until Mr. Merzak gets back. Just let me know what you need."

"I'll keep that in mind, Reverend, thanks."

Reverend drove the limo with a rush to the Gladstone building, disregarding speed limits, and whipped into the circular drive to the entrance at three minutes after seven.

"I keep this in the building garage during the day," Reverend explained. "They've got my cell number upstairs. Call me if you change your mind or need me for anything."

"Thanks, again, Reverend."

They shook hands and Butch got out and went to the front door. It was unlocked. He expected it to be locked, not realizing that this building never slept. Gladstone operations were constant, day and night, every day of the week. It was a company that never slept. Its assignments were too important for the luxury of sleep. There was a security guard at the reception desk. He eyed Butch carefully.

"Can I help you," he asked politely. His badge said Continental Security. He was not a Gladstone man.

"Here to meet some folks at Gladstone."

"All right, let me give them a call."

The man punched some numbers into his phone console and waited for the connection.

"Your man is here, Ms. Simon. Yes, of course." He looked up at Butch. "Ms. Simon will be down to escort you to their offices. You can have a seat over there. She might be a minute or so." He pointed to a carpeted section of the tiled lobby where an assortment of furniture was arranged.

"Thank you," Butch said.

The guard nodded and went back to whatever he was doing before Butch came into the building.

Butch walked over to the nearest couch and tossed his briefcase on it. He didn't wait long.

Cathy breezed off the elevator less than ninety seconds after she had gotten the guard's call. She looked and acted fresh and almost perky. Butch hated perky and was glad she wasn't actually so.

"Good morning," she said. "You know I thought about it last night after we dropped you off. What I was supposed to call you…"

"Try Butch, it works."

"Thanks, that's easy. Come on up. We'll get you some access codes assigned and given some expense money. Then an ID card and record your biometrics. Once we have the routine stuff out of the way…oh yeah, accounting needs you to sign some papers…once that is all done then we can get going on the records and figuring this thing out. Okay?"

"Lead the way," Butch said as he grabbed his case.

The processing that took more than an hour was frustrating for Butch because he was eager to get at the case, but there was no way around corporate procedures.

"Now, you're all set. You can come and go to Gladstone offices day or night, draw more expense money as you need it, and function pretty much as a Gladstone employee with top clearance."

"Great. Thanks, Cathy, now let's get started."

"Follow me."

He dutifully followed her from the accounting section to the far end of the floor. She stopped in front of a lighted office that was sparse in its furnishings.

"You can use this for anything private you want to do or to be alone and work on things, but I thought for starters you might want to work in my office. I have access to the database we need. The computer in there just links to the Internet and a printer, not to our network. My office is down here next to Chet's. He has the corner office."

"Of course," Butch laughed.

Once in her office, she situated herself at her computer and dived into the database, all the while giving a running account of what she had already accomplished.

"Chet didn't ask me to, but I started running names right after the first theft. I figured that this was no random hit. They came specifically for the plastic explosives, knew where they were, and knew they could get away with them without too much difficulty. Only an insider could or would do such a thing. First of all, the average bad guy has no clue our training facilities even exist. This wasn't some guys who wandered on to the property and scrounged around for Semtex. We were targeted, they came armed to kill, they came with equipment, they knew what they were doing. Someone with inside knowledge. More than likely a former employee. Someone with knowledge of the sites, knew what was there, had been there…to both of them…and knew where the plastics were kept. What do you think?"

"How about a current employee passing the information on to a confederate?" Butch suggested.

"That's a possibility, but I don't think so. Too risky. Too easy to check on those that know about the plastic, look at their connections, etcetera. Besides, everyone currently working here has been thoroughly checked out.

"Okay, then, I think you're on the right track, but how do you narrow the suspect field? Gladstone has probably had lots of employees over the years. How long have they been in business, twenty-five years? Lots of folks, right?"

"True, but I learned that the second site didn't go into operation until five years ago. That means our suspect has been gone within the last five years to know all about number two."

"Good, that helps narrow it down," Butch agreed.

"And I thought about it a great deal and I figured the guy we want wasn't a guard. No offense to the guards, but our guy is probably real smart and our guards have been and are…well, average, no high powered smarties in the lot of them. No, I thought our guy had to have been one of the trainers or one of the analysts here at the headquarters office who went to the sites and had working knowledge of them."

"Go on."

"Eliminating the guards and going at names in the last five years slims the potentials significantly. Besides, our turnover of employees has not been very high. So I checked all of the trainers and found that all but two are still working for us here in California...or somewhere else in the world...or have left the company and southern California and working for someone else. I then checked administrative staff...analysts, planners, and project people...who would have had knowledge of and experience at the sites and found that all but three are still working for us here...or somewhere else in the world...or have left the company and southern California and working for someone else. That left five names...five men who could be suspects, I think. Oh, and I took any women, and there were a few, out of the mix. Here are the files of the five men."

"Bravo," Butch said, clapping his hands slightly in mock applause. "There could be other possibilities, like someone coming back to the area, but this is a damn good start. Let's take a look at those."

She handed him a file folder.

"This is Neal Stone, He lives in Canoga Park. He was a trainer and now works for a security firm in the Valley. You know, Butch, I don't think he's someone who left the area...our man."

"Probably not, but why do you think that?"

"I just believe it's someone who has stuck around. I don't know...it's just my...intuition, I guess."

Butch thumbed through the Neal Stone file and read Cathy's recap of the man's status.

"This guy looks solid. Stable life, nothing to cause suspicion."

"Here is David Haskins, living in Venice," she said, handing him the folder. "Now works for an industrial consulting company doing risk analysis."

Butch exchanged folders with her and scanned her report. He shook his head.

"Don't think so," he frowned. He handed the folder back to her.

"I found out," she said, tapping a folder on her desk, "that this guy is dead. Ron Kamura. He was called a strategic planner and left the company two years ago to go to work for Northrup."

"You're sure he's dead? A phony death is a nice cover."

"No, no, he's dead all right. Killed in an auto accident on the 405 Freeway last year. Obit was in the LA Times and also a small article about the accident. Two others were also killed then."

"Okay that leaves two," Butch said.

"Right. Gordon Johns and Kyle Dixon. Both of these guys were training technicians. They didn't actually do any training, but they helped in the preparation and planning and scheduling. They also were responsible for any materials used in the training. Both men had technical backgrounds which meant they knew about explosives and ordinance."

Cathy handed Butch the Johns folder.

"Lives here in Santa Monica," Butch said.

"Yeah, they both do."

"Let's see," Butch said as he scanned her cover sheet, "left Gladstone three years ago to go to work for the California Highway Patrol…"

"That's what he told HR," Cathy interjected, "but the CHP has no record of him..."

"Looks like he might be a prospect."

"I think so."

"Can't find him employed anywhere?" Butch asked.

"Not so far."

"We need to check him out."

"That's what I figured, but I wanted you to see the whole group that fit my criteria."

"How about this other guy?" Butch asked as he picked up the last folder from Cathy's desk.

"Kyle Dixon. He left four years ago to head up a non-profit. Something to do with the environment..."

"...The Alliance For A Better Environment," Butch intoned quietly and looked away from her, staring at the wall in concentration.

She waited a minute before she said, "What?"

He didn't respond, caught up in his own thoughts.

"What is it?" she insisted.

"This is a guy who might have an axe to grind."

"Aren't you jumping to conclusions?" Cathy asked. "He's gone on from here to..."

"...to spearhead a cause," Butch interrupted.

"...to run an innocuous non-profit organization."

"Focusing on the environment." Butch affirmed.

"So what does that mean?"

"Well, it means that people who get deeply involved in hot-button issues like the environment can often harbor a lot of anger for whatever reason or reasons. Whether or not they act on that anger is something else, but the potential is there, it seems to me. Look at some of the destructive actions radical environmentalists have taken: burned down a large building up the mountain at the Vail resort, bombed labs around the country, wreaked havoc on car dealerships…there are plenty of examples."

"Eco-terrorism?" You think he might be planning something like that?"

"Plastic explosives can do a lot of damage. Why would someone want plastic explosives?"

"How about Gordon Johns? What do we do about him?"

"We check him out…we check them both out…starting with their immediate supervisor at Gladstone if that person still works here. Can you check?"

"Easy," Cathy said and picked up the phone.

Human Resources quickly determined that Russell Timmerman had been the boss of both Johns and Dixon and that he was a current Gladstone manager. Minutes after a phone call to Timmerman, Butch and Cathy were seated in his office.

"Butch is helping us while Chet is out of the office," Cathy explained. "He's an old friend of Chet's, a professional investigator, and with…with an…an excellent background. He has clearance from the top."

She didn't really know what background Butch had so she fumbled a bit when she tried to say something about it, assuming for sure it had to be good if Chet got him involved.

"Thanks for meeting with us on short notice," Butch said after Cathy had made the introduction, "this happens to be very important as I'm sure you can understand."

It was difficult to tell if Russell Timmerman's florid face was a reaction to the anxiety of being interrupted or from job frustrations or something else that angered him. Perhaps he drinks too much, Butch thought, maybe he has Roseacea or some other skin condition. But he was red-faced and very small beads of perspiration had popped to the surface on his forehead. He spoke with raspiness in his voice that was an annoyance to Butch which he chose to overlook. Timmerman smiled, but it was a phony smile, a smile that said I am tolerating you two, but don't take too long bothering me.

"We're investigating the robberies of our two training facilities and we think we have two potential suspects. Gordon Johns and Kyle Dixon. They both worked for you a few years back and we wanted to know what you could tell us about them. Whatever you remember."

"Yeah, well, sure. What do you want to know?"

"Let's start with Johns. What do you remember about him?"

"Ah, let's see. Johns, he was the one from UC Berkley. Very bright, very quick. Kooky though, a little erratic for our business. He knew it, knew he didn't belong with our kind of operation. Very talented with his analytical ability and sense of how we could train the folks who are our clients. Gifted in areas of technology, using explosives, hiding weapons on you, that kind of thing. Very good while he was here. Left to become some kind of strategic analyst with the California Highway Patrol, a special unit they were putting together to be prepared for terrorism. He would have been good at that."

"He never got there," Cathy offered quietly, "and as far as I can find out, he's nowhere."

"Maybe dealing drugs if he has no official employment."

"What?" Butch almost yelled.

Cathy's stare burned a hole in Timmerman.

"He liked to smoke pot when he was working here. Never on the job, but recreationally on his own time. And he talked about drugs, the ridiculousness of the drug laws, the drug culture, the power of drugs, and that kind of thing. I never gave it much thought until right now. His pot smoking never interfered with his job while he was here. I thought it was harmless. Nothing on our time."

"Give me a break," Cathy screamed. "Are you kidding?

"No, I just thought…"

"You didn't think," she snapped at him and then felt badly at yelling at the man. "Sorry, that was uncalled for and I apologize."

"Well, I did ask him to move on," he said, ignoring her outburst at him. "I told him that maybe it was best under the circumstances…before I had to fire him. When I told him that, he said it was okay because he had this chance for a job with CHP."

"CHP screens for drugs," Cathy said, "just like we do."

"I know. I told him he would fail his screen if he were asked to take one and I'd have to fire him."

"How did he get hired here in the first place?" she asked. "Never mind, it doesn't matter."

"Do you believe he could be a candidate for going to our training facilities and stealing plastic explosives?" Butch asked Timmerman.

"I don't think so. He had another agenda of some kind, but I don't think it would have been something like that."

"Why?" Butch demanded.

"He was…," Timmerman stopped and thought about what he wanted to express, his face now redder than ever. "He was too soft…too passive about things even with his ability to do his job here. For our program he wasn't passive, but for everything else he just didn't seem to have the energy for much. I think the drug thing was very important to him and, in retrospect, must be why he reacted the way he did."

Cathy rolled her eyes, but Butch kept a steady gaze on Timmerman without reacting to what the man had just said.

"Tell us about Dixon," Butch said.

"Yes, indeed, Dixon. Had everything Johns had in the way of intelligence and ability, but with more attention to our job. He was outstanding. Very hands-on at the training sites. Very, very good with everything. Didn't relate well to other employees, but I think that was because he was so smart. Went to Cal Tech for awhile and then quit for some reason. Right after that he came to work for us. Really quick and bright. There wasn't much he couldn't figure out and do. Knew explosives better than anyone I ever knew. Must have been that Cal Tech instruct…"

"He have any other interests? On the outside, I mean."

"Oh yeah. Big on the environment. Talked about it all the time before he left here. In fact, he left here to head up a…"

"We know," Cathy cut him off.

"Was he always caught up with that stuff?" Butch asked.

"No, not early on. It developed in the time he was here. He got pretty intense about it. He could get all wound up with the negatives. Nothing changing he said, nothing happening fast enough for him. He could get himself in a knot about the environmental issue, that's for sure."

"Angry?" Butch asked.

"I think so," Timmerman replied, "I think quite angry."

"Angry enough to do something about it?"

"You think he's our man?" Timmerman asked.

"What do you think, Mr. Timmerman?"

You never know who will act out," Timmerman said. "I think possibly so. He let slip once…in the last few months when he was here…something about seeing his shrink. I just thought it was about his marital problems, but maybe it had to do with something else. Maybe his anger about the environment."

"Marital problems?" Butch said. "How did that come out?"

"I don't know; it just did one day. Said his marriage was not going too well. I didn't want to hear about it, so he didn't say much more. When the shrink thing came up I just assumed it had to do with marriage counseling or something."

"I ask you," Butch said quickly, "is he our man?"

"If he's one of your targets, well, I would say...probably. He certainly has the potential."

"Thanks, Mr. Timmerman. We appreciate your input."

Butch wheeled out the door and Cathy followed without saying a word. When they were well out of earshot from Timmerman's office Cathy unloaded.

"Can you believe that guy? Duh, your man is admittedly using drugs and you don't can him immediately? What a joke."

"Timmerman knew the reality of the situation. He took care of it."

"Johns was probably doing drugs before he came here," Cathy asserted. "You tell me how he got hired."

"Beat the system," Butch said solemnly. "Lots of ways to do that."

They went back to her office and Butch tossed Dixon's and John's folders on the desk.

"Now what?" she asked.

"Well, we don't tell the authorities just yet, that's for sure. What we do is find this guy Dixon and get his story. And we have Arnold check out Johns just to play it safe."

"Okay."

"By the way, have you arranged a pistol for me...and holster?"

Without responding, she picked up her phone, punched in a number, and waited. There was a answer.

"Arnold, will you get Mr. Greiner's pistol and the holster Chet had for him? Thanks."

She smiled at Butch.

"And if Dixon is hot?" she asked.

"We get the FBI involved. They'll get the other bozos into the action. Homeland Security, ATF, Riverside Sheriff...everyone who needs to know and be involved."

Cathy's phone rang and she was slow to answer as if she were still reacting to what Butch had said and the meaning restricted her movement.

"Simon," she answered.

She listened as the caller spoke and silently mouthed the words *it's Timmerman* to Butch.

"Thanks," she said after several moments of listening and dropped the phone back onto its cradle.

"What was that?" Butch asked.

"Russell Timmerman remembered after we left his office that Kyle Dixon was absolutely ingenious coming up with ways to kill people. Ingenious is the word he used. The more he thought about Dixon the more he thinks the man is dangerous, perhaps lethal. How about that?"

"Plastic explosives are lethal, or can be. Let's see what we have here...a very angry man headed full bore with a cause. Then let's add into the mix the fact he has emotional problems of some kind and is seeing a shrink. That's a guy who could blow up something. I'd say that's our man. Now we have to find him before he does something bad with the plastic."

Arnold knocked at the open doorway. Unlike last night, today he was wearing a well-tailored business suit that snuggly fit him as if he had been sewn into it. He was carrying a black semi-automatic and black holster.

"Got your gun. It's a Glock…it's loaded. Hope the Glock is okay, it's what Mr. Marwood assigned for you. Nice holster. Also a couple of extra clips."

"Thanks, Arnold. Now we have another assignment for you to tackle while Cathy and I try to catch up with Kyle Dixon."

After describing Gordon Johns' background, Butch directed Arnold to confirm where he lived and determine what he was doing.

"Read the recap sheet Cathy made and make notes of anything you need, addresses and so forth, and leave the file here," Butch said as he pointed to a chair in front of Cathy's desk.

The big man sat down, pulled a packet of pink three by five cards from his inside suit coat pocket, and began to read her notes. He pulled a pen from inside his coat and began jotting on one of the cards.

Butch was not surprised at Arnold's preparedness; although he didn't seem the type. His actions were incongruous with such a hulking, behemoth presence that might otherwise connote lesser ability. In other words, Arnold was not a dope and Butch had sensed that the night before.

Cathy began copying names and addresses from Kyle Dixon's folder as Butch stood and watched.

She looked up at him and smiled. "I thought this would help us."

"You bet," Butch said, "it will, but I better make some notes, too…in case we have to split up."

"All set," Arnold said, standing. "I'll stay in touch." He pointed to his cell phone.

"Thanks, Arnold," Cathy said. "Good hunting."

He grunted and was gone.

"Where do we start?" she asked Butch.

"Let's check out the last address that shows for him. We'll see where that takes us."

15.

Kyle charged into the reception area of Alan Simmons' office unannounced, presenting the bravado of a bull fighter ready for a confrontation with death. He stood in front of the reception desk without saying a word as if the young woman there would surely know what he wanted. Perhaps she would anticipate his need and facilitate the removal of his anxiety. She was unable and unwilling to do any of that. Donna Watson knew from experience all about Kyle and she didn't like any of what she knew. She knew him to be a colossal pain in the butt.

"Dr. Simmons is with a client," she said with a certain finality that meant for him to back off and go away. She knew he would not and was prepared for that.

"When they break," Kyle said flatly. "I'll see him for a few minutes."

"We're very tight with scheduling. He has barely…"

"I'll see him when he breaks. Don't argue with me."

She sensed something different about him, something alarming, and it put her on edge. Perhaps he had a psychic break that made him dangerous, she could not be sure.

"I have an appointment next," the man said who was seated across from the desk in one of the comfortable lounge chairs.

"You stay right there until I'm out of here," Kyle said menacingly.

The man looked away and did not respond to Kyle.

The wait wasn't long. Alan came to the door to his office and motioned to Kyle. Donna followed Kyle into Simmons' office.

"I tried to tell him how busy you were, but he feels he's more important than our other clients."

"It's all right, Ms. Watson, we'll give Mr. Dixon a couple of minutes."

She turned on her heels and Simmons followed her to the door.

"John, thanks for your patience," he said with a smile and a wink to the man in the reception room, "I'll be with you right away."

The man who had spoken up to Kyle grimaced through a wan smile of his own and nodded.

"What the hell is going on?" Simmons said after Donna closed the door.

"It starts tonight. I wanted you to know. Fire and Brimstone starts tonight. I am satisfied that we are on the right track and we now go forward."

"Who the hell are we?" Simmons was angry.

"The we, are the ones to take society forward…to a new understanding of where we are and what has to be done to protect us from the future. I told you about Fire and Brimstone. It's the only way and it begins tonight."

"Why are you telling me this? What is it you expect me to say or do? I know that I haven't helped you understand…"

"But you have helped me tremendously…given me focus, the surety to know what I am doing is right. I had to tell you. I would hope that after all the time we have spent together that you would understand what I am about. What I need to do. But you don't, do you?"

"Yes, I understand. I understand that you have a distorted sense of reality, that you think there is all this wrong out there and that only you know what is right for society. I beg you to stop now with any plans you have to press your alienation on the rest of us. I beg you to rethink what you think, to reevaluate what it is you want to do. I don't know what you have planned, but I think it is probably destructive and there will be no good that can come of it. Nothing good can come from negative action. Count on that."

"We are going to cut off the water and electricity to lots of people in southern California and they will become aware of what is important. That will not be negative. That is the awareness that is necessary."

"That will be criminal," Simmons yelled at him, "that will be foolish and destructive."

"We'll see," Kyle said, "we'll see. But I wanted you to know what was going to happen."

"Why, for God sake? I don't want to know."

"Yes, you want to know about something important that changes society. You'll be satisfied that you knew it was going to happen."

"I…I'm not happy at all. To see you throw your life away in a manner that hurts others, that sends pain to your family, and that…"

"Wish me well, Al." Kyle turned and was out of the office.

"Don't call me Al, you son-of-a-bitch."

Simmons screamed the words, but no one heard him. He figured that now for sure, Kyle would never be in his office again.

16.

Butch was not really an automobile aficionado, but when he saw the one assigned to him, he whistled. It was a brand new Lexus LS-460, shiny black.

"Well, now. This is very nice. This I can appreciate."

"It's loaded," Cathy said, "Any extra you can get is on this car. It is luxury personified."

"You want to drive it?" Butch asked, holding the key toward her.

"No, no, you drive. It would make me too nervous to drive. It won't bother you."

"Okay."

They headed out of the Gladstone underground garage as Cathy programmed Kyle's last known address into the navigation system.

"Just so you know, Butch, this car has a third-party owner, so it can't easily be traced back to Gladstone. That's so no one can run the plates and quickly ID where you're from. I put a letter in the glove box that authorizes you or me as a driver. Just in case the cops stop us. Also an insurance card."

"Interesting. This thing going to tell us where we are going?"

"I think so, but I already checked that out. I just wanted to see how this works. Turn left."

The drive to the house where Kyle's wife Laurie and three children lived with Laurie's sister Hanna took less than half an hour. It was located south of Santa Monica in the Venice section of Los Angeles in a quiet, unpretentious neighborhood between Lincoln Boulevard and Centinela. It was the worst looking house on the block. The navigation system told them they had arrived.

The beige stucco bungalow needed help with various kinds of repairs and the small front area was in disarray with weeds, scrawny plants, and several discarded toys. A small tricycle stood sentinel at the foot of the front steps. The scene was depressing to Butch, because he knew it reflected an attitude and a state of mind. He remembered what Timmerman had said about Kyle seeing a shrink and it seemed to fit with what he saw here.

A young woman answered the door when Butch knocked. The bell had not worked.

"Yes," she said warily, ready to close the door. "What do you want?"

"Looking for Kyle Dixon. We'd like to talk to him. Does he live here?" Butch held up his ID card that showed he was a licensed private investigator. "Name is Greiner, this is my client representative Cathy Simon." Cathy showed her company badge.

"No, he doesn't live here," she snapped. "He used to."

A small child appeared and clung to the young woman's leg.

"What do you know about Mr. Dixon?"

"Why do you want to know?"

"We need to clarify some things."

"Gladstone International," the young woman said quickly as she looked at Cathy. "That's who Kyle used to work for. What's going on?"

"May we come in and chat with you for a few minutes," Butch asked calmly.

"Sure, come on in. This has got to be good. I'm really curious; he hasn't worked for them for four years. Now you want him? What did he do?"

Butch and Cathy followed the young woman into a small, poorly furnished bare floor living room cluttered with toys. She asked them to sit down.

"How do you know Kyle?" Butch asked as he and Cathy sat on the soiled cloth sofa.

"He's married to my sister Laurie. This is his baby daughter Sadie. She's three, almost four. Born after that SOB ran out on Laurie. He never was around for her birth, the bastard."

"Where is he now?"

"Why do you want him...what'd he do?"

"My client had two robberies recently..."

"Gladstone?"

"Yes. These robberies...how and where they were conducted...indicate that someone with proprietary knowledge was involved. Mr. Dixon had such knowledge..."

"An inside job, you mean. What'd he steal."

"We don't know that he stole anything, but we have a number of suspects and we need to eliminate them one by one as we talk to them and confirm their whereabouts during the times in question."

"What a bunch of BS. You would not be after him unless you thought he was connected somehow. Where are the police in all of this?"

"We're trying to help them as much as we can."

"Oh, really. There's been nothing in the news about this. Why is it being covered up?"

"It isn't being covered up, but it is a sensitive matter and..."

"What did he steal?"

"We don't know if..."

"Okay, okay. What was stolen?"

"Certain sensitive material was taken from..."

"What?"

"Plastic explosives."

"Jesus Christ...he's going to blow something up, that nut. He's just rabid enough to use that stuff."

"Why do you say that?"

"Oh, man, he's a fanatical radical when it comes to the environment. And you know who got him started? My sister. But he went way beyond her; he is one angry dude about the environment. He is wound tight about that...in a knot, big time. He would use that stuff. I never thought about him doing something really really terrorizing, but taking stuff to blow things up...hey, he's the man for the job. For sure."

"Do you have Kyle's address?"

"Yeah, it's in Riverside. He has an office there, too. Let me get our book."

She jumped up with a struggle and limped out of the room.

"Well, well," Butch said to Cathy. "And so we move ahead."

She was back in less than a minute, thumbing through a large leather planner. Butch noticed that she labored when she walked and wondered about her physical condition.

"You watch the kids while you sister works? Butch posed.

"Yeah. Laurie's a nurse over at St. John's in Santa Monica. Two of the kids are in school. It's just Sadie and I here during the day. Do you need to talk to Laurie?"

"I don't think so if you can give us the addresses in Riverside and tell us anything else you know. Then we wouldn't have to bother your sister while she's working."

"Here they are."

Cathy had a notebook poised and copied down the addresses and phone numbers.

"He's been crap as a provider. Three kids and he's given little to support them. He was just around recently and gave Laurie a check for five grand, but he owes a hell of a lot more than that. You know, you might check with his mother. He stays with her…at her house…when he comes here from Riverside. She has a business…a gallery…over on Olympic Boulevard. Her name is Doris Krause. It was Dixon, of course, but then she married this Krause guy who died. Her maiden name was Taylor, which is the name of her place. Taylor Gallery. Talk to her, she can probably tell you more. Here's her address and phone number."

Cathy made note of that also.

"I appreciate your help very much…ah, Miss…"

"Hanna…Hanna Hart. My sister was a Hart. And she's got too big a heart to put up with Kyle all these years. I'd have put him in jail for non-payment."

Thanks, Hanna, you've been a great help."

Back in the car, Butch looked at Cathy.

"Kyle is not nice," Cathy said, "even if he isn't our robber."

"He's our robber, all right. But let's talk to the mother. He sounds to me like a mama's boy, anyway. It will be interesting to hear what she has to say. Ten bucks says she tries to cover for him."

"No bet. Do you think she knows what his plans are?"

"No, probably not. She knows he's up to something, but my guess is she has no details. We'll see."

Getting back to Taylor Gallery in Santa Monica put them within five minutes or so from the Gladstone offices.

"Recognize the neighborhood," Cathy asked.

"Yeah, sure. I know where we are. You don't know this, but I'm quite familiar with LA."

"Oh really? You'll have to tell me about that sometime."

"Be glad to. I had some fun here in LA once upon a time. Long time ago."

They pulled into the parking lot of Doris' gallery and the navigation system confirmed they were where they should be.

"That thing is comforting," Butch said. "Let's hope it's as good when we really need it."

No one was to be seen when they walked inside the gallery. Butch looked at a small bronze statue of a nude woman in a garden setting while Cathy fidgeted. She didn't seem interested in looking at much of the art work or antiques until a large oil painting caught her eye.

"Can I help you with anything," a tall blonde girl said. She had appeared from nowhere and strode toward Butch aggressively. She wore pea-green corduroy slacks that were so tight the lines of her pubic area clearly showed. A light blue denim shirt did not hide her large bust and she moved rather easily on red leather platform heels. With this ensemble, she could have just come from a movie audition; she was that good-looking and that provocatively dressed.

"Yes, we're looking for Mrs. Krause."

"Did you have an appointment with her?" She had stopped a few feet from Butch and stood with feet spread apart.

"No." Butch was curt enough to match her aggression. "Is she here?"

"Maybe I can help you."

"I don't think so. We like the art, but we're here to talk to Mrs. Krause about her son."

The blonde took a step back.

"Tell her we're here," Butch said quietly, "and tell her why we're here."

The blonde spun agilely and elegantly on the platform heels and retreated.

"I'll tell her," she said without looking back at him.

Several minutes went by before Doris appeared.

"Doris Krause," she said extending her hand as she approached. "You wanted to see me?"

"Butch Greiner, Mrs. Krause, this is Cathy Simon. We represent Gladstone International. I'm a private investigator working for them. Miss Simon is the assistant to the head of their security division."

He showed her his PI card. Cathy flashed her badge.

"What about my son, Mr. Greiner?"

Butch knew he had been right about her. This was going to be like combat, with words as the weapons. He had suspected she would be defensive of her son and the tone was there in her voice. It was the tone of protection; it was the tone of defiance. Be delicate, he cautioned himself; see how much you can get from her before she balks and refuses any more information.

"I understand your son is heading up an environmental organization out in Riverside. What's it called?"

"Alliance For A Better Environment. We recently had a very successful fund raiser here in Santa Monica. My son is involved in very important work."

"Very dedicated to his cause, I guess." Butch noted she used the word "we" when she answered him.

"He's a very bright young man. It's critical that someone like Kyle is spearheading the need for change. He understands; he truly knows the need."

"He's living in Riverside?"

"Yes. Why all the questions?"

"But he stays with you when he's around here?"

Her eyes narrowed. It was going to get tougher with her.

"What is this all about?"

"We're trying to sort out some things, put some missing pieces together to solve a crime. That's what I do for a living. Miss Simon is responsible for protecting her firm…"

"And…so?" She took a step back, folded her arms, and glowered. She was ready for battle.

"All we want to do is talk to Kyle, clear up some things. Can we find him at his place in Riverside? Or an office? I assume the Alliance has an office."

"Yes, it does. Working to get the word out. He's very busy at that."

"Do you have an address for the office?"

"Not really, its in downtown Riverside. Now, what is this all about? I answer no more questions until you tell me what is going on."

"Gladstone has had a theft…a couple of thefts. We have reason to believe it was an inside job. Your son worked for them once and we're checking out a number of folks…former employees. To see what they know. It's a routine investigation."

"Get out," she yelled. "You're involved in harassment, I think."

"Tell Kyle when you talk to him that we want to see him. Cathy, give Mrs. Krause your card."

Cathy did and Doris stared at it.

"Have him call that cell phone number. It would be very helpful."

"Get out," she said again, this time quietly, but firmly.

Butch didn't move.

"Is your son guilty of something?"

"What?"

"You're very defensive. You must suspect that your son has done something…"

"No…"

"Why cover for him then?"

"Get out or…"

"Or what? You'll call the cops. I don't think so. You want the cops as far away from you and your son as possible."

She took a step forward in anger with no idea at all what she would do. Butch still didn't move. They were toe to toe, so close he could smell her. She was obviously a vital older woman and he knew she was frustrated and torn about her son.

"We're going," he said finally. "Have him call. Maybe we can get everything straightened out."

"What do you mean?"

He could smell the garlic on her breath and her sweet perfume and the sweat that had overcome her. The conglomeration of odors was strange and almost intoxicating.

"I think your son wants to blow up something. I don't know what just yet, but I'd like to talk to him before he does."

"What are you talking about?"

"Plastic explosives were stolen from two of the Gladstone properties and I think your son was involved."

"Never."

"Have him call us…any time, day or night. It's critical he does."

"Good-bye, Mr. Greiner."

"He needs to call." Butch and Cathy were on their way to the door.

"Good-bye, Mr. Greiner."

"This could be very bad," Butch yelled at her as he and Cathy went out the door. He wanted the last word.

They were back in the car on Olympic boulevard heading east.

"Let's check out his organization on the Internet."

"Right," Cathy said quickly. "We're only blocks from our office; we can stop there and get what we need. And you can try out your biometrics."

Butch smiled and drove to the Gladstone building where he parked in front.

"I'm impressed," she said, "you do know your way around."

"Like I said, I've been here before."

In the lobby, the security guard supervised the scan of Butch's right index finger and then of his right iris. Cathy also scanned her entry and in a few minutes they were in her office.

"Here it is. The Alliance For A Better Environment website."

She compared the address and phone number to those in her notebook that Laurie's sister had given them. They matched. Butch dialed the number she had written. Christy Warren answered.

"Alliance For A Better Environment," she said with a smile. "May I help you?"

"Kyle Dixon, please." Butch tried to sound affable, as if he could be a potential donor.

"Not in. Could I take a message?"

"Well, I need to speak to him as soon as possible. When will he be back? Or how can I reach him? Does he have a cell phone?"

"I don't know when he'll be back and I don't know how to reach him. He checks in with me. He's out soliciting funds right now. If it's real important, you might try him at his apartment tonight. He said he wouldn't be in the office for awhile."

"Give him my number when he checks in, okay? Tell him this is very important."

"Sure."

Butch recited Cathy's cell phone number to her.

After he hung up the phone, Butch glowered at Cathy.

"Yikes, you look like you've eaten something bad."

"Yeah, right, maybe this assignment."

"What…?"

"She said she didn't know when he'll be back in the office. He's out soliciting funds. Not likely, Cathy, not likely. My guess is that he's ready to use the plastic…soon. He'll stay away from the apartment. He has some other place, a place where he can assemble a bomb and not be noticed."

"Like where?"

"Something rural, most likely. I know this is getting away from us too fast. I know Chet wanted the authorities out of this as long as possible, but we've got to get law enforcement after this guy. We can't cover enough ground fast enough."

"What do you mean?"

"Talk to the FBI guy who talked to Chet. Let him notify any of the other jurisdictions he sees fit. We've got to limit our liability on this thing before it gets out of hand. Otherwise, the Feds will be asking why we weren't forthcoming with the info about Kyle."

"Call Fuller…in Riverside?"

"Yeah, if he's the guy."

"He's the one." She showed him the number. Butch picked up the phone to punch it in. Miles away, in Fallbrook, Kyle was busily getting ready to set his plan in motion.

17.

Creating havoc with the Southern California infrastructure was something Kyle had considered for a long time. In truth, bringing it about was not a last minute decision on his part, it was the result of more than a year of planning and preparation. The decision was almost preordained from the mindset he carried, mixed with his own frustrations with society, and his inability to cope with it.

Fourteen months before, he had met and mesmerized Connie and Leon Herrons at an environmental rally in Banning. He had organized the protest at the construction site of an upscale housing development and had fired up the crowd with a fifteen minute harangue about the misuse of land by greedy capitalists who violated the legacy of open space and constantly raped society. Leon was then an out-of-work laborer and Connie was waiting tables in a Banning diner. Both of their kids were grown and had moved from California the year before. The couple was ripe for something to do that meant something. They latched onto Kyle's cause like a terrier to a rat.

He recruited them for the Hayfield operation and financed their every move. This made it possible for Leon to pursue employment with and eventually get hired by the Los Angeles Department of Water and Power. He was assigned to the Hayfield pumping station in a remote area adjacent to Joshua Tree National Park more than 175 miles east of Santa Monica. This pumping station was a critical juncture in the transmission of water from Lake Havasu on the Colorado River to Southern California.

He helped Leon with the LA DWP job application and had brother-in-law Kevin Rothstein write and sign a letter of recommendation. Kevin's networking and connections helped pave the way for Leon to have a chance for the job.

Kyle had vigilantly monitored hiring and job postings to be aware of the impending Hayfield job.

Kyle had spent considerable time researching the water and electrical distribution systems for Southern California and was technically fluent in vulnerabilities that could be exploited. He considered Hayfield just such a weak point. Carefully, he brought Norm Burch and Kevin Forrester into the Hayfield project. They would deliver the placement to the Herrons.

What Kyle had envisioned for this first night of Fire and Brimstone was complex and depended upon those he had recruited to carry out the details of their assignments. He called them the Dixon Brigade. Besides himself and the immediate group at the ranch, there were the Herrons, Burch, and Forrester, plus five couples. Four of the couples were married and the fifth was a lesbian duo from Yucaipa. He had met with each of the couples separately and explained what they would do and how they would do it. As with all the others he had influenced, the couples had attended several of his rallies. He provided them with maps of where their targets were located and the potential timing. Only the day needed to be communicated to them. Each couple believed they had a special assignment to further the cause. None of the couples knew about the others.

As Kyle worked through the morning heat to finalize the various placements that would be used that night, Carrie, Ellis, and Ted were stealing the various vehicles they would be driving. The truck for the Hayfield placement had been stolen the night before. Mark stayed at the ranch as Kyle had requested. Something else needed to be done.

"Mark," Kyle said as he worked with some wiring, "I'd like you to call these numbers and let them know that tonight is the night."

Mark looked at him curiously.

"What are these?" he asked. "Who are these…?"

"An important part of the Dixon Brigade, my friend. All are part of Fire and Brimstone."

"How?"

"They will be setting fires at five strategic locations, five miserable construction sites that are taking away open space, five sites that have to…"

"When did they come into the equation?"

"They've always been part of the plan, Mark. Oh, not these specific people, but the idea of the construction sites was there. I knew we had to do something about them. I got these folks involved over the last few months. They're all real excited about the challenge…of participating in an important cause. I had to give them something to do. I thought burning the sites was perfect for them. There was no way I could let them be part of what we are doing. The number of people involved is already big enough"

"What else is there man that you haven't shared with me?"

Kyle stopped what he was doing. He looked at Mark with an expression of hurt feelings.

"Listen, sorry, I don't have this thing written down. It's kind of all in my head. I didn't want it written down. I think you know everything. This…these people I didn't think about until today."

"Shit." Mark said, drawing the word out for emphasis.

"What?"

"There's got to be more details. I can't do this on a minute-by-minute basis."

"Well, ask me some questions. What are you wondering about?"

"Here we are to D-Day. What do we do after tonight?"

"We move to Santa Monica. Now, get going with those calls."

Mark shrugged and started for the house.

"It's okay," Kyle called after him, "everything's going to work out all right. It has so far. No one knows what we're doing."

Mark kept going and did not hear the last of what Kyle said.

By eleven-fifteen that morning, a van and three sedans were parked in the avocado barn. Carrie and the two ranch hands had done their job. Kyle stood surveying the vehicles, nodding approval.

"These are perfect for what we want," Kyle said.

"How's this all gonna work?" Ellis asked.

"Like this," Kyle said pulling a folded map from his hip pocket as he walked out of the barn. "Come on; let's go up to the house. Have a beer, scope it all out."

They all marched up to the kitchen following Kyle. Carrie pulled beers from the refrigerator and everyone except Kyle plunked down around the table. He stood in command, ready to pull the strings on what would take place. He had asked Carrie to get some note pads and pens from the office and then they were ready for his dissertation. Each man had his beer and was ready.

"Ellis, you take one of the cars to this location. Make note of where it is. You'll have two placements to install. Put them at the base like this."

Kyle proceeded to make a sketch of an electric transmission tower.

"Get them tight up against the steel and that's that. The timers are already set. Ted, the same thing for you. Here's where you go. Check the map and write it down. Install the placements and that's it. Come back here and wait for me to contact you. You, too, Ellis. Mark, here's where you go. Then I want you to meet Carrie and me at the entrance ramp to I-15 coming down Route 74 from Perris. There's a lot happening here, guys, so you just have to go ahead with your part of the plan and everything will fall in place."

"What happens?" Ellis asked.

"Turmoil," Kyle answered. "You come back to the ranch...and Ted you get back here also. No one knows anything. No one is going to run out here after you, so don't worry. Go about the business of the ranch. If anyone shows up..."

"You mean the law?" Ellis said.

"Yeah. It's not very likely, but if they do, you stay cool, tell them you know nothing and don't say anything else."

"Why would they come here? Ted asked. "What would get them here?"

"I used to work for Gladstone. Someone might trace that down...eventually. But you know nothing and you'll be clean."

Ted stared at him.

"In the meantime, Carrie and I are going to take out the pumping station at the Perris Dam. We're moving on to Santa Monica after that for operations there. This is the way we bring the entire Southern California basin to its knees so that attention is paid to the issues we want addressed."

It was hot and the men guzzled their beer. Carrie sucked on a small glass of tequila with squeezed lime. Ted, Ellis, and Mark looked at the notes they had made and each thought that it was too easy and therefore more dangerous than Kyle would say. But they would not challenge him and they would not question the assignments he had given to them.

"Relax," Kyle said quietly. "It's all going to be okay. Take a nap, rest someplace, take a walk, but whatever you do don't worry about what is going to happen."

For a long time the men just sat and drank beer. Eventually, Ted and Ellis took chairs on the porch and went to sleep.

Carrie and Kyle went upstairs to their bedroom. Mark sat staring at the wall. He was in a beer-induced stupor helped along by the hot day. He was caught in a malaise that made him virtually paralyzed. This would never work out right. He was sure of it.

In mid-afternoon, with everyone at the ranch but Kyle in various states of semi-sleep restlessness, Norm Burch and Kevin Forrester arrived. They each wanted a beer. Kyle was putting the finishing touches on the placements that would be used and particularly the Hinds and Perris Dam placements. He greeted them outside the barn and led them up to the house. He popped caps on two Anchor Steam bottles and asked the men to relax.

"You've got a few hours to go, maybe you want a nap...lay down or something..."

"We're fine Kyle. Show us what we're dealing with."

He took them down to the barn where the truck they would take to Hayfield was waiting.

"It's all loaded and ready to go. Get it to Chiriaco Summit and you'll be fine. Tell Leon to park the left side toward the station: that's important; it's a directed charge. In other words, it wants to blow that way."

"That's like the Murrah bomb in Oklahoma City," Burch offered.

"Placement," Kyle corrected, "I call them placements."

"Whatever."

"What you said is somewhat true. Only there they placed the plastic in the building lobby and it detonated two seconds later. This one goes almost all together. It's a tight sequence with the fertilizer and then the plastic in quick succession. Kaboom. It will sound like one, but it's really two. Anyway, after you make the exchange with Leon in Chiriaco, get back on I-10 and keep going east. Disappear. No one will ever trace you. But you'll have our thanks for contributing to our cause. We couldn't do this without you guys. Know what you have done is really important."

The two men settled into chairs on the porch and Kyle went back to the barn. He could not sit still regardless of the heat.

"No wonder there's a siesta," he said under his breath. "No one should be working in this heat."

He carried two placements to each of the cars and put them in their trunks. Then he assembled the Perris Dam placement in the van in a similar manner as the Hinds placement using fertilizer, kerosene, and plastic explosives. When he was finished, he went back to the house.

Ted and Ellis were still in semi-stupor, Mark was sitting in the kitchen with Burch and Forrester. Kyle ignored them and went upstairs to where Carrie was lying naked on his bed. He lay down beside her. Nothing was said for a long time.

"It's underway," he said finally. "At last we will have the stamp of disapproval cast on a misbehaving society."

He rose and went to his briefcase on the table nearby. She rocked up on her elbow to see what he was doing. He came back to the bed with a sheaf of papers in his hand and sat down with his back against the headboard.

"Let me read you the letter."

Attention. Citizens take note. Fire and Brimstone is upon you. What is happening is necessary to provoke full awareness of the importance of our water and our electricity, to open eyes to the need to protect our environment, and to guard against the terrible use of land as we spread out in all directions with little sense of what we are destroying for ourselves, of the land, and all the living things that need the land for survival. Stop mindless building and expansion that destroys and wastes open space, stop the waste of energy, and stop the misuse and overuse of our water supply. Only by being without these two elements – water and power - can society understand what has to be done. You will suffer and that is unfortunate, but it is necessary for you to understand what must happen. You will suffer and your suffering will be a learning process. You will suffer and you will ask for and demand change in policy, in programs, and in the perception of what is right for our society. Suffer you citizens and understand. Suffer you citizens and be a part of a new dimension of responsible action. You must demand change. You must ask your mayors and councils and zoning boards to make changes in policies that damage our environment and that waste our land. We will continue to make life inconvenient to lots of people until the changes are pressed for and instituted. Our future depends on the actions of all citizens who care about what must be done. Demand positive action now before it is too late. You all must care.

This action letter has been sent by those who are taking action because they care.

"I signed it The Protector. Well, what do you think?"

"Good, it's good. Who will read it?"

"All the major newspapers in the LA basin will get it. I mailed it yesterday. Then they will know. The people will know."

18.

"One moment for Special Agent in Charge Fuller." The cheerful female voice was responding to Butch's explanation for the call and its importance. The line was silent for a few moments.

"Fuller. What have you got?"

"This is Butch Greiner, Agent Fuller..."

"Special Agent in Change," Fuller reminded him.

"Yes, I got that. I'm here at Gladstone International corporate headquarters in Santa Monica. I've been hired by Chet Marwood, who is the head of Gladstone security, to fill in for him while he's out of the country. Trying to find out who might have pulled the two robberies at our training facilities in your area. You talked to Chet before he left. He wanted to look into the possibility it was an inside job..."

"Yeah, he sort of stiff-armed me about sending our guys to check it out. He asked for some time to see what was what with your records. Did you find anything we can use?"

"Yeah, we think so. We have a suspect we believe could be our man. Former employee. If he is our man then he has some kind of plan for the explosives."

"No kidding? Regardless of whether he's your former employee or not, the thief plans to blow something up. Wouldn't you say that's a reasonable assumption?"

"I would," Butch said. He had stated the obvious only in the sense that it related to Kyle, but he was not surprised by Fuller's reaction. Fuller now probably thought he was some kind of dope. He should have kept his mouth shut.

"Well, isn't that interesting? Some guy and the gang he has with him want to blow something up. Whether it's your guy or someone else, he wants to destroy something and has plans for it. Let me read you something that got to me a few minutes ago. It came from Bud Daniels over at the Riverside Press-Enterprise. Bud got it in this morning's mail. He wanted to know what the hell is going on. I, of course, did not have an answer for him. This letter is no coincidence and you know it."

Fuller read Kyle's letter.

"He signed it The Protector. This means he's going to blow up places that have to do with water and power."

"Read that first part again," Butch asked, "where he says something about water and electricity."

"Okay…here's what it says: '*What is happening is necessary to provoke full awareness of the importance of our water and our electricity, to open eyes to the need to protect our environment, and to guard against the terrible use of land as we spread out in all directions with little sense of what we are destroying…*'"

"Substations, water lines, that's what it means. He's going to try to stop water and electricity from getting delivered in southern California."

"That's what I think."

"The thing is," Butch offered, "his letter got out before he's done anything. Have you heard of anything happening?"

"Not a thing."

"Not part of his plan, I'm sure. Which means it starts tonight."

"We're dealing with a nutso," Fuller said.

"You're dealing with Kyle Dixon, I think," Butch responded.

"Yeah, I was going to ask you your guy's name. Kyle Dixon, that it?"

"Yes. We'll fax you everything we have. I don't know what your manpower situation is, but we'll head out to Riverside and see if we can be of help."

"We can handle it, don't worry."

"This will take a lot of head count to cover all the bases. Don't blow smoke at me; you'll need all the help there is."

Butch could hear Fuller sigh in frustration.

"Stay in contact," he said.

"You'll know our every move."

Butch dropped the phone onto its cradle and smiled. Cathy smiled back at him. She was not sure why he smiled, but it seemed impish and her reaction was automatic.

"So we head for Riverside?" she asked, knowing the answer.

"We can't just sit here," Butch said.

Once they were back in the car headed for the Santa Monica Freeway, Cathy wanted to know what had just transpired with Fuller.

"I only heard your side of the conversation. What was the big deal?"

"The big deal was that a newspaper guy passed on a letter he received this morning. Fuller read it to me. It sounded like an explanation for something that has not yet happened. At least that's my guess. A premature answer for something that will probably go down tonight. The letter was signed The Protector. Kyle Dixon is our protector and is going to take away water and power so we understand how important they are."

"And?"

"And what?"

"What does Fuller do about it? What does he protect? There are lots...there are just scads of targets it seems to me. Aren't there?"

"There are. He gets everybody involved. All of the FBI in southern California, Riverside police, Riverside sheriff, every bit of law enforcement in the southern half of the state.

But what do you do? Post a cop or deputy at every electric pole? The magnitude of this thing is overwhelming. We won't know what or where until something happens. That's the brutal truth."

Butch rocketed the Lexus onto the east bound Santa Monica Freeway and Cathy was silent. Butch looked over at her. Tiny beads of perspiration formed a glisten smatter at her temples. She gripped the edge of her seat with her left hand and the right pulled at the shoulder strap.

The speedometer was close to ninety.

"I think you should slow up when you go though the interchanges downtown," she said softly.

"I will. Don't worry."

Butch loved driving in southern California. It was one of the few things he did like about being here. He could go fast wherever the traffic flow would allow. When it opened up, he let the needle bump the ninety mark as much as possible. The Lexus just hummed and it was exhilarating and he knew there was little chance he would be stopped. Other cars still passed him.

Kyle's office was in a two-story nondescript building not far from the Riverside FBI; an easy five-minute walk. Neither Butch nor Cathy realized this when they arrived. Kyle's three non-profit money-raising groups were noted on the office registry next to the elevator, all in Suite 210. There was no other identification on the door other than the suite number.

"Interesting," Cathy said. "No name on the door."

"Didn't want to spend the money," Butch sniped.

They went inside the office.

The attractive young woman was eating something when they entered which she quickly hid from view and almost finished chewing before she greeted them.

"Hello, you caught me. I was having a little snack. Can I help you?"

"Maybe you can. I'm looking for Kyle Dixon. It's very import…"

"You're the one who called. I recognize your voice."

"Very perceptive of you."

"I told you I didn't know where he is."

"We had to be here in Riverside anyway," Butch lied, "so I thought we would stop by. See if maybe you've heard from him since we talked."

"No, I haven't. What is it that is so important? I manage the office for Kyle, maybe…"

"Anyway, we wanted to take a look at the Alliance's office, see what made the… What do you call it? The movement, the cause? How do you describe it?"

Christy wasn't smart enough to pick up on the edge of sarcasm in Butch's voice, but was wary of anyone prying. Kyle had trained her to be alert to nosey news media people that might want to give them a hard time. She thought Butch might be a reporter. Up to this point, he had not identified himself nor Cathy, nor had said what their business was.

"Listen, are you a reporter?"

Butch laughed and Cathy turned away to keep from bursting out loud.

"Would that be bad?

"Kyle says to be careful of reporters, they can make trouble."

"No, Miss... You are?"

"Warren, Christy Warren."

"No, Miz Warren, we are not reporters. However, we can make a lot of trouble. My name is Butch Greiner, this is Cathy Simon. I'm a private detective and Cathy works for my client, Gladstone International. We think Kyle has gotten himself in a lot of trouble. So if you know anything about Kyle…where he is, where he can be reached…you better tell us."

"I've told you. He left me in charge, said he would contact me, he would be on the move. That's it."

"Where else does he hang out besides his apartment?"

"What? What do you mean?"

"When you two are together and you're not at his apartment, is there another place you go? A cabin in the mountains, a little farm house somewhere? Like that."

"I don't follow you…"

"Aren't you and Kyle lovers?"

"Ah…sort of."

"Sort of?"

"Yes, we are. So what? I give him comfort and…"

"I'm sure you do. Now, where else do you go?"

"Nowhere…his apartment…my apartment. Restaurants, coffee shops. Listen, why is a detective looking for Kyle? Has he done something?"

"Not yet, but we think he's going to do something. Something not good."

"Look, Mr.…"

"Greiner."

"All I know is that we are trying to do something for the environment and Kyle has an important mission…"

"And you're screwing him and helping him and taking charge of the office. Right?"

She stared at him, her lips apart as if she wanted to say something, but nothing came into her head.

"You just sit tight, Miz Warren. The FBI will be here soon and they'll want to talk to you. Don't leave, don't do anything foolish, answer their questions, and you'll be okay."

Butch motioned to Cathy and they were out the door.

"She doesn't know what's going on," Butch stated as they went down in the elevator. "Let's go to the FBI offices and check in with Fuller."

"We've missed lunch," Cathy said, "I'm getting hungry."

"We'll catch lunch after we see Fuller. You have their address?"

They were in Fuller's office within fifteen minutes, but not without some tribulation about parking. Butch was willing to park anywhere; Cathy rejected the red curbs. Finally, they found a spot and made the walk. Butch reminded her that closer was better and she was not persuaded. She was satisfied with where their car was situated.

"Nice meeting you two. Really appreciate getting this guy's name. Kyle Dixon. Not much on him. Couple of minor things in the past that had to do with protests. Civil disorder. Resisting arrest. Disorderly conduct. That sort of thing. All in LA county. He's been an activist, I guess. Couple of speeding violations...well, actually six to be exact."

Fuller was reading from a sheet of paper he held.

"Agent Tobin reported from the apartment. Nothing unusual."

"We just came from his office. You need to turn that place. The young gal secretary there doesn't know anything. Told her he'd be in touch, said he was going to be on the move scrounging up donations or something. A cover story, I would guess. He's got to be able to build bombs someplace. Somewhere that he can wire timers and put stuff together. Not an apartment. Someplace remote. I would check county real estate records and see if he owns property that is rural. A farm, a cabin…something like that."

Fuller looked at him.

"He's out there. God knows where. He's getting bombs ready for delivery, easily operating without suspicion. He has to have a place where he isn't noticed. Comings and goings, vans, trucks, and that sort of thing. He has to have a building to work in. A barn, a warehouse where accumulation and assembly and preparation happen. Check his name for property ownership. That's the best I can offer right now. Other than that, I would say that tonight there will be some places blown up and we're going to be about three steps behind this Kyle. He knows where he's going and what he's going to do. We don't."

"Thanks for the encouragement," Fuller snapped.

"We're hungry. We missed lunch. We're going to get something to eat. Any suggestions?"

Fuller thought for a few seconds then shook his head.

"Naw, just the usual fast food. Nothing special."

"You have Cathy's cell phone number. Let us know if you learn anything."

"I will," Fuller confirmed.

"He won't give us poop," Butch said as they left the building and headed for the Lexus.

"Why do you say that?" Cathy asked.

"Too many bad experiences with his type…"

"FBI, you mean?"

"Yeah, they want all the glory, anything they can cram into their personnel file. That's how they get promoted. Oh sure, there are some exceptions. I just haven't met up with any. I'm jaded, I guess. Should reserve judgment; let him prove me wrong. But I doubt if we'll ever get anything from him.

He has no reason to; we're not part of law enforcement. We'll see what happens."

"Tacos, okay?"

"Yeah, sure. We're close to Mexico aren't we? Why not? Ohio tacos stink. Sorry about being so negative in regards to Fuller...and the FBI. Old baggage."

"That's okay. It doesn't bother me; I'm just trying to learn. Cut back toward the Freeway. I saw a place called Benito's or something like that. Yeah, there it is."

Butch pulled into the parking lot and they went inside. It smelled of tacos, the odor was authentic. True Mexican.

"A margarita con sal," Cathy flipped at the waitress when they were seated. "And a chunk of lime."

"Si, and you, señor?"

"Water."

The waitress was off and Butch looked at Cathy.

"Con sal?"

"With salt," she said.

"Yeah, I know a little Spanish."

"Too pretentious?"

"No. Too...familiar, too..."

"Pretentious." She laughed.

He liked the way she laughed and why she laughed and he suddenly realized he felt some connection to her, some stimulated involvement that he could not readily assess. It bothered him because he could not quite grasp what he was feeling. It felt too much as if he were attracted to her. Could he handle that? He didn't know if he could, it had been so long since he had such feelings. She was attractive in an athletic way he appreciated. No, she was more than attractive, he thought, as he watched her laugh slip away to an easy smile.

"Sorry, I'm really not a pretentious person. My humble beginnings are too close in my memory for that. I guess I just like saying it. It fits with the times and where we live and how things work out."

"It fits," Butch confirmed.

The margarita came, they ordered and ate, and Butch paid the check.

"Let's head back. I'd like to get a run in if I can. We've done all we're going to do around here for today."

"You're a runner?"

"Triathlons. I do a lot of cross training. Running, biking, swimming. Today would be my biking day if I were home, but since I don't have my bike here with me, I'll run. It'll work my legs."

"I bike," she offered. "I have a mountain bike. I've never biked in the mountains, but I ride around Santa Monica."

Traffic was already at an agonizingly slow pace, a crushing press of vehicles on the move somewhere. Butch tried to relax, painfully impatient with not being able to go ninety. Nine and nineteen were possible, but not ninety. He contented himself in consolation with getting to know this gorgeous young woman seated beside him. He had no idea how taken she was with him, how eager she was to reveal herself and make the connection with him.

It was a tortuous drive in its slowness, but otherwise uneventful and they arrived back at the Gladstone building somewhat strung out. Butch wasn't sure whether it was the effect of the jammed, slow traffic or getting to know Cathy that made him feel whipped. For her part, she knew the reason and liked knowing it happened.

"See you in the morning," Butch said in an offhand way, trying to be nonchalant.

"Where are you going to run?" she asked.

"I don't know. Probably in the neighborhood. Maybe run down to the beach. I make it a pretty good workout."

"Would you like some company…running?"

"Ah…sure," he hesitated.

"Well, my apartment is here in Santa Monica. Not that far from where you are. I could drive over and we could run together. I need the exercise. Lots of people run down the boulevard on San Vicente. We could do that all the way to Ocean Avenue. Then take a walk on the beach."

He stared at her.

"I run too…as well as bike. I just don't compete…yet."

"Okay," he said slowly.

"I'll be at your place in fifteen minutes."

Butch had little difficulty negotiating the way back to his Gladstone apartment. Inside, he found the bed professionally made. He had only casually thrown up the covers that morning. Magazines carefully arranged on the coffee table. The kitchen cleaned and the glass he had used was washed and put away and the marks of a vacuum evident on the carpet. He had not been aware that daily maid service came with the apartment. This sort of thing could really spoil a person.

He changed into his running clothes and shoes, put his wallet and a key in a pocket, and went downstairs and outside to wait for Cathy. He was pleased that she wanted to run with him and excited she was coming to join him. He was surprised with his reaction and a bit unnerved by it.

He checked the bulky watch he wore only when working out: Time- 5:19PM, Temp- 83°F, Elev-83', Hum- 37%. He stretched for several minutes while he waited for Cathy and sensed some exotic flower smells wafting to him from somewhere nearby. He was relieved when her Toyota Camray slipped into a parking spot in front of the building next door. Relieved and excited at the same time.

"Hi,"

"Hi, yourself," he said. "Didn't take you long."

"You expected it to take awhile?"

"No comment."

She laughed and headed down the street toward San Vicente. Her short legs made a choppy stride, but she seemed to move easily enough. Butch couldn't help but admire her shapely legs as he took after her and the pleasant curves of her behind. He figured he should run along side and not be so distracted. She stopped at the corner of San Vicente, waited for half a dozen cars, and crossed to the boulevard where she picked up her pace.

"Nice setting," Butch said as he ran beside her.

"I thought you might like this." She did not look at him.

After several blocks, Butch increased his stride slightly and gradually ran faster until he reached his normal speed. Cathy could not keep up and fell behind. Eventually, he realized she was not with him and slowed so she could catch up to him. They continued side by side, without speaking until they were almost to Ocean Avenue. Butch stopped and surveyed the traffic.

"Let's walk over to the park and take a rest."

"I'm for that," she said, breathing heavily.

They worked their way over to the park and Cathy stretched and sat on one of the benches. Butch stood nearby and looked out at the ocean.

"Great view."

"Yeah, it is," she said. "Boy, you are in great shape. You're hardly breathing. I'm gasping for air like...like I'm going to die."

"I work at it."

"You win your age group, I bet."

"Usually," he said, unembarrassed with his own admission of success.

"Take it easy on me going back. I'm going to ache enough tomorrow as it is."

"We'll run-walk. Save your legs."

They were walking, nearly back to his street, when she asked him if he would like to have dinner. He did, but wasn't sure if he should, if he could stand the emotional tension that inevitably would come with it.

"Hadn't thought about it. You have a place in mind?" He was stalling, afraid to make a decision.

"Yes. A little French restaurant over on Montana. Small, quiet, very nice, excellent food, and super wine list."

"Hmmm," he hedged.

"You game? Or are you too tired? From the tough day and time difference and all...the travel, jumping right into things."

She didn't say it as if it were a challenge, but he knew it was. It was her way of provoking his masculinity, of getting him to say yes. It worked.

Chez Louis was comfortable for Butch and he felt a certain easiness here with this young woman he found so desirable. For the first time in a long time, his spirits were lifted and he forgot all about Kyle and things getting bombed. Their meal and wine were perfect as they bantered. They were getting to know each other better in a personal way that filtered out the professional stuff and stuck with life essentials. I like this, you like that, we like the same things, and discovering they like a great deal of the same things. They ordered cognac for dessert.

"This has been very nice," Butch said as they touched glasses. "I'm glad you suggested it."

"Thank you, it is wonderful here. And pleasant to be with you."

Butch stared at her, not knowing what to say next. He felt like a schoolboy.

Cathy's cell phone rang.

"Hello."

The caller was Laurie Dixon.

"Miss Simon?"

"Yes."

"I wish you would have talked to me."

"And this is?"

"Laurie Dixon. Kyle Dixon's wife. You talked to my sister. You should have talked to me. I can tell you some things."

"Such as?"

"You are dealing with a maniac. He is obsessed with this environmental thing; he will make a point in some way, no matter what it takes."

"Hold on, Mrs. Dixon, please talk to Butch Greiner."

She handed the cell phone to Butch.

"This is Butch Greiner, Mrs. Dixon."

"I just said, you are dealing with a maniac. He is obsessed. Beyond normal. You've got to stop him, he will do something extreme. I think he has something planned. I saw him the other day and he gave me some money for the first time in a long time and I got the idea I would never see him again. He gave me that impression."

"Slow down, Mrs. Dixon, let me ask you a couple of questions. First, though, you're right. We should have talked to you and I apologize for that. Your sister told us about the apartment and the office in Riverside, but I wondered if there would be someplace else that he could be...a farm..."

"The ranch," she said flatly.

"The ranch?"

"Yes. He owns an avocado ranch in Fallbrook that used to be his father's. He goes there a lot. It's his escape place."

"Where is it?" Butch asked.

"Oh, I don't know exactly. It's outside of town a ways. I've been there a few times, but I can't tell you how to find it. I don't know the address, if it even has an address. Some rural route probably. I don't even remember the name of the road it's on. It's been awhile."

"You've been a big help, Mrs. Dixon. Sorry we didn't talk earlier. I think that's probably where he is. We'll try to get to him before he does something drastic."

"Keep in mind, Mr. Greiner, he has no conscience. He is capable of doing anything."

"Yes, I was afraid of that."

Butch closed the cell phone and handed it back to Cathy.

"We better get going. Get a good night's rest. We're going to Fallbrook tomorrow. That's a long old drive, I think."

"It is," she sighed. She was disappointed with how the evening was ending, but the circumstances could not be avoided. Perhaps another evening, she consoled herself.

19.

Norm Burch looked at his watch, frustrated with waiting. The Herrons had not arrived yet. He stirred his coffee and poked at the fruit pie in front of him, not sure what fruit it was, not caring. His anxiety and nervousness were making Kevin Forrester uncomfortable. Norm and Kevin were partners in the switch, in the delivery. They had brought the placement van from Kyle's ranch to hand off to the Herrons. The vehicle was stolen, they knew that, and they knew it had to move on with the Herrons before it was identified as a stolen vehicle. And they had some idea of the magnitude of the placement in the van; Kyle had warned them about that aspect. Stolen vehicle, placement that could kill them and everyone in the restaurant, these were certainly issues to put them both on edge.

Connie Herron was driving when they pulled into the parking lot. She was calm, she was positive about what she was doing, and she commanded the Camray with like assurity. She and her husband Leon were known here at Chiriaco Summit as frequent customers, as workers at the Hinds pumping station at Hayfield Lake, which was four miles east.

Leon and Connie came into the restaurant with nods and hellos to several of the waitresses and one or two other customers. They spotted Norm and Kevin, came to their table, and sat down without being asked.

A waitress was right there, attentive, ready to take their order.

"Burger, fries," Connie ordered, "And bring me a diet soda…whatever."

"Me too with the burger, medium rare," Leon said, "no diet, just water."

"Make mine rare," Connie said.

"We didn't know you were coming for dinner," Norm said sarcastically.

"Shut up and give us the keys," Leon snapped.

"There are no keys, asshole, it's wired. It's unlocked over there, the green van." Norm pointed without being obvious. "Flip the switch and you go. Kyle says get it in position like you guys talked about. Before eleven tonight. It goes at eleven no matter what or where."

None of them said anything and the silence was overpowering.

"It was not nice meeting you," Norm said, finally, "good luck and safe journey; wherever it is you are off to."

He and Kevin got out of the booth they were sharing and headed for the door. Norm stopped abruptly and came back to their table.

"I want to thank you for picking up the check. We appreciate that."

Leon flipped him the bird and looked out the window.

Norm missed the insult because he was already headed back towards the door.

Norm and Kevin went outside into the cool desert evening air. Already a zillion stars flooded the sky even though the sun had barely set, but that panorama was lost on them. They were more interested in being on the move. Kyle had provided them with a late model Chrysler car and in several minutes they were on I-10, eastbound, job completed, money earned.

Norm dropped Kevin off at his sister's house in Bodine, Missouri, and moved on to Clarkston, in upstate New York. Each man went on with his life in a new career, under new circumstances. Neither man would be traced nor come under the scrutiny of law enforcement. The men believed they had done their part for the environmental cause.

Connie watched as Norm and Kevin exited the parking lot.

"Good riddance," she said softly. "Guys like that can screw up an entire project. God forbid they have anything else to do for Kyle."

She finished her burger and fries first and waited impatiently as Leon played with his. He finally pushed his plate aside.

"Finished," he said, knowing how antsy his wife was.

Connie drove the placement van and Leon followed in their Camray. She inserted her ID card at the Hinds gate and headed for their house. Leon carded himself through and followed her.

Connie pulled two beers from their refrigerator, popped them open, and handed one to Leon.

"Ten-thirty," she said simply.

"Ten-thirty," he affirmed.

They watched television without talking to each other until ten-twenty five when Connie punched the remote to kick off the TV. They went outside and looked around. No one had seen them come back into the secure compound when they returned from Chiriaco Summit and no one was paying attention now.

Again, she drove and got the placement van right up to the pumping station and parked as close as she could. He drove up behind her as she crawled out of the right side of the van. She got into the truck and they drove off the compound onto I-10 and sped westbound. Eventually they headed north on Route 395 and worked their way into Oregon until they reached her sister's ranch near Pendleton. After several weeks, they moved on to Yakima, Washington, where Leon's father had a farm.

Meanwhile, Kyle and Carrie had reached the Perris Dam with a placement truck. Traffic on the Ramona Expressway was light and no one paid any attention to them. It was a simple matter of parking and leaving. Kyle got the truck almost against the fence nearest to the pumping station. He got out of the truck and moved casually over to the Honda Carrie was driving.

"That will take care of that," he said smugly. "This place will be out of commission for a long time."

They went back to the ranch, switched cars to the one they already had packed, and headed for Riverside where they picked up the catering truck Kyle had put in storage. He drove the truck and Carrie followed, excited that she would, at last, be meeting Kyle's family. She had no idea there was a wife and three children.

It was an easy matter for Mark, Ellis, and Ted to place the plastic explosives at the bases of the electrical transmission towers they had been assigned. They met at a parking lot in Murietta Hot Springs to get rid of the stolen cars, and into Mark's Tahoe that had been dropped there. They headed north on I-15, bound for Santa Monica and the next round of destruction. They were satisfied that they were righteous and it was not likely they would ever be caught. Kyle had convinced them of this.

The five couples of arsonists had yet to make their moves, but they were all poised and ready.

20.

Shortly after ten o'clock, the first fire erupted at a large condominium construction project in Beaumont and spread quickly through the adjoined, partially completed structures. It was reported to the 911 operator at ten after ten and Riverside County fire trucks were dispatched. Within the next fifteen minutes 911 received three more calls to report huge fires raging in Cherry Valley, Woodcrest, and Moreno Valley. The Hemet Fire Department received a call at ten fifteen reporting fire at an unfinished north side condo development.

Five substantial fires were now simultaneous in progress that would essentially destroy three condo projects and partially ruin two upscale housing developments. The five teams of soldiers in Dixon's army had done their work using the fire starter kits that Kyle had devised and provided to them.

Only two of the five fires were knocked down and somewhat contained by eleven o'clock when the Hinds Pumping Station bomb detonated. The blast could be felt at Chiriaco Summit and heard for many more miles around. The fertilizer portion exploded first with the Semtex letting go less than two seconds later. The one-two punch blew away the entire west half of the pumping station to ground level and took the top off the remainder. The three huge pipes which were conduits for carrying the water over the elevation rise were torn open and water immediately surged into the open. Water from the pipes and from the destroyed pumping station spilled across the desert onto the dry Hayfield Lake bed and eventually would run away through Red Cloud Wash. Pieces of the placement van would later be found scattered around the desert, some more than a mile from the pumping station.

Within seconds of the Hinds Pumping Station explosion, four high-voltage electrical transmission towers crumpled to the ground as the result of the explosive charges Mark and Ted had put in place. A large area of the eastern Coachella Valley was suddenly without power.

The Perris Dam placement exploded before the towers hit the ground, obliterating the pumping station and letting loose a flood of water that rushed out across the Ramona Expressway and into the residential subdivision on the south side. The blast had almost no effect on the dam itself.

Two more transmission towers fell that were the responsibility of Ellis and thousands more homes and businesses were without power.

The Riverside County 911 switchboard overloaded and failed. It was jammed with thousands of calls about what had happened: fires, explosions, massive power outage. People were screaming for answers. For many, the assumption was that Southern California was under attack, probably by terrorists. They were correct, but these terrorists were not the kind that might be assumed.

Henry Gonzales was babysitting with his wife at his daughter's house in Corona when he was reached on his cell phone. It was the shocking news about the Hinds Pumping Station. While he was getting a sketchy report of the incident the deputy stopped talking to him in mid-sentence.

"What's going on?" Gonzales demanded. He could hear someone yelling in the background.

"It's very bad, sir," the deputy sputtered, "a very bad...godawful situation."

"What? What the hell is it?" He could hear more yelling from other voices.

"Sir, the 911 system is toast...overloaded. Can't take any more calls. A lot more has happened..."

"What?"

"We just got word that the pumping station at Perris Dam has been destroyed...water is running everywhere. We've got crews headed there, sir, but there's worse reports...power is out over a wide area, we're not sure exactly how much yet, but it's big. Electric towers were knocked down...it's like an attack."

"Now we know why and what," Gonzales said.

"What's that?" the deputy asked.

"Never mind. Who else have you contacted?"

"You were first, sir."

"Call the Sheriff, let him know what's going on and he can deal with the County Supervisors. I'll get with the FBI."

He punched off his phone and pulled a small notebook from his pocket to get Jim Fuller's number. Fuller's voice mail answered and Gonzales left a brief message. Then he called Andy Tobin's cell phone. Tobin answered.

"Andy, this is Henry Gonzales, I wanted to let you know what has happened..."

"It's on television," Tobin said.

"What are they saying?"

"Big explosion in Perris...at the Dam there, lots of flooding, power outages, electrical towers been blown up..."

"I just got a report about that and the Hinds Pumping Station..."

"Where is that?"

"Way east of here. Blown up, water running all over..."

"Someone trying to cut off the water supply..."

"Right, and the power," Gonzales said. "The cause our thief and his gang had was us...getting at us."

"Jesus," Tobin exhaled.

"There is so damn much going on at once that I have no clue where to start first."

"We try to get Kyle Dixon," Tobin said, "that's what we do." "You better get with the water boys and find out what they need. Stay in touch."

Tobin hung up and Gonzales stared at his wife, who had put down her book and was staring back at him. He grabbed the remote and clicked on the television. A talking head was describing the situation, explaining that camera crews were right now going to the disaster sites, that reports would be coming soon, that an early estimate was that possibly half a million Southern California Edison customers were without power, and that flooding was engulfing possibly hundreds of homes in Perris. At this point, there was not much information which was definitive, but a great deal of speculation to incite fear and panic.

"What a mess," he sighed.

His wife asked what had happened and he shared with her what information he had been given by the deputy.

"I've got to go. When Lisa gets home tell her what you can and plan to spend the night. I don't know when I'll see you again."

She nodded stoically, gave him a strong embrace, and he was on his way. On the drive from Corona to Perris he kept wondering where Kyle Dixon might be and how the devil would they catch him.

Andy Tobin got busy with his phone contacting each of the field agents from the Riverside office, making assignments to the Hinds Pumping Station and the Perris Dam locations, and asking the others to come in to headquarters. At this point he had no idea of the locations of downed electrical towers. He also had no idea where Jim was, but assumed he was with his girl friend and would show up in the morning. He could not wait for the boss and instinctively took the actions he did and would do all night long. He notified Toby

Grant, Special Agent for Terrorism, in the Los Angeles FBI office what had occurred and learned Toby had no idea what had gone down.

"I'll get to your office as quickly as I can," Grant said, "and mobilize some other agents. You guys will need all the help you can muster."

Next, Tobin phoned Jack Cameron, Special Agent in Charge, of the San Diego FBI office to inform him. Cameron already had a heads-up about the bombings.

"One of my agents who lives in Temecula called me a few minutes ago," Cameron explained. "Told me power was out all over that area. Said he'd gotten a call from a buddy who told him there had been some explosions in Perris and some other places around there. So, you think these were bombings?"

"Yes," Tobin said emphatically.

"Then you need help," Cameron said, "I'll get some agents up there right away."

Thanks, Jack."

Tobin phoned Hicks Sylvester, the agent in the Riverside ATF office, and Chad Coley, Sylvester's counterpart in LA. Both men said they would join him as quickly as possible

He slumped in his chair and waited for agents to arrive, scribbling some notes on a yellow legal pad to help him figure out how this should be tackled, trying to determine where he would get enough lab people to get the forensics done before the crime scenes got spoiled, and speculating who would be jockeying for lead dog on the investigation and who would get blamed for the bombings even to have occurred. He also wondered where Kyle Dixon was and how long it would take to run him down. He was already perspiration-soaked and the night was just beginning. It was going to be awful, he thought.

21.

LA Times reporter Barry Walker's phone rang shortly after eleven. Barry covered the Inland Empire that included the impacted area southeast of Riverside. A friend in Perris alerted him to the explosion at the dam. He said his neighbors were near panic. What did Barry know? Barry had no inkling of what had just occurred. He had just brushed his teeth, ready to end his day when the interruption came. He thanked his friend, punched the speed dial number on his cell phone for his Riverside Sheriff's office contact and got no answer. He phoned Jim Fuller. No answer. Likewise Zack Conlon, Riverside Police Department. Next number, as he fingered through his contact list, was Henry Gonzales. Henry answered and he was not cordial.

"Who is this?"

"Barry Walker...LA Times. What's going on?

Gonzales did not answer for a few seconds, trying to decide what to say.

"Do you know where the Perris Dam is?"

"Ah, no," was the honest reply.

"Look it up. Ramona Expressway. Meet me out there and I'll fill you in. This is serious stuff, I would appreciate it if you would get to me before you report anything. Okay?"

"Why?"

"Right now there are too many unknowns...just work with me on this and I'll get you what you need down the line."

"TV guys are going to be all over this and they won't wait for anything. You know that."

"I'll give you the straight story...not them."

"Shit," Barry said and slammed his phone down.

Driving from Riverside, it took Barry more than an hour to get to the Perris Dam site and find Henry Gonzales. There was no way he could get anything written that would be in the next morning's edition of the Times. He consoled himself with the reality that even under the best of circumstances time-wise, he would not have made the press deadline. His in-depth story the following day would be extensive, filling most of Section A, and he would present information no one else had obtained. This night he was sullen and dejected as the television crews were getting the story, getting the attention, and dominating media news.

Television news directors had the advantage. They could dispatch crews and equipment and make the breaking story instant and real even if it were in the middle of the night. Within minutes of television crews being on the scene in Perris and several of the electrical tower collapses, newsrooms around the country were aware that something awful had happened in southern California and were ready to pounce on the story. Soon every major TV station in California was focused on Perris and many across the country were eyewitnesses to the unfolding disaster that was progressing minute by minute. Scenes of darkened intersections with backed up traffic, fire crews still at work, the crumpled steel of transmission towers, and the blown apart pumping station at Perris Dam filled television screens across the country. And the news of Hinds Pumping Station had yet to be revealed to the public, although law enforcement and other authorities were already at that scene and were dealing with the water release problem.

Riverside County authorities and responsible law enforcement were jumbled in their uncoordinated attempt to deal with the bombings, and Federal law enforcement was similarly spastic in its response. This was a situation that Kyle had predicted and counted on so that he and the others could move away with little chance of being detected.

The dark cloak of night was their benefactor, their aide in easily moving from Riverside County to Santa Monica. After getting the catering truck inside the gallery, Kyle drove to his mother's house and parked in front. It was shortly after two o'clock in the morning. Of course the house was dark, of course the security was on, and, of course Raymond would probably have to be dealt with if they were to succeed over the next two days. Kyle saw Mark's Tahoe parked up the street and was satisfied everything was proceeding according to his plan. Mark could be counted on and could be trusted to get a job done right.

Mark, Ted, and Ellis got out of the Tahoe when they saw Kyle pull up and the five of them approached Doris' house. Kyle unlocked the front door, quickly went to the security system control panel, and entered his code. The electronic buzz stopped and the blinking panel lights went dark save one green safe light. Kyle turned on the foyer lights and led the way to the stairs with the others following. Mark had closed the front door and brought up the rear of the ascending column of eco-terrorists.

Kyle showed the three men the guest room with one double bed and the bathroom they would use.

"You guys will have to figure out the sleeping arrangement," he whispered "We won't be here that long so it shouldn't make any difference. Somebody's got to sleep on the floor. Draw straws."

He and Carrie went to his room. She stripped naked in a wink, but Kyle flopped onto the bed still dressed, emotionally stressed, and totally exhausted from the past few hours. Her nakedness could not arouse him and he was unconscious in seconds.

The house was quiet save for the woosh of conditioned air that was being pushed about. It was the subtle sound of a slight wind, a background sound almost imperceptible. Raymond Estancia could hear the sound, lying there quite awake in his apartment above the garage. He had heard them enter and proceed up to the second floor. He knew it was Kyle and he wondered who the others were and why they might be here. And why in the middle of the night? He figured the reason was no good, something illegal, something that would bring turmoil to this house. He wondered if Doris heard. If she heard, knowing it was Kyle, would she care? It was difficult for him to go to sleep and he resented Kyle for the interruption and the lack of sleep.

The damnable irony of Kyle's coming to Santa Monica less than three miles away from the Gladstone apartment would have frustrated Butch had he only been aware. As far as he knew, Kyle was out there someplace, with that someplace covering a large territory. He was in the hands of deep sleep when the apartment phone tore into his consciousness. The sound was penetrating as it emanated from phones in the kitchen, living room, TV area, bathroom, and next to the bed. One had only to walk a few steps in this place to answer a phone. The quintet of sound was always insistent; when asleep, at night, the sound was shocking.

He jolted upright, knowing instinctively that something was wrong.

"What?" he asked. He sounded cogent even if he were still at the edges of sleep.

He checked the clock. Five fifteen in the morning, daylight just sneaking up on the city.

"It's happened," Cathy said. "The bombs have gone off. It's all over the TV…"

"Where did it happen?"

"Some pumping station way out eastern Riverside County that serves the aqueduct from the Colorado River to Lake Matthews and…"

"A what?"

"Wait a minute, there's more. Another pumping station in Perris by a dam…"

"To cut off the water supply…"

"There's still more. Six power line towers were knocked down with explosive charges…"

"To cut off the electrical supply. The eco-terrorist has made his mark…"

"There's more…"

"What else?"

"Last night there were five mysterious fires started at residential construction sites around the same area in Riverside County that were called in even before the explosions. No one seems to know if they are related…"

"Guess what?" Butch said. "They're related."

"I would assume so."

"I'll pick you up in a few minutes."

"Where are we…"

"Out to his ranch."

Long before Butch and Cathy could reach Fallbrook, Kyle, dressed and ready for action, had roused Carrie and the three other men. He went on down to the kitchen where Supe was intently watching the small television. Her concentration was broken only for a moment to greet Kyle pleasantly and then turn back to the small screen. She could barely comprehend what she was seeing and hearing. Not because she could not understand English, but the complexity, severity, and extent of the problems being reported were beyond her experience and education. She shrugged and turned back to Kyle who was also caught up in the news broadcast.

The results are in, he thought to himself.

"Maybe now people will begin to appreciate some things," he said to her. "like electricity and water."

"Si, we need them. Bad without them. Very bad. A long time ago I live in village in Mexico with no running water and no electricity. Is difficult to live that way."

"And you really appreciate them."

"Si, I do. That was a long time ago…when I was a little girl. It was very hard on my mother, but she still did a good job taking care of us kids."

"People need to understand what they have and how things are getting ruined."

"God, I'm hungry," Carrie said, coming into the kitchen. "What's for breakfast?"

Mark, Ted, and Ellis were right behind her.

"It won't take long," Supe said, "Eggs, bacon, toast…I no expect you, but no is problem."

"God damn," Ellis said with a tense, raised voice. He pointed at the TV. "It's Kyle. How the hell…?"

Kyle was almost stupefied. He could not believe he was seeing a photo of himself. How could this be? Everything was going so well. How could they be on to him so fast? He leaned against the counter staring at the news broadcast, listening to the reporter talking about him. He tried to gather his senses while Carrie and the others jabbered about what this meant. Supe went about her cooking. She had stopped listening to what she could not comprehend. There was work to do. She had no idea what it meant to have Kyle's face on television.

But Raymond knew. He was watching the news and decided he should wake Mrs. Krause and tell her what was happening. He rapped on her bedroom door and she called to him.

"I'm awake, Raymond, I was reading. What is it?"

He opened the door.

"Kyle and some others are in the house ma'am. They arrived during the night. They're in the kitchen right now..."

"I think that's all right, Raymond. My son knows he always has refuge here...even with friends."

"A woman, also."

"Ah, I see. And you disapprove?"

"No, ma'am, I..."

"What is it then?"

"I've been watching the news and...I think there's a problem..."

"Like what?"

"Kyle's photo is being shown on the news as an...well, they're referring to him as an environmental extremist who possibly committed some bombings. They're calling them acts of terrorism. Eco-terrorism."

"Nonsense," Doris issued loudly and went to the top of the stairs and called down. "Kyle, Kyle, darling, come on up. Let's talk."

She turned, went back in her bedroom, and clicked on the TV.

As Kyle came up the stairs, Doris called to Raymond.

"Thank you, Raymond, I'll check with you before I go to the gallery."

Raymond did not reply; he knew a response wasn't necessary as he well knew he had been dismissed.

Kyle embraced his mother and kissed her cheek even before he spoke to her.

"I've started Fire and Brimstone," he said quietly.

"I guess you have. Let's hope the message gets through to the people...and the powers that be."

"We can't stay," he said quickly. "It won't be long and they'll be here looking for me."

"I'll take care of Raymond and Supe. Where will you go, dear?"

"To the gallery first. I've got the roach coach there that I told you about. We put it there last night."

"You and a young woman?"

"Yes, her name is Carrie. She wants to meet you."

"No, dear, I'm not going to meet her or any of the others right now. Later, at the gallery. You know, eventually the gallery will be unsafe for you. That's what I meant when I asked where you will go."

"I don't know yet. I wasn't planning on having them be on to us like this."

"On to you, dear, they're on to you. Perhaps I have a solution. We'll talk about it later, at the gallery."

22.

"It's all like one big city, but the places you want to go to are far apart and the driving is atrocious," Butch said. "I don't know how anyone stands it." He had the Lexus cruising at seventy-five.

"Get used to it, I guess," Cathy answered. "I was born here, so it's all I've ever known. I do pity people with the brutal commutes, though. I feel lucky to live so close to Gladstone."

"You're lucky you can afford it. They must pay you a lot of money."

"Not really. I share a place with an old friend. She works in Santa Monica, too. For a film producer over on Olympic Boulevard. It's a good arrangement for both of us."

The music for the commercial they were not paying any attention to ended and the excited morning team for the talk-radio station came on air with more information about the bombings.

The female news person was almost yelling when she said, "Every hour more details are coming out about those bombings that have shocked and freighted people living in the Inland Empire...Riverside, Riverside County."

"That's right, Amy," the male news person yelled back at her as if she were a block away, "we know now that six electrical towers were bombed that have knocked out power to nearly five hundred thousand Southern California Edison customers. The morning commute in parts of Riverside County are awful because of traffic signals not working, gas stations not being able to pump gas, garage door openers that don't work and that sort of thing...lack of power effects practically everything we do."

"That's right, Bob, and think about air conditioning or rather...no air conditioning. The weather service is calling for temperatures in the mid nineties for this afternoon in Riverside County. This means problems ahead for super markets…in fact all stores are in trouble without electricity."

"What about Kyle, you idiots?" Butch snapped at the voices as if they could respond. "Tell us what you know about who did this."

Cathy laughed. "They don't hear you."

"I know. It's too bad. I wish they could."

"I bet you do."

The two morning radio blabbers went on about traffic problems, water on roadways, authorities scrambling to regain order amidst the chaos, while still trying to be cheerful. What was known for sure was that no one knew for sure what was going on across Riverside County. The effects of the outage on the electrical power grid for California were considered negligible at this point. Because adjustments were made quickly through a series of automatic computer controlled corrections, the sudden jolt from thousands not using power was readily accommodated. There were a few anxious seconds, but the system worked as it should. From a power generation standpoint, the outage was actually helpful in such hot weather. A spokeswoman for the Riverside County Office of Disaster Management said that she had been told that power would be restored in a day or two for most customers and no more than four days for the remaining customers. At this point, she announced, there was no loss of water supply, and none was anticipated. The Southern California Water District officials had assured her that everything was under control for maintaining water to residences and businesses in Southern California. She also tried to allay any fears that the water supply had been poisoned, this in reaction to such rumors that were running across the county from cell phone to cell phone.

"Didn't Kyle's wife tell us that it was an avocado ranch?"

"Yes, I think so. Why?"

"Well, I think there's probably a growers syndicate or co-op in Fallbrook. The area is big for avocados. We check with them, see what they have on Kyle. At least it's a place to start."

They arrived in Fallbrook well after eight o'clock. No businesses were open. Only the coffee shops and breakfast places. Butch and Cathy stopped at Neal's Cafe.

A strange looking girl showed them to a booth. She appeared to be suffering from some kind of hangover, but was able to take their coffee order. The regulars stared at these strangers, sure they must be foreigners from LA or San Diego. Butch smiled and said good morning to one unusually fat woman who refused to take her eyes from him. She smiled and nodded.

"Is there a growers co-op office in town?" Butch asked the scraggly one when she returned with their coffee.

"Yes sir, there is. Right out Main Street on your left. The plant is just south of here near the edge of town.

"Thanks," Butch said.

They ordered breakfast and the girl went away. Butch noticed for the first time that the paper place mat said "Avocado Capital of the World."

"Really something isn't it?" the waitress said, as she plopped down their breakfast orders. "Power's out in Temecula where my sister lives. She says it's a mess up there. The guy who did it is on TV. His picture, anyway. He wrote a letter telling why he done what he done. They've been reading it...the news guy has."

"What's he say?" Butch asked, knowing full well what Kyle said.

"He says we've got to appreciate what we got more. Take better care of the environment. My minister says that, too."

"Probably both good ideas."

"I think so," she said as she walked away, "but I don't think we need to blow stuff up and cut off folk's electricity to do it."

After breakfast, they lingered some over more coffee and watched the wall-mounted television with fascination along with the rest of the customers. Riverside County was a full-blown disaster area and Governor Calish had mobilized the National Guard to the tune of five hundred men and women who would assist in maintaining order and help local authorities. Butch saw Jim Fuller behind Calish at one point, but he never spoke, nor were any questions thrown at him. This was Calish's photo-op.

"It's after nine. Let's get out to the co-op offices and find out where Kyle's ranch is."

"What are we going to do, just run out there and walk in on him?" Cathy asked.

"No, we're not going to rush in like idiots. We'll approach carefully. If they're still there we wait for the FBI. If they're not, we can look around. There might be something to help us. In any case, when we get it located, we call Fuller."

The helpful young woman at the co-op office knew Kyle, knew where the ranch was located, and drew a simple map for them to easily reach it. Twenty minutes later, they slowly drove by the entrance to the property. The ranch house was a hundred yards from the road. Butch could see the barn in the distance beyond.

"I didn't see any vehicles, did you?"

"No," Cathy whispered. "Turn around and drive by again."

Butch continued a quarter mile or so and was able to make a U-turn. No one from the ranch house would have been able to see their car through the trees and brush. He drove by the entrance again, this time even slower. There were no vehicles in sight.

"Let's leave the car here."

Butch eased the Lexus off the road and cut the ignition. He called Fuller, could not get through, and left a detailed message. Before he got out of the car he pulled out the Glock and racked in a shell.

"Let's cut through here and work our way through the cover of those trees."

After several minutes of staying low behind bushes and dodging among trees they were close to the ranch house.

"Looks deserted," Cathy said quietly.

"Let's have a look around."

"No warrant."

"Don't need one, we are not the law. We are just trespassing snoopers. We don't need a warrant. Get your gun ready. Just in case someone is here."

Cathy did and looked to him for the next move.

"The house first. Be alert and stay behind me."

She gave a slight nod and they went up to the porch. Butch noticed a lone Anchor Steam beer bottle by one of the chairs. The door was locked. One solid kick broke it open. Butch stepped inside with gun raised and ready. A quick tour downstairs and up assured him that, in fact, Kyle and the others had bailed.

"Now, let's take a few minutes and see if we can find anything."

"What are we looking for?" Cathy holstered her pistol and poked at the mess on the kitchen table.

"I'm not sure. Any notes or phone numbers or scribbling…I don't know. Something that might indicate more targets."

"He's not done?"

"No, Cathy, Kyle and his gang are not done…I don't believe."

"Why? What makes you think that?"

"Can't tell you. A sense about this that I have. Makes me think they're not done. More punishment needs to be inflicted. The question is where and what?"

They continued to look around the kitchen and living room of the ranch. Nothing. There was a small room off the living room that had once been a den and appeared to have been converted into an office. In the center of the desk, Cathy found a single note with the word *Gallery* printed and underlined.

"This is the only thing I've seen that might mean something."

Butch didn't pick it up, but stared at it for several seconds. "Yeah, makes sense. Mother covers for him, that's where he moves his operation. That's where we need to be."

Butch strode quickly out of the house and went to the barn. The small grade door was locked. He walked across the way to a stack of wood, grabbed a log, and went back to the barn. He drove the log into the handle and the door popped open. He used the same log to break into the compartments Kyle used to build the bombs. All of the evidence was there. He punched Fuller's number into his phone again and waited. No answer, leave a message.

"Goddamnit. Did you get Tobin's number?"

Cathy flipped through her notepad and found Tobin's cell phone number. Butch punched it in. Tobin answered on the first ring.

"Tobin, Butch Greiner. Where the hell is Fuller?"

"Very busy. He goes on TV in twenty minutes. Busy in makeup."

"I'm at Kyle Dixon's ranch near Fallbrook. You guys need to give this place a thorough going over with your lab guys. This is where he built the bombs."

"Fallbrook is not in our jurisdiction, Butch, that's the San Diego guy's territory. Better call Jack Cameron. It's his to work. We've got a lot on our plate, Butch, stay in touch. We're on this and we'll get this guy."

"Bullshit," Butch screamed at him. "You don't have any idea where he is or what he is going to do. You guys couldn't find both cheeks if you had an entire room of mirrors."

"What?"

"Yeah, what's Cameron's number."

In less than two minutes, Butch was online with Jack Cameron, Special Agent in Charge of the San Diego office of the FBI. He explained who he was and what was happening.

"No offense, Mr. Cameron, but your people need to turn this place. There has to be a lot here. It looks like they left it intending to return."

"Thanks, Greiner, we'll get right on it. Appreciate what you've done…what you may do. Stay connected to us and don't get too pissed off with the Bureau. We all want to get the bad guys. I know how helpful you can be. Keep at it."

"Thanks for the encouragement, Jack. We're going to be tenacious about this, don't worry."

Butch motioned to Cathy and they walked back to the car and started the drive back to Santa Monica.

"I lost my temper and didn't ask Tobin if they had done all the right things."

"Like…what?"

She was curious about Butch's admission.

"Oh, like get an All Points on Kyle, notify their LA office where Kyle might be, contact the Santa Monica police…there's a long list. With Fuller now a TV star, I'm not sure what will be done right. As it is, there are going to be a whole lot of law enforcement people falling all over one another trying to be the heroes in this case. Television makes careers. Being in the news helps careers. Those guys just can't resist."

23.

The LA Times headline screamed: *Terrorist Strikes.* Barry Walker's in-depth article told a great deal about eco-terrorist, Kyle Dixon, and in its conclusion made the mistake of chiding Kyle in the subtlest of ways by implying that his plan failed in its effect. Those responsible for the transfer of water from the Colorado River to Southern California had already implemented their emergency planning and assured authorities there would be no disruption in the water supply in spite of the damage to the two pumping stations. Water run off and flooding had been contained and minimized. Southern California Edison was equally as optimistic about restoration of power.

In truth, it would be weeks before the water would again surge from the river and it would take days longer than anticipated to bring electricity to the outage area. The suffering, complaining, and civil unrest as a result were more tumultuous that anyone had expected. People did not just accept the situation. Folks bitched at their local politicos, there were public protests to confront police and National Guard, and many of those who were affluent and well-connected politically put tremendous pressure on the decision makers. Suffering meant little or no water for those effected, it meant no air conditioning in blistering temperatures, and surely stopped most of commerce in those areas. Only the drug dealers continued unabated, untouched by the inconveniences others faced, content that their businesses had no down cycles. Those without power felt captive in their own homes, waiting for something to be done to solve the problem. Schools were closed for the summer and children ran about with little restraint as their parents contemplated closed workplaces and limited resources for such an emergency; such resources as water, food, and other supplies to carry a family through crisis time. Few families had prepared for such an emergency.

In the meantime, Kyle's second letter was received by media outlets across Southern California. The LA Times published it on the front page and the television and radio stations broadcast its content repeatedly.

Dear Fellow Citizens:

The problems of the environment will not go away. I have given you a preview of what is to come if an effort is not made to conserve energy and minimize the use of water. Our precious land has been overrun and misused by greedy and unscrupulous developers without regard for green space and minimalist planning that is in our best long-term interests. Those charlatans are aided and abetted by shameless politicians and bureaucrats. We must call a halt to such waste and misuse of resources and land, we must take control of our society's great natural realm, and we must say no to such so-called progress in the name of prosperity. Fire and Brimstone is not complete. More of you need to feel its effects so that you listen to my warning.

It was signed The Protector.

"Ellis, we need to steal at least three cars. We need those for tonight's operation. Carrie and Ted will work with you. Bring them here, we'll get them loaded and then we'll be ready. The truck is all set. I took care of that while it was stored out in Riverside. We need to work fast; I don't know how long we have before the authorities will get here. Probably not long."

Kyle and the others were standing in the rear of his mother's gallery. It was not yet ten o'clock in the morning. The air was already stifling in the closed building, signaling the coming torrid day.

"You'd better get..."

Doris was in the back door and speaking before Kyle could finish.

"I have the answer," she said sternly. "Kyle, come in my office. Good morning, gentlemen...and lady," she threw back as she moved on.

She walked away to her office in the other half of the old building. She dropped her purse on the desk and pushed at some papers she had left from the previous day. There was no meaning to her gesture, merely a nervous reaction to the stress she felt. She did not sit down. Kyle followed her dutifully and stood waiting for her pronouncement.

Sol Jacobs' estate. He's in Europe and I have a key. He won't mind, I'm sure. It's for a worthy cause. Keep a low profile...no rowdy stuff. This is a very quiet Santa Monica neighborhood."

"What do we say if someone sticks their nose in?" Kyle asked.

"Just tell them you're working on some decorating while Mr. Jacobs is away on vacation. Tell anyone you are Mr. Jacobs' stepson and the others are employees of your company. I doubt if anyone will say anything, but stay calm and casual. Everything will be all right. The staff has been given the time off until Sol gets back, so they won't interfere."

Carrie and the others had followed Kyle to his mother's office.

"Thanks, mom," Kyle said. "I'd like you to meet my group. This is Carrie...you know Mark...Ellis and Ted."

"Well...Carrie," Doris said slowly. "Do you have any idea what you have gotten yourself into?"

"Yes, Mrs. Dixon, I do."

"It's Krause, now, but that's okay, an honest mistake."

They all gathered around a Santa Monica map that Doris pulled out so they could determine where Sol Jacobs' house was and where they would meet up later.

"Nice to meet you Mrs...."

"Krause…"

"Mrs. Krause. I think your son is a genius and I know…"

"You better get going, there isn't much time."

"Sure," Carrie said.

Ted, Ellis, and Carrie left to steal cars.

"Get going before customers start to show up," Doris said. "Go on over to Sol's. Stay in touch, dear, let me know how things are going."

"I will, mother, and thanks."

Kyle and Mark drove to Sol Jacobs' house which turned out to be quite an estate. Landscaping precluded it being seen from the street. There was a three-car garage with only one car in the slot closest to the house. It was a late model Rolls Royce. Plenty of room to hide cars and provide protection from the prying eyes of the neighbors.

For Ted and Ellis, stealing cars in Santa Monica was not nearly as easy as it had been in Riverside County. But not impossible. Just before noon they lifted the second car, a Buick Lucerne, and had it stashed in Sol's garage. They went to work on number three.

Kyle and Mark had thoroughly gone through the Jacob's estate and believed they could work here satisfactorily for several days if necessary. The plan was to leave in two days. After they felt comfortable with the location of the house, they went back to the Gallery to get the catering truck. There was no reason it could not be parked within the confines of the secluded estate. Kyle felt this would remove the gallery from being a target location even if authorities came snooping around.

The gallery was where Butch and Cathy were headed. The drive to get there in Santa Monica was confounding for Butch in its slow, nonsensical crawl along high-speed freeways designed for volumes of traffic to move quickly.

An agonizing walking pace became a trotting pace and when he could accelerate to forty, he thought he was in heaven. Such was the daily driving menu on Southern California freeways. Slow was fast and fast was otherwise. Fast, in another situation, would be a quantum leap in any progression to get to the destination.

As they headed north on I-15, National Guard troops were present at each intersection through Riverside County, ready to direct off-ramp traffic, filling the roll of traffic lights that did not function. Military vehicles seemed to be everywhere. On the Freeway, running on the surface streets, cutting across the overpasses, the olive-drab trucks and personnel carriers crawled with men ready to keep the situation from getting out of hand.

"People do this every day," Butch said. He slumped in his seat as the line of cars ahead of him stopped. "Drive to survive, that's the way it is in Southern California. Jesus, the military is all over the place."

Cathy's cell phone rang.

"Hello."

"Fuller here. That Greiner guy around?"

She handed Butch the phone without answering.

"Greiner."

"Where are you?"

"Beats the hell out of me, but we're probably half way back to Santa Monica. Don't see any more military guys."

"Why didn't you call me?"

"Why didn't you answer when I called?"

The air was silent. Fuller wasn't sure which lie he wanted to tell. He would avoid the issue.

"Everyone is looking for this guy Dixon..."

"Yeah...no kidding?"

"Where is he?"

"In Santa Monica. He's going to blow up more stuff. I don't know what, but he is not through and he is not going to wait. Tonight, more gets hit. There's probably nothing you can do about it any more that the others he did."

"You've been on his ass," Fuller said with intuitive confidence, "how close behind are you?"

"I don't know."

"Aw, bullshit, you've been operating your own investigation from the start. You just give us tidbits to make it official. You want to nail this guy yourself. Don't kid me. We have the responsibility. Now, where is he?"

In Santa Monica, like I said. His mother's house, his mother's art gallery, his wife's place…it's a guess. Who knows? Maybe he has another location to hideout until he hits tonight, I don't know, but he will hit tonight to carry out his plan."

"What's your next move?"

"I'm going to check out the art gallery. What are you guys doing?"

"Sitting here sucking our thumbs, wondering what will happen. We're working on this with a full effort, smartass, don't worry about us."

The air went dead as Fuller punched off his phone.

"So much from the FBI," Butch laughed.

"How do we handle Kyle's mother?" Cathy asked.

"I'm not sure. We play it by ear. She was hostile before; my guess is she will be more than hostile this time. She's protecting her son. She might send us on a wild goose chase or stonewall us, I'm not sure. We'll see."

The rest of the drive into the LA basin was uneventful although not as fast as Butch would have preferred. Fuller called again to report the ranch was yielding terrific evidence, but that there had been no word from the LA boys. Butch was not surprised. It had not been their case, they had not yet seemed to grasp the enormity of what had occurred and the fact it would soon be in their lap.

Butch parked near the front door of the gallery.

"This could be unpleasant. This woman is very protective of her son."

Cathy nodded understanding and they got out of the car and approached the building. He stopped as they got to the front door.

"Be ready."

"I am," Cathy whispered.

"Your gun. Safety off, ready to return fire."

"You think Kyle's mom would shoot us?"

He scowled at her.

"Be ready."

She flicked the safety. A round was already chambered.

Once inside, they could hear talking from beyond the front partitions. No other customers were there. They recognized Doris' voice. She was talking to a young woman. They took several steps forward when Doris came out from behind one of the partitions that had artwork displayed on it.

"What…? You two. What is it you want? I don't know where my son…"

"He's here in Santa Monica, Mrs. Dixon, he's…"

"The name is Krause and he's at his ranch in Fallbrook."

"That's a lie and you know it."

Carrie stepped out from behind the partition behind Doris, hands on hips, and glared at Butch and Cathy. Butch remembered later that she had looked menacing and the thought of a menacing woman seemed incongruous to him.

"Who the hell are you?" Carrie demanded.

"We're representing Gladstone International, Miss, and we want to find Kyle Dixon. We think he is…"

"Oh, sure…"

Carrie moved quickly to her right as she said the words, pulled her pistol in one quick motion and fired two shots in rapid succession at Butch and Cathy. The shots were high and wild and went into the wall above the front door.

The confusion of a close encounter gun fight is at best difficult to remember for the living participants, a true test of their composure and sensibilities during the action. The recreating in Butch's mind, and in a report he later wrote, has Cathy returning fire first, the shots scattering wildly as only they do when a person has never been in such a fight before. Butch fired second, but with the accuracy and profound effect that comes from experience. One of Cathy's bullets hit Doris in the side as she was turning to retreat to her office and another smashed into her left hip as she went down. Neither shot would have hit her if she had not moved, of course, but that's how it went. Butch's tight pattern of fire tore into Carrie before she had moved three steps and she was dead before she hit face first on the finished plank floor. She would no longer have to worry about quitting smoking or going to AA meetings.

Even Butch was stunned by the events that just occurred and he leaned against a table that held a large bronze statue. Who to call first?

"You okay?"

Cathy nodded yes.

"That's why you have to be prepared in these situations."

"Thanks. I thought I was." Cathy broke down in tears, an involuntary sobbing that shook her whole body.

Butch put his arms around her and she balled into his embrace for a moment and then straightened and hugged him tightly.

"Sorry."

"Don't be sorry," he said and rubbed her back and ran his fingers through her hair. He could feel the heat of her pistol against his belly. "You'll be all right. Take a deep breath and let it out slowly."

She pushed her cheek against his and he could feel the tears, the wetness, their moist warmth as if he were also crying.

"I'm okay," she said as she pulled away from him and shook her head and sniffed. She slowly holstered her pistol.

"I'll check on Doris, you call 911. Get an ambulance here right away. She may make it."

"The other one dead?"

"I'd bet on it," Butch said as he moved to Doris.

The woman was in great pain, but her wounds were not life-threatening as long as she got medical care quickly.

"You bastard," she slurred as she rose on one elbow to focus on Butch. "You are interfering with my son's work. You are…"

"Shut up until the ambulance gets here," Butch growled at her. "Keep talking and I'll shoot you again just to keep you from aggravating me."

Doris slumped to the floor and was silent.

"Where is Kyle?" Butch spoke sharply and the effect was the same as poking Doris with a stick. She recoiled visibly.

"He's on a mission and you won't stop him." Her head hit the floor as she lost consciousness.

24.

Governor Callish was imposing in person and dominated the TV screen with the presence of any high-profile Hollywood star. He was describing the status of conditions in Riverside County speaking from the powerless Promenade Mall in Temecula. There were complaining signs of protest in the background. Loud shouting, yelling, and catcalling could be heard as the Governor tried to make his remarks. The din of unrest and dissatisfaction rose when Callish introduced a spokeswoman from Southern California Edison. She never finished what she wanted to say. No one wanted her excuses. Someone screamed and the crowd of hundreds began edging toward her and the Governor. They were standing on a small platform that had become an island in this sea of angry folks on the verge of becoming a mob. State Police and Riverside Sheriff's deputies moved in to keep order and the pushing and shoving escalated. A riot was breaking out and the Governor and Edison woman were hustled back from the crowd to a waiting SUV that got them out of danger. Authorities quickly subdued the crowd, but there were injuries to both law enforcement personnel and citizens. It was a morass of conflicting bodies that sustained bruises, cuts, skinned knees and elbows, twisted ankles, and black eyes. There were fourteen of those citizens hauled away in Sheriff's vans, but ultimately, no one was charged. Public aggravation and unrest was building and bursts of festering public outrage could get worse unless electric power was restored.

Butch watched this disgrace on the small television set in Doris' office. The sound had been turned down, but the picture said everything awful about what had occurred. It was an interesting phenomenon to him that the public could withstand the inconvenience of power loss or water rationing caused by weather or natural circumstance, but could little tolerate such inconvenience when caused by manmade exploits. The vagaries of public opinion and mass hysteria, he assumed were at work here. He had checked the rest of the building to make sure no one else was there when he heard the EMS siren.

The medical team glanced at Carrie's sprawled body and moved to Doris, who was cursing vehemently between moans of pain and bobbing her head up and down as a reaction to the trauma. They didn't seem to hurry, but every one of their moves was calculated and precise, deliberate and choreographed as a ballet. They moved her to the stretcher and had her in the ambulance in only a few moments, without wasted motion.

As Doris was being wheeled to the door, two Santa Monica uniformed police officers entered. One of the officers, a short redheaded young woman, spoke to her.

"Can you give me your name, ma'am?"

"Krause," Doris moaned.

"Is there anyone we should notify?" the officer persisted as she walked alongside the stretcher.

"Go to hell," Doris yelped, her jaw clenched against the pain.

"Yes, ma'am, have a nice day," the policewoman answered.

Her partner, a young guy wearing glasses, addressed Cathy.

"Who's the dead one?"

"I have no idea," Cathy replied.

"We don't know the entire cast of characters, yet," Butch said. "But this has to do with the investigation of Kyle Dixon who is wanted for the bombings in Riverside County. The woman who got taken out of here is his mother…"

"Who are you?" the policewoman asked.

Butch explained who they were, what they were doing, and why.

"I assume you have permits for the guns you used."

"Certainly," Butch said.

Cathy answered, "Yes."

While the officer was questioning them, her partner was on his radio notifying detectives and the medical examiners office.

"Detective Gross will be here in a few minutes. He'll want to get a rundown on what happened. Crime scene team is on its way, too. Why don't you two just chill for a few minutes until Gross gets here?"

"If you don't mind," Butch said, "we'll chill in the mother's office. We can sit there and I can touch base with my FBI contact."

"Okay," the officer said.

Cathy flopped onto the leather couch across from Doris' desk. She pulled her knees up to her chest and rested her head on her knees. Butch dropped into Doris' chair, put his feet on the desk, and punched in Fuller's number. Surprise, surprise, Fuller answered.

"How's it going," Butch asked, "I haven't seen you on TV lately?"

"No shit. The Governor's down here running around like a banshee, going from one photo op to another, getting little accomplished, and ready to take credit for anything good that happens. And we're grinding it out, one lead at a time, not getting very far."

"Did Kyle have a girlfriend?"

"Let me check here with what I have. Where are you anyway, Greiner?"

"Santa Monica. The gallery Kyle's mother owns. We had ourselves a little gun battle here and Kyle's mother was shot by the young woman you met who was with me. I shot a young woman who fired at us the second she knew who we were and what we were doing. He's not here, wasn't here when it happened, but sure as hell he was here, and I think he's got to be nearby. Haven't a clue where, though. Your boys in LA better get on the stick or they're going to get left behind. It won't look good for the bureau. Fumble, bumble, will be the press you get. You'll all be tainted for screwing up. Again."

"Aw, damn it, I talked to them in LA. Toby Grant was supposed to be on it."

"Anybody suggest staking out this gallery and the mother's house and his house where the wife and kids live? No, well they should. He's moving around here somewhere and using someplace as a base of operations. Tonight, he's going to blow stuff up around here, you can count on it."

"I can't do their work for them," Fuller whined.

"Anyway, what do you have on a girlfriend?"

"We interviewed a Christy Warren who worked for Dixon as a secretary at his Riverside office where he ran those environmental non-profits. She said she suspected a Carrie Barnes might be his girlfriend because she hadn't heard from Kyle like he said she would and this Carrie quit coming around looking for him. She suspected the two of them had run off somewhere together. Your body might just be the Barnes girl. We ran a check on her. Did time, was on parole, and worked at a coffee shop here in Riverside until last week when she quit. Blonde hair, five-nine, a hundred and fifteen pounds. Witnesses at his apartment say a woman of that description lived with Kyle. No one knew her name."

"I'll have Detective Gross give you a call," Butch said.

"Who's that?"

"Supposed to be the one coming to head this investigation. Talk to you later."

Detective Terry Gross stood in the doorway as Butch punched off his cell phone.

"Name's Gross. I'm with the Santa Monica Police Department."

"Butch Greiner." He didn't stand and he waited for Cathy to introduce herself.

"Cathy Simon, Gladstone International security department," she said, raising her head slightly from her knees.

"Give me a brief outline of what happened. I'd like a full and complete statement at headquarters as soon as you can." He pulled a note pad and pen from his sport coat and was poised for the story.

Butch quickly explained what had happened, why they were there in the gallery, who Doris was, and the potential for the dead woman to be Carrie Barnes, and how he knew so.

Detective Gross listened and made notes and when Butch had finished, directed his attention to Cathy.

"That how it went, Miss?"

"Yes, exactly," she said softly, looking up from her knees.

"She's never shot anyone before, let alone be in a gunfight," Butch explained. "She's pretty stressed out."

"I can understand that," Gross said.

"You might want to put surveillance on the mother's house," Butch said, "and his house where the wife and kids still live. I don't think the FBI has done that yet."

"Why didn't you notify us about what was going on?" Gross asked.

"Because we were working with the FBI and Riverside County Sheriff. Here in Santa Monica he hasn't done anything, but the FBI still has jurisdiction. Bombing is a Federal crime, they coordinate with Homeland Security. You weren't a factor when Cathy and I came back to Santa Monica."

"It still would have helped," the detective groused.

"I know Kyle has been here," Butch said. "I don't mean to tell you your job, but I would check with the neighbors, other businesses around here to determine what they saw."

"Thanks, we'll do that."

Santa Monica police officers had run yellow crime scene tape around the parking lot and across the back entrance to Doris' gallery. Police cars crowded the streets in front and back of the building and now a van for the forensics team from the medical examiners office was prominent at the parking lot entrance. Television crews were just arriving.

This picture of official investigation greeted Kyle as he drove towards the gallery. That sense of panic that might otherwise grip someone less obsessed, less determined, and less sure of his mission did not take hold of him. He was outwardly calm, inside resolute, although an involuntary surge of perspiration made his armpits clammy. He slowed slightly, drove on, and went by the gallery and back to the Jacobs house.

The morning had been successful by Kyle's standards. The cars he wanted had been lifted and were ready in the garage and in the driveway of Sol Jacobs, out of sight from the street, set for tonight's action. He understood that Ellis had been exhilarated by the challenge of getting cars in the urban confines with which he was confronted and Kyle enjoyed that exhilaration vicariously. Each car had the necessary explosives inside and the big placement was assembled in the roach coach.

He had no sense of panic, but there was a pang of realization that Carrie and his mother were probably lost to him for some yet unexplained reason. Something happened at the gallery, some confrontation, something not good. When he got back to the Jacobs house, he went directly to the den where there was a large TV and grabbed the remote. He powered it on and pushed the channel button until a local station was shown with a special report from Olympic

Boulevard in Santa Monica. The outside of his mother's gallery was in the background behind the young Asian woman reporter who was describing the shootout that had occurred in the building behind her.

"One woman is dead," she said excitedly, "and another woman in critical condition has been taken to St. John's Health Center."

"Who is dead?" Kyle asked the TV.

"The deceased victim's name has not been released," the reporter continued, "but the survivor is tentatively reported to be Doris Krause, mother of Kyle Dixon who is wanted for the bombings in Riverside County."

Carrie was dead. Somehow it barely registered with Kyle. He felt little connection to her and the reality of her death was as remote as if her death were of an anonymous stranger in any other news story. Kyle wondered if Laurie would know her mother-in-law was there at the hospital. Would she see her? It was, he considered, an interesting twist of fate. He assumed his mother would be all right. She was always all right. She was tough.

Mark, Ellis, and Ted trailed into the den. They had heard Kyle come in and were curious that there had been no greeting of any kind from him. Then they heard the television.

"Hey, Kyle," Ellis said.

"What's going on?" Mark asked.

Kyle shushed them.

The four men stood there silently, stunned by what the reporter was saying.

"...we have with us the two people involved in the shootout that just happened here at Taylor Gallery in Santa Monica and Detective Terry Gross of the Santa Monica Police

Department. Detective Gross can you tell us what happened inside just moments ago?"

"We have one deceased young woman and an older woman who suffered one or more gunshot wounds who was taken to the hospital…"

"How did this go down, was there a confrontation? What caused this shooting?"

"Well, understand, Sinja, that this incident is just in the beginning stages of investigation and I'd rather not comment until all of the facts are in and we have the full story. I'm sure a spokesman from the Santa Monica Police will have an official statement later today, but right now I can't say much about what has happened."

"Can you give our viewers an idea of what the reason for the shooting might be about?"

"I can tell you that this gallery is owned by the mother of Kyle Dixon who is wanted for questioning in the bombings that occurred in Riverside County. He is a suspect as I understand it. Whether there's any connection to what went on here, I can't say. We'll have to wait until all the facts are sorted out…"

"But wouldn't it seem likely there is a connection? Sir, what can you tell us? You were involved in the shooting weren't you? And Miss…?"

"Simon…Cathy Simon. But I really can't say anything right now."

"You, sir, are?"

"Butch Greiner. I'm a private detective working for Miss Simon. We are trying to find Kyle Dixon for questioning about another crime that took place. We have reason to believe that he is here in Santa Monica and I would like to challenge your viewers to be on the alert for him. Report anything suspicious that you observe. There is very strong evidence to suspect him of the Riverside County bombings."

By now there were eight or nine microphones thrust at Butch as he spoke.

"You TV people need to keep broadcasting his photo. That's all I can say right now."

Kyle screamed, "That's how the bastards were on us so quickly. A private detective who was hired by Gladstone. Damn, there was no getting around that personnel database."

"That's what I warned you," Mark said. "They would figure it as an inside job right away."

"Nothing can be done about it right now. But one of those two killed Carrie and shot my mother."

"Do you care that much about Carrie?" Mark asked.

He posed the question casually, not meaning to be cruel or critical of Kyle's involvement with the girl. He understood Kyle's sexual appetite and allowed for it in their work.

Kyle did not respond.

News of the shooting reached Barry Walker on his car radio as he struggled to stay awake on the drive to Santa Monica. He had grabbed snatches of sleep as he worked through the night to find out more about Kyle Dixon. The LA Times archives had provided a great deal of the background he searched for and he was able to determine the connections to his mother, her gallery, her home, and her special friend Sol Jacobs. For Walker, it was a no-brainer that Kyle would head back to Santa Monica to inflict more infrastructure damage. Santa Monica was where he grew up, an area he knew well. But where would he bide his time until he could place more bombs?

He fought to stay awake as he drove, struggling to work out in his mind where Kyle might be. Not at his old address surely nor his mother's house. With the news of the shooting, the gallery was eliminated. Perhaps Kyle could use Jacobs' place or a place Jacobs owned. It was a long shot, but one that he would check. Sol Jacobs was a partner in the law firm of Bensler and Stein. He had learned that bit of information in one of the Times articles about Doris and Sol attending a charity event in LA sponsored by the Ralph's supermarket chain. A call to his friend Karen at the Times LA office provided him with the law firm's phone number.

"Bensler and Stein." The young woman's voice answered so rapidly it was difficult to discern what she said.

"Bensler and Stein," Walker repeated, his brain foggy from lack of sleep.

"Yes, it is. Who would you wish to speak to?"

"Sol Jacobs."

"Mr. Jacobs is not in. Can his associate help you?"

"No. I need to talk with him. Is there a way to reach him?"

"Just a moment, please."

The line was dead for what seemed like an eternity to Walker.

"Mr. Jacobs is on vacation," a new woman's voice said. "I'm Janet Brown, Mr. Jacobs associate. May I help you in some way?"

"No, thanks." Walker pressed the END button on his cell phone and closed it.

He was groggy and knew he needed to get off the Santa Monica Freeway before he ran into somebody. He needed to get a cup of coffee or one of those energy drinks to give him a boost. The San Diego Freeway was coming up next and after he passed that he would get off and find a gas station. He also needed a restroom.

Once off the I-10 onto Bundy, he cut over to Santa Monica Boulevard and found a Chevron station. After the restroom and a jelly-filled sweet roll, he sipped his black coffee and phoned Karen at the Times. Several minutes later, she was able to come up with an address in Santa Monica for Jacobs.

She was also able to give him directions to the location. Walker drove to the house and parked across the street.

Although he had some sense that he should call someone, let them know where he was, what he was doing, his fatigue worked against such prudence. Notifying his editor perhaps or maybe the police would be a good move, but his dogged desire to get the story, even interview Kyle, helped form his decision to check out the place. And because he could not see anything other than an upper portion of the house, his curiosity coaxed him into being foolish.

Walker got out of his car, steadier now with the assistance of caffeine and sugar bolstering his system, and walked to the large wooden gate that spanned the driveway. There on the stucco pillar next to the gate was a call button and speaker. He pushed the button, but got no response. He could see the gate was suspended on wheels that rode on a steel track to open and close. The clearance at the bottom of the gate was about six inches or so. He knelt down with his right cheek almost to the pavement to peer under the gate. He could see what appeared to be a catering truck and a car parked in front of a three car garage.

He rose and pushed the call button again. No answer. So, he walked to what he thought was the edge of the property, or at least where the front wall ended, and there was a large oleander bush. He pushed his way through between the end of the wall and the bush and disappeared from view of the street.

Walker was enmeshed in foliage and reached out with his left arm to determine where the wall was located. He thought it might be lower, running alongside the property, and he would have a chance to scale it. He pushed toward his left in an effort to touch the wall and pushed through the bushes and onto the Jacobs property. There was no side wall, only the wall across the front. The stand of oleanders was the protector on this side.

He headed for the front door, feeling slightly dizzy from the exertion of plunging through the bushes, and stumbled as he climbed the three steps to the small half-circle porch. He landed on his left knee and scuffed a light gray patch into his chinos. The door opened before he could gain his balance and rise.

"What the hell do you want?" a voice barked.

Walker looked up at Kyle Dixon. He recognized Kyle immediately and his heart rate accelerated. He struggled to stand. He was really dizzy, now.

"Looking for you. People are saying bad things about you and I wanted to get your side of the story. I'm Barry Walker of the LA Times, Riverside bureau."

Kyle knew the 'getting his side of the story' business was a lie, but appreciated the man's quick wittedness.

"Come on in then."

Walker saw three other men standing in the background when he entered and one of those men motioned him down a hallway to the large living room at the rear of the house. Large picture windows looked out onto an Oriental garden which had the obvious touch of a master gardener.

"Sit down over there…on the sofa. Would you like something to drink? A beer, soda…?"

The idea of a beer appealed to Walker, but he thought if he drank one he would pass out for sure.

"Yeah, a Pepsi would be great."

"We got Coke."

"Coke's fine."

"Good. What's your name again?"

"Barry Walker. I'm with the LA Times in Riverside." He pulled out his pen and reporter's pad. "I live in Loma Linda.

My wife says we have no power at home." He spoke nervously, not sure what to expect."

"Ted get Barry a Coke will you? Sounds like he has a dry throat."

"Yeah, I've been up all night…"

"I bet you have."

Ted went for the Coke as Kyle and Ellis sat down. Mark remained standing by the doorway.

"Could I please have your cell phone, Barry?" Kyle asked politely.

Walker took the phone from his inside jacket pocket and handed the phone to Kyle. Kyle tossed it to Mark who slipped it into his pants pocket.

"We don't need any interruptions while you interview me. Go ahead, what would you like to know? No, wait a minute, let me ask you a question. How did the police decide to focus on me? I've never done anything wrong."

"There's this private detective who brought your name to the FBI in Riverside and the FBI notified the Riverside County Sheriff…"

"Really…?"

"Guy by the name of Greiner. He was hired by Gladstone International. I guess you worked for them once…"

Kyle did not confirm that piece of information, he just looked at him as Ted came back with the Coke and handed it to Walker. He took a generous swallow and put it on the coffee table in front of him.

"Go on."

"Well, he and this woman with him from Gladstone figured you were the one who stole plastic explosives from Gladstone, so they got to the FBI man named Fuller. Henry

Gonzales thinks you were pulling a long string of robberies in the county…"

"This Gonzales have any proof?"

"I don't know for sure, but I don't think so. It's just speculation. What's your side of this Kyle?"

"You know, Barry, I've been involved with the environmental movement for a number of years raising money to try to increase awareness of the dangers we face if we don't make some changes. I said so in my letters to the public. Your paper printed those letters. This is serious business for all of us, Barry. But it's no secret that I…we, are conducting a campaign of Fire and Brimstone to bring the public to its senses. What they are saying about me is true, Barry, but it is a just cause. And we're not through, yet. That's why we need to keep you here until we have finished and then you can write your story."

Walker was in the grasp of Ted and Ellis as he stood to protest. Mark grabbed his ankles and the three of them carried him to an upstairs bedroom where they used gray tape to bind his ankles, knees, and wrists. A complete wrap of tape held his arms tight to his body and his mouth was also covered with tape. He was so exhausted that in moments he was sound asleep.

"All set," Mark reported when he found Kyle in the den watching TV news.

"Good. My mother is alive and recovering and Carrie is dead. Shot twice by that Greiner. That son-of-a-bitch has caused us a lot of trouble. I wish there was some way to get to him, some way."

"Easy does it, Kyle," Mark soothed, "easy does it. We have other fish to fry."

"I know," Kyle said, "I know. But I can still wish."

25.

Word spread quickly through St. John's Health Center that Kyle's mother had been brought to ER. She received some emergency treatment to stem the severe bleeding and was rushed to surgery. After surgery she was placed in an intensive care unit with a Santa Monica police officer posted to keep watch on her room. Doris eventually regained consciousness and Laurie was at her bedside, sitting quietly, waiting for contact with her mother-in-law. Doris tried to blink away the haze of post-anesthetic blurriness that discomforts and disorients patients recovering from surgery. She was aware of someone, but did not know who it was.

"It's Laurie, Doris, I wanted to make sure you were comfortable and all right. It's Laurie."

"Laurie...Laurie?" Doris' speech was slurred.

"Yes, Kyle's wife...Laurie."

"Am I going to die?"

"No, you're going to recover just fine. You've had a terrible shock to your body, but you are going to be okay. I wanted you to know I was here for you and make sure you were comfortable."

"Laurie?"

"Yes, Kyle's wife."

"Kyle's wife?"

"Yes, Doris, Laurie.

"Oooh...yes...Laurie."

"I'm right here." Laurie patted Doris' arm.

"Oh, Laurie, you sweet girl. What happened to me? I dreamt there was shooting...it was awful."

"Don't think about anything right now, just try to rest. Get some sleep. I'll check on you...make sure you're okay. Get some rest and don't try to think about anything."

"Who did this to me? Someone shot me, I know it. Someone shot me. There was shooting and I felt pain in my side."

"Just rest, just rest, don't think about anything."

"It was that man, that detective...he shot me..."

"No, no, just be quiet, just rest. You need to rest so that you get better quickly and feel better."

"Kyle...where is Kyle? Have they killed him?"

"No, they haven't killed him and I don't know where he is."

"They're going to kill him, you know. Going to kill him. One way or another, they're going to kill him. Just like at Waco with all those people burned to death...and the McVey boy. One way or another, the government will kill my Kyle."

"Just relax. Try to stay quiet. Don't talk right now, just rest." Laurie continued to alternately pat and rub Doris arm.

"I want to talk to Kyle; I want to make sure he's all right."

"I don't know how to contact him, Doris. He may be busy right now."

Laurie thought it was probably a silly thing to say to Doris, but the words seemed to satisfy the woman and her eyes closed. I'll bet he's busy. Busy trying not to get caught, busy getting ready to do some other damnable thing, and busy trying to figure out how he's going to survive this ordeal.

"Tell Kyle I'm okay," Doris said quietly without opening her eyes.

"I'll try." She knew that was also a dumb thing to say, but Doris was still.

Laurie had finally been able to calm Doris and she went to sleep without opening her eyes again. Laurie went home to her children and her sister. She wondered if Butch Greiner had indeed shot Doris.

Butch and Cathy were at the Santa Monica Police Department headquarters. They had finished giving complete official statements detailing the circumstances of the shooting. Each was licensed and trained to carry a firearm, so no charges were made against them. The police report indicated that each of them had fired in self-defense. When the statement sessions were completed they were escorted by Detective Gross to a conference room where three men sat blank-faced, waiting impatiently. The stares were their best interrogation-style visages. No give away to what they were thinking or feeling. Also great for poker.

Gross introduced the three. There was Toby Grant, Special Agent in Charge of the Terrorism Section of the LA FBI office. Grant was a pudgy, balding man, a far cry from the poster-perfect image of an FBI agent J. Edgar Hoover loved to show off to the public. And Tito Chacon, Lead Detective in the Special Investigations Section of the West LA office of the Los Angeles Police Department. Chacon was six feet tall, a well-built Hispanic with close-cropped black hair, and an infectious and somewhat disarming smile that belied his strength and courage. Finally, there was Chad Coley, ATF Agent in their LA office. Coley was a studious-looking man who wore clunky, old-fashioned glasses, was dour at all times, with a pessimistic vision of his job, and with a pallor which suggested he might not be in good health. He blew his nose frequently and carried a box of tissues with him.

Grant spoke first. "You two piss-ants have caused me one hell of a lot of trouble..."

"Then get your act together and do your job," Butch snapped as he interrupted the agent.

The stunned agent's mouth hung open. Even Cathy was startled by the quick verbal crack Butch had given the man.

"Listen..."

"You listen. We went to Fuller with what we knew right from the get-go. It's my understanding from him that you were notified what was going on and to take action here in the LA area. That you sat on your hands is not our problem. Now, let's start at square one and see if you guys can do your jobs, there can be some cooperation, and we can get Dixon before he does too much more damage."

Lieutenant Chacon tried to suppress laughing at Butch's comments, but made a weak effort at doing so. He spoke next.

"What do you think is going to go down with this guy and what can we do?"

"He's here in Santa Monica and he'll do something around here. Around here means it could be in Santa Monica proper or it could be in West LA, or both. He has a great deal more explosives than he's used and he's going to use them somewhere around here on something. Street patrols need to be stepped up; someone needs to get on TV and warn citizens to be on alert for anything suspicious. Kyle Dixon is a terrorist and the same kind of alertness is crucial as it is for any terrorist. I don't know what it's going to be, but I would heighten security on the aqueduct coming into the San Fernando Valley and any power generating facilities that might be vulnerable. Other than that, I don't know."

"How much plastic does he have?" Coley asked. "Can he do a lot of damage?"

"Big time. And we've learned they have grenades. Not concussion grenades, but the real thing. God knows what he'll do with those. And they have plenty of armament if there's a stand-off."

"They," Chacon said, "you keep saying they, but all we've heard about is this one guy Dixon. How many are there?"

"If Gonzales with the Riverside County Sheriff's office is right, the 'they' are the same four that pulled a long series of robberies in that county. So, there is Kyle Dixon and three others. Right now. The young woman I shot is probably, or was probably, Kyle's girlfriend Carrie Barnes. More than likely, she was with them for the bombings, not with the robberies. We're looking for four men who are armed and dangerous."

"Any ideas where they might be hiding," Grant asked.

"I would guess that wherever it is has some connection with the mother…"

Grant's cell phone rang. The group was silent as Grant listened and took notes. Finished, he clapped the phone shut.

"That was one of our agents at the mother's house. The household help – a cook and a butler – refused to cooperate and we've taken them to the Federal Building charged with obstruction. However, witnesses in the neighborhood say our targets were there. No other details, yet, but our guys are working on it. Four men and a woman were seen arriving, even though it was the middle of the night and were seen leaving this morning."

"That's why," Butch said, "you have to alert the public to report suspicious behavior…"

"The Governor emphasized that this morning when he was on TV," Chacon said. "After our perps were already gone."

"You were saying something about the mother," Grant said. "Go on with that."

"Everything points to the mother being protective of Kyle. I think she knew what he was planning and what he had done. I don't think she was a part of it other than letting them use the house to crash and maybe the back half of the gallery to store cars or vans. I checked it out and there was a fresh oil puddle from some kind of vehicle with a leaking oil seal. The domestic help is not talking because she put the pressure on them and will reward them for their keeping quiet. I don't think she knows what he's going to bomb next; so, I wouldn't waste time trying to get her to say something from a hospital bed. She wouldn't tell you even if she knew."

"What kind of connection you have in mind?" Coley asked.

"Not sure. Kyle is very bright, the mother smart and savvy. They would know they couldn't stay at her house very long nor at the gallery. How the girl got left there at the gallery, I don't have any idea. But the mother would have the old wheels turning in her brain to figure a way to hide these guys and their vehicles. Maybe a friend. Or it could be a business associate she knows has a place to use where questions would not be asked."

"We'll check out that angle," Grant said.

"You guys have a lot to do and if you don't have anything else, we're out of here. It's been a long day and, frankly, this might be a long night."

"You think they've got something planned for tonight?" Chacon asked.

"Absolutely. They can't wait. Believe me, they have a sense that every hour the authorities' chances increase for getting closer to them. If they wait, I think the FBI can get to them before tomorrow night. I say nighttime because that's when they hit before. Kyle won't change his MO. He wants the cover of darkness."

"Stay in touch," Grant said, and slid his card across the conference table to Butch. The other two men also gave Butch their cards.

Cathy took out one of her cards and put it on the table in front of her without saying anything.

"Her cell phone number is here," Butch said. "Keep us in the loop. Please."

Butch took Cathy by the arm and they exited Police Headquarters into the early evening hot air. The sudden change from air conditioning was a jolt as heat radiated from pavement and buildings. Palm fronds hung limp and lifeless as if they had wilted and died. A sea breeze had yet to kick up to relieve the heat. Cathy stumbled.

"You okay?"

She nodded.

"Hang on to my arm 'til we get to the car."

"I think I'm going to throw up," she said, her hand to her mouth. She gagged and choked, but didn't vomit.

"You want me to take you to your folks place?"

"Oh, god, no. I'll be all right. I think I need to eat something and I sure would like a beer."

"Then you will throw up."

She laughed and kept her hand to her mouth.

Butch helped her into the car and headed out of the police parking lot.

"You want to come to the apartment? Relax a bit, have a beer, a little snack. They've got all kinds of snacks there for me. We can figure out what we want to do for dinner."

Sure, I'd like that. I can throw up there."

In less than fifteen minutes they were in the Gladstone apartment munching pretzels and drinking cold beer from the bottles. Shoes off, Cathy slouched in an overstuffed chair with Butch across from her on a sofa, his shoes still on, feet on the coffee table, and head laid back staring up without seeing anything but a blur of creamy ceiling.

"Feel better?" He asked softly.

"A little. The pretzels have helped some. The Bohemia sure tastes good."

He gave a little smile. "Good."

"Sorry about getting weak-kneed on you…feeling mushy and wimpy…"

"Don't even think about it..."

"I just...even with all the training I got from Chet...everything he told me about the real thing. It didn't help. It was all so surreal, so unreal, so fantasy-like..."

"Of course it helped. You got your gun out, brought it into position, and got off two rounds before I did. Don't second guess yourself. You reacted the way Chet would have wanted you to, the way he taught you. It's a situation of stress layered with stress that knots your guts and numbs your brain. Only good reactions work in times like that. Reactions that only come with training. Or else, the other guy kills you."

"Thanks. I still feel weak and inadequate...and sick."

"You'll get over it."

They were silent for awhile and only the sound of crunching pretzels could be heard. Butch slugged down the last of his beer and went to the kitchen. He came back with two more beers and a plate with slices of cheese and summer sausage, and crackers. He put the plate on the coffee table near Cathy. She had pulled her knees up to her chest and made herself into a ball of remorseful emotion. He studied her for several minutes before he spoke.

"Do me a favor."

"What?" she moaned.

"Stand up and extend your arms to your side."

She hesitated, uncurled from the chair, slowly rose, and stuck out her arms.

"Like this?"

"Yeah. Now, take five deep breaths, slowly, and let the air out of your lungs slowly."

She did as he asked.

"Now, rest a minute, then repeat that."

She did so and dropped her arms to her sides. She cocked her head as she looked at him and made a face. It was as if to ask, "What the hell is going on?"

"Spread you feet apart a little bit and do ten arm lifts."

He stood up and showed her what he meant.

She got her feet apart, completed six arm lifts, and started to laugh. She bent over laughing, hands on her knees, and shook her head side to side. She then stood up straight and came to him, putting her arms around him in a tight embrace and pressed her face to his cheek. A surprised Butch didn't know quite what to do with his hands, but decided to pat her back.

"Thank you," she whispered. "Thank you."

She slipped back from him slightly, took his face in her hands, and kissed him softly on the lips. This action was a real shock to Butch, who did not know how to respond. She sensed his reluctance and moved her head away from him and smiled. She kissed him again, this time firmly, lips barely parted, a full, loving kiss of affection that presented the passion she felt.

He returned the kiss this time and feelings swept over him that he had not felt for years. Not since Cindy had such emotions gripped him. He tried to move away, but Cathy clung to him, her head on his chest.

"Sorry, if I…if I shocked you," she murmured.

He was silent. He really didn't know what to say. He felt embarrassed, somewhat emasculated in spite of what had just occurred, and unsure of himself, his feelings, how he should or shouldn't react. What was right? He had wondered when this time might someday come and now it was here and he was in a muddle about it. He realized he had his arms around her in an embrace and also realized it felt good and he did not want to release her.

"How are you feeling?" she asked quietly as she leaned her head back and studied his reaction.

"Just fine. Still a little stunned by what happened, but surviving nicely."

They let go of each other almost simultaneously. Cathy went to the cheese and Butch dropped back onto the sofa.

"Thanks for getting me out of my funk," she chuckled. "That was clever. I know I needed to snap out of it, I just had to have a little kick start. Thanks."

"I know the first experience like that is tough, but you have to move on from it."

"You know, all of a sudden I'm really hungry and this cheese is not going to get it done for me. What do you say we get some dinner."

"You know the places, just name one, and we go. I could do with a good meal."

"There's a great seafood restaurant on Main Street almost to Venice that I think you might like. The food is excellent."

"Let's do it," he said, picking up the keys, "fish sounds great."

There would be a short wait for a table and they bided their time at the bar, each with a glass of white wine. The conversation during the ride to the restaurant had merely been chit-chat, a satisfactory release from the tension each had felt in the apartment a few minutes earlier. But now, Cathy directed the subject to Kyle and their prospect of catching him.

"Where do think he might be?"

"As I said to Chacon and Grant, I've got to believe he's nearby. His mother figured out something for them…a place to hide."

"And then what?"

"They get their bombs in place tonight and...kaboom, parts of Santa Monica and West LA are without power and water. There will be chaos around here with traffic lights out, air conditioning gone, businesses unable to operate, and all of the modern conveniences we take for granted will be out of commission for awhile. This area will be as bad off or worse as the parts of Riverside County that have been effected. Pretty messy. Let's hope no one gets killed from any of the explosions or in the aftermath. Traffic will be snarled, tempers will be frayed, and it'll be interesting how these super-sophisticated folks of Brentwood and Santa Monica handle the situation. Sometimes the elite snobs don't fare well in a crisis."

"Aren't there any tough elite snobs?"

"Probably a few and a few who could be resolute and resourceful and patient, but who have forgotten how to be tough. I'm not optimistic that this crowd around here won't become a rabble. Those lower down the economic scale don't get so excited about such things because they don't have as much to lose...they don't have all of the luxuries to be deprived of."

"That's probably true."

"It's my take on it. I don't have much faith in the public, anyway. Look at how those people in Riverside County have behaved. They didn't even wait twenty-four hours before they were up in arms. It'll take twenty-four minutes in Brentwood."

"You know, Butch, I'm having trouble with the idea of how Kyle reconciles the bombings and where he thinks he can go or what he can do after he's done bombing. How do you think he works this out in his mind? He can't get away with it. He must know he's going to be caught."

"I think he believes that he is not going to get caught and I think he has some sort of escape plan worked out."

"Like what?"

The dapper host politely interrupted with the announcement their table was ready. Once they were seated, Cathy repeated her question. The waiter came to the table before he could reply.

"Ah, I see you already have wine. Should I give you a few minutes to review our wonderful menu?"

"I think so," Butch said. "Unless you know what you want; you've been here before."

"I need a few minutes," Cathy said, holding the menu to her chest.

"Very well," he said, and was gone.

"Nothing conventional, of course, but something relatively easy. Like a private plane or boat. Maybe hidden in some kind of vehicle. Just have someone drive him out of the LA basin. There's a great deal of wilderness in this country. With the right accomplice or accomplices he might never be found. Don't think there isn't a certain amount of sympathy for what he's trying to accomplish."

Butch looked at the menu, Cathy followed suit, and they were silent as they considered the choices. The waiter returned, they ordered, asked for two more glasses of wine, and for the first time since they kissed, looked squarely at each other.

"Did I scare you?" she said softly, not wanting their table neighbors to overhear. "Too aggressive?"

"Nicely aggressive, affectionately aggressive. And yes, you..." He stopped, groping for the right word that would explain properly. "No, not scare. I think jolt might be accurate..."

"Jolt?" She smiled.

"Yes. Yes, indeed. I haven't kissed a woman in a long time. Since my wife died. I've had somewhat of a bad time getting over her death. Took a long time to sink in, to become a reality that I could accept."

"I'm sorry." She looked distressed.

"Don't be sorry. How could you know?"

"I feel badly for you. I didn't mean *I* was sorry, I meant I was sorry for you."

"Thank you."

The meal was as outstanding as Cathy had said it would be and afterwards, as they waited for the valet to bring the car around, Butch asked her if she felt better.

"Here, let me drive," she said quickly as the car slid into view in front of the restaurant. She adeptly pulled a bill from her purse that she gave to the valet and slid in behind the wheel before Butch could protest.

"Didn't know you were so eager to drive this thing," Butch said laughing as he sat beside her.

"I'm not…ordinarily."

"Why now?"

"Because, you would have taken me to my apartment."

"Oh?"

"Yes, and I want to go back to your apartment."

Butch's eyebrows rose slightly.

"And why would that be?"

"Don't be coy with me, mister. You know why…to be affectionately aggressive with you."

He said nothing during the remainder of the short drive. His mind was flashing all kinds of thoughts about the age differential, his ability to perform, and his willingness to engage in lovemaking with this attractive young woman. He could not deny that he was excited about the prospect of sex with her, even though he was filled with the anxiety produced by doubts. He tried his best to steer clear of thoughts of Cindy and what this might mean in regard to his memory of her. He tried not to think about having sex with Cathy as cheating on her, of spoiling her memory some how. After all, it had been that memory which had prevented him from even attempting to have a relationship with another woman. All this time, all of those thoughts, all of the mental gymnastics surrounding guilt and self-doubt and remorse and self-pity and anger, all mixed with a sexual desire that did not go away. This had created within him an emotional quandary and a stultifying pattern of denial that was a barricade to moving on with his life.

From the moment they kissed, he was pushed to a new awareness, one he was reluctant to accept, one that nagged at him, and which he could not deny. Stop deluding yourself, a voice inside of him screamed, get laid. You'll feel better.

"You're deep in thought somewhere," she offered as she pulled the Lexus into the underground garage.

When they got out of the car she took his hand and kissed it. Almost as if he were a little boy, she led him to the elevator, up to the apartment, and inside. Once there, she kissed him passionately. The next few moments could be the awkward time. What to say, what to do? But she took care of that, also.

"Why don't we take a shower? You can wash my back."

That was easy.

Cathy walked to the master bedroom, unbuttoning as she went. She kicked off her shoes with an easy motion and stepped out of her pants. She never looked back and expected Butch to follow her. He did and sat on the bed and undressed, all the while watching her take off her blouse, her bra, and then her panties. She didn't mean it to be a striptease, but that was the affect and he was aroused.

It had been so long since he had allowed this kind of arousal to energize him, to flow through his groin, and tighten his stomach muscles. And give him a well-bloomed erection.

She looked at his naked body for a moment and went into the bathroom to get the shower started. He followed her into the large tiled shower stall, self-conscious about the obviousness of his excitement. The warm water, the feel of her skin, the tender way she touched him and washed his body was a pleasure he did not remember ever experiencing. Even with Cindy. He struggled not to feel guilty about that, to not apologize to her spirit in some way. He needed to banish such thoughts and stay in the moment and appreciate and luxuriate with this gorgeous naked woman with soap suds cascading from her trim, athletic body. He was almost overwhelmed. Could he withstand an orgasm? He wondered.

He stood there letting her towel him off, enjoying that kind of attention for the first time in a long time.

"I guess you've recovered from feeling sick," Butch said.

"I have," she almost giggled, "and I never did throw up, thank goodness. Do you like this…getting washed and dried?"

"Yes, I do. It feels…"

"Wonderful?" She kissed him.

"Yes."

She dried herself and they climbed onto the king-size bed after pulling back the comforter. They sat facing each other, legs intertwined, knees touching, and hands joined.

"Now, I know you're still scared. Relax, this won't hurt a bit."

She stood up, balancing herself on the bouncy mattress, pushed him gently onto his back, and straddling his hips, lay down on top of him. They kissed and he ran his hands over her body as she caressed his face. He could feel her breasts against him and there was something racy about that, some old message that got played from when he was a boy first thinking about sex and wondering what it would be like to touch a girl's breast. How would that feel? What would it be like? This is how it really feels; warm and tender and intimate, and connected.

"Do you mind that I'm on top?"

"Not at all." He could barely breathe from his excitement. This was a new experience; this assertive woman, this woman hungry for him. His lithe, athletic body was taut and vibrating with anticipation.

She rose up on her haunches and had him inside of her before he realized what was happening. The glory of the union did not last very long and he survived its climax. She lay down against his chest again and kissed his cheek and lips and patted his other cheek. He could tell she was smiling.

"I...I couldn't..."

"Shhhhh," she whispered, putting the tips of her fingers to his lips. "Don't say anything."

After the time of after-sex bliss, which was a separate pleasure in itself, Cathy moved off of him. She lay there beside him, eyes closed, and rubbed his belly.

"I wasn't very good about this," Butch said. "I think I can do better."

"Now, that you're not scared?"

"Right."

"It's okay, you'll get another chance."

Butch looked at her naked body, so beautifully formed, so luscious, and marveled at what had occurred. What had occurred was something he had avoided for so long. In the years since Cindy's death, he had doubts that it ever would be there for him, such passion, such carnal pleasure. But it has occurred and now he wondered if this were the right time and place, and the right woman. He resisted thinking about what it meant and savored what was.

26.

There wasn't enough beer in Sol Jacobs' house. The three bottles found in the refrigerator were soon gone. While Mark and Kyle watched the grim television news, Ted and Ellis roamed the large house looking for something else to drink. They wandered in and out of bedrooms in their search, not so much because they thought they would find a drinking treasure, but out of sheer curiosity. When they reached the room with Barry Walker, they ignored him and continued looking around. Neither of them had ever been in a house of this magnitude before and they were fascinated by what they saw. Art was everywhere. Paintings, glass pieces, ceramics, textiles, oriental rugs, and sculptures of marble and bronze were on display. Whoever owned this place had to be rich. They could not have imagined such a place if they had not actually seen it.

"Look at all this stuff. It means money, big-time money," Ted said. "What do you think he does?"

"Probably one of them big Hollywood producers," was Ellis' take. "Or he owns a company of some kind. Anyway, the mother knows him. Maybe he's a musician. There's that big piano in the living room."

"Yeah, he's got dough, that's for sure."

Their meandering of the spacious house got them through the bedrooms, all of the rooms on the main floor and back to the kitchen where their search had begun. A large pantry off the kitchen was their last nosing about spot and in there was a floor to ceiling cabinet filled with Sol Jacobs' wine collection. The two searchers finally found it.

"We should have started here, I guess. You like wine?"

"I can take it or leave it," Ted said. "Don't know that much about it. This is expensive stuff, I bet."

"I know what you mean. I don't care that much, but it's here. Let's open one."

"Right. Which one?"

"You pick."

"Okay. Red or white?"

"Red, I guess," Ellis decided.

"Hmmm, here's one from France. Ah…says nineteen eighty-five. Name is Lafitte something or other. Let's give 'er a try. But it's going to take a corkscrew."

They took the bottle into the kitchen and after going through several drawers, found a corkscrew.

"There's foil around the top," Ellis said, "let me cut that off."

He pulled a knife from his trouser pocket, flipped it open, and carefully peeled away the dark foil. Ted inserted the corkscrew and withdrew the cork with a pop.

"Whoa, that's a sound. Where'd you learn how to do that, Ted?"

"I've done it a few times. Not on an expensive one like this, but I knew what I was doing. Hey, look at this price tag. Ninety-three bucks." He whistled in astonishment and placed the bottle on the counter.

"Let's see," Ellis said, "I got to see that." He did and shook his head. "Find some glasses, I got to try this."

"It's old. Think it's still good?" Ted asked as he opened cabinets. He finally found one with all sizes and shapes of glasses.

"They say it don't matter with these French wines."

"Look at all these glasses. Why would you need so damn many glasses?" Ted chose two that he thought were right and set them on the counter next to the bottle.

Ellis poured each glass nearly full. He picked up one and took a big swallow.

"Man, is that sour."

"Let me try it." Ted drank some from his glass. "It's okay. Not what I'm used to, but it's not bad."

"What are you guys doing?" Kyle asked as he came into the kitchen.

"Testing the wine from this guy's supply," Ellis answered.

"Tasting, you mean," Kyle said quickly. "That's all right, but don't drink any more than that bottle. We've got a lot of work to do and I want you guys able to get it done without screwing up. Understand? No getting shit-faced."

"You bet," Ted said and took another swig.

Kyle saw the bottle of Lafitte and laughed. "You guys know what this is?"

"Ninety-three bucks worth," Ted said. "I know that much."

"Try three hundred ninety-three," Kyle said. "Don't spill any."

He left the kitchen and went back to the news where Mark was locked on to what the young woman field reporter in Riverside County was blabbing. Behind her, a construction crew was hard at work on repairs to the Perris Dam pumping station. The devastation which had occurred was well evident. The reporter talked about the considerable damage to the Hinds Pumping Station, but no pictures were shown. Kyle could see how well his placement had done. Then attention was switched to another reporter who was interviewing homeowners from the subdivision directly across the highway from the pumping station.

Several were in tears, sobbing, crying out for some kind of help. Still others were just flat out angry. Thirty-five homes had sustained some kind of damage, with ten houses almost totally destroyed.

"We don't seem to be able to get the authorities to understand that we were also bombed," said a tall brunette who had two small children grabbing at her. She picked up the smaller one. She spoke calmly without sounding hysterical and the reporter continued to interview her.

"We can understand your concern," Don James said, he the reporter now on camera. "I imagine the explosion was quite horrific…"

"You have no way of knowing…unless you've been through something like this. You don't realize how loud it is and…and the concussion. The blast just knocked us down. I know some of my neighbors…" Tears welled in her eyes and she could not continue speaking. Her husband stepped forward and put his arms around her and the child. The woman wept.

He shook his head back and forth, fighting back the tears, unable to speak at first. He regained composure and said, "My wife is trying to say that we know some of our neighbors are dead. We don't know who exactly, but several. That's the word, anyway. Firemen put out the fires, but no one else has come around yet to see what we need."

"We all are concerned about your situation," James said. "All our viewers are very sympathetic to the emotions you folks have about this. I'm told the Governor will be here shortly to assess the damage." He turned toward the camera and walked forward, away from those he had been interviewing. "That's the story here in Perris…serious injuries, heavy damage, and an untold number of deaths. It's a bad postscript to the bombing, a situation of sadness and frustration as these folks wait for the Governor. Back to you, Jill."

Several small brush fires that had been started in this area were mostly contained, but three of those ignited from the blasts that took down the electric towers were still creating havoc for the Riverside Fire Department. Two were on the verge of being put down, but the third was still raging with minimal containment and spreading towards a cluster of houses. The reporter on the scene of the out-of-control fire gave his description of the battle and threw it back to the studio. Kyle flicked the MUTE button.

"No one was supposed to get killed," Mark said. He was depressed by what he had just witnessed on the news. "Victims turn public opinion against us, not for us. What we have tried to achieve gets ruined by victims."

"All the public are victims," Kyle countered.

"You know what I mean. This whole thing that we are doing is a struggle for ideas. We want to direct a public philosophy that tips the balance toward our cause. People equate these kinds of victims with evil and we become the evil they focus on. They forget about the reasons for why we had to draw attention to how they are the victims of their own doing. Now they are victims of our doing."

"Sacrifices have to be made," Kyle said casually. "Sometimes lives are lost to achieve the end result. There is example after example down through history of how this is so.

"I need a beer," Mark said.

"There isn't any. Have a glass of wine. They've got a bottle open in the kitchen."

"Having these kinds of victims is going to bite us in the ass," Mark said. He headed for the kitchen.

"Don't worry about it," Kyle called after him. "The truth is the truth and people will realize what it all means.

Kyle, operating in his own parallel universe, did not understand that under no circumstances would their actions to bring environmental awareness have any positive effect. He was not attuned to what the populace might think about what they had done and were about to do. He had no common sense for understanding how deprivation of modern conveniences would impact catastrophically. He only had the ideal that such deprivation would signal alarm and, thus, alliance with their cause. The result, he assumed, would make them heroes for challenging the establishment by showing what must be done to save the environment. He was cut off from reality, in his own partition of ego-involvement, his own neediness for being superior, and the self-acceptance that he was right, no matter what anyone else thought about what they were doing.

The wine had been drunk. Ellis and Ted were sitting in the kitchen laughing about something or another when Mark came for a drink.

"We'll open another bottle, simple as that," Ted said magnanimously, certainly willing to drink expensive wine that someone else had purchased.

Ted went into the pantry and surveyed the wine cabinet. He had no frame of reference to choose a wine. No instinct, no learning, only the stupid notion that whatever he chose would be right for them. He was correct; he could not go wrong no matter what he selected. He stared at the racks for several moments and then pulled out a bottle of white. It was from California, an excellent Chardonnay, and, strictly by happenstance, ready for drinking. He opened it with gusto and poured Mark a glass.

"It's got to be good, it's expensive."

Mark took the glass from Ted and sloshed it around a bit.

"Don't open another bottle of wine," Mark instructed. "This is it. More, and you get stupid. We need to be clear. We do what we do and we are out of here."

"Do we come back here or what?" Ellis asked.

Mark looked at him.

"I mean...no one has said. We don't just hang around here 'til the cops crawl on top of us. When do we get on the boat and where is it? What's the action?"

"Kyle will let us know," Mark said. "We get this done, we move on, lay low, and everything will be okay."

"We're counting on that," Ellis said.

Mark sipped the wine Ted had given him. He savored it and smiled.

"Lots of body, full of fruit and the flavor of Caribbean spices with just a hint of vanilla."

Ted and Ellis laughed.

"Shit, just like some pompous ass on television," Ellis whooped.

"I know these things," Mark retorted. "I can make the judgment."

He went back to the den, leaving Ted and Ellis to the bottle.

"Let's get out the maps and work everything out." Kyle was all business as he pulled his briefcase from beside the chair where he was slouched.

He spread a map on the coffee table and probed with a pencil at one of the red notations he had made.

"This is the pumping station on San Vicente. It's where the big one goes with the roach coach. Hey, get those guys in here; we need to get this scoped out and they need to pay attention. I have maps for everyone and each of us has to do his assignment."

"Come on in here, you guys. Quit sucking up that wine and listen up. This all happens real fast."

Ted and Ellis came from the kitchen without the bottle, but with filled glasses they held as they listened to Kyle's directions.

"Here's the way this is going to work," Kyle began. "Mark is going to operate with me so we can get the truck parked and I can walk away and get in the car he's driving. That Chev you got this morning, Ellis, we'll use that as the command car."

Ellis and Ted were a bit glassy-eyed from the wine, but attentive to what Kyle was directing.

"We each take a car?" Ted asked.

"Yes. Ellis takes the BMW to the Fairfax location, you take the Lexus to the Santa Monica sub-station and another one on Centinela. Mark and I will get the place in the hills. Get your placements set and come back here. We'll make our move then."

It was Ted who was the first to evoke doubt about what they were doing and how, in god's name, were they going to get removed from all of this. Kyle had to have some sort of plan, a plan that until now had been taken for granted, accepted as the way things would go on without the authorities touching them. It was mystical thinking, of course, but it was their way of coping and continuing with the operation.

"What kind of move," Ted insisted.

"You're not worried are you, Ted? Afraid I wouldn't provide for you?" Kyle was insistent.

"Ah, no...no, but..."

"But what? Take it easy. I have it all worked out. Come back here and relax, have another bottle of wine, and chill. Then we'll be on our way."

The long shadows of late evening fell across Sol Jacobs' house, the neighborhood quiet, households conducting mealtime rituals, and Butch and Cathy having dinner less than two miles away.

There is an irony in proximity, timing, and connection. All three were in effect right now. Kyle had no way of knowing that Butch was nearby, although he knew Butch had identified him, was after him, and smart enough to be close on his trail. Butch had created more problems for him than he could have imagined or anticipated. He had made no contingency plan for being found out so quickly. On the other hand, Butch was more savvy and believed Kyle was somewhere in Santa Monica. He just didn't know where. He had speculated to Cathy about catching up to Kyle before he did more bombing, but really did not expect that to happen. He thought Kyle would do something tonight and they weren't any closer to stopping him.

News hawks from daily papers, radio, and television were hard at work to find Kyle, as well as the authorities and Butch, and they also wanted to talk to Butch. Butch and Cathy were, in a sense, incognito. Other than through the connection of Cathy's cell phone, no one save those who had her number knew where they were. Reporters from various media outlets, including representatives from national news sources, were clamoring to interview Butch. He had become prominent in the massive investigation since Jim Fuller had mentioned his name at one of his several press briefings and his name had been bandied about on radio and TV newscasts. Fuller would not reveal Cathy's cell phone number, Gladstone would not give it out, and, try as they might, those reporters probing diligently with cell phone companies could not get access to her number. They could not make the connection.

And, the Los Angeles Times was missing a reporter. As mercurial as Barry Walker's editor thought he was, the young man could always be counted on to stay in touch with the office. There had been no word from him since he had left a message that he was headed to Santa Monica. He had said he thought he could get to Kyle, but his editor did not know how or where or any of the details. Barry would fill him in later. Barry never called and now the editor was worried. He notified the FBI and they were not encouraging. In fact, the Agent who took the call was greatly perturbed that the FBI had not been brought into Walker's tracking. That the editor had not been told did not matter to the FBI.

Barry Walker was struggling to stay calm. He knew that staying calm was necessary to survive. But he had no control of the mucus that ran from his nose and the congestion that was building in his throat. The tape across his mouth restricted his breathing and made him feel as if he were choking. He struggled to turn to his side and lean toward the bed so that he could blow his nose and allow the mucus to fall away. He could wipe his nose on the pillow by extending his turn and stretching his head. He had slept soundly for several hours and woke to the constriction that gripped him and could hear voices downstairs and the sound of a TV. His predicament was a shock to him; the memory of his being carried upstairs and subsequent taping more like a dream sequence than a reality he could comprehend. He knew now, it was real, awful in reality, terrorizingly real, frustratingly real, the real that could well mean his death. He was sure Kyle would come upstairs and shoot him, a severe punishment for finding Kyle, discovering the hideout, audacious enough to want to interview him for...*the story*. *The story*, the end game for a reporter, but should not be the end of his life. That is what Barry Walker assumed. The end game here was going to be his death.

Suddenly, it was silent downstairs. No TV, no voices. Kyle had not come up to this room and shot him. It did not matter, however, he still could not move very much and he was weaker than he had ever felt in his entire life. He had been forgotten. Maybe, just maybe, someone in the future would discover him and he would be okay. He relaxed with that thought and willed himself to not have so much mucus ooze from his nose or slide back into his throat. He fell into semi-sleep, floating in the nether world, lifeless, but alive, and hoping for freedom.

Kyle climbed into the back of the catering truck as Mark watched him, and from the rear door could see that Kyle was pressing on something.

"Setting the timer?"

"Yeah. Ten-thirty...same as the other packages."

"Doesn't matter when," Mark said, "as long as we have time to get the other placements and get out of the area."

"Ten-thirty is a good time."

Kyle drove the truck away from Sol's house and Mark followed in one of the stolen cars. He led the way through several turns in the neighborhood until they reached 26th Street, then headed north to San Vicente Boulevard where he turned right. He drove along San Vicente just at the speed limit until he recognized he was close to the turn he would make. It probably was not necessary to make the turn, but it was a precaution he was going to take.

The neighborhood was quiet and unsuspecting. They would be vulnerable victims of Kyle's delivery, his lesson for the masses. They would suffer the lesson of understanding, his understanding of what was lacking in society's awareness. They would suffer beyond anything he had imagined because he had never really thought through the full consequences of his destruction. They would be totaled into the number of sufferers already feeling the devastating consequences of Kyle's schooling for his unheeding fellow citizens. Residents close to this site, those a mile or so away into the hills, and hundreds of thousands of others in the area would be impacted by the repercussions of Kyle's handiwork. No one would accept his premise or side with him, and ultimately, many of these victims would want him executed.

Kyle parked the truck on Gretna Green, around the corner from San Vicente Boulevard. Mark pulled around the truck and parked thirty feet ahead. He walked back to the truck as Kyle cranked down the window. It was dark now, although some streaks of blue-gray light still streamed over them, the last remnants of sunset.

"Nice and calm," Mark said, trying to assure himself they would not be seen, wanting Kyle's response of reassurance.

"I know; we're in good shape. No joggers, either. Wait in the car and I'll swing around and park this thing in front of the building."

Without a reply, Mark headed for the car as Kyle started the truck, made a U-turn by jockeying back and forth, and drove slowly towards San Vicente. He stopped at the corner, made sure traffic was clear, crossed eastbound San Vicente through the boulevard, turned westbound, went to the next boulevard access, and came back east. He pulled into the building's driveway, parked parallel to the large main doors as close as he could, and cut the engine. He took the keys from the ignition and locked the doors as he exited. He walked back around the corner to the car and got in beside Mark.

"Well, that one is set," Kyle said.

"Think anyone will notice?"

"I think, Mark, that a few may notice, think it strange, and disregard it. It's not lighted there so it's not as obvious to those zipping by. People in LA ignore stuff like that anyway."

He checked his watch. Eight-forty-five. They needed to move on to the next stop.

Kyle had parked the catering truck in front of the LA Department of Water and Power Brentwood Pumping Station. This building on the southwest corner of San Vicente Boulevard and Gretna Green sits on property excluded from and adjacent to the Brentwood Country Club. Kyle had designed the combination fertilizer and plastic explosive placement that was packed into the back of the truck to detonate much like the placement he used at the Hinds Pumping Station. It was to be somewhat directional with its blast. The truck was now situated so it would create maximum damage to the pumping station.

"This same kind of placement did a job on the Federal Building in Oklahoma City," Kyle said as Mark drove, "it should take care of the Brentwood Pumping Station. We'll see how people do around here without water. They might come to appreciate the precious water when none comes out of their showers or washes their dishes. Some places in the world, in fact, lots of places, the people try to get clean and wash clothes and dishes all in a nearby river. Maybe these people can start to relate...and understand what they have."

Mark drove down Gretna Green to Montana, turned left and went to Bundy, turned left at Bundy, and drove north on Bundy. They continued on Bundy, past San Vicente, to Sunset Boulevard and jogged over to Kenter. They drove on Kenter for a short distance and went left onto Homewood until they were in the hills of Brentwood Heights.

"Right about here," Kyle said. "There...there's a spot behind that Jag."

Mark positioned their stolen car a few feet behind a brand new Jaguar convertible with the top down.

Kyle reached into the back seat and pulled up a slightly filled daypack and then a second.

"One for you, one for me." He also retrieved a heavy-duty bolt cutter. "I've got this."

They got out of the car, slipped on their packs, headed across the street, and then walked back in the direction they had come from Kenter. There was little light save from the houses across the street and they moved unnoticed in the shadows. Kyle had previously pinpointed and selected the Kenter Canyon Terminal Tower substation as a target because he believed it represented a significant power input source for Brentwood. His idea of maximum effect.

They moved through spotty sections of bushes and slender eucalyptus trees. The smell of eucalyptus oil that mixed with lemon blossoms and jasmine blooms was strange. They were immersed in an aroma they hardly recognized and that surely did not register with them. They were too intent with their mission.

A dog barked and yipped a ways off to the left, but did not seem to come any closer. Kyle stopped, sensing someone or something else was out here in the brush. Perhaps they did not have the dog's attention. He looked around. Lights from the houses behind them, lights on the hillside across the way; points of evidence that others were near and yet removed from them, unknowing of the danger that crept into their world. No wind, save the slight updraft of warm air escaping from lower down, wafting into the night. It was getting cooler and odd sounds carried over open space. They were the distorted odd sounds of people talking, music playing, and the edgy noise of vehicles on the streets behind them and from streets below. They were alone, but not alone in this affluent mass of hillside houses built with scant regard to terrain. Something moved ahead of them. Not a scurry of fearful steps of flight, but rather the deliberate move of a hunter, a stalker, a predator of some kind. Knowledgeable of what it was about, sure of its actions, and mindful of its intent.

They stepped forward into a small clearing and there, ahead of them about fifteen feet, were three full-grown coyotes, tongues dangling from the sides of their open, panting jaws, teeth flashing reflections from a yard light behind Kyle and Mark. They were nonchalant in their own press to kill someone's dog or cat for dinner, and patient knowing this was their territory and they knew what they were doing there in the dark. Kyle walked toward them and as he did, pulled a container of pepper spray from the side pocket of his pack. He increased his pace as they stared at him without moving and he sprayed a continuous zap of nastiness at them that mushroomed and caught them with its potency. They yipped and were gone.

"Damn," Mark said, hushed.

"You have to be ready," Kyle said, he, too, with hushed voice. "I hated to do that, but we have to meet our objective. This has been their land for a long time and I'm sorry we've taken it away from them. They don't know they're losing. They keep doing their thing. There have been no accommodations made for them and people wonder why their kitties or their precious poodles disappear. It is simply how it works and the coyotes are in the right."

They moved on to the gate. Kyle snapped the security chain with the bolt cutters and they were quickly inside the lot. The tight mass of electrical equipment stood as bold representatives of the modern world, carrying the power to that modernity which Kyle refused to accept. Up the hill was the faint sight of thin lines that transported the power, the incoming source to the substation. Thousands of streaming volts hummed a mantra to society's functioning needs. A pulse of sorts, that provided a life of efficiency and ease to the users.

"You have three placements. Tape them to these bases here and there and there," Kyle directed. "I'll get the far ones."

Mark went to the closest support anchor and pushed the clear plastic bag against the base and taped it securely. He looked at the timer.

"Ten-thirty?" he whispered.

"Yes," Kyle answered.

Mark went to the second base as Kyle went about getting his three placements taped in position. It was done. Kyle closed the gate, wrapped the chain so it looked secure, and they began their move to the car. The random barking of dogs could be heard, the one nearest them still snarling, still calling to his master about something out there somewhere moving about. They worked their way down the street, and over to the car. Once inside the car, Mark turned it around, and headed down the hill and back to Sol's house. Their part finished.

Ellis was on his own and he was okay with his solo assignment. He shared an apartment with Ted and knew the two of them were usually relegated to minor tasks other than the cars he lifted. He realized the importance of what he was doing tonight and appreciated Kyle's confidence in him. And having time away from Ted was somewhat of a relief. He knew exactly what he was to do. He had the assignment with the most exposure and he relished the fact. After all, he was the one stealing the cars, and that exposed him to getting caught far and away more than what he would do tonight. He left Sol's house in a car that had especially delighted him when he stole it. It was a light beige seven hundred series BMW. He loved the BMW, loved the ride, the handling, and response when he tromped on the accelerator. He got to Bundy and headed for the I-10 Freeway. He took the I-10 east to the Fairfax Avenue exit, pulled off, waited for the light at Fairfax, and went ahead on Apple Street. He took a left on Washington Boulevard and then another quick left on Thurman Avenue. He drove up Thurman a short distance and turned left onto Glennie Lane, having circled back towards Fairfax. He drove down Glennie and pulled into a parking slot next to Genesee Park.

He was very calm about what he was doing as he grabbed the black athletic bag from the seat beside him. He got out of the car, checked to see if he was being observed, and walked along the fenced park playground to Fairfax. He turned left onto Fairfax and walked back to Apple Street. There was relatively heavy nighttime traffic, the usual clamor of humanity in this overwhelming city, but he was sure no one paid any attention to him. He walked to the electrical transmission tower that stood dominantly at the corner of Fairfax and Apple and seated himself near one of its four bases.

He could hear the sizzle of electricity that charged overhead in a stream of power that would soon be stopped. There was something frightening in the sound and he shivered. His involuntary reaction was a fitting parcel of his street person act passing time, perhaps recovering from a booze induced haze. He reached into the athletic bag and pulled out a water bottle covered by a brown bag. He took a swig. No one paid attention to him. Cars zipped by in all directions and no pedestrians were there to see what he was doing. He pulled another brown paper bag from his satchel and pushed it into the inside corner of the base. He sauntered over to the second base and put another brown paper bag there and then the third and the fourth, systematically fixing placements to each of its four bases. No one noticed him working diligently, rapidly, efficiently as he put them in place. This intersection was brightly lighted with street lights, advertising signs, and the glare from stores and shops. Headlights flashed over him as cars turned and passed and turned and passed, the drivers oblivious to what he was doing, unknowing of what he represented. He was seen and unseen by the mass of people who went about their lives. He was visible, yet unnoticed; a warning to those who could recognize what he signified, but otherwise an aberration of the urban landscape. He walked away and back to the BMW.

On his drive back to Sol's, Ellis stopped at the Ralph's supermarket at Bundy and Wilshire and bought a case of Corona beer. He wasn't that crazy about the wine.

Ted was full bore into his assignment. He had been hesitant about working alone, but said nothing to the others of his anxiety going solo. He tried to calm himself by mulling over a certain contentment with driving a special car he asked Ellis to steal for him. It was a late-model Lexus. He gripped the steering wheel tightly as he drove from Sol's neighborhood, concentrating on the luxury of the vehicle, and blocking out any fears he might have. Cutting through side streets, he angled south to Colorado, and headed west. When he reached 9th Street, he turned right, went one block to Broadway, and turned left. There is an alley that runs from Broadway to Colorado between 9th Street and Lincoln and there he turned left.

At the intersection of Lincoln Boulevard and Colorado Avenue, on the northeast corner, is the Santa Monica electrical substation of Southern California Edison. It was contained in two sections that ran from Lincoln to 9th Street. There was no security other than block walls and chain-link fences. It operated automatically as most substations do, reporting its functions and distribution to the SCE's master control board that linked their system with the California power grid. The alley Ted used separated the two sections of the substation. He parked behind an auto repair shop that was next to the substation. The open yards of the substation property were unlighted save for light coming from the surrounding street lights and businesses.

He waited for a few minutes and then powered down the window. He listened to the buzz of all that energy being redistributed and directed, like the sound of a zillion bees hovering over a hive. This was a main center for electrical power in the area. He opened the athletic bag beside him and checked the eight packets inside. Timers set for ten-thirty, as Kyle had explained. He got out of the Lexus, walked down the alley toting the athletic bag until he was at the double-gate on his right. A large chain and padlock held the gates closed, just as Kyle had described. It was easy enough to crack the chain with bolt cutters. He entered the substation yard, closed the gate behind him, and quickly went about setting four placements at regular intervals among the mix of transformers and switches and wires and connectors that made up the substation.

He moved from the first section, making sure the gate appeared to be chained, and across the alley to the second section gates. Same maneuver with the bolt cutters and he was quickly inside to set the other four placements. He pulled the gates closed and wrapped the chain so it would seem to a casual observer that it was doing its job. Back in the Lexus, he slowly and carefully turned around, and headed back down the alley to Broadway. Broadway to 10th Street, 10th to Colorado, and then east on Colorado. He was soaking wet from sweat, his throat constricted with fear.

Ted pulled a bottle of water from the athletic bag and began drinking. It helped some, but he was still scared and shaking a bit. He tried to calm himself by pushing his head back against the headrest. It eased his anxiety a bit, but the sweat still flowed.

When he reached Centinela, he headed south. At Iowa, he made a left and shortly a right into the alley that ran from Iowa to Nebraska. He drove slowly through the alley until he was fifty feet or so from Nebraska, stopped the car, and killed the engine. He was stunned by what he saw. There in front of him was the West LA distribution headquarters of the Department of Water and Power with its electrical substation that was four times the size of the one where he had just been. And this one was fully lighted. What was Kyle thinking?

He was momentarily frozen with fear trying to decide what to do. Continue as Kyle had told him or move on? Kyle had said both locations would be easy, but take your time and be cautious, be aware. This didn't look easy. The damn thing is lighted, lighted like day; the other was not. What were the consequences of not doing what Kyle had directed? He decided he did not want to find out. He checked the last eight packages from the athletic bag and got out of the car. He looked around the quiet residential neighborhood. The houses were small, unassuming. He walked to the end of the alley and checked up and down Nebraska. No cars, no one walking their dog. He went across the street to the double-gate in the chain-link fence that was chained and padlocked as the others were. This time, however, there was a large steel plate welded to the fence in front of the chain and lock in an attempt to prevent exactly what Ted intended to do. He reached his hand behind the plate and moved the gates. There was just enough play in the length of chain so that he was able to get the bolt cutters behind the plate. Pop went the chain.

Still no cars, no one to witness what he was doing. He entered the lighted substation yard, closed the gates behind him, and waited as he looked over the area. He saw no one and swiftly moved through the yard putting the packages where Kyle had instructed. He crouched as he went, that instinctive maneuver to minimize size and form, and in some places duck-walked behind transformers and equipment to make sure he was not seen. He was cautious with every move. Kyle had said no one would be in the yard that time of night, but be prepared and use your pistol if you are confronted.

The persistent hum and buzz of moving electricity and electrical equipment reminded him to be careful of that danger, also. Don't touch any of the steel support frames or inadvertently stumble and fall against anything. There was a large building on one side of the yard and from beyond that he could hear the sounds of heavy machinery. Otherwise, he seemed to be alone.

After all of the packages were in position, he left the yard, making sure the gates were closed, and walked back to the Lexus. He threw the bag over to the passenger seat and stood listening. A barking dog somewhere, traffic on Centinela, the steady hum of electricity. In a city of four million, how could it be this quiet? He drove out of the alley onto Nebraska and returned to Sol's.

Twenty-six small placements and one large placement had been delivered, set to bring West LA and Santa Monica to its knees. No one reported anything suspicious even though radio and television broadcasts one after another stressed the importance of watching for the unusual, something out of the ordinary. It had been a relatively easy matter for the four men to get accomplished. They had gone to the planned locations and done what they wanted to do. Now, they were reunited at Sol's with Corona beer. Kyle's instruments were fixed to administer the awareness necessary for people to understand.

To others, the thought process might well be considered convoluted, demonic, and reprehensible. But to Kyle and his followers, what they were doing made sense. It was crucial for the long-term survival beyond these minor bumps of bringing awareness to the people. Nonetheless, cracks were beginning to show in the stoic emotional armor the others wore in support of Kyle.

Kyle thumbed through a manila folder that he had pulled from his briefcase. He examined a series of sheets and shook his head, almost in disbelief, certainly in mild frustration.

"It's too bad we couldn't get these other targets I identified. The aqueduct coming into the Valley from up north, those stupid wind farms around Palm Springs…the Getty Museum."

"Isn't wind power supposed to be good?" Ted asked.

"Yes, yes it is. But not at the expense of the landscape. Mile after mile, acre after acre, creating an ugly backdrop…that's not what we want. Location of wind farms has to be more thoughtful in terms of visual serenity."

"More news," Mark said as he played with the TV remote.

The picture showed a body of water in the background, the reporter standing close to its shore, microphone in hand, his interview subject standing placidly waiting to speak.

"This is Jim McClelland, senior engineer for the Water District. Jim, thanks for taking time to talk with us. I know that our viewers are concerned here in Southern California about their water supply. We've had two major pumping stations bombed…certainly a threat to continued supplies of water for folks. What can you tell us?"

"Well, Perry, first of all, I want to assure all of Southern California that there is no need to worry about water supply…"

"Bullshit," Kyle snapped at the TV set. "There is plenty to worry about. Lake Matthews can't hold out forever and it will take forever to get those pumping stations back on line no matter what he says."

"...have a real challenge to get our pumping stations in order and functioning, but Lake Matthews was designed for just such a contingency. There are enough acre-feet of water here to last way beyond what it will take to get Hinds and Perris Dam up and running again."

"That's great news, Jim..."

"He's lying to keep people calm," Kyle yelled. "Where's the phone, I'm calling the LA Times and letting them know the truth about this."

Kyle jumped up, grabbing his briefcase as he did so and went to Sol's phone on the desk in the corner of the TV room. He pulled a notebook from the briefcase, flipped to the Times number, punched it in, and waited with an indignant huff as if he were an advertiser whose ad had been botched.

"I need to speak to an editor," Kyle screamed. "I don't care, just get me an editor. Yes, all right, city desk."

He waited and fumed while he was being transferred to an editor.

"These guys will get it right...hello. Yes, this is Kyle Dixon. Yes, I am...never mind, just listen. There are reports that the water supply has not been affected and that is just not true. The TV people are lying, the water people are lying. They don't want the public to panic, but the public needs to rise up and react to this. This is what it is all about. You what? No, damn it, I set the placements, I know what I'm talking about. What? Yes...yes. No...no. Oh, screw yourself. Enjoy the consequences of being stupid."

"I'm not sure that this is..." Ted began.

"Shut up," Kyle directed with a snarl. "Doubts will kill us all, doubts will reduce us to sniveling idiots not capable of tying our own shoes. What we have done, what we are doing is right. Not sure of what? That we're righteous? We are and you know we are. Time and history will be on our side. The critical factors of the environment will be at the forefront for everyone. Global warming, conservation, reducing energy consumption...the very essence of how we live and survive is at stake. 'I'm not sure.' Don't give me that nonsense."

Ellis pulled his head back and stretched the muscles in his neck, muscles that had grown taut with the tension, that had immobilized his head and shoulders. He knew something was wrong, something skidding off course from the direction they had all originally talked about and planned. He believed Kyle was right, but there was that edge of something that gnawed at him, some feeling that pulled at his instinct for survival. His instinct told him to cut and run, but he thought about that. What if he did? Would Kyle shoot him? Maybe? He decided to stick it out. For the time being anyway.

Mark was scared. For the first time since they had talked about this project three years ago, he was filled with doubts. They were still free, still outside the grasp of law enforcement. How long could that last?

"When do we get out of here?" Mark asked.

"Later, after we experience the blast at the pumping station, after we know that we have achieved what we wanted. Relax, drink some more beer. We're okay. It's others who have to worry."

The four of them sat watching the news on TV, taking verbal shots at the talking heads and reporters with snotty remarks and sophomoric potty humor. The snipers were led by Ellis, his way of staying calm, with Ted and Mark willing assassins in the assault. Kyle retreated, first to a corner of the den and then to the kitchen. After a bit of nosing about, he found a liquor stock in a cupboard that Ted and Ellis had overlooked. He grabbed a bottle of Dewars and poured himself a drink. He dropped in a few chunks of ice and a dab of tap water. He leaned against the counter and stared at nothing. He was weary, but would not acknowledge so; he was furious with Butch, but did not want to recognize this. He simmered, ready for fulmination that matched the placements they had positioned, ready to detonate his emotions in rage for being cleverly found out and tracked by this man. He walked back to the den and, sure enough, there was Butch's face being portrayed as a potential avenger, one who would bring this demon, Kyle Dixon, to justice. It seemed ludicrous to Kyle.

He wished he could set about to kill Butch, to stalk until found, and shoot him. He knew he could not do that, there was another issue on his mind. He wanted to see his mother. She was not that far away and he believed he would be able to see her. He would wait for the results of the placements that had been set and then he would drive to St. Johns. She was there and she would want to see him before he moved on, perhaps never to be seen again. Circumstances would make that decision.

"After we experience what happens we'll be on the move. Leave the stolen cars here, then on our way. We'll be out of this stuff for awhile…"

"Where…?" Ted started to ask.

"Never mind. We'll all be fine. But I've got to see my mother first. We swing by the hospital, I say goodbye to her, and away we go. Easy as that."

"Isn't that ridiculous," Mark asked, "and dangerous for us?"

"I want to see my mother," Kyle said.

"What about us?" There was a strained edge to Mark's voice. He was angry, but trying to control himself dealing with Kyle. Something had changed. What was supposed to be an important mission had drifted off course, tainted by Kyle's skewed psyche. How had he missed the signal that Kyle was veering into his own world, that remote world of the disconnected. He, too, had been caught up with executing the plan, so caught up that until now the death and destruction were theoretical, academic, best results from best planning.

He suddenly realized that the only chance he and Ted and Ellis had was to get away from Kyle as soon as possible.

"So? What about *you*?"

"Going to the hospital is an unnecessary risk and every minute we waste screwing around here is time we could use for our escape. Time lost for taking advantage of the chaos."

"You don't seem to understand, Mark; I have to see my mother. I can't just let her lie there wondering about me. I can't leave without knowing she is okay. It's something I have to do."

Ted and Ellis had moved to stand by Mark and the three of them faced Kyle with all the air of defiance their body language could muster.

"I'm not sure you have a grip on your senses," Mark said calmly. "This is critical for us." He gestured to indicate the three of them. "Critical for us."

"What are you saying?"

"What I am saying is that I don't think you're making a good decision. A decision that matters to us…"

"It's a bad decision?" Kyle looked puzzled.

"I think so."

"Then maybe we should part company right here…"

"Look, I didn't mean it that way. What I wanted…"

"What you want is for me to change my mind. To change. That has always been the case. I've had to change. That's what I asked Alan. Why should I have to change?"

"You don't have to change. Just make a decision…"

"A decision that you approve of?"

"Kyle, we've been friends for a long time. I don't want to see our friendship come apart like this, but we have to get out of here, we have to get away. You said you had a plan...that you haven't fully shared with us. And you want to waste time. We should be on the move right now."

"Not until I experience what I missed before and not until I see my mother."

"Let's get the hell out of here," Ted said. "No way he's changing his mind."

"We won't lose much time for what we need to do. Besides, I'll make it worthwhile for all of you."

"How?" Ellis asked.

"Money. Cash money. You guys can't get far without money anyway. You're better off staying with me. It won't be as risky as you think. Be patient. It will all work out."

"You sure?" Ted asked.

"I'm sure." Kyle smiled.

It was that automatic, plastic kind of smile Mark had come to expect from Kyle, the smile politicians are capable of flashing whenever a camera appears. But there was something about his eyes, a vacant quality. That empty look of pathos made Mark realize for the first time they were in trouble. At this point, he had no idea what to do about it. It would not help to have more conflict with Kyle right now. He had to wait.

The three men agreed, Mark reluctantly, hesitantly, but he did. Mark felt in his gut that it was a mistake, but considering the options without much money and no solid plan of their own, there was no other real choice. Fleeing willy-nilly was not the answer. They were stuck with Kyle.

27.

Adrift in a delirium from the aftereffects of passion, Butch and Cathy had their naked bodies pressed together in restless sleep. Windows were open to let a fresh breeze push by the curtains and carry the night air across the room. The air was cool and moist, and it flitted about their faces before touching the skin so lightly it could barely be sensed. Certainly not by these two satisfied lovers, their energy spent, their senses suspended for the time being as they languished in their own dream-world.

The blast from the Brentwood Pumping Station bomb created a shock wave that hit the apartment building before the thunderous noise roared over them, jerking them awake with a severity that sucked reality from them, impairing their ability to reason what had occurred. There was the smell carried by the shock wave that identified a bomb, but Butch couldn't grasp that yet. He rolled out of bed instinctively, yelling for Cathy to do the same, and crawled to the dresser where he had left his pistol. What good would that do? It didn't matter, it was an instinct. Cathy was beside him, crouching, naked and shivering, unsure of anything.

"That's our boy," Butch said through clenched teeth. "Damn. What the hell would he bomb that's so close?"

Cathy shook her head, partly in response to Butch and partly in disbelief.

"Get dressed. We have to get moving before the madhouse sets in."

"What do you mean?"

"Police, fire crews, FBI, news crews, gawkers…it's going to be a mess."

"The office. We can work there and better keep in touch with what is going on."

She stood there looking at his naked body and was torn by the trauma she was feeling and the desire to touch him. She went to him and they held each other and she trembled from all of the emotion that whipped through her and from the cool night air that danced on her skin.

"Get dressed," Butch said, again.

The shock wave that had reached them was devastating to buildings closer to the pumping station. Directly across San Vicente, the glass in all of the apartment windows facing the street was blown out; curtains, drapes, and blinds shredded and gone. The landscaping was in tatters as plants, bushes, and small trees were savaged and blown away. The five closest buildings to where the catering truck was parked sustained structural damage, but were left standing. This was fortunate for those living there, but especially those on the upper floors of the apartments. All along San Vicente, within one-half mile in either direction, there was damage. The two largest Coral trees in the boulevard closest to the blast had every leaf stripped from them.

There were two vehicles passing by at the time of the explosion, one headed west and the other eastbound. The large SUV headed east was closer and received full effect of the blast. It was blown onto its side and into the boulevard section where it slid on the grass for thirty yards across to the westbound lanes, turned over onto its top and smashed into a tree. The driver, a Brentwood attorney, was critically injured, but still alive when rescuers got to him.

The westbound car, a Saab convertible, was bounced from the left lane to the right lane, over the curb, and into a tree. The young woman driving the Saab was traveling in excess of forty miles per hour at impact. She lived for a short time, but died before rescue workers could get her extracted from the crushed car.

As Butch suggested it would happen, pandemonium took over as fires broke out and there was no water pressure in the hydrants to feed the LA Fire Department pumper trucks. Those pumpers had to depend on water that they were carrying. The call would go out for more pumpers as the numerous fires gained advantage.

Much like the Coleridge poem said, there was water everywhere, but none to use. Water gushed from the totally demolished Brentwood Pumping Station and ran in all directions, flooding the Brentwood Country Club golf course behind it, out onto the streets, and with steady, multi-plumed white geysers from within the devastated ruins of the Station.

The catering truck itself created various sized pieces of deadly shrapnel that were impaled in trees and walls, and scattered for blocks around. A single woman jogger was a victim of the shock wave that violently knocked her to the ground. She sat on the curb several hundred yards from where the station once was, crying, thanking anyone who would listen that she was lucky to be alive. She sobbed as she told of hearing pieces of something, some kind of materials fly by her as she was flattened by the concussion. She could not be consoled and cried on her cell phone for her friend to come and help her. She eventually let police take her to the hospital.

This area, this neighborhood, was home to many influential people in politics, movie production, the entertainment industry, and business. A great mass of cell phones were scrambling to connect, jamming the wireless circuits. The calls were of complaint, for action, for help, for information, to relay messages, to report, and to bring a monumental concentration of news media to the scene.

First on the scene was the LA Fire Department, as was usually the case in times of disaster. First call the fire department, then call the cops. The cops are never to the scene first, they drag in later. The first Fire Department commander to reach San Vicente and Gretna Green knew right away his guys were in trouble. Eight serious fires were already in progress and it was going to get worse. He called in alarm Two and five minutes later notified communication that an alarm Three was needed and be prepared for Four. People were screaming from their apartments and other dazed citizens wandered about trying to figure out what had happened. They all seemed to be in their pajamas and robes with many in silly fuzzy slippers of some kind and an assortment of other odd footwear.

Fire Captain Keith Reynolds tried to stay calm as he spoke into his radio asking for police help right away. He was told the closest patrol car was four minutes away. It arrived eight minutes later and that officer had no idea what to do. It would be another fifteen minutes before an adequate police presence was available for crowd control and to help with injured and the other victims. For the first hour after the bombing, it was a frenzy of wasted wild energy in terms of dealing with the situation. This was a neighborhood in shock, authorities stunned, a dumbfounding lack of coordination, and with no idea at all what to do about the water that continued to flood the area.

That was the San Vicente, Gretna Green situation. The substation on the hillside up above, less than a mile and a half away, let go within one minute of the Brentwood Pumping Station explosion, its sound ignored by those overwhelmed down on San Vicente, but still an awful factor for those nearby. Parts of condensers, transformers, relays, switches, and other metal components were hurled in all directions. Those hot molten pieces, traveling at near ballistic speed, caused structural damage to nearby houses and shredded landscaping. They also started numerous fires. High tension lines cut loose from the substation whipped back towards the last transmission tower and slashed at houses and foliage in their path. This also caused fires to be ignited in several locations. In seconds, the canyon seemed ablaze everywhere, the fiery tentacles darting toward multi-million dollar homes, unchecked, persistent, and primed to race for miles if they were not held at bay.

Most of the nearby fire fighting resources were headed for San Vicente; this canyon calamity was not yet recognized. The fire was going to burn for awhile and it was going to take a significant number of houses in its path.

It is uncertain which explosion happened next, the Fairfax electrical tower or the substations in Santa Monica and on Centinela. Regardless, they all occurred in less than one minute of the San Vicente blast.

When the Fairfax tower came down, three people in automobiles and two pedestrians were killed immediately. Two others died later as a result of the collapse. The tower had staggered for a few seconds after the four bases were cut loose by the explosives as the electrical lines it carried secured it momentarily. It broke free and dropped onto Fairfax with a rending of steel and a crashing of glass and plastic from automobiles and trucks and store fronts. Neon signs exploded, plate glass windows cracked and flew apart, and pieces of debris hurled through the air with strange whistling sounds. And then it was quiet save for the moans of the injured and the brief jagged squawks of security alarms. The quiet was short-lived before people started screaming and running around crying and yelling for help. The topmost section of the tower fell into the Department of Water and Power substation yard across Fairfax and destroyed several transformer sections that exploded and sent additional shrapnel into the surrounding neighborhood. The area immediately went dark.

Snapped power lines had whirled around like whips cracked for amusement, throwing sparks across the cityscape as if they were fireworks on the Fourth of July. Several roofs began to burn and a serious conflagration was underway. Traffic snarled in seconds with rear-end collisions and a succession of fender-benders jamming streets in all directions. Hoards of people came from nearby apartment buildings to see if they could be of help, but the turmoil was so great it was difficult to determine where to begin.

With the loss of electrical power, the impact on the power grid was immense. Rolling brownouts and outages occurred as the computer controls in the grid jockeyed service, made adjustments, and struggled to restore power. There was, however, a large section of LA dark and powerless. Hollywood Hills, Studio City, and Encino struggled with the outage as well as other communities west of downtown LA and into the hills dividing Los Angeles and the San Fernando Valley.

The loss of the Santa Monica substation was another serious blow to the California power grid. Even though block walls and a chain-link fence contained some of the blast effect, the concussion of sonic forces and flying debris still brought destruction to surrounding structures. Every window in the Denny's across Lincoln and the restaurant across Colorado were blown out and their walls were pitted and penetrated with shards of steel and masonry. Significant damage was in all directions and suddenly most of Santa Monica was without power. An area instantly zapped to darkness. And loss of modern conveniences. A world that would struggle to cope.

Coping was essential for police and fire departments, and plain average citizens. Homes went black, at least where there had been lights on; restaurants were plunged into temporary darkness until emergency lighting snapped on, street lights were off; traffic lights stopped functioning; and security systems went dead.

At St. Johns Health Center, it was not more than seven seconds before the powerful generators of their standby electrical system kicked in, so that a very brief crash of darkness was experienced. There were a few gasps by patients and staff alike, but no panic and business-as-usual continued. Fortunately, none of the operating rooms were in use at the time, but even if they had been, things would have gone on smoothly. St. Johns could function indefinitely on the emergency power system as long as the generators were supplied with diesel fuel.

The last placements to let go were at the Los Angeles DWP substation on Centinela. The results here were probably more devastating than any location other than the pumping station on San Vicente. The hurling outward from the blasts of dozens of large, molten pieces of metal created a rain of destruction beyond anyone's imagination. Fires were ignited in homes and commercial buildings in a frightening circular swath around the epicenter. It created panic and injury and, ultimately, death. And it brought darkness that brought despair and desperation and deprivation. Few around here knew what this was all about and few would have cared about Kyle's cause if they had known. Now, hundreds of thousands across southern California were without electricity.

The consequences of the five nearly simultaneous bomb blasts were that emotions went from the initial chaos and panic to confusion and frustration, and finally, to anger. Subsequent news stories in the LA Times, New York Times, and the national news weeklies were in large measure vignettes of the eye-witnesses, the survivors. Each story was a defining moment for the individuals as a result of the disaster which had taken place.

Nestled in the comfort of his favorite overstuffed chair, Myron Kallman was sipping iced tea, watching the National Geographic channel on his new HDTV. He was sitting in the den of his apartment across San Vicente from the pumping station, his back to the windows which face the street. Fortunately for Mr. Kallman, when the unexpected blast occurred he was protected by his chair. Glass, fragments from the windows, and shrapnel from the catering truck were carried by the sonic wave against and around the chair, but not into him. He did not escape injury, however, as the chair was hurled violently across the room and against the wall. His right wrist and elbow were shattered, the forearm broken in three places, nose smashed to one side, and the orbital bone by his right eye, cracked. His forehead was badly torn open and bleeding profusely, as was his nose.

When Mr. Kallman regained consciousness, the room was dark and he could hear sirens of all kinds screaming nearby and whining in the distance. He felt lucky to be alive. He tried to move, realizing he was on the floor against the wall with his chair on top of him. Still caught in shock, his pain was not yet a reality. When he moved his right shoulder and arm to extract himself from beneath the chair, pain rushed in with an excruciating pulse that almost made him pass out again. He knew he was injured badly, that his right arm was useless, and could feel the blood running on his face from his forehead and from his nose. He could taste his own blood and it was an odd sensation to him, one he had not experienced since he had been a teenager in an auto accident. This was not the first time his nose was broken and his head split open.

He turned on his left side and inched his way with a series of otter-like moves. At eighty-three, through the intense pain, Mr. Kallman made a gallant effort to free himself. He was able to sit up, but could not see much of anything. There was not the normal glow of street lights he was used to when all of the den's lights were dark. He could hear yelling, but not what was being said and it was meaningless to him. He kept wondering what happening. How could this be? Then he remembered there was an emergency light in the hall closet. Could he get to it? He would not try to stand up just yet. He would crawl using his left arm, letting the right arm hang loosely and drag along. He felt along the wall for the doorway opening to the hallway, moving slowly, fighting the inclination to pass out, gritting his teeth against the pain, and questioning if he could make it. He had to make it.

His cell phone rang. It was in his right pants pocket. He rose up on his knees and using his left hand, slid the phone up until its small antenna poked out and he could pinch it. He was able to thumb it open. I never knew I had such left-handed dexterity, he thought through the blur of pain. The lighted screen told him it was his daughter, Miriam.

"Miriam?"

"Poppa, you okay?"

He took several seconds to answer. "I'm alive, if that's what you mean. Otherwise, I'm not okay."

"I heard the explosion…"

"Nearby…I don't know. Its dark…no lights. No lights outside. Lots of sirens and yelling. Something happened, I don't know what. I know I hurt…"

"What's wrong…?"

"Lots of pain…a lot of pain…"

"What…where…"

"Can't work my right arm…hard to breathe. I think my nose is broken…my head is bleeding…"

"I'll get there as quick as I can…"

"Where are you?"

"Jerry and I are at Schoen's house…"

The call was dropped, the phone silent. He punched in her speed-dial number, hit send, and nothing happened. That was that, he thought, and returned to the agonizing process of trying to get to the emergency light. It was there, on the first shelf. He could feel it. He pulled the light to his chest and felt for the control. Flick, it was on, and he could see back through the hallway to the den and some of the damage. He crept back to the den on his knees, pushing the light along on the floor, balancing with his left arm, and finally got to the front of the apartment. It was a war zone, he thought, if ever there was a war zone it looked like this. Everything, and that was everything, in that den room was destroyed. Pictures on the wall were smashed and trashed and thrown to the floor.

And the art work. Paintings and prints were mashed together in a corner. Every piece of collectible studio glass was broken and scattered.

Mr. Kallman wanted to weep, his body racked with tears, a way of releasing the volatile feelings contained within him, but he resisted the release. He registered the emotional pain balanced against the physical pain that held him in a vise of morbidity and knew he was going to survive. After all, he had endured much worse. It was a price he had paid, that he was paying for being alive. For others of his age and circumstance had died without reason in brutal conditions so long ago. This he could deal with, this he could overcome. Whoever the bastards were that did this, they would be caught. And they would be punished. He was sure of it.

Billy Pierce rode the fire-rescue truck that was quickest to the scene at San Vicente – Gretna Green, in front of Mr. Kallman's apartment. What he saw stunned him, scarred him emotionally, projected him to some relieving plateau that removed him from the pain, the suffering, and the devastation he viewed. He was cutoff, outside of what others saw and felt, and able to function without reaction. Billy had some idea of what happened, that the bomber who struck in Riverside County was now at work in his territory, and that all of the nonsense he had been watching on the TV at the fire station and at home had become his nonsense. He had taken it on in his mind, wishing he could be there helping the situation, wishing there was something he could do. Little did he know that the circumstances of need for help would come to him, that he would be faced with far more than what was experienced in Riverside County.

Billy had been making fire-rescue runs for twenty-four years. This would be the worst run of all, worse than the earthquake of 1984, worse than any training video he had seen, worse than any scenario he could have imagined.

He was the first rescue person to get to Myron Kallman. He had heard cries from the apartment building where Mr.

Kallman lived. Random screams, yells for help, and some heavy-duty swearing from someone. Billy took the stairs two at a time, his rescue-aid bag smacking against the wall as he charged toward the sounds. Mr. Kallman was slumped against the wall near the doorway of his apartment. It was as far as he was able to get before Billy broke open the door.

"Hey, you okay?"

"No...I'm not. My cell phone doesn't work. Why? Why is it my cell phone doesn't work? This is when I need it. I got cut off from my daughter, They tell you, 'Look, you buy this thing and its good when there is an emergency.' Well, let me tell you, this is a real emergency and it doesn't work. What's going on? What happened? Was it that bomber guy they showed on television?"

"We have no way of knowing, Mr.... What's your name?"

"My arm is broken, my wrist, my shoulder...it's awful. It hurts very badly. Can you help me? Get me out of here?"

"Yes, yes I can. Let me get a stretcher up here and we'll get you to a hospital."

"Cedars," Mr. Kallman said emphatically, "I want to go to Cedars...Cedars Sinai. That's my hospital. My doctor, Aaron Mishbaum, practices there. It's the best. Get me there. He'll know what to do."

"Take it easy," Billy said in his best comforting voice. "We'll take care of you."

Billy kept Mr. Kallman calm until a stretcher crew hauled him away to a waiting ambulance that took him to St John's Health Center.

Billy continued his search of Myron Kallman's apartment building. Mr. Kallman had been lucky, others were not so fortunate, others who were in the building while the additional residents were out for the evening, out of town, or away on business. The man who was cursing had both legs broken and could not see, although Billy could not tell if he had been blinded. The woman who had been screaming was passed out when Billy got to her badly burned body. She was lying in her living room, mostly nude, her nightdress and nightgown torn away from her by the shock wave. She was bleeding profusely from the many fragments that had pelted her body. She was in critical condition and in balance as to whether or not she would survive. No one was killed initially in any of the apartment buildings across from the pumping station, but the injury toll was horrendous and the injuries were severe. The death toll would come later.

As Billy exited the apartment building, he was more than ankle deep in water that surged from the pumping station. He had not realized it until now, but Mr. Kallman's building was on fire as were the buildings on either side. He heard someone yell that there was no water pressure just as more fire fighting equipment arrived.

"This building is empty of people as far as I know, "Billy yelled at the battalion chief. "We've got the survivors out and no one was home in the other apartments...as far as I could determine."

Billy stumbled towards the boulevard just as the front of the apartment building next to Kallman's fell away and collapsed into a heap of rubble. He did not know who was checking that building, but he ran towards where the front entrance had once been. He intended to get inside and see what was going on there. The explosion that flung Billy all the way to the street was enough to bring the entire structure to a staggering release as it fell away from its standing and smashed into the buildings on either side. Its sudden upheaval threw others tumbling and its flying debris seriously injured rescue works, reporters, and the inevitable onlookers fascinated with the horror of it all. No one was killed, but the injury toll more than doubled with that aftereffect incident.

Billy could not see and knew he had been struck blind. Someone was talking to him, he sensed, but he could not make out the words. He reached out, water washing over him and in his nose and mouth, and realized he was on pavement; the street probably. What was the person saying? He couldn't tell. He got to his knees and tried to stand. He could not get up and fell forward onto his hands, splashing through the water. Someone helped him to his feet, talking all the while with words he could not understand, and got him removed from the scene. He sat in an ambulance, unaware of the other victims who would travel with him to St. John's. For the first time he could feel the pain that racked his body, pounded in his head, and he could now hear ringing in his ears. He still could not see.

LA policemen Justin Bryce and Lonnie Flowers had just stopped for coffee on Santa Monica Boulevard when the bomb detonated at the pumping station. They heard it, did not know what it meant, but knew it was trouble of some kind.

"We'll get a call," Lonnie said sassily when Justin looked at her after the sound. "We'll get a call if it means anything. I want my coffee...I need my coffee." She slumped in the booth where they sat, hoping against hope that the sound meant nothing.

Justin's two-way sounded in less than two minutes. It was the call from dispatch. Get up on San Vicente, all hell had broken loose.

Siren blaring, Justin drove north on Bundy just as fast as he could make the cruiser travel. Jerking through the Montana intersection as he adjusted for traffic made Lonnie's coffee spill across the front of her uniform.

"Can't you..." she started to say as the car bounced again.

"Emergency. Hang on." Justin was a demon driving to the scene of the bombing at San Vicente and Gretna Green.

Lonnie brushed coffee from her jacket and pants, and hung on as the cruiser raced north.

They were not prepared for what they saw. Driving on San Vicente towards the epicenter of the blast brought more and more destruction and pandemonium into view. They had no clue what their first action would be when they got to the scene. Nothing they had learned, none of their training had let them know how ravaged a neighborhood would be from a terrorist bomb. That, they decided quickly, was what this was all about. The terrorist had to be Kyle Dixon, they assumed. Justin figured he was in the process of blowing up southern California. That's what he would do…blow us all up as much as he could.

The most shocking part of their first vision on encountering the blast scene was the flood of water that coursed every which way. Water was running away in the San Vicente gutters, but not fast enough to lower the level in front of where the pumping station had once stood.

Justin parked the cruiser a block from the main aftermath section and they slogged their way through the running water to where a fire captain was directing his men battling the blaze in Mr. Kallman's apartment building. They seemed to be on the verge of getting it under control. That's when the gas explosion next door threw flames and building sections at them, and refocused the attention of the firefighters doing combat with the various blazes.

"Jesus Christ," Justin yelled, "look at that guy. He's on fire."

They rushed to Billy and slapped out the flames that had ignited his clothes. They got him to his feet and helped him away from the turmoil of survivors, rescuers, and onlookers. Out of the water onto the boulevard and to safety. An ambulance had just pulled up and they got him loaded and to a hospital.

After they had Billy in the ambulance, they went back to the corner where the action was intense. Justin found the fire captain who seemed to be directing all of the fire fighting and rescue efforts.

"What do you need us to do?"

"Get the water turned off. Get us some juice. We're shit out of luck without hydrants to hook up to. All water has to be trucked here to fight this. Get somebody to stop traffic on San Vicente back at Wilshire. Get the gawkers out of here. Get us room to do our jobs. And tell the Governor to activate more national guard if he wants to keep order here so that rescue can go on, fires can get knocked down, and that insurrection doesn't take place."

"Aaah...roger that," Justin said hesitantly.

He called dispatch, but no one responded. He waited a few seconds, tried again, and again there was no response. He waited, looking at Lonnie, checking out the fire captain, and tried again. This time dispatch answered.

"What's happening where you are?"

"We need lots of help. Traffic guys have to lock off San Vicente, we need control officers at intersections, detectives to talk to witnesses, and someone needs to tell the Governor that Guard troops are necessary to keep things under control."

"Casualties?"

"Who knows? What the hell difference does that make right now...?"

"Chief wants to know..."

"Tell the son-of-bitch it's critical and that's what he needs to know right now."

"Will do," the dispatcher sighed. "Stay safe."

Justin looked to his right and could see the glow of fire inside another building.

"Look at that...the fire up there. I don't know how they're going to fight all of the fires going on without water pressure. Pumping station gone, they're screwed."

Lonnie did not know what to say. She could see the flames flickering in several apartment buildings.

"Let's try to get other survivors to medical help," she said. "It's all that we can do, I guess."

By now, hundreds of area residents had streamed out of their houses and apartments to find out what had happened and view what could be seen. With the power outage, only emergency lights illuminated the grisly sight, surreal with their elongated shadows deep and foreboding, ominous in their own right, certainly emphasizing the horror of it all. The surrounding flooding did keep the throngs of people from crushing toward the center of the action and closer to the lights, but still made it even more difficult to deal with the crisis.

It would have been a crisis for the average person, but these affluent neighbors were not average, they were instead, an elite privileged crowd who would have difficulty bearing up without electricity, without water, and unable to function the way they would like. It was a situation difficult to deal with for most, ghastly for these folks.

The crowd of onlookers peered from the darkness, trying to see what was going on, their view dim and distorted of the scene the portable lanterns and spotlights presented. For some the realization came that they were now victims of that maniac bomber who struck in Riverside. From one to another it was said and his name was passed about and he was cursed. The questions flew with the intense resentment. How could he think he was helping anything by destroying? Many had read his declaration in the Times, had heard the words repeated on television news, both local and national, and they knew of his claims. Kyle Dixon was not the leader of a revolution for enlightenment of the environment. He was the vilified maniac who was trying to destroy us. Like some kind of Greek chorus, the somber epithets of condemnation were spoken by many at the same time, a wave of sound that washed over the crowd and incited stronger curses of complaint.

Chico Gomez sat on the curb, his head in his hands. He could barely speak, but he tried to tell Lonnie his story when she found him there. He pointed to the Honda Prelude sitting in the middle of San Vicente.

"I think I die," he said to her.

"You're going to be all right," she said. She recognized he was in shock. "Come sit in our patrol car, then you can relax, be more comfortable."

"No, I sit here."

"Okay, okay. Just take it easy. Did you see the explosion?"

"Si, I did." He moved his head from side to side still holding it with his hands.

As the crowd of the curious milled about, Gomez was finally able to tell Lonnie that he had been headed west on San Vicente to deliver a pizza. He saw the flash, there was a loud noise, and his car was hit with flying debris. Not knowing what else to do, he stopped his car. She noted the smashed windshield. Some piece of something had hit the lighted delivery sign that had been on the roof and knocked it away. Parts of it were later found in the street behind where the car sat. The Prelude had not been in great condition before the blast, but the pelting it received had turned it into a pockmarked and thoroughly battered junker. After Gomez had given his story to Lonnie, he calmed down and went to look over the extent of damages to his car. Someone had taken the pizza.

Among the anxious horde of onlookers were reporters and news people of all kinds. It was a news bonanza for all of them. As a result, there were literally hundreds of gripping personal stories recounted in succeeding days. They ranged from the heart-rending accounts of individual losses to the stern, sterile scientific recitation of injuries, wounds, and medical treatment. Anyone who lived within a mile felt intimately affected, within two miles vitally involved, and if you lived west of the San Diego Freeway this was your own disaster. Much could be said for those who lived in the same relative proximity to the Fairfax explosion. It was yours, it impacted your life, and it was very, very personal.

At another time and place in history, after the reward posters had been nailed up, Kyle Dixon would have been hunted down like the mad dog he was by a posse of irate volunteer citizens. They would have caught him and they would have summarily hanged him on the spot. The more benign anger of these Angelinos would not accommodate such an outcome even though some of them thought about how it might have been and what they would like to do.

28.

Kyle Dixon slumped in a white painted wicker chair on Sol Jacobs' patio as he faced the small, overgrown enclosed backyard. One light from inside cast an odd pattern of brilliance across the grass and onto several of the Oleander bushes. He rattled the ice around in his glass. For the first time his thinking was splintered by the nasty sharp point of self doubt. Perhaps his mission might not be successful; that he could not change minds and attitudes. Perhaps there was no way to turn the unwieldy juggernaut of self-indulgent society away from wasting the land and its resources, to be better custodians of their environment. He wasn't so sure and he was terribly bothered by that fact. He sipped his Dewar's and admired the Oleander and tried to shake off his doubt

He kept checking his wristwatch, waiting for the sound he knew would come. At ten thirty and fifteen seconds, he sensed the shock wave even before he heard the tremendous concussion. His reaction was tantamount to that of a composer hearing his music played for the first time. He was awed by its power, for him a magnificent sound of success. He had wanted to be nearby, a witness this time. To feel its power. He had missed the other bomb blasts in Riverside County, the logistics making that impossible. This was sheer pleasure for him. He had planned, calculated, built, and delivered. What he had wanted to take place, had happened. He forgot about the glimmer of doubt that only a few moments before had penetrated the shell of surety he had developed, doubt lost in the fever of success from his ability.

Mark was the first of the others to come outside.

"Goddamn, that was loud. Did you know it was going to be like that?"

"The Hinds placement was like that, but we weren't there to hear it. The newspapers said it was heard a long way away. It will be interesting to see how far away this one is heard."

"That isn't our goal," Mark said. "To see how far away our bombs can be heard."

The house had gone dark even before he had spoken.

"That took care of that," Kyle laughed. "The substation is gone. Too bad we can't hear the reports from Fairfax. It's got to be bad there. This will get everyone's attention. Plenty to deal with. Just like my letter to the public said, there has to be an awakening. This should do it. This should bring people to realize what this is all about. We will have the masses on our side at last."

Ted and Ellis came outside.

"We move on?" Ellis asked. "Eventually they'll get here, too, won't they?"

"Oh, probably. With that private detective working overtime, he'll get here or at least determine the connection and sick the law on us."

Using flashlights, they systematically gathered their belongings and loaded the car.

"I'll drive," Kyle said.

"You still insisting on seeing your mother?" Mark demanded.

"Of course, we are going to St. John's so I can see my mother. I want to see my mother before we head out. We went all through this issue."

"Your mother…" Mark started to say.

"What about my mother?"

"Nothing," Mark said. "It's just that she knows how capable you are…and…and she's smart. She can figure out you're okay and that you have to be on the move." He was hoping he could still change Kyle's mind.

"I know that's true, Mark, but I want to see her."

"Let's just hope we don't get caught because of this" Ellis said.

"No, we won't. There is so much commotion going on with casualties being brought to the hospital that no one will pay any attention to us."

"What do you want us to do?" Ted asked.

"You work as lookouts. We're going to be armed. We may have to defend ourselves to get out of there. I don't think that will be the case, but we have to be prepared."

"I say this going to the hospital stuff means trouble," Ellis said, shaking his head.

"I need to see my mother," Kyle snapped. "Everything has worked out so far. Stick with me on this and we'll be gone."

"Seeing your mother in the hospital was not part of any plan," Mark said with bulging neck muscles. He was voicing the frustration fueled by his doubt.

"It is now," Kyle hissed at him.

"We might…" Ellis was nervous.

"There is so much confusion we won't have a problem. Cops have their hands full, FBI is chasing its tail…we'll be okay. I talk to my mother and we're on our way."

"Where…?" Mark asked.

"I told you. We leave by boat. We cruise away to be safe and secure. Don't worry."

"Where is the boat, where do we go? Why the mystery?"

"You'll see. It will all work out."

Upstairs, lying helplessly in the dark, Barry Walker did not need witnesses or television news or anyone else to inform him of what occurred. The men had left and he heard them return. It was all very simple to understand. The bomber, Kyle Dixon, with his flunkies, had struck again. This time the consequences would be worse than his previous attacks.

This time, more people would be effected, and in ways far more devastating than before. He could hear their voices off somewhere. There was a bit of yelling, then muffled conversation, and again the drone of debate. Side to side, issue by issue, a conflict of some kind took place among the men downstairs.

He had been so foolish coming here, so naïve, so unmindful of the potential consequences of dealing with this guy Dixon. He should have been careful, he had not been, and he regretted it. I should be pounding out a story about this by now, he assumed. I should be in a position to reap the rewards of getting so close, of sensing his whereabouts. I should be pulling back to compose the description of what society was up against. Fools rush in and I have been a fool. He wondered if he would live to tell about it. He was tired and weak, he was dreadfully thirsty and the angry pangs of hunger dug at his belly. He had no food or water for hours.

The voices were silent. Had they left again? He held his breath to better listen for the slightest sound. Nothing. They were gone.

Kyle parked the car on Twenty-First Street, up the block away from St. John's. He got out and started walking towards the hospital and the others dutifully followed. He turned, pushed the door lock button, heard the qualifying tone of security, and headed up the street. No one said a word and they proceeded in a bunched group. Kyle led them around the complex until they reached the loading dock. They waited until the lone security guard was distracted inside and moved quickly into the facility.

There was, in fact, tremendous commotion taking place within the hospital, the public address system continued to bark instructions and make calls for doctors and staff. No one paid any attention to them. Kyle headed up the first stairwell they encountered and exited onto the second floor. He went to the first nurse's station he saw.

"Can you check on Mrs. Krause?" he asked the nurses' aide who was sitting behind a computer terminal. "I'm Dr. Ferris, I'm in on consultation and not sure where she is."

"Dr. Ferris?" the woman said slowly. "I don't know any..." She was looking past him at the other three men.

"Yes, from Santa Barbara. You wouldn't know me. These are family from up north and I'm trying to give them some..."

The woman had looked away and entered an inquiry into the computer. "Four seventeen, Dr. Ferris."

"Thank you, thank you." Kyle nodded with a wave of his right index finger and moved to the elevators.

The woman stared after them for a moment and then went back to her work. The man looked vaguely familiar, but she could not place him. There was shouting down the hall and she quickly forgot about Dr. Ferris and the other men.

The elevator would be too slow and Kyle pushed back into the stairwell and took two steps at a time going up to the fourth floor. Mark, Ellis, and Ted dutifully followed.

Doris Krause had survived the two gunshots, weathered the operation to keep her from bleeding to death, and now suffered the pain of recovery. She was a strong, resilient woman, determined to match the trauma and pain with her own brand of tenacious courage. She had the ferocity of a middle linebacker and the mentality of a big-game hunter. She was not a woman to be taken lightly, although pain and drugs had subdued her to some degree.

Kyle's wife Laurie was there at her bedside, holding Doris' hand and daughter Kelli and son-in-law Kevin were at the foot of the bed. The last person they expected to see was Kyle. His entrance was emotional from a variety of perspectives. He went straight to his mother to embrace her and kiss her lightly on the cheek. Laurie was stunned, dropped Doris' hand, and stepped back. Her shock held only for a brief moment.

"What the hell are you doing here?" Laurie was red faced. "Right now there are dozens of people, maybe more, streaming into this hospital in need of care because of you and your crazy goddamn scheme. What's wrong with you...?"

Kevin gripped the footboard of the bed in a tight grasp without saying anything, but wife Kelli let fly.

"You bastard, you betrayed us. After all we have done for you. Raised money, directed donors your way, kept your books... And you do this shit? Bomb people? To what end, you idiot? I trusted you, I..."

"Shhhh, please, shhhh, don't yell. It's done, it was an important cause, people had to wake up..." Doris coughed and gasped a bit. She needed a drink and Laurie, the attentive nurse, responded quickly.

"Mom, you don't condone what he did, surely?"

"Well, I think that his cause is worthy..."

"Of course it's worthy, but Mother, he's killed people. People died tonight, people are critically injured, and more people could die."

"I know dear, but..."

"This is insane. He can't do anything wrong in your eyes, can he?"

"My son is brilliant...brilliant. He has..."

"Oh stop, this is ridiculous..." She headed for the door.

Kyle stepped between her and the door and they eyed each other intently. She with red-faced rage and he with the cool demeanor of one disengaged from reality.

She looked closely and knew he was functioning in another state of mind. She backed up, away from the door, and sat down. She too became calm and under control. Kevin leaned back against the wall beside her. She felt in her pocket for her cell phone and traced her thumb over the raised numbers, working the picture of their positions in her mind. She recognized number six, pressed it, found send, and pressed it. She had called up nine-one-one. She had no idea if what she had done would do any good, but it was the first thing to come into her mind to react to her brother and the fear she felt about him. She didn't know what else to do. She did not know that Laurie had already triggered the nurses' call button.

The light blinked at the nurse's station and the on-duty LPN headed for Doris' room. She was stopped midway down the hall by Mark. He was not sure she had been called, but his intuition told him so. Otherwise, why would she be in such a hustle?

"Who called?" he asked as he stepped in front of the rotund woman charging to her assigned duty.

"Mrs. Krause..."

"...four-seventeen?"

"Yes, but..."

"Its all right, I'll take care of it. I'm one of her sons."

"Oh, all right...thank you." She went back to the nurse's station to complete a form she was working on when she was interrupted.

Mark walked quickly to four-seventeen and inside, the door shut behind him.

"Someone pushed the call button," he said. "Someone who wants to get hurt."

Laurie looked at him with contempt that would have killed him if such mind power were possible. She glared.

He saw her look.

"You…you did it, you bitch…"

Kyle held up his hand to Mark as if to say "stop I'll take care of this," and he turned to Laurie.

"Did you push the call button?"

"Yes," she snapped.

"If you do that again I will shoot you. Now, sit down…there."

Kelli and Kevin were immobilized with fear, her brother's disconnect from reality fully clear to them. They believed he was capable of killing all of them.

"You need to understand what all of this means," Kyle said quietly.

His calmness made them even more frightened. Kelli did not respond, she would not.

Doris had her eyes closed, distraught from her children's conflict. She motioned to Kyle. He did not see her at first, but Mark nodded to him in the direction of his mother.

"What?" he was solicitous with her.

"Please don't argue, don't fight. They don't understand what you are doing. Just go ahead…" She stopped talking; tired, frustrated, and unwilling to change her support for her wonderful son.

This was a situation none of the others would have wanted to transpire nor thought in their wildest imaginations could come to pass. They all waited for Kyle to speak, to alleviate the tension.

Not more than six blocks away, Butch and Cathy sat in her office at Gladstone International.

"Let's put the TV on in the conference room. We can get an update that way. You'd think that maybe Fuller or Chacon or someone would touch base with us. Why haven't they?"

"Their hands are full. We're the least of their concern right now. You have their cell numbers in case we want to talk to them?"

"Yeah, right here." She pointed to her notebook.

"This is worse than what happened in Riverside County. The golf course is flooding, water is running like rivers on San Vicente and Gretna Green. No power anywhere around here. What's our standby situation?"

"We're good for days. So is the hospital. Bad for most everyone else."

"Fires burning all over the place. He wanted to cripple the city and that is what is going to be the result. Crippled and limited in its response. No one, for sure, able to go after him."

"If you're right, he's around here someplace watching his handiwork. Where?"

Butch stood in the center of the conference room staring at the television news. Cameras were showing live pictures from Brentwood. Chico Gomez was being interviewed.

"It was awful, man. I think I going to die…"

"This is Chico Gomez," the reporter said, "eyewitness to what occurred here tonight. Tell us, Mr. Gomez…"

Butch pushed the MUTE button.

"He was with his mother, then he disappeared, but he didn't go far. He stayed somewhere that was connected with her. She made it possible for him to hide out. Someone she knows, maybe a…a…"

"Friend?"

"Man friend, maybe. Who would that be? Someone she knows well enough to send him and the other jerks to for protection. He'll move on to a hideout. He knows he can't stay here in Santa Monica."

"She's really covered for him…"

"Right, and he would want to see her before he headed out, and he will be heading out and away someplace. He won't want to face the heat…the real heat."

"St. John's," Cathy said. "His mother is right around the corner in St. John's…two minutes from here."

Without another word they exited the office, the building, and were in the Lexus making the short trip to the hospital. It was a slug of a drive, an agonizing attempt to make time, and to avoid getting bogged down among the mass of vehicles pushing to get to the same location. Two blocks from the hospital, Butch parked in a strip mall, and they started walking. Butch set a brisk pace and Cathy was able to keep up with him. In a few minutes, they were in the lobby. It was a madhouse.

When he was finally able to get some help they determined that Doris was on the fourth floor. The elevators were jammed. He and Cathy ran up the steps.

"This is the workout we've missed," he said as their effort made them breathe heavily and sweat break out on his forehead.

Kyle hugged his mother and she quietly wept, the odd tear lines streaming on her cheeks. She patted his back. He pulled away from her and kissed her cheek. He could taste her tears and the sensation gave him a brief, very brief, feeling of melancholy. It was a feeling he was not used to and the uncomfortable reaction startled him for a moment. But he said nothing and shook it off as he might have brushed a fleck of lint from his clothing.

"Talk to you later," he said. It was a reassuring tone, one that was intended to calm her fears.

He motioned to Mark and they went out the door.

"You bastard," Kelli screamed after him. "You think this is like some college prank? You've killed people. You'll pay…"

The door slammed shut.

"He has to pay, mother, there will be consequences. How, in God's name could you support him, help him, agree with him?" She was enraged. "He used you…us. We all tried to help him and this is the result. He is a mass murderer…and an idiot to boot."

Laurie leaned against the window and sobbed. How could she have known that it would turn out like this? Kyle had made such sense once, a long time ago. Now, she had no idea who he was.

When Butch and Cathy reached the fourth floor there was less pandemonium. The hospital functions seemed to be carried out in a routine way. They made their way to the central nurse's station.

"Yes, I'm looking for Doris Krause's room."

"Four seventeen, but the room is full right now. All of the family is there…"

"All…?"

"Yes. Her daughter and son-in-law and her sons."

Butch pulled out his cell phone and saw that it was not getting a good signal. He went down the hall away from the central core and the signal improved.

"What is Chacon's number?" He gestured for Cathy to look it up in her notebook.

As she said it he punched it into his phone. He got Chacon's voicemail and left a detailed message.

"Miss," Butch said, addressing the young woman behind the counter. "Call the police, keep calling if you have to…if you can't get an answer at first. Tell them that the bomber, Kyle Dixon is here in the hospital."

She gasped.

"Go on, call. Keep calling if you can't reach somebody."

"We're in Santa Monica," Cathy reminded him, "you need to call Terry Gross." She looked up his number, punched it into her phone, and handed the phone to Butch. Gross answered.

"Gross, this is Butch Greiner, we met earlier. I'm here at St. John's with Miss Simon. Kyle Dixon is here. Yes, visiting his mother. I know, but…"

Butch was silent for several seconds. He snapped her phone shut and handed it to her.

"He says wait for the cavalry…a SWAT team. Don't confront…wait. Keep the room under surveillance until they get here. Damn…"

"Miss, where is four-seventeen?" Cathy asked.

"Down that corridor," she said pointing. "About half way. Please be careful."

"We can see the doorway from here," Butch said. "We can hold our position and see what happens."

As they moved down the hall toward Doris' room, Butch motioned her against the wall.

"Get ready…this may be another tough situation…"

"I am ready."

After a period of waiting and watching, guns ready, hands sweaty, Butch checked his watch.

"Six minutes have gone by. He's already gone."

He holstered his pistol and strode to the room where Doris Krause lay crying. He pushed the door ajar. Better be safe. A woman was holding Doris' hand and brushing her hair with her hand. Butch did not see Kyle. He pushed his way into the room and Cathy followed, her gun still drawn, at her side. She holstered it as soon as they were inside the room.

"How long has he been gone?" Butch asked.

"Ten minutes," Kelli said as she continued stroking her mother's hair. "He's out of his mind…who knows what is next."

"You are?" Butch said."

"This is Mrs. Krause, she is…"

"You are?" Butch said again.

"Kelli…Kelli Rothstein. I'm Kyle's sister. His ex-sister," she emphasized.

"Always the sister," Butch said, "that's something you can't change."

Doris was weak, but she was still feisty, and she despised the fact that Butch was after her son. In her mind, the efforts that Kyle was making were sincere and socially important. She believed in what he believed in and stood for in the environmental movement. She would not relent, she would not apologize for him and, surely, she would not accept Butch as authority to contain her son.

"Let him be, he has done right." Doris said the words through parched lips and with a somewhat swollen tongue. She was angry, she was without capacity to think clearly. At this point, she could be very hostile.

"You are…?" Butch directed his attention to Kevin.

"Kevin Rothstein. I'm the son-in-law and the brother-in-law. And I know this is a damn mess and I know that Kyle will not be dissuaded. He is a law unto himself, he is a…"

"Kevin," Kelli yelled, "shut up. This man will sort things out, he doesn't need you to set…"

"Lay it on me Kevin," Butch interrupted, "give me the story. About Kyle."

"He is self-righteous beyond anything I have ever seen. Black and white, ugly and beautiful, he sets the conditions for how and what will be qualified. He thinks no one in society is doing anything right, so it has become his crusade to right the wrongs to our environment. But it is not a crusade as such, in terms of an analogy. In my mind, it is a vendetta, strokes of vengeance like some omnipotent power who says no matter what, I shall bring the sword of justice to bear. My evaluation, my judgment, and my justice. He is a complete megalomaniac. Check with his shrink, he can tell you."

Kelli looked at her husband and shook her head. Doris was stiffened with an apoplectic fit of rage that would have, could it have been extended and acted out, certainly suffocated Kevin.

"Did he say anything to you?" Butch asked Laurie.

Laurie had shrunk to the background throughout all of the encounter with Kyle and with Butch. She was so traumatized, so helpless in her observation of what was taking place. She was a ghost figure, unnoticed by Doris or Kelli or Kevin or Kyle. But Butch could see her clearly, cowering in the corner, trying her best to be invisible. Long ago she had divorced herself from the man Kyle, emotionally extracting herself from their relationship, and yet willing to maintain a connection with this ridiculous family for the sake of her children. Although, she still had feelings for Doris. Doris was the grandmother, Doris had been very supportive of her, and Doris was willing to champion her cause with the celebrated son who could do no wrong. She knew Butch wanted her to say something, she could see it in his face, knew he wanted her to react. She was numb. She was rendered almost speechless from what had transpired. She did not know if she could even talk.

She shook her head, no.

"Isn't that a bit strange?"

She nodded.

"Where is he going to escape?"

Laurie stared at him blankly.

He turned to Kelli. She knew the question was also directed at her.

"I have no idea," Kelli said. Her voice was husky from wanting to cry, but she was determined to be in control as long as her mother was.

Butch looked at Kevin.

"What do you think?"

Kevin shrugged, collected his thoughts, and put his brain in motion. He stared zombie-like.

"How would they know?" Doris sobbed, "Kyle told us nothing...I don't know. You didn't ask me."

You wouldn't have told me, so I didn't bother."

"I've been trying to figure out," Kevin said, "how Kyle thought he could get away with doing what he has done. I thought maybe in his twisted mind he thought he would be a hero to the hard core environmental crowd. That he thought he might somehow not be punished. I guess only his psychiatrist would have the answer to that. You know..." Kevin was working on something. "I handle his books. There have been a number of strange checks written recently. Maybe one of these..."

"For what?" Butch asked quickly.

"Let's see. I don't remember exactly. They were to a couple of companies. Plus, some other smaller amounts to individuals. Smaller amounts, but still fairly substantial..."

Like how much?"

"Thousand, two thousand. I have no idea what any of that means, but I...I thought it might mean something. It's the only thing different recently that I would be aware of. Any checks to a person or company in Newport Beach previously were to Alan Simmons his psychiatrist, so I was surprised by these. Most other checks were written to someone or a company in Riverside County or down in Fallbrook."

"Alan Simmons?" Butch repeated. He motioned to Cathy and she made a note.

"Yes, those were fairly regular over a long period of time."

"Mrs. Krause," Butch turned to Doris, "where did you send Kyle to hide out? He wanted to use your gallery, but we upset those plans. Where did you send him? He had to be someplace, some home, some warehouse or whatever where he could hang out until he placed the bombs. Someone you knew…a friend or acquaintance. Where was it?" Butch was intense.

"Mother," Kelli gasped, "what did you…"

"Shut up," Doris choked out. "You can all go to hell."

"I didn't think you'd tell me, but I thought I'd give it a try. Which of your mother's friends might be a good possibility, Kelli?"

She pursed her lips and wrinkled her brow as she thought who it might be.

"I think it could be Sol Jacobs," she said softly after a few moments of concentration. "He would be the most likely candidate."

"Who is he?"

"Sol is mother's special friend and he's out of town for a couple of weeks. His house would be the perfect place for them to hide. It had to be Sol's house. Of course it would be Sol's house."

"Where is his house?" Cathy asked.

She intoned Sol's address to Butch as if she were reciting her drivers license to a traffic cop.

"It's not far from here, actually."

Kelli then slumped in her chair with the frustration and disgust she had for her mother's complicity with what her brother had done. She was devastated and wondered if she would ever recover from this and whether she could ever forgive her mother.

"Leave him alone," Doris screeched with the breathy, tragic voice of despair.

"Yeah, right. Get well, lady, you'll need your strength to stand trial for being an accomplice in all of this. The government will want your hide. Count on it."

"He has others with him, Mr. Greiner, be careful," Kevin said. "I don't know how many, but I think at least three."

"Thanks for the warning. We will be careful."

Butch turned quickly and left the hospital room with its usual smell of healing flesh and bad breath and bodily functions, and the stench of family dysfunction that was very difficult to explain. Cathy followed him and knew they were going to Sol Jacob's house. Butch had that direction action about him and she knew she had to hustle to keep up with him.

29.

The lights dimmed, flickered, dimmed again, and then regained full power. Los Angeles Mayor Leon Megradosa paused for a moment to look over at the hostess as if to ask, "what's wrong here?" and then went on with his expounding. He was holding court at a small dinner party of friends, political cronies, and several strong financial backers who were seeking a return on their investment. There were thirty-five guests, a small group in terms of many other LA parties, especially political gatherings. Mr. Mayor was in fine form telling how he would handle the situation he figured the Governor had mainly botched. The subject was partisan, he was partisan, and he had all of the answers. At least it seemed he did when they heard him blather about how and what he would have done. His cell phone rang and that call would change everything for him. It would be a shocking dose of reality as an aide explained that all hell had broken loose in West LA.

Megradosa was a short squat man, with powerfully toned muscles. He was an avid body-builder, intelligent, well-educated, and with exuberant energy that flashed from his exciting smile. He had graduated from Southern Cal in the top ten percent of his class and immediately put his political science degree to work. Within twenty years he was mayor of one of the largest cities in the world, directing and decreeing, appointing and naming, finagling and dealing, and working as hard as he could to stay in power. He had a great deal of help. What he heard on his cell phone would put everything he had worked for at risk. He suddenly wished he had not downed two well-made margaritas. Con sal. He adored the taste of the salt against the lime background. He wanted a third, but had resisted the temptation when the waiter had come by just before the cell phone call.

Before he responded to the aide, he shook his finger in some sort of gesture even he didn't understand, but was supposed to mean that "I've got to move away where I can talk." Before he spoke, he walked to the side of the room where no one was engaged in conversation. He was in the palatial Hollywood Hills home of Harvey Bergman and it was Harvey's wife, Gloria, who recognized his need for privacy. She casually led him away to Harvey's office. She closed the door behind her as she exited. The lights dimmed and flickered again.

"What the hell are you saying?"

The young woman on the other end of the call took several minutes to explain about the bombs and the power outage, the water running in the streets, and the terrible loss of life.

"How many have died he asked dispassionately. It was not a matter of caring or not caring, it was simply a way to chart the extent of how bad this thing would be for him. High death count equaled big problems and a more difficult reelection campaign.

His phone rang again as soon as he punched off. This time it was the Fire Chief and his report. Phone off and it rang immediately. Now, the Police Chief and his report. Phone off and it rang and it was Governor Calish.

"What's your plan?" Calish boomed into his ear.

"My plan is to get to West LA as soon as I can get there. Assess the situation and make the decisions I need to make…"

"I've already called out more Guard troops and I have ordered martial law to be in effect. We can't have loonies running around wild or criminal types taking advantage of what's going on."

"Don't you think you should have talked to me before you acted. I'm the Mayor, after all. You're overrunning my powers to…"

"Oh stuff it, Leon, this is a crisis. Bigger than you. Where are you heading?"

"Its somewhere on San Vicente. I'm leaving now…"

"Too bad to break up the party. I'll meet you there."

LA was not unprepared for disaster. After all, this City of Angels had withstood several serious earthquakes. She sustained tremendous earthquake damage in 1994 and action plans were in place for all of the city's agencies. The suddenness of the attack was still a surprise, but the reactions were structured, steady, and undaunted. Personnel from the City, the Department of Water and Power, and police and fire departments were already pursuing assigned tasks before the Mayor had been told what had occurred. The 'what ifs' had been documented and planned for, and the 'how tos' were underway.

Water was turned off to the Brentwood Pumping Station and flood waters began draining, running away like a giant bathtub unplugged. There was a sloppy residue that remained and dirty water stains would show for days, but the rescuers no longer slogged knee deep in water. The water to fight the fires came from the pumpers alone and they fought a gallant battle to get under control and eventually doused what could have been a conflagration. Fires in the hills were another matter.

Loss of electrical power was another critical component of the cascade of problems. There would be no electricity to large sections of LA and Santa Monica for days, and, even then, service would be spotty with periodic outages. Short-term, the power grid was affected as rolling blackouts and brownouts persisted for more than twenty-four hours, but the system eventually righted itself and control was restored. Long-term, there was considerable work to be done to get new towers erected and lines strung.

Los Angeles quickly became a militarized zone that included check points to restrict vehicle and foot traffic in and out of the major effected areas. LA police were, according to their plan, in place to control traffic where signal lights were not working. The complexity and magnitude of the results of the bombings were almost incomprehensible, but first responders were efficient, dedicated, and patient as they dealt with an angry and frustrated public. This was a public caught in a tangle of dead and dying victims and those injured who were seeking care. And then there were the bewildered and frightened elderly, folks least able to withstand the shock and trauma and cope with the deprivations.

Kyle Dixon had achieved the results of his mantra, "they shall suffer and the suffering shall serve notice of what is required." The suffering was intense, but it is doubtful anyone viewed this as a clarion call to environmental awareness. The public only wanted him to be caught and punished. The condemnation of death being too good for him was widely expressed.

Television and radio crews jockeyed to get the best locations, and reporters scrambled to get the best and even better stories. Like buzzards surveying carrion, then picking it apart morsel by morsel, the news media sorted through, finding the grisly and the mundane, and seeming to extract emotional agony from either.

Governor Calish arrived on the San Vicente scene first and the media quickly converged near him as if he were some powerful magnate they could not resist. Mayor Megradosa was soon on the scene playing catch up to the Governor, hating the fact he had been relegated to second banana in his own domain. Let the Governor screw around in Riverside, who cares, but not here in LA. What Megradosa failed to heed was that Calish was also in reelection mode. Visibility and positive press were key. There was nothing quite like a full-scale disaster and the succeeding crisis to provide free exposure that would save millions in campaign dollars. Just don't blunder.

The Governor sloshed through the water like General MacArthur returning to the Philippines and his pants were soaked to mid calf. Megradosa trailed, wishing he were not wearing a twelve hundred dollar tailored suit and four hundred dollar hand-made Italian shoes. They stopped on the boulevard across from where the pumping station had once stood and looked over the damage all around them. The cameras were rolling, microphones open, and reporters yelling. Calish held up his hand. The media gaggle quieted. Like some prophet of old, ready to address his minions, the Governor was in command, and commanding. He spoke very calmly and quietly for emphasis.

"I have already ordered California National Guard troops to be deployed here and in other locations and I want to assure everyone listening and watching tonight that order will be maintained, that services will be restored quickly, and the needs of everyone directly effected will be addressed."

He went on for another seven or eight minutes, allowing Megradosa to suffer silently in his secondary role before relinquishing the attention by complementing the Mayor on the city's action plan and asking him to say a few words. The Mayor was complementary in return and thanked the Governor for all of his help. Since both men were from the same political party there was less acrimony than could be expected if they were not.

"You can be confident my fellow Angelinos," the Mayor continued, "that an intensive manhunt is underway right now to locate and apprehend Kyle Dixon. Although we do not know for sure these bombings tonight were his handiwork, his signature is apparent, and he is a logical suspect. His letters to the media indicate that he conducted the Riverside County bombings. We have no reason to believe that anyone else other than Kyle Dixon conducted these bombings tonight. We will catch him…we will catch him. Now I know that this is not the only area suffering. In the hills behind us where power lines went down, people have lost their homes and are also without power or water. The area of Fairfax and the I-10 is also in turmoil with fires and lack of electricity.

Santa Monica has a problem with no electricity. So many of us are in difficulty tonight, but we will get through this just as we have done with the earthquakes we have endured. We will get through this with your help and cooperation. Thank you and thank all of the many rescuers and responders."

There was no applause. People standing nearby were too stunned to respond in any way. There was still too much work to be done, injured people yet to get transported to medical facilities, and too much damage to allow spirits to be moved by the words from two disconnected leaders who would walk away and go home to the usual comforts.

Kyle could hardly have conceived of the havoc that he would create. He, too, was disconnected from the realities of everyday lives, caught as he was in the disjointed, fractured reality in which he conceived his mission. Even as he fled and listened to the radio reports, he could not imagine the extent of the catastrophe he had presented Riverside County, Los Angeles, Santa Monica, and other Southern California locales. He had meant to send a message; he had instead sent the angel of death. He had wanted to create awareness of his cause, but he brought devastation and anguish and the loss of life and property. Misjudging society is the crime of malcontents and revolutionaries, as well as misguided leaders, and all of them wonder why they are misunderstood. Pushing society to change with violent means is a clear miscalculation of the people's tolerance for nonsense and forcing sacrifice where it is not required.

Governor Calish and his entourage of limos and SUVS went to a friend's house in Holmby Hills, which he used as his command center for several days before returning to Sacramento. He was not one to drink alcohol, but instead had a large dish of strawberry ice cream and a slab of deadly cheesecake courtesy of the local Cheesecake Factory. For him, all of the bombings in Southern California were an opportunity to show off and flex his political muscles. The situation arrived at the right time for him. It was an advantage and when an advantage falls in your lap, you grasp it and triumph.

Mayor Megradosa sullenly rode away in his limo and police escort and got back to the Bergman house right after the last of the other guests had gone home. He and his wife Louisa and the Bergmans poked at and only half ate a late night snack of corned beef sandwiches and pasta salad which the Bergman cook prepared for them. For the Mayor, all of what had transpired was a nightmare. He was sincerely concerned for the victims. He knew that he was also a victim and could not help wondering what this would do to his career. His inner thoughts were wrapped around his feelings that it is all a terrible shame - for him. He had another margarita. Con sal.

30.

Trying to make sense out of what had happened made no sense at all. Butch was frustrated, but encouraged. He felt as if somehow they were closing in on this maniac. What was interesting to him was that although the authorities had all of the information available to them that he had, they were unable to move with dispatch or expediency from one step to the next. They were lost in bureaucratic nonsense that diluted focus, shifted manpower, and eliminated thoughtful deliberation on how this bozo could be run to ground. Those failures were compounded by the manpower problem that now existed for the Los Angeles and Santa Monica Police Departments, the FBI, the LA County Disaster Management Authority, and all of the other authorities affected by Kyle's onslaught against southern California. Too few were trying to do too much with too little resources. The trail of damage and the needs of recovery were so extensive that it seemed chasing after Kyle was almost an afterthought to the authorities who should be after him. It was not, of course, but that is what it looked like to the uninformed observers that included most of the media.

Investigations were quietly, deliberately moving forward and whereas, at first, only Kyle's photo was shown on the television newscasts, his three accomplices were identified and their photos were now included. The "band of four" is how the media described them. The current state of public awareness and notoriety was not in the context that Kyle intended. He was fully willing to accept martyrdom to achieve the results he wanted for the cause which in turn meant he would be credited with forcing society to change. To be branded a killer, a menace, a pariah to be hunted down and judged was an anathema to him. He could not reconcile himself to that low status and could not understand how that had become the result of what he had done. It was, in his mind, critical to talk to Alan Simmons. It was his good providence that Alan already was part of the plan. He knew they had to move quickly; the damned detective was getting close.

Butch was close. At one point, only several hundred feet apart as his entrance and Kyle's exit took place at St. John's. The irony would have been stunning to either of them had they known. Butch drove with Cathy to Sol's without that knowledge as he groped to find answers to Kyle's whereabouts. Sol's place might give some answers.

"We need to touch base with Gross again and then Grant. If Gross has SWAT action directed at St. John's it's too late. They need to be put on ice for the time being."

"How about Jacob's house?"

"If that's where they really were operating from they won't be going back there. They're most likely on their way to the start of Kyle's escape plan…whatever that is."

"Seems eerie without any of the lights on," Cathy offered.

"It is indeed and far from safe."

The headlights from the Lexus cut a wide band of visibility in front of them as they carefully headed for Jacob's house, but on each side and behind them was darkness. Other cars were on the move, their headlights stabbing at the night, casting shadows that bounced through the trees and on buildings like some strange creatures rampaging. Who were these other people, Butch wondered, what were they doing, and where were they going? Trying to get home from somewhere, most likely, worrying about what they would find in their own homes. Would they be lucky enough to have electricity where they live? They probably don't even know there might not be water.

"It's ringing." She handed the cell phone to Butch.

"Grant, this is Greiner again. Call off your SWAT guys, Dixon is gone from St. John's and so are we. We're headed for Sol Jacob's house. He's a close friend of Mrs. Krause,

Kyle's mother. Out of town and we think this is where they holed up to set tonight's bombs. We're on our way there now." Gross wanted to send the SWAT contingent. "Don't bother, they won't be there. Better send some lab folks if you have any available." Butch read the address from Cathy's notebook and closed the phone.

"Well?"

"He's pissed that we're out in front of him."

"Figures," she sighed.

"Grant also needs to be brought up-to-date, pronto. We have to keep the FBI in the loop. Besides, they're the ones who are eventually going to be the long arm of the law. With so many jurisdictions involved only the FBI can take the lead after Kyle."

Cathy got Grant on the phone.

"Mr. Grant, this is Butch Greiner. Yeah, you bet, quite a night. In so many ways you can't imagine."

He looked at Cathy when he said that and she smiled in a way that excited him. He felt a bit guilty about that self-indulgence in the midst of such chaos, but that's the way it was and there was no changing or reconciling what was.

"We tracked Dixon to St. John's Medical Center in Santa Monica. He went there to see his mother…we missed him. He's on the run. We think they used a guy's house here in Santa Monica and we're on our way to check it out…see if it gets us anything. I've alerted Terry Gross, SMPD, recommended he get lab people there, but you might want to do that also. Friend of Kyle's mother. I'm betting they didn't go back there. I know, I know, there are so many crime scenes you're stretched thin, but this place would be important to dust and examine. Okay, we'll be careful." Butch closed the phone.

"What did he say?"

"Don't touch anything."

"Gee, that's helpful."

"He also said thanks for the call."

"It's the next street," Cathy pointed. "Turn left."

There had not been another car for several blocks. The neighborhood was quiet and dark, although here and there the flicker of candles and the dancing beams of flashlights and other emergency lights gave a surreal quality to things. Butch parked the Lexus in front of Sol Jacob's house near the end of the driveway. They got out of the car and stood there waiting for the automatic headlights to turn off so they could adjust to the darkness. The lights turned off and they continued their wait. Even after several minutes it was difficult to see much.

"I'm starting to see more," Cathy said quietly.

Butch nodded without saying anything and unholstered his Glock.

"Keep waiting?"

"Yes."

"I can see pretty well. I see the gate…the wall."

"Okay," he said.

They went up the drive to the gate.

"We can't get in this way. Let's work our way to the right."

Much as Barry Walker had done, they followed the fence around to the side. Butch used the small high-intensity flashlight he had carried with him to aide their progress, but clicked it off as they surveyed the house and assessed the situation.

"Cars in front," Cathy whispered.

"They left what they didn't need," Butch whispered in return. "They're in one vehicle. Let's check out the place."

"Not going to wait for the Santa Monica police?"

"When do you think they'll get here? They have so much on their plate; God knows when that would be. My guess is the FBI gets here first."

"Wait for them?"

"No." He went to the front door. It was unlocked. He clicked on his light and entered with Cathy quickly following.

Visitors had used this house; there was no doubt about that. They were visitors who didn't give a damn about being tidy and knew they would not be graded for neatness. Bits and pieces of all kinds littered the den, kitchen, and living room; trash that included fast food wrappers and bags, used napkins, half-squeezed condiment packets, plastic utensils, and beer bottles. Wine bottles rested where they had been finished and empty wine glasses were on tables in each of the three rooms. A large bottle of Dewar's, cap off, was on the kitchen table.

"Let's check upstairs, see what kind of damage they did there."

Cathy stayed close to Butch as they climbed to the second floor. Just to be safe, he shut off the light so they would not be good targets. They groped their way upward, step by step. At the top, Butch stopped and listened. He could barely see vague shapes and door openings. He clicked the light on again and they checked out the bedrooms one by one.

In the master bedroom the light flashed over Barry Walker. He was still alive, but unconscious.

"Help me get this tape off of him," Butch said, as he moved quickly into the room. He placed the light on the dresser so that it shone on the inert body.

Cathy carefully picked at the tape around his face as Butch worked at the ankles and knees. Walker did not move. She was trying not to tear his skin, but the tape had been on long enough so that it had a mean grip. She was able to get a fingernail under one edge, slowly easing it away as the rasping sound of release made her cringe.

"I don't think he can feel it," Butch said, "get it up some more..."

She did and Butch slipped the blade of a small pocket knife between skin and tape and cut it apart.

"Now, just pull it away."

The ripping noise was excruciating. A raw, red welt began to form across Walker's face and he groaned in pain. He blinked several times and his eyes went shut. Butch cut the rest of the tape binds and pulled them loose. Walker's wrists were almost as raw as his face.

"Now what?" Cathy asked. "He needs medical attention."

"Call 911, see if there are any units available."

She punched in the call and waited. There was no response.

"Overloaded...everyone is calling 911."

"You grab his ankles, I'll get him under the arms and we hoist him downstairs as best we can."

"He stinks," Cathy said as she realized for the first time there was an awful odor about the man.

"You would too if you were tied up and couldn't get to the bathroom."

"Yuck."

"It's not like on TV."

"I know, I know."

Butch pulled Walker into a sitting position, put his arms around the man from behind, and locked his fingers together. Cathy took an ankle in each hand. They pulled him from the bed and he hung like a hammock between them.

"Damn."

"What? Oh, the light."

"Put his feet down while I hang on and move the light into the hall."

Cathy took the flashlight into the hall and placed it on a small table in such a way so that it would not fall to the floor. She grabbed the ankles again and they took Walker to the top of the stairs.

"Same routine. Move the light downstairs so that it shines up in some way."

Cathy bounced down the stairs with the light and placed it at the end of the banister. She took off one of her athletic shoes and put it on top of the light so it could not roll.

"It's not shining up the stairs, but…"

"That will work," Butch called to her.

She bounded back up the stairs, took firm grasp of the ankles, and slowly they eased Walker down, step by step. Each of them was leery of losing balance, starting to fall, and dropping the man to keep from getting hurt themselves.

"Not easy carrying dead weight," Butch huffed.

"I know, and I'm scared of…"

"Don't say it. Take one step at a time, nice and easy. We'll make it, just hang on to those ankles. It won't take long."

It seemed like it took forever. A sweaty, agonizing forever with Walker moaning and groaning throughout the ordeal.

They laid him on the floor by the foyer and he continued with odd sounds, but did not open his eyes. Butch opened the door and they were greeted with the flash and jump of lights out front. There was the sound of car doors slamming and excited voices talking. Cathy grabbed her shoe and brought the light to Butch.

"Who is it? Are they back?" Cathy asked, a catch of excitement in her voice.

"No, it's either the Santa Monica guys or the FBI. There has to be a button here to open that gate."

Butch took the light and swept the walls of the entry area as Cathy knelt down to slip into her shoe. There it was. A panel with a speaker and two buttons. He first pushed what he thought was the speaker button.

"Who is it?" he said into the panel and released the button.

"FBI. Is that you Greiner?"

Butch pushed the other button without answering. The gate motored back away from across the drive allowing Toby Grant to trot toward the house followed by two other agents.

"What did you find?" Grant demanded as his greeting.

"Trash and bottles. And a body."

"A body."

"He's alive, but he needs medical attention. He's unconscious. They had him all bound up with gray tape, even across his mouth. He's a mess; couldn't get to the bathroom, of course. We tried 911, but they didn't respond, so we just now carried him downstairs. We were going to take him to the hospital…"

"Any wounds?"

"Not that we could see. We only had this flashlight."

"Did they beat him?"

"I don't think so. Here, take a look."

Grant and the agents moved into the foyer.

"Keep trying 911," Grant directed one of the men who nodded and went outside to use his cell phone. "Check for ID?"

"No, we just wanted to get him help as quickly as we could," Butch said.

Grant felt underneath Walker on the left side in search of a wallet. It was there and he tugged at the pants pocket to get it free. After a few moments of squeezing and pulling, he had it in his hands.

"Here we are," Grant said. "Let's see...Barry Walker...a reporter for the LA Times.

"Am I dead?" Walker asked with slurred speech, one eye open. The blurry, crazy moving patterns of intense light and awkward, jarring shadows made him squint the one eye.

Cathy knelt beside him. "No, but you need medical help, I think...and a shower."

"I haven't had anything to eat or drink for hours," he mumbled. "I could use some water..."

"They're on their way," the agent said as he came back inside the house. "They're strapped for units, but they'll do their best."

Without a word, Cathy took the light Butch held and worked her way to the kitchen. She quickly returned with a half-liter of bottled water. She cracked the cap off and knelt down to see if he could drink. She tilted the bottle alongside his face so that he could turn his head and sip. He was too weak to sit up.

"That helps," he whispered. "Thanks."

"Did Kyle Dixon tape you up?" Butch asked.

"The jerks with him...three guys..."

"Doesn't look like they roughed you up any," Grant offered.

"No, no, the three fools he's got with him suddenly grabbed me, carried me upstairs, and put the tape on me."

He sipped more water.

"I feel real sick," Walker moaned. His eyes rolled back and he was out again.

"I wanted to ask him if he heard anything; like where they were headed." Butch said. "He might have heard something."

Grant was looking around flipping his light here and there, muttering to himself, trying to assess what could be accomplished here. The two agents traced his meanderings of light and they too voiced odd comments about what they saw.

"Neal, call Homan and see if he can get a gen set here, pronto, we need lights on this crime scene. Get some Santa Monica cops here to close it off from reporters and souvenir hunters. And get hold of someone in the lab and let them know they have to work this place."

The two men went outside to use their phones. Grant shined his light on Butch.

"Okay, smart guy detective, you're the visiting fireman. Give us some enlightenment from your advantage of vast experience and expertise. Where the hell is this asshole headed?"

"I appreciate your high regard for my capabilities, Grant, but I'm as much in the dark as you. No pun intended."

"That figures."

"How did you get here so fast?" Butch asked.

"We were on the move this way. Check out the other situations. Lots of problems. Your call came at the right time."

Walker was conscious again and tried to get to one elbow. Cathy gave him more water and now he was better able to drink.

"Did you hear them talking? Did they say where they might be headed…discuss any of their plans?" Butch hoped for the best, but it was not to be.

"I didn't hear anything like that. They hauled me up on that bed and taped me up and never were around me again. Sorry, I can't help you."

"You must have been tracking him. Was there any information you uncovered that might indicate how this guy thinks he can get away?"

"No…I don't think so."

One of the agents came inside to announce that an EMS crew had arrived.

"That was quicker than I thought it would be," Grant said. "They'll get you to the hospital. You'll feel better when you've been cleaned up and get some food in you. We'll get a statement from you later. You just get your strength back."

"Thanks," Walker moaned.

With the assurance they had for their ability, the two EMS techs flipped him onto a gurney with all of the alacrity of soccer players kicking home a goal. Likewise, they wheeled him to the ambulance nonchalantly, and whisked him away to St. John's.

"That's a whole other story with that reporter," Butch said to Grant.

"I'll say. Like I said, we'll get to him later. Right now, we've got to find this guy Dixon. And you're no help."

"I think we're going to pull back and review what we know. We'll head back to the office and figure our next move. We'll stay in touch."

"No ideas?"

"None."

"Get out of here. I'll talk to you later."

Butch and Cathy found their way to the Lexus and made the careful drive to the office. National Guard troops were already at the major intersections and here and there lights shone in office buildings on Olympic Boulevard where generator sets were in place and operating. Lights were coming back on where emergency systems had taken over and the bleak darkness that prevailed earlier was now superimposed with random and selective lighting. It was still an eerie view, strangely lighted buildings and the constant overlay of weird shadows that wrapped around the Santa Monica cityscape.

Once in Cathy's office, having struggled through manual security checkpoints in the Gladstone building, Butch threw himself into a chair and pondered the next move.

"You're sulking," Cathy said.

"I know."

"Quit sulking, it depresses me."

There was quiet for several minutes before a Eureka moment struck him.

"Alan Simmons…"

"Kevin talked about Newport Beach and the money spent there and the fact that the connection in his mind was Alan Simmons."

"And?"

"That's where he's headed with the other three bozos. Somehow Alan Simmons…wherever he lives in Newport Beach is the destination for the escape plan…"

She was already searching for Simmons' address. It flashed onto her computer screen.

"That was quick…here it is…Alan Simmons address. My, my, high rent district…"

"Of course it is and that is where we are headed. Kyle is already on his way. Call Grant and let him know. Tell him to use whatever it takes to get men there."

"What is Dixon going to do?"

"I have no idea. Maybe Simmons has a boat. Note the phone number and we'll call him on the way."

"It's a long drive."

"Damn it, everything is a long drive in southern California. Why should this be different?"

31.

No one said a word for a long time. They passed National Guard barricades, unlighted intersections, and block after block of houses and businesses without electrical power. The results of their efforts were dramatically in place. Kyle drove as if nothing had happened, devoid of emotion, centered on where they were going and what they would do. Finally, it was time to move on. He rejected the term "escape." They were rather, in his mind, reassigning themselves to a new location where they would not be subjected to criticism or the judgment of the ones who could not understand. After all, understanding what was at stake was at the very heart of the issue he was presenting. One must realize what must be done before acceptance can be made for the steps to be taken to change society. No one seemed to "get it" and he was frustrated. His letters to the Times should have clarified everything, but they had not seemed to do so. Why? Why? He could not understand the reluctance of people to "get it." He could not relate to modern society and did not want to relate. He was the conspicuous outsider wondering why he was not inside, although pretending not to care. He cared, and he resented his outsider, alienated, and disregarded position. A fleeing monster who would be hunted down and brought to justice.

Traffic on the Freeway was light. TV and radio news reports had stressed the importance of staying put, staying in your home. Minimize Freeway congestion so that emergency vehicles, police, fire, and other authorities could get to critical areas and take care of the terrible situations that confronted southern California.

"It sometimes takes time for people to realize what is necessary..." Kyle was pontificating.

"They're thinking about survival right now," Mark snapped. "With no water and no electricity, they're thinking about how they will cope with the situation at hand. They are not thinking in grandiose terms of how their deprivation meets your lesson plan for the masses..."

"Oh, shut up. Did you think this was going to be easy? Of course not. We draw back, let people assess the situation, understand what is at stake, and we get recognized as champions for what is right. People understand right. What has been going on is not right. You know it, I know it, and everyone knows it is not right. The wrongs...they will know we are trying to right the wrongs."

"I don't know how they will know..."

"I have another letter...a position paper, and they will understand."

"And in the meantime, we need to evacuate the area. Don't you think?" Mark never looked at Kyle when he said it.

"That's what we are doing."

Kyle eased over to the diamond lane through sparse full-flowing traffic that was less than typical volume for this time of night. He punched on the radio.

"...right now the scene in west LA and Santa Monica is desperate. Fire crews from other districts of the LA basin are racing to the effected areas with equipment to aide in all of the fires that are now burning out of control. Helicopter water tankers are being mobilized for drops in Mandeville Canyon where there are several fires burning out of control. We have a reporter on the scene at Fairfax and the I-10 Freeway and she says...it's our Molly Minturn...that conditions at that location are under control, but still serious. Several businesses are on fire and the fire has spread into the surrounding neighborhood. We've lost contact with Molly, but hope to get her back on line as soon as we can. In the meantime, we've learned that the flooding at San Vicente and Bundy is under control, the water level is going down, and rescue crews have evacuated everyone they are aware of who needed help. That's some good news on a night when bad news and disaster is the norm. We'll break here for some messages from our sponsors and then be back with more coverage on the night that brought LA to its knees. Stay tuned."

Kyle turned off the radio.

"They have no clue where we are," Kyle boasted. "Onward and upward."

He kept the speed steady at eighty miles per hour in the diamond lane as they sped south to Newport Beach.

For Mark, it was if he were in the front car of a roller coaster, without control, holding on for dear life, and knowing for sure that he would eventually fly off the rails into space. And certain death. Ellis wasn't sure what was happening, but he still had faith in Kyle. Kyle had everything planned, everything scoped out and arranged so far. He surely would have their getaway detailed and under control. Ted wanted a beer, had to go to the bathroom, and figured if these smart guys were comfortable with what was going on, then he would relax and see what comes next.

"I gotta take a leak," Ted voiced.

Kyle immediately swung out of the diamond lane, edged over to the far right lane, and pulled off the Freeway onto Crenshaw Boulevard. He worked his way through traffic for three blocks, and pulled into a Chevron station.

"We'll all go," Kyle announced. "If there is any trouble…I mean if someone recognizes us, just get back in the car and we're out of here. Try not to shoot anybody."

The three others nodded, not fully comprehending the seriousness of their situation.

No one paid any attention to them. It was a hot night, a crowd of bikers were harassing the cashier, and nothing mattered but beer and ice and the price of gas.

Mark wondered what would happen if he simply walked away from the station, away from Kyle and the other two, down Crenshaw, into the night, and made his own way from their mess. And then what? Besides, now it was his mess, too. He got back in the car and hated himself for lacking the courage to do what he just thought about doing. They would never get away, he thought, and he was a pawn of his crazy friend driving this car.

When had Mark first thought that Kyle was screwy? He sat there wondering when it had been and why he had not acted. He did know that he was trapped in his own guilt and sense of inadequacy. At least he knew it now. When had that revelation come about?

Several hours from now this drive could not be made. The National Guard would be maintaining a lockdown over southern California essentially freezing movement of all but the necessary emergency vehicles. The freeways would be almost traffic free, save for the few Guard Humvees, delivery trucks, and authorities' cars given access. Kyle got back on the southbound San Diego Freeway, still carrying less than its usual load of traffic.

"Everyone comfortable?"

The others were silent. It wasn't fear exactly, it was something else, some tainted image of Kyle leading them to a secure, hidden location where they could drink beer, relax, and let things blow over. Neither Ted or Ellis grasped the full extent of what they had done. But they were beginning to have doubts. Their blind zeal had insulated them from what the news presented. When they watched the news on television, it was as if they were viewing the exploits of some other guys, not the results of their complicity with Kyle. After all, he had thoroughly explained what would happen and why it was important and necessary. What they saw on TV did not match the vision he had given them, so it must somehow be something else, something not of their doing. Their convoluted and cockeyed reasoning had taken them to this point. They were finding it difficult to keep the perspective Kyle wanted them to have.

"Good, because the next stop is in Newport Beach."

"I have to tell you..." Ellis began. He said the words tentatively and Kyle knew what might be forthcoming.

"Listen, guys," Kyle said, "now is not the time to lose faith. In a couple of hours we will be out of California, on a big boat, headed for a private island where we can relax, and where we can take time to recharge for the future."

"Future?" Mark said quietly.

"Yes, our future."

"How do we do this," Ted asked.

"With the help of Dr. Simmons. He has the boat."

"He'll help us?" Ellis asked.

"Of course he will, although he doesn't know it yet. But he will. He won't have a choice.

"Simmons has a boat?"

"Yes, Mark, a big boat..."

"Who is this guy Simmons?" Ted wanted to know.

"He's a shrink," Mark said. "Kyle's shrink. How did you find out he has a boat?"

"I know a lot about Dr. Simmons. Where he lives, what he does with his spare time, the women he sees...I have kept track of him over the years. I figured if I entrusted my life to him I ought to know who he was and what he was. I know about Dr. Simmons very well."

"And he'll help us?" Ellis asked again.

"Yes. He will help us."

"Why?"

"Because he wants to stay alive, just like we all do. Simple equation. Help us, live; don't help us, die. And die in an ugly way. Besides, he owes me some loyalty, some empathy for what I have struggled with. He will help us, don't worry."

The high speed of traffic on the San Diego Freeway was a bonus for them. California Highway Patrol had other worries. Cruising at eighty and no one paid any attention. Getting to Newport Beach would not take that long. The high speed, the easy flow of vehicles; it was hypnotic and Kyle dropped into the world of his own mind, into a zone few could comprehend. He had almost forgotten that the other three men were in the car with him. He was lost in thoughts of what the magnitude of their actions might be and how that would impact his constituents. There was no way to trust media accounts. Reporters were talking about how angry people were, not about how they realized the mistakes of how they lived, how they violated the environment, and how they wasted nature's resources.

Kyle left the San Diego Freeway onto the Fifty-two Freeway, eventually exiting on Pacific Coast Highway, eastbound in Newport Beach. The drive from Sol's had taken forty minutes. Unbelievable, Kyle thought, an unexpected bonus from their actions.

Alan Simmons lived in a two-story house on Bayside Drive across the water from Balboa Island. To describe the area as upscale was to understate the luxury of the homes and their fabulous setting overlooking Newport Bay. His house was designed so that from almost any room the water could be seen. There was a patio with custom-designed tiles and a pool large enough for lap swimming, which Alan did every morning. Beyond the patio and pool, Alan's possession of pride was moored to the dock that jutted into the Bay from his property. The *Paprika*. One hundred fifteen feet of gleaming white and blue yacht.

It was a boat beyond his means, one he could not afford, but one he wanted. There it was. He figured he would enjoy it as much as he could, as long as he could, and, what the hell, if it got repossessed, so be it. He worked diligently to keep the boat, and if an impending combination publishing and lecturing deal worked out he would have the boat for awhile. Taking the boat out to cruise was another matter. That required a captain and crew. They were expensive to hire even on a part-time basis and not always available. He had only used them twice since he bought the boat. He had no intention of commanding the helm himself, so he was not interested in any courses or training for power boat seamanship. That could be someone else's worry; he would merely enjoy the comforts it presented, even at dockside. Plus, he basked in the status and position it gave him at cocktail parties when he dropped words of his "big boat." into the conversation.

Alan's answering machine was screening phone calls. He had ignored them all evening. Had he received the call from Butch earlier a great deal of difficulty might have been avoided. And now Alan was upstairs asleep in the master bedroom with a naked Mrs. Nadia Jenski. She lived four doors from Alan and made the walk to his house always with great anticipation and excitement. These walks were made in arrangement with Alan and his availability. She was discreet about them and only one nosy neighbor was aware of their trysts. They had been having an intimate relationship for almost two years and she had no clue of Alan's other personal involvements with mature, needy, and sexually passionate women whom he had seduced and continued relationships. Each relationship was an integrated, self-contained, and separate adventure of his interesting and complex life. His ability to juggle his schedule so that it interdicted satisfactorily with the lives of these women was a marvel in planning, attention to detail, and memory. They all loved him and, in some confounding measure, he loved each of them in a small way.

Mrs. Jenski was a robust woman, not easily controlled once she had a couple of martinis and pulled off her clothes. She knew what she wanted from Alan and she forced delivery. Almost six feet tall, zaftig and strong, voluptuous and athletic, she could maneuver him around a bed like a calf roper at a rodeo. Their love-making had started on the first floor in the living room. It had culminated on the king-size bed. Each physically spent; they were wrapped up in some fantasy land of sleep.

Her usual program was to rise early, dress, and get home before daylight, before Mr. Jenski awoke. He was a very sound sleeper, in a separate bedroom, who gave Mrs. Jenski plenty of space to do her thing. Vlado Jenski was a professor of biochemical statistical analysis at Cal State Irvine and he understood his wife's need for freedom in living her life. Had he known what she was doing down the street at Alan's, it is doubtful he would have cared much. Maybe a little regretfully, but not a whole lot. Tonight, she would not get a chance to leave Alan's house as she had planned.

The band of four parked their car on a side street off Bayside. Kyle got out of the car first and popped open the trunk. He stepped back from the car onto the grass and sniffed. There was a sweet moist smell in the air and it was potent to him, as if he had never smelled it before. Night blooming jasmine; the odor was a special mnemonic of scenes and occurrences in time past. He looked around. The neighborhood was quiet, asleep, and unsuspecting of what was to come.

"Get your stuff," he whispered. "I'll take that other bag there…thank you Ellis, this bag is important for all of us."

Each man grabbed the duffle that contained his personal belongings. Kyle shouldered his duffle and another bag that appeared to be heavily laden with something.

"What you got there?" Ted asked quietly.

"Cash," Kyle said calmly. "The money we need to get where we're going and the bonus for each of you. Cold, hard cash."

He headed to Bayside, turned the corner toward Alan's house a half mile away, and the others dutifully followed without another word.

The patio screen door to Alan's house was not locked. Passion negated such prudence. Kyle slid back the door and the band of four entered with Ted closing the door behind them. There was faint light in the room from a squat, fat candle that was still flickering, barely dodging being extinguished by the soup of liquid wax that would soon drown the flame.

"He's in bed," Kyle said softly, "upstairs. Probably with some woman. He rarely sleeps alone."

"You've really checked this guy out," Mark said.

"I know him like a book. He has his ladies. He sleeps like a baby. I've been in and out of this place before. I know every step around the house. We'll let him sleep for a bit, then we'll get him up and get working. Take a look down there." He pointed toward the patio where they had just entered. Kyle walked to the kitchen and flicked on a small fluorescent light over the stove. There was now more ability to see. He pinched out the candle.

Ted and Ellis walked to the door and peered into the darkness. The dark shape of the boat was visible beyond the orange glow of the security light by the dock.

"Damn, that looks big," Ellis said.

"It is. It's big. It will take us where we want to go."

Kyle sat in a large overstuffed chair in the living room, a cast of light from the kitchen bouncing from his forehead.

"Dr. Simmons keeps strange hours so no one around here will be suspicious with lights on at this hour. He has a weird schedule. Understandable when you think about how he deals with the women in his life. We'll wait. You guys take it easy. Get some sleep if you need to." He checked his watch. "Hmm, one-thirty. Guess we shouldn't wait. Let's get the good Doctor up so he can help us."

Kyle went to the stairs motioning the others with him as he went. He flicked on the lights in the master bedroom and there was the naked Mrs. Jenski in a fetal position next to the spread eagled Alan Simmons.

"Rise and shine love birds. We have work to do."

Mrs. Jenski started to scream, but Kyle grabbed her face and held his pistol to her head. She choked, coughed, and did not scream.

"We have a mission that you will help us with and we need your cooperation. You do as you are told and we won't shoot you."

"Kyle you can't..." Simmons began, the sheet now pulled over him as if it gave him protection.

Mrs. Jenski did not make a sheet grab. She didn't seem to care that she was naked, she cared more about been shot. Up on her elbows, she closed her eyes and let her head hang back as if to resign herself to some ill fate. A lamb to slaughter, she had become the epitome of victim. At least on the surface.

"This is like with the KGB," she moaned. "No rights, no dignity."

"Excuse me," Kyle snapped, "you're fucking the guy down the street. Don't talk to me about dignity."

"You're a Nazi," she slobbered and saliva ran from the corner of her mouth.

"Get dressed...both of you. Now."

"Kyle..." Simmons began his plea, "this is the wrong way to go about..."

"Whoa there, good doctor, get dressed, and then we'll talk. I do want to talk to you. I want to tell you how it's going to be."

Simmons and Mrs. Jenski stumbled around the room for something to cover them, fumbled to get dressed, and bitched constantly under their breath.

"I've got to pee," Mrs. Jenski said.

"Get in the bathroom and get it done and leave the door open." Kyle was unsympathetic with her feelings and uncaring of her privacy. She was a potential threat to them.

For Mrs. Jenski's part, it was her first step in gaining control of the situation.

Mark and Ellis and Ted stood back and stared at what had taken place as if they were watching reality TV. This was, in fact, better than TV. Each of them felt it, each of them knew it, but they said nothing. Kyle was a commando king and they were following orders.

She finished in the bathroom, pulled a filmy wrap around her, and stood at attention just outside the bathroom door. Alan was dressed in slacks, casual beach-wear shirt, and in bare feet. He, too, stood ready, waiting for the next command.

"Let's go down stairs, get something to eat, and decide what we do with the mistress. By the way, Alan, how many do you have?"

"What do you mean?"

"Mistresses. How many do you have? Three…four…six…ten? How many?"

"I don't know what you…"

"Oh give me a break. I know of five women you've been screwing. They may not all be current, so that can't be the up-to-date accounting. What is it right now, besides this lovely woman. Your name is…?"

"Nadia…"

"Ah…Nadia…"

"Mrs. Jenski is…"

"Yes?"

"Mrs. Jenski is the love of my life…"

"Really?"

"There are no others as you claim."

"I know some women who will be very upset to learn that Mrs.…"

"Jenski…"

"That Mrs. Jenski is the sole proprietor of you affections."

"It's true…"

"Doctor, Doctor, Doctor…save us the denial, it's unbecoming. Now, let's go downstairs and sort out what we have to do."

Kyle led the way and the gaggle of others followed. Once on the first level, Kyle sent his three men to the kitchen to get something to eat and seated Mrs. Jenski on a sofa. He made Simmons sit on a chair in the dining room.

"If either of you makes a fuss or creates some kind of noise I'll shoot you right between the eyes. Is that clear?"

"Yes," Mrs. Jenski said, her voice barely audible.

Alan was silent.

"Well?" Kyle said, looking at him, pointing his pistol at him.

Alan stayed silent as he looked back at Kyle. He had regained control of himself after the initial shock. There he was, awakened by four men with guns, caught naked in his bed with a naked woman, a naked neighbor at that, and hardly enough sleep to overcome the previous night's adventures with Mrs. Jenski. His regained internalized control meant he could be stolid and impassive and take command of the situation from the patient. He stared back at Kyle as if he were a child who had been a bad boy and who needed a talking to. This had the effect he wanted.

"Don't look at me like that."

Alan was silent; he did not need to say a word.

"Let's talk," Kyle said. "We should talk. I'll tell you what we are doing."

"Let's go in the study," Alan said, "it's my home office."

He lied, of course, he had no home office. Alan calmly placed himself in a superior position as he hiked his butt onto the table that served as a desk and flipped on the lamp beside him. Without Kyle realizing that he had done so, he tilted the lamp shade so that the light shined onto Kyle's face as he dropped into the nearby chair. It was like some stereotypical police interrogation scene and Kyle had no clue at that point. Simmons knew full well what he had on his hands and he was stalling for time, hoping against hope that the authorities could be more efficient than they had been in the last few days.

Kyle squinted, the light darting at his eyes, and he still did not get what Simmons had done. He was so intent on what he wanted to say and do, and what he was thinking, that any other actions were irrelevant to him. Simmons recognized Kyle's preoccupation. He wondered what Kyle would do to Mrs. Jenski. If he could be clever enough, Kyle would do nothing.

"It's obvious to me, Kyle, that there are some loose ends that need to be accounted for. Why don't we talk about that?"

"The keys to the boat are where? Kyle asked abruptly.

"The boat?"

"Yes, isn't that your boat out there?"

"Ah…"

"Ah, shit. Yes. Where are the keys?"

"In the drawer over there," Simmons said mechanically. "I thought we were going to talk about you and what was going on."

Kyle went to the drawer in the table and found the keys. A tag that hung from the key ring had the name *Paprika* handwritten on one side. He eyed them for a minute and then dropped them into his pants pocket.

"What are we going to talk about? For the time being I have completed my mission. Time to leave and regroup."

"You can't escape so maybe I can help you with the authorities. You will have to reconcile yourself with the police...the FBI...all of the people who are after you. You have committed crimes that will not be forgiven lightly. Perhaps, if you put yourself in my hands, I can intercede for you and minimize the penalties that they will surely want you to pay. You are in deep trouble, let me help."

"You are going with us Alan. And now I suppose we'll have to take the neighbor lady. Or we can shoot her and leave her here."

"Shooting her is not necessary."

After he said it, Simmons wondered if maybe that might be the best result for him under the circumstances. Where was his conscience? He hated to give up Mrs. Jenski, but it might be the easiest way, considering the options.

"We have done what we had to do and although there have been a few casualties, we have not been forced to take one life in cold blood. Others have died, yes, but they were victims in a war of necessity. We don't want to shoot her. Although, maybe we should shoot both of you and be done with it and move on with our business."

"She is obviously an innocent bystander to all of this...I am the one who has counseled you and tried to help you and certainly you..."

"There are no innocent bystanders, Alan. We are all on this ride together, with this earth struggling for survival against the onslaught of man, and we all have a responsibility to preserve its existence. A duty to guarantee survival, in fact, I believe there is a charge from something superior...a demand...an order for us to make sure it continues with as little harm as we can do to it. We are all in this thing together. There must be sacrifices."

Simmons' brain was whirling, trying to think of a direction that he had not already taken with Kyle. As a patient of long standing, Kyle was, he thought, a matter of known quantity to him, a bound ledger of feelings noted and quantified, described and detailed, a man who's profile of symptomatic and idiosyncratic behavior he clearly understood. Surely he could outsmart and refocus this miserable wretch. It was simply a matter of keeping him engaged in dialogue. Through dialogue he would persevere, he had no doubt of that.

"All consequences are not equal," Simmons said with a finality that took Kyle by surprise.

"What do you mean by that?"

"There are circumstances whereby the resulting consequences of well-meaning actions are ameliorated by the overwhelming importance of what motivated what was done. Yours is such a case. Everything you have done in the preceding weeks and months was the result of your firm belief that it must be done for the good of society. Justification abridges consequences."

"Which means?" Kyle stared at him.

"You say to the authorities, look, I did these things, but I did them for the betterment of mankind. There is a higher purpose for what I have done. Hear me, Kyle, if you continue running away like a common criminal, you negate the importance of the mission you undertook to get society's attention. You have their attention...don't throw that away..."

Kyle looked at him without speaking. He weighed what Alan had said. It made sense, too damn much sense. And why?

"You're full of crap. Therapist mumbo-jumbo..."

"Really? You know I am right."

"What I know is this: that in about an hour from now we will be on your boat, with a crew, and out of here on our way to Isla de Gato off the coast of Ecuador. We can regroup there. We won't be extradited and we will have a chance to see what is done in response to our message to this jaded and...and...forlorn society."

"Nice word...forlorn. And you are not?"

"I think that I am...enlightened."

"A savior?"

"Hah. Think you're cute, talk meister..."

"You make a plea as if you are a savior, I just wanted to..."

"Shut up and sit there without moving."

"Or?"

"Or I will shoot you right between the eyes. If you think that this is all a joke then I can't help you."

The voluptuous and dynamic Mrs. Jenski had recovered quite quickly from the initial shock of being woken lying naked in her neighbor's bed and had gathered her senses and was assessing the situation. She was not to be easily contained; there was too much pepper in her persona for that. She already sensed that she might be on the threshold to gaining the upper hand. Her see-through wrap made that possible and she knew the power of its revelation. Men were so easily titillated. The sight of her recently naked body, mildly sheltered by the nylon scrim, fully diverted the attention of the three jerks that were leering at her. She graded the three men who were with her in the living area as ninnies of the first order and began figuring how she would deal with them. She had deliberately slipped on the sheer cover that ordinarily would have been used at poolside over a bathing suit. It was something she had kept at Alan's and that she had used that night to excite him. Now these men were excited by the same vision.

She used the fact that the three men were able to see her zaftig body and more than ample breasts as a way of cornering their total focus as she tried to decide what she could possibly do. If she could get hold of one of their guns, she would kill all three of them. She was sure of it. Alan didn't know, and certainly none of the others would have guessed, that this woman was experienced with handguns. In fact, all kinds of guns. She had grown up on a ranch in Wyoming and had handled pistols and rifles since she was a kid. She was also a woman with few fears and that, too, came from ranch living. These ninnies did not seem like much of a threat to her. But they had the guns and she did not. She fully understood what that meant even if they were inept.

She let the top of the coverlet slip open to reveal her nipples. It was a way of keeping their attention from wavering. Ellis succumbed first. He sat next to her and put his left foot on the antique coffee table. He had stuck his pistol in his belt. He put his arm around Mrs. Jenski without touching her and with an air of familiarity. Two old friends chatting about old times. Just harmless bantering.

"You're very pretty." It was a tentative, quite mundane line that he said softly.

"Yes, I know," Mrs. Jenski replied.

She let her hand drift to his thigh and he was snagged like a game fish on a light line. But he didn't resist as the fish would have, he merely lost his sense of danger. She pulled the pistol from his belt and shot him in the face with one motion and turned quickly and shot Ted in the chest. He flopped back against the wall and reached for his pistol when she fired a second time. The second shot tore into his gut just below the ribcage. He was already dead as he slid down the wall to a heap. Mark dodged towards the kitchen as she fired twice at him. He hit the floor, skidded on the tile, and was out of her view.

Kyle was startled by the shots, but reacted quickly and stepped from the study. Her head turned toward him and for a splintered fraction of time they looked at each other with the same primal intensity. He shot Mrs. Jenski once in the chest and she fell back on the sofa, her body shuddering in death. He walked towards her and shot her a second time in the chest.

Alan Simmons never moved from where he was sitting. He tucked his head and pulled himself into a somewhat fetal position, still on the chair.

"Stay there," Kyle ordered. He went to the kitchen and stood next to the prone body of Mark. "You all right?"

"I'm hit. I can feel it…"

"Where?"

"I think my side…my…my butt…my hip."

He became unconscious. The bullet had penetrated just below the left buttock, slammed into the femur, and sliced the main artery. Mark was bleeding to death internally and did not know it.

Kyle walked back to Alan.

"So much for the neighbor lady. But your neighbors will be calling the police. Get some clothes in a bag, get all of the cash you have stashed, and let's get on the boat."

"What?"

"Clothes, money. Get moving."

"I don't know what you mean…money…"

"Come on. I know you have cash hidden here. Let's go. Our crew will get here soon and we're on our way. You've always talked to me about facing reality, Doc, and that's what I'm doing. The reality is that I need to leave, pronto."

Ty Roman had decided to head for the *Paprika* early. He figured this Dixon character wouldn't mind if he were there before the time he said. Be at the boat by two in the morning, Dixon had firmly requested. He had paid Ty plenty to get the boat ready and fueled without Simmons' knowledge. After all, Simmons left the care and handling up to Roman.

Two men stepped from the shadows as he walked along the dock to the boat. He choked as he tried to swallow his surprise and fear. He was caught off guard and he stumbled with the two duffle bags he carried. Each man was dressed in dark clothes and wore an armored vest. They carried M-16s that were now pointed at him.

"FBI. Your name?" The taller man asked in a whisper.

"Roman. What's wrong?"

"Keep your voice down. Where are you going?"

"That boat down the way there…the *Paprika*…Dr. Simmons' boat." He whispered the words as if he were revealing a bit of gossip.

"Why at this hour?"

"This guy hired me to get the boat ready. Called me yesterday and said to be here at two. Skipper the boat. Take him and Doc Simmons to South America. Said when he hired me it was a surprise for Doc. Don't tell him. It's a vacation he needs. That's what he said. I figured leaving at night like this that maybe they had some kind of scheme they were working on, but hell…"

"Don't you watch the news?"

"Naw, it's all bad. I watch boxing sometimes and a little baseball, but…"

"And the name Kyle Dixon doesn't mean anything to you?"

"Well, he's the guy that…"

"I know, but beyond hiring you. You haven't heard about him on TV or the radio?"

"I don't think so…"

"Damn," the agent exhaled. He looked at the other agent and shook his head in disbelief.

"Can you tell from here if Simmons and the others are on the boat?" It was the shorter agent who asked.

"No lights on. I'd say no, it doesn't look like it. Like I said, I'm early. He said by two and I figured no later than two so I came on."

"How'd you get here?"

"Walked. I live on a guy's boat in the marina. We have an arrangement. When he brings one of his girl friends, I get lost for awhile. They never stay overnight. He doesn't like them to stay overnight."

"Convenient."

"Yeah, it is. All my work's in the marina anyway so the setup suits me okay."

The short agent signaled to someone back in the shadows and a young woman approached. She was not wearing an armored vest and was dressed in slacks and a blazer.

"Take Mr. Roman back to the rendezvous point up the street and get his ID and statement."

She nodded and led Ty Roman away, still toting his bags, and wondering what the hell he had gotten himself into with this Dixon guy.

When they turned over Roman, the two agents moved towards the house where Lyle and Simmons were engaged. These men and several women were set in motion by a call from Toby Grant in LA. The Orange County Sheriff's office and the Newport Beach police had both also been notified and had officers headed for the scene very quickly, but they were ordered to hold back and wait for the FBI. Grant had waited with his call to both of those agencies because he was worried they might act too soon. This was an FBI operation; they would be in the lead. Notifying the Sheriff and the Newport Beach police was good protocol and they could provide backup. He figured they were best at directing traffic, anyway.

More agents in SWAT gear were moving into position. The house was flanked on either side by houses similar in design with limited access between them. It was nearly a zero lot line type of arrangement. This presented severe logistical problems. First of all, for all practical purposes, they could not readily surround Simmons' house. Secondly, if shots were fired, there was the potential to have stray bullets go into the flanking houses and hit innocent victims.

Arnold Moore was in the house next door that was one of the problems. He watched in the dark as the stealth moves the agents made brought them up the street through the shadows, around bushes, and close in on his house. He had not turned on any lights and had used his cell phone to call police when we had heard the shots. He did not expect such a quick response. He could tell they were not the Newport Beach police. Arnold was a semi-retired trial lawyer and knew what he should see. This was not the police; they looked more like FBI. Sure, the FBI, but what the hell were they doing here and what happened in Simmons' house? He moved to another window for a better vantage point as he eyed the calculated moves. There must be a dozen or more. He went to the family room in the rear and spotted others edging ahead in the shadows.

Bill Guthrie of the Santa Ana FBI office stood at the far corner of the front of Arnold Moore's house away from the Simmons house. He stood in the shadows watching agents work their way into place, much like Arnold was doing inside. Guthrie headed the Orange County Joint Terrorism Task Force spearheaded by the FBI. The JTTF had been on alert since Kyle had begun his bombing rampage and it did not take long to get agents from Long Beach, Orange County, West Covina, and other areas mobilized to this location. Toby Grant's phone call triggered a pre-set plan of action and Guthrie was watching the result. Slowly, Alan Simmons' house was covered as best they could by a large, heavily armed contingent of FBI agents. In the background were dozens of state, local, and county officers.

32.

"Goddamnit, there's blood everywhere. Look at this. Look what you've done."

Alan Simmons stood in his living room surveying an ugly sight. Mrs. Jenski dead, had flopped back onto the lap of dead Ellis. A torrent of blood poured from her chest that had been torn apart by the bullets from Kyle's gun. Her blood seeped into the fabric of Ellis' jeans, while the excess dripped down his legs onto the carpet. His blood had run onto the back cushions of the sofa, his head resting there as if he were taking a nap. His face was barely recognizable, smashed as it was from Mrs. Jenski's retaliation. A streak of blood smeared its way down the near wall to Ted's crumpled body. He had bled an odd pattern of dark crimson onto the champagne-colored carpet. A wide stripe of blood followed Mark's skid to a stop on the kitchen floor and a pool of blood by his thigh revealed that he would not last long without medical help.

"Why did you shoot her?"

Simmons was incensed, now partially recovered from the initial shock of what had just occurred. His face blushed with his rage, and yet he caught himself, collected his thoughts, wanting to regain control of the situation. He had no way of knowing that the phone call he ignored while he was having sex with Mrs. Jenski could have spared him the ugly predicament in which he was now enmeshed.

"Simple. She would have killed me. She was damn good with a pistol. Did you know she could shoot like that?"

Simmons ignored the question.

"You did this. Not willing to use reason, not willing to accept a meaningful course of action. Their blood, the others, all of the blood of your escapade to gain attention has culminated in this. Pools of blood ruining my house..."

"What matters is if we get people to understand," Kyle said, "to acknowledge what they need, that it is precious, that it must be respected and cared for, and that their very day-to-day existence is fragile at best unless steps are taken to preserve what we have."

"What?" Simmons was stunned with what he just heard.

"What do you mean 'what'?"

"I mean you are not making any sense. You have destroyed, you have hurt people, people have died, Southern California is in knots, people are struggling, can't go to work, and you have accomplished nothing but misery for millions."

Kyle stared at him.

"It's all come down to this…right here," Simmons yelled at him. "Three dead people and another ready to die. This is it. All of your talk, all of your planning, comes down to this. And now what? Sail away to safety? I don't think so."

"Let's get on your boat. We've got a trip to take…"

"I'm not going anywhere…"

"You're going with me. You are a part of all of this with me. You knew what I was doing, what I was going to do, you were inside my mind. You were inside my psyche, probing and prying, poking and peeking, a voyeur of my thoughts and ideas and reasons. You had a hand in all of this, at my side, in my head, and sympathetic to my goals. You are a part of this and you have to leave with me. Let's get on the boat. There isn't time now to pack or worry about anything else there is only time enough to board and get our captain to take us away from this…"

"What captain?"

"Why, Ty Roman, of course. I've hired him to take us to Ecuador…"

"He can't do that by himself…"

"He'll have to, because that is the condition of things..."

"Look, I know you need me. I know that is my position in your life. But it is time for you to face the inevitable...you cannot escape this..."

"I will...we will..."

"You will not. It is time for reconciliation, time to admit you are stalemated with society in Southern California, and time for you to meet with the authorities to present your case. It is time and I can help you. I can provide you with the guidance, counseling, and emotional protection that you will need to affect your reconciliation and to foster understanding and acceptance of who you are and what you stand for."

Kyle stared at him.

"To run and hide is to say, 'I was wrong and I need to be punished when you catch me...if you catch me'. To run is to admit defeat at the hands of the system you feel needs to change. To run is to deny the value of what you have worked for. To stay and deal with the authorities is the high ground, the superior position in a fundamental argument that you pose for society, and the ultimate message to the violators of the principles you feel are being trampled. To stay is to ultimately win out. It is the victory you want. Running away removes victory; staying and dealing with the authorities trumps any nay-sayers and detractors."

Kyle slumped against the refrigerator. His pistol banged on the metal door as he let his arm drop limply in a gesture Simmons had difficulty fully understanding, yet a result he was trying to achieve.

"I wanted us to go to Ecuador. Now, I don't know. You're so full of shit I should shoot you. But maybe you're right. I don't think so, but maybe. Let's get on the boat. We can talk more about it there...get away from all this blood..."

"Kyle Dixon," the voice of Bill Guthrie boomed on the bullhorn. "This is the FBI. The house is surrounded. You cannot escape. Come out with your hands up and surrender. This can be accomplished peacefully and no one gets hurt."

The glare of high-powered lights darted in the windows like the morning sun. More than a dozen of them were aimed at the house. There was nowhere to run, there was nowhere to hide.

Guthrie had no idea of the body count inside. His agents were ready, there was plenty of backup, and EMS was on the way. The stage was set and lighted. Other big shots in the FBI, ATF, Homeland Security, the Governor, mayors, other politicians, and those who wanted their name connected with this arrest were now racing to Newport Beach. The media frenzy that was building was akin to a large swarm of attacking Piranha. Butch and Cathy got to the first police barricade just as the bullhorn command sounded for Kyle.

"Any money on whether he'll be taken alive?" Butch asked Cathy as they got out of the car.

"I wouldn't even want to guess…"

"Not with a bang, but a whimper," Butch said.

"What does that mean?"

"Never mind, I'm just waxing poetic."

As they approached the yellow tape that was strung across the street, a Newport Beach policeman barked at them.

"You reporters?"

"No, we're not."

Butch showed his identification and explained who he and Cathy were and what they were doing and that they had just come from being with FBI agent Grant in Santa Monica. It made little impression on the officer.

"Can't cross the line," he said impassively.

"Who is in charge?" Butch asked.

"FBI guy…Guthrie…this is an FBI operation. They don't want anyone mucking it up."

Butch did not respond and took Cathy by the arm and ushered her away from the officer behind the crowd which was quickly gathering.

"Follow me," Butch directed, "we'll do an end run."

He moved by the crowd, between two houses, and reached the rear where he could see the docks and line up of big boats. No cordon had been set up yet. With Cathy at his heels, he worked his way from house to house until he could see men in protective gear and rifles at the house next door to Simmons'.

"Who the hell are you?" a voice from the shadows demanded with a hoarse stage whisper.

"Greiner, working for Grant in LA, looking for Guthrie."

"Through there. He's up front."

Butch and Cathy moved between the houses until he reached the corner of Arnold Moore's house. The man with the bullhorn was crouched down near Arnold's front stoop. They got to Guthrie without being stopped.

"Butch Greiner. I'm the detective who has been after Kyle Dixon. This is Cathy Logan from Gladstone. We just came from Toby Grant in LA. Maybe we can help."

Guthrie looked shocked by their sudden appearance behind him. "How?" he frowned, "and how did you get past the security…?"

"My cell phone has Dr. Simmons' number set for redial. Punch Send and maybe you can talk to him."

Guthrie took the phone without a word and pressed the Send button. As it made the connection, he scowled at Butch. After an eternity, someone answered the call.

When the phone rang, Simmons froze. He heard the first ring somewhere else in the house before the kitchen phone picked up the signal and chimed in with a different sounding tone. He could not move.

"It's for you." Simmons said the words in a slow, odd way; his tongue thick, his mouth dry with fear.

He still did not move, although he desperately wanted a drink. Anything. Vodka would be nice.

Kyle was still slumped against the refrigerator like a battered boxer ready to go down for the count. The phone rang several more times before he reacted. He beat the answering machine.

"What do you want?"

It was a question that emanated from his frustration with the glare and the demand to surrender. His escape thwarted, with no Plan B, his confusion was monumental. Who was interrupting his thoughts with a phone call at such a crucial time?

"I'd like you to come out the front door peacefully, your hands raised, and surrender so we don't have to come in after you. Let's not have any more bloodshed if we can help it. We need to do some talking…"

"Why do you want me?"

"Let's just say there are a few issues that need to be cleared up…"

"What do you think I did?"

"You are a person of interest to the FBI in regard to some suspicious explosions. We need to talk to you about that stuff, and there are some other folks who would also like to find out about some other problems."

Butch listened to Guthrie's end of the dialogue and marveled at the man's composure. It sounded like a childish conversation, but he knew it had its purpose. Guthrie was obviously an agent who had done this before. Nothing forceful, nothing intimidating, just a calm way of getting cooperation, a way to avoid a gun battle.

"Let me...let me think about it. Call us back in five minutes."

"Who is with you?"

The line was dead.

"He wants five minutes, so we'll give him five minutes."

He looked at his watch.

"Thanks," he said to Butch as he held up the cell phone. "This may save us some trouble."

The young woman who had taken away Ty Roman made her way to where they were positioned in front of Arnold's house. She was one of Guthrie's agents.

"Yeah, Baxter, what have you got?"

"Several reports were called in, sir, by neighbors telling of several shots fired in the Simmons house before we got here."

"Interesting. Wonder who shot whom?"

"I don't think he would shoot Simmons," Butch offered.

"Why not?"

"I just believe he's too emotionally tied to him. Simmons has been his therapist and counselor for years. I don't think he would do it. At least not yet. I think Simmons is the key to the decision Dixon makes. Now we find out how good Simmons is. Can he get Kyle to surrender? Can he survive? I think he's probably working on it."

Simmons was working on it.

"That was the police wasn't it? They want you to surrender."

"No, it was not the police, it was the FBI. And yes, they want me to surrender. I told them I wanted five minutes..."

"You said "us" when you spoke to them. You know this is not a simple decision, but I can help you like I said before. You need my protection."

Alan Simmons did not think that Kyle would shoot him, but he was not certain. After all, he had seen how calmly he shot Mrs. Jenski. Perhaps Kyle could shoot him as easily. Probably not, considering their bond which he believed was still intact. He relied on that aspect. He counted on the psychic connection between the two of them that had been reinforced over the many years of counseling. Kyle was hesitating because he needed assurance that Simmons would be as supportive as he claimed he would be.

"It will be an ordeal, but I will be there with you every step of the way. There is a wonderful attorney I know who can help you. He understands the many nuances of psychology and, thus, he will understand what you have been through and what you need. We will help you."

Kyle leaned against the counter without looking at Simmons.

"Fix me a drink."

Simmons dutifully reacted by pulling a bottle of vodka from the liquor cabinet and a can of tonic from the kitchen closet. He mixed the two hurriedly, guessing at what ratio he should use, spilling some of both on the counter top. He handed the sloppily made drink to Kyle.

Kyle gulped half of it before he responded.

"Thanks. This may be the last one I'll ever have."

"Nonsense…"

"He's dead," Kyle said, pointing to Mark. "Bled to death before we could get him any help. I didn't even say goodbye…"

"It was out of your hands," Simmons said in an inane way that he intended to keep Kyle calm.

Kyle looked away and went to the TV room moving through the display of death without regard to the bodies and blood. He clicked on the large television.

"Let's see what our so-called friends in the media have to say about this situation. Might be interesting."

There they were, in an exotic, mesmerizing scene from Newport Beach. How magnificent for the media to throw the spotlight of grim notoriety on this wealthy enclave. There was Simmons' house brightly lighted, a gleaming focus of hatred and derision. The media was in the process of piling on with all of the negative angles they could muster, pointing fingers, blaming, holding a variety of authorities responsible for the nightmare days southern California had been and was experiencing.

"…thanks to the work of private detective Greiner, Kyle Dixon has been run to ground here in this house in this luxury community by the bay in Newport Beach. Owned by prominent psychologist and well-know therapist, Dr. Alan Simmons, this house is where Kyle Dixon has finally been cornered. Our reporters on the scene tell us that this man Greiner is on the scene to help the FBI…" The television newscaster was in the studio with a split screen showing the well-lighted Simmons' house and the crowd of police and FBI agents holding their prey at bay.

The phone rang.

Guthrie waited for Dixon to answer. It had been exactly five minutes since they had spoken.

"We'll see," he said to Butch, covering the phone with his hand. "What do you think?"

"He'll stall," Butch said. "Simmons doesn't have him ripe yet."

"Oh yeah, really?"

"My guess." It was what Butch believed and he didn't care what Guthrie thought.

There was an answer and Guthrie removed his hand from the phone. He listened intently for several seconds before he reacted.

"No, no, that's not in the cards. I don't care, that's not where we're going."

Guthrie listened as Kyle yelled at him. Butch could hear Kyle yelling even though the phone was at Guthrie's ear.

Butch gave Guthrie a questioning look.

"He wants you to come inside. He wants to talk to you."

"Tell him I'm not here, tell him I'm in Santa Monica interviewing his mother…"

"He's watching television news. They say you're here."

"God damn," Butch exhaled, "the news people are so helpful."

The locusts had descended. Satellite trucks jammed the nearby streets, reporters of all kinds crowded the barricades, cameras fired away, and video crews were sending out a steady stream of visual sensationalism and meaningless images.

"In there?" Butch asked. He could hear Kyle screaming through the phone that Guthrie held at his side.

Guthrie put the phone back to his ear and listened to Kyle's rant.

"Talk to him," he said and handed the phone to Butch.

"You want me? Why?"

Butch listened as Kyle screamed at him for twenty or thirty seconds.

"We'll call back in two minutes to let you cool down, then maybe we can talk."

Butch snapped off the phone.

"What the hell are you doing?" Guthrie barked. "You trying to queer this thing?"

"Let him simmer down. He wants the upper hand that he's not going to get. He'll stew for a couple of minutes, then we'll talk. He's about ready to cave, but he wants to say something to me first."

"What can he say that makes any difference?" Cathy asked Butch. He just wants to shoot you. I think he's that angry about you."

Butch selected Simmons' number and punched Send. Dixon answered immediately.

"It's over, Kyle, time to listen to Dr. Simmons. Dr. Simmons has the right answer for you, I'm sure…

"I want to talk to you in here. I told the other guy that, I told you that. Now, get in here…"

"Whoops, whoops, hold on. You are not in charge. And I am not coming in. And I am never going to talk to you. You can walk out or be carried out…those are your two choices. Check with your Doctor right there beside you and figure out which one you want it to be. I'm going back to Santa Monica to make sure your mother is charged with aiding and abetting. Maybe I can even get her to testify against you. Your call, shithead, walk out with Dr. Simmons or get flipped onto a slab at the Orange County morgue."

As Butch talked, Guthrie was shaking his head and trying to get the phone from Butch. Butch clicked off the phone and handed it back to Guthrie.

"What the hell are you trying to do?" Guthrie screamed at Butch.

"Simplifying your life. Let him work it out with Simmons and he'll come out. He'll realize it's his best option. Simmons will make sure he understands that."

"Don't be so sure…"

"I'm not so sure. Nothing is sure. But I think it's the way this will go."

Kyle looked at Simmons in a questioning way that required an answer. The bodies were there, the blood had flowed, and he, too, could be a part of the carnage.

"What I have said is true," Simmons explained softly, as if he were detailing something to a child. "The time has come. We will go out and face the authorities and we will explain what needs to be explained and I will be at your side."

The snap catch of what Butch vowed about his mother gnawed at Kyle with potent results. His mother was an innocent, he would see to that.

"My mother is not part of what I have done…"

"That must be told correctly," Simmons said, realizing at once the trigger Butch had used. "Another reason why now is the time to step forward and be forthright and accept your position in this drama. You are the consummate protagonist and the moral high ground must be obtained."

Right," Kyle murmured, "right."

"Let's go…"

The phone rang.

Simmons answered it this time as Kyle leaned submissively against the kitchen table.

"We're coming out now. For God sake don't shoot us."

Guthrie blasted with the bullhorn for the agents to stay calm, hold their fire, and allow the fugitive to surrender. The front door opened and Alan Simmons and Kyle slowly, carefully, edged through the entryway onto the stoop and out on the front lawn. Agents were to them in seconds and Kyle had his arms wrenched behind his back, his wrists jammed together with a white plastic manacle strip, and read his rights. Dr. Simmons was escorted away by two other agents as Kyle screamed.

"He is with me, he must be with me, I need him to be with me…"

"Sorry," Guthrie snarled, "Dr. Simmons will be moving on without you."

Kyle yelled and fought, struggling against the restraint as several agents led him towards a waiting FBI SUV parked down the street by the barricade.

Then Kyle saw Butch and really went ballistic.

"You bastard, this is all your fault. You've helped stop progress, you've thwarted a movement that has to take place, you've…" He started to weep.

"Naw," Butch said, not getting closer to Kyle, "not me. It was this sweet little girl right here who figured it was you. You think you're smart, but she's smarter."

Kyle was speechless. He glared through his tears as he sobbed, but he was defeated. The agents moved him forward.

"I guess you were right," Guthrie offered grudgingly. "It doesn't matter. We got him. And he will fry."

"Maybe," Butch said, "maybe not."

"What do you mean?"

"What I mean is that Kyle Dixon is a fruitcake. As bright as he is, and he was is that, Kyle's brain was stretched to the limit of his ability to reason. He reasoned himself beyond reason. At least, how most of us reason out these things."

"An insanity plea?"

"I think it's in the cards. Look at him with your guys…crying like a baby. I'm not sure he thinks he's done anything wrong. You, Mr. Establishment, are in the wrong."

Guthrie shook his head, started to walk away, and turned to face Butch and Cathy.

"Look…thanks for your help."

"You're welcome. You guys need all the help you can get."

"I know," Guthrie smiled, and turned away.

Alan Simmons house was secured as a crime site, the forensic team had already moved in, and the media crushed around trying to find the best stories. Butch and Cathy were hounded by reporters who got nothing from Guthrie or anyone else in the FBI.

"Statement," someone yelled to Butch. TV cameras were in action, microphones shoved at his face.

Butch pushed the closest of the microphones back from him and surveyed the mass of media folks who had pressed near almost as hyenas to a carcass.

"The most that can be said is that Kyle Dixon is in custody. Anything else needs to come from the authorities at a later time."

"Mr. Greiner how did you know that Dixon was…"

"My associate and I will be glad to grant interviews after the officials in this case have made a formal announcement. That's all we can say right now."

Butch took Cathy's arm and pushed through the crowd of reporters and TV news people until they got to their car. They were bombarded with questions the entire way, but they were resolute in their silence. Butch headed the Lexus for LA and the morass of media madness slipped away behind them.

33.

"'Not with a bang, but a whimper.' That's what you said about Dixon...the way he was hauled away whining and crying. That's the way you said it would be. I'm not educated enough to get the reference. It was a reference?"

"Yes, and you're smart enough to know it's a reference. That separates you from the crowd."

"What crowd?"

The great mass of dullards you can point to out the window as we drive along."

"You snob."

"I'm an elitist, I admit it. But most of those folks don't know about T. S. Eliot."

"So, that's the reference?"

"Yes. From his poem, *The Hollow Men*. I thought the line was appropriate for Kyle Dixon...the way I thought he would end up."

"I guess so, but I didn't think he would let himself be taken alive. I thought there would be a shootout or he would blow himself up in one last dramatic statement. I guess he was too cowardly for that ending."

"No, I think we have the good doctor to thank for that not happening. Alan Simmons, clinical psychologist, licensed therapist, did his job well. He saved his own life, which was his first interest, and then he saved Kyle for us."

"For us?"

"John Q. Public. Our public wants some answers and now, Kyle will be able, if he is so inclined and I think he is, to give those answers in full."

"What's the Q stand for?"

"Quintessential. Meaning, the pure concentrated essence of our society. John Q. is the embodiment of the everyman, our collective alter ego, our fictional agent for asking the tough questions."

Cathy laughed.

"Don't believe me?"

"I do and you make it seem so simple."

"Well, that's my job."

"How do you think Kyle will be executed?

"Probably by lethal injection like Timothy McVeigh

"Yikes."

"You know…Kyle did not really enlighten the public about the environment even though that's what he claimed was his goal. But he did reveal how fragile our water and power infrastructure is and how dependent we are on them. Southern California is going to suffer for awhile."

"The environment is important," she said absently through fatigue-sodden cognizance, "we've got to pay attention to it."

"Without killing innocents in the process," Butch offered.

They became silent.

The rest of the drive back to LA had the pall of anticlimactic somberness to it as Butch and Cathy sorted out their feelings and searched for words they wanted to share with each other. Not altogether uncomfortable, but silent, and to some extent, melancholy. For each of them it was a question of: now what? What would happen to their new found intimate relationship and what would be the long-term prospects. For Cathy, it was a simple short-term matter; she wanted to get back to the corporate apartment Butch was using and make love again. That simple, that easy.

For Butch, the next move was complex. Having nailed Kyle Dixon was relatively easy in his mind, deciding what would happen between he and Cathy was much more difficult. There was the tantalizing lure of this young woman. There was this confrontation within himself in order to resolve his feelings about the quick, seemingly effortless way they ended up in bed together. He had not thought that could ever have been possible again. Time and space were the determiners of how many decisions are made. This was one of the instances where those two issues conflicted with the practical and the potentially desired. Where he lived and worked and where she lived and worked were compound confounding elements. The time distance apart in their ages was the other. One was relatively easy to overcome, the other was more difficult to resolve.

Butch guessed that he was too old for such an emotional consequence to hustle him along the way it had and he wrestled with that. Yes, Cathy was an emotional consequence. At least for him, she was. These last few days the focus had been on hunting down and capturing Kyle Dixon. There had been little time to think about and explore the possibilities of a relationship with this lovely young woman who had made it so easy for lovemaking. Lovemaking: something that had been missing for him, an activity, an aspect that had not presented itself since his wife had died. It was back, it seemed normal, and it was delicious.

On the Santa Monica Freeway through central LA, there seemed to be the normal blaze of street lights and advertising signs, the lighted apartments and houses. That is until they reached the Fairfax area. Here, they moved through a zone of darkness for a couple of minutes and then lights reappeared. As they moved through the cloverleaf conjunction with the San Diego Freeway they could see that west LA and Santa Monica were still largely unlighted. Emergency generators and batteries helped somewhat, but the area was mainly without power.

When they returned to the apartment building where Butch was staying, the garage security gate was open. They parked and went up the stairs. The elevator was useless. Backup batteries in the lobby and hallways were already beginning to fail, their weak yellow glow a testimony to the problem. Once in the apartment, Butch pulled out his small flashlight and flicked it on.

Cathy followed him to the bedroom and began taking off her clothes.

"Get undressed," she ordered, "we're off duty…as of now."

He was caught within her emotions in a sensual, romantic, and physically abandoned set of passion. His emotions were, on the other hand, twisted and distorted so that he could hardly recognize them. The passion was wonderful, no doubt about that, but somehow, in some way, without having resolved in his mind the issues with this young woman, he felt he could not get completely immersed in what was taking place. Her lips, her tongue, and her hands changed his fluttery perspective quickly. He became involved. Completely.

In the sweaty aftermath of their sexual ballet, Butch lay exhausted and spent, naked and uncovered next to Cathy as she drifted along in a fitful sleep. He was not tormented, he knew that was ridiculous, but he still was conflicted. This physical stuff with her was glorious. Where would all of this lead and how could he tell her of what was whirling around in his head?

Sirens could be heard in the distance. They had been sounding periodically ever since they had returned to the apartment. Butch had opened the windows to the night air, a night that was rapidly coming to a close. Now, as he watched, the first faint slits of daylight appeared in the northeast. It was still dark in the city and the sirens continued. All of the sounds, what he could barely see, and the room around him became a blur. And he was deeply, soundly asleep.

Cathy's cell phone ring startled them both awake. Butch looked at his watch and it read six.

"I don't know where the hell it is," she fumbled in the semi-darkness of morning light.

"The floor over there," Butch pointed.

"Damn." She was entangled in the sheet and fell to the floor. She crawled to where Butch pointed. "On my belt…"

By the time she found her slacks, tossed and turned them until she got to the cell phone holder, the ring tone had stopped. She punched buttons to retrieve the call.

"Dawson?" She looked at Butch quizzically with cocked head as if to ask, "Why is he calling me at this hour?"

Butch shrugged.

She punched Send and waited. A voice came on.

"Yes sir." Her answer was curt and official. Whoever was on the other end was a big shot.

She started to cry even before she punched off the phone. She sobbed and clutched Butch and they fell back together on the floor. She shook from sadness and pain. He held her and waited for her to calm down and get her composure.

"What?" Butch asked softly. "Or should I ask who?"

"Chet." It was all she could say and continued sobbing quietly.

"What about Chet?"

She could not answer right then.

"He's dead?"

She nodded.

Butch held her and eventually, ten minutes or so, she stopped sobbing, and was able to speak.

"It was Spence Dawson. He wants me to meet the plane at the Santa Monica Airport. They're bringing him back on a private jet. It lands in less than two hours."

"Where's Donna?"

"She's back east with family. She was visiting while Chet was gone. Butch, she said good-bye to him a few days ago and now…and now she never had a chance to talk to him again."

She started to cry, tears flooding from eyes that should not have any tears left.

"She's been around this business for a long time. She knew about the risk. She knew she might never see him alive again."

"I don't think that makes it any easier…does it?"

"I suppose not."

Butch thought back to his loss and wondered how Donna would react. She was a capable woman, strong, resilient, and once a CIA operative with a successful career in her own right.

"I'm going to shower," Cathy said in a matter-of-fact way which contrasted with her grief just moments before.

In her mind she was back on the job; she had cried enough, it was time to get going.

"Right," Butch answered, "me too."

They showered together, but it was more practical than romantic, a way to save time. They still touched each other lovingly and with some enjoyment even though they were distracted. They dressed and headed for the Santa Monica Airport. The ride was a grim procedure, facing the inevitable. It was also a matter of maintaining patience since they were slowed at main intersections where the traffic lights were inoperable and re-routed by traffic control at various points where work crews or emergency vehicles blocked streets. Auto accident injuries, heart attack victims, seniors with a variety of ailments, all needed assistance.

"Mr. Dawson sent a Gladstone jet for Donna," Cathy said as they inched their way along Centinela.

"That's good," Butch said. "Who's flying Chet in?"

"He didn't say specifically...just that 'they're flying him here.' He didn't tell me who "they" are and I didn't think to ask."

"What about a funeral home?"

"Mr. Dawson is taking care of that. He said to wait for them at the airport. Make sure they get the…"

"…the body," Butch finished.

"Yes."

They got to the fixed base operations at midfield of the airport twenty minutes before the time Cathy was told touchdown would occur. Rather than have to wait in the private service terminal, they were directed to one of the hangers Gladstone used for its two corporate jets. There was a waiting room just off the main hanger area where they were greeted by a service manager.

"You can have a seat in here," he said affably. If he knew the dead body of Chet Marwood was due to arrive, he didn't show it.

"No thanks," Butch said, "We want to wait in the hanger."

"Well, our policy is that…"

"I'm sure you have a policy. My friend…who also happens to be her boss, is arriving soon in a box. We'll wait for him by the tarmac. They'll be a hearse coming to get the box. Let us know when they get here."

"Yes sir," the man said.

As they stood by the large doorway looking out onto the tarmac, Cathy talked about Chet.

"He was such a mentor to me. He brought me into Gladstone, taught me stuff I needed to know, and gave me lots of responsibility. He trusted me. He trained me, tutored me, taught me tough ideas about protecting yourself, and he trusted me to make the right call. I think I learned something new every day that I was with him. I can't tell you how much I will miss him."

"I know what you mean. We went through some wild experiences together. He could be counted on…in many ways."

Cathy looked at him.

"Maybe some day I'll tell you about…some of it…"

"Not now?"

"No, not now."

The small jet glided in from the east and they watched it land and taxi toward them. It rolled into the hanger, stopped, and cut power. After a few moments, the rear door opened. Four men climbed down, looked around, acknowledged Butch and Cathy's presence, and three of them climbed back into the plane. The man who stayed on the ground came toward them. He was slightly taller than the others and older, and Cathy could tell that he knew Butch. But he did not greet Butch, in fact, ignored him, and spoke to her.

"You from Gladstone?"

"Yes…I am. Cathy Simon…"

"We've got Mr. Marwood's body…"

"I know…"

"We're turning him over to you. He's your responsibility."

He turned and walked back to the plane.

"Notice the plane has no numbers or any other identification on it," Butch said.

"I see that. Why?"

"Why do you think?"

"They don't want to be identified."

"Something like that."

You know him don't you?"

"That asshole? Yeah, I worked with him once or twice."

"He didn't even say hello or look at you."

"No, he'd like to pretend I don't exist."

"That bad?"

"That bad."

Slowly, but surely, a large wooden box was carried out of the plane, down the steps, brought near where Butch and Cathy stood, and placed on the cement floor. There was no paper work, nothing more said, and the men from the plane walked out of the hanger to a waiting limo.

Cathy stared at the box, a crate, really. Hands on hips she walked around it and shook her head.

"Just like that. Sent home in a wooden box and dumped off at an airport. Nice ending for someone doing his job, representing his company in the line of duty for his country."

"What would make it better."

"This stinks."

"He's dead," Butch said, "that stinks."

"A casket would be nice…"

"Just be thankful we got him back," Butch said harshly.

"What do you mean…?"

"The alternative would be worse. Not getting his body back. Forever wondering. We don't always get the bodies back. Donna will be thankful, under the circumstances, to have the chance to properly bury him. To properly honor him."

"I guess you're right."

They waited. There were sounds of a jet taking off in the background.

"They've got power," Cathy noticed.

"Stand-by gen sets. Keeps them operating like the hospitals and some of the office buildings."

It was quiet and they waited. After a few minutes the service manager came into the hanger.

"The hearse is here," he announced. "I'm having one of my staff direct them around so they can take your friend…"

"Thanks," Butch said. "This is the box I mentioned. Try not to say anything to reporters if they come around. We'd appreciate that."

"Mum's the word," the man said.

"Yeah, right," Butch replied under his breath, but Cathy heard him.

The service manager stood nearby waiting to see what was needed.

They all waited in awkward silence. Cathy's memory of Chet's serious face was distinct and vivid, as if he were there explaining something to her. He was there, all right, in a plain wooden box, and he would not be speaking to anyone.

Chet Marwood had almost reached fifty, ruggedly built, and still in great physical shape. A former college linebacker for Appalachian State, at six feet four and two hundred and fifty pounds he was still agile and athletic, unruffled by any situation. He could, however, be highly frustrated by Gladstone administrative bureaucracy and the corporate BS that came with his vice president's job. He knew his stuff and did his job extremely well. Butch knew that Chet still had a sublimated sense that he wanted to hit a bad guy. A carry-over from his football days when it was so fun to hit someone and make it hurt. Butch tapped the box lightly with one toe, a gesture of respect, of acknowledging fond memories, and to relieve the sadness he felt.

After several minutes the hearse appeared and backed through the doors of the hanger until it was close to the box. A distinguished, gray-haired gentleman emerged from the passenger side and greeted Cathy. He had been told that he would be met by a young woman representing the company.

"I expect you are Miss Simon."

"Yes," Cathy sighed.

"Sorry to meet you under these circumstances, but I think we all understand that this is part of the cycle of life. It's good to accept the cycle of life. I'm Carl Wittenburg, our funeral home is in West Hollywood. I got the call from Mr. Dawson. We'll take care of everything, don't worry. We understand everyone's grief and we will make sure Mr. Marwood is specially taken care of."

He motioned to the hearse and three young men and the driver got out, and as Mr. Wittenburg opened the rear door, they lifted the box, and placed it inside the vehicle.

"I understand that Mrs. Marwood will be counseling with us when she arrives in Los Angeles, but I do appreciate your waiting for us and being responsible right now. Thank you."

The luxurious Lincoln hearse took Chet Marwood away unceremoniously. Tears were in Cathy's eyes again when she spoke to Butch.

"Mr. Dawson wants to meet with me this morning," she said ominously, as if she were reporting an impending hurricane. She sniffed.

"Let's go," Butch answered. "We'll get you to your place and your car, and you can have at it with Mr. Dawson. He probably wants you to take Chet's job."

"That's silly," she said and laughed. It was her first light moment of the day. A glimmer of relief from the sadness.

"Fifty bucks."

"You're on." She laughed again.

After he dropped off Cathy, Butch worked his way back to the apartment, changed into his running togs, and headed down the street to San Vicente. LA city crews and private contractors were hard at work clearing the remnants of destruction from the blast at Gretna Green. Three different sets of forensic teams were still on the scene trying to find every piece of evidence that could be located. He noted the clothing IDs: FBI, LAPD, and CHP. Each unit assigned to a specific area to scour, each unit diligently searching for whatever they could find.

Butch stayed in the center of the blocked off street until he was well west of the intersection and then shifted his running to the boulevard grass. He ran to Ocean Avenue, on Ocean to Alta, up Alta to 26th, 26th back to San Vicente, San Vicente back to his street and the apartment. Running made him feel better and he tried not to think. Not to think of how he felt about Chet's death, not to think about what the future might or might not hold in store for him with Cathy. He concentrated instead on Kyle Dixon.

Society would like to think of Kyle as an anomaly, Butch pondered, but he wasn't so sure that was true. He thought perhaps there were many more Kyle Dixon's sprinkled about and a multitude of sympathizers to boot. After all, Kyle had found cohorts to readily assist him with his cockeyed plan of destruction. Kyle probably rationalized it as something righteous and wonderful, but it was merely a plan of destruction and mayhem perpetrated on the people of southern California.

How many more madmen were waiting in the wings to follow suit? Kyle had established a new low for civil disobedience to make a point about some issue. Would others, could others, take his model further? Kyle was the poster boy for those who thought they knew better about things than the rest of society. He was smarter than everyone else and believed he had some innate right to decide what was best for the rest of us. He thought he could achieve some kind of enlightenment by making others suffer.

As Butch entered the apartment lobby he heard the grinding sound of the elevator. The power was restored to the building. The doors slid open and a man stepped out.

"Morning."

"Morning. When did this start working?"

"Just. A few minutes ago. I talked to a friend of mine who said the power might not stay on, but this building has it for right now. Have a nice day."

"Yeah, right, thanks," Butch said and went up to the apartment.

He flicked on the TV before he went through his ritual cool-down stretching regimen. Cathy was center screen, seeming larger than life, a star for the media, and an excellent spokeswoman for Gladstone.

"Was he a former employee of your firm, Ms. Simon?" The question came from some unknown member of the media.

"Yes, he was."

"How did you focus on Mr. Dixon?" another reporter fired at her.

"Well, we had some thefts from two of our training facilities, and having the information we had, we made a determination that the person we should be looking for was Kyle Dixon."

"Can you elaborate on that?" another threw at her.

"I believe there are a great many details that will eventually be revealed, but for right now I think that it is up to the FBI to provide information relating to this case. I am merely confirming that we were a part of the investigative process that led to the FBI's arrest of Mr. Dixon. Thank you."

Cathy exited the scene back into the Gladstone building and the newsroom cut away from the remote feed back to the studio.

"There you have that part of the story," the glib, pretty-boy newscaster said, "Cathy Simon, a security officer with Gladstone International giving a brief statement about Kyle Dixon, a former employee of Gladstone."

"And they were looking for him, Neal. Isn't that an interesting wrinkle to this breaking story?" Neal's on-air partner, Cheryl Gomez, was as glib as he was and somewhat disconnected to what was occurring. She was concentrating on being attractive. After all, it was LA, you never knew who might be watching.

Butch switched channels to a national news cable network to see if there might be something more about Kyle. There was: Kyle was in the Orange County Detention Center in Santa Ana and would be going in front of a Federal judge this afternoon. The legal proceedings were underway, already crunching forward in that restrained, yet relentless way that it usually did. Step by step, procedural debate by procedural debate, issue by issue, in the steady pursuit of justice.

The nattily dressed female reporter talking in front of the Detention Center explained what would happen next, told us that Kyle had an attorney, and that word from authorities was that there was a suicide watch posted for Mr. Dixon.

Butch flicked the TV black.

"God forbid he kills himself," Butch said out loud, "better that the government should take care of that job. Only when and if it gets done years will have gone by, there will be no restitution, and no solace for the victims. Justice will be done and justice is blind, very blind."

There were more messages on his cell phone that he had ever seen before and he did not recognize any of the numbers. He tried one of them.

"KTLA," the voice answered.

He canceled.

He tried another.

"City desk."

He canceled.

He tried another.

"Fox News."

He erased all of the numbers and punched in Cathy's. Lo and behold, she answered.

"Hi," she said. The tone was upbeat and she sounded more mature than when he last spoke to her.

"How you holding up?"

"Good, very good."

"I just saw you on TV. I didn't think I would be able to get through to you now that you're a media personality."

"I'm still me and I'm okay. Busy as hell…"

"How'd it go with Dawson?"

"Very well. I'll tell you all about it at dinner. Make a reservation someplace nice and pick me up about seven. Maybe Joie de Vivre on Montana, if they're open for business. You're a celebrity…let them know who you are and you can get us a table."

"Yeah, the press is after me. Fifty some messages on my cell phone. They had to work some to get my number."

"That's what I said, you're a celebrity. See you tonight."

She was gone to the ether and he missed not having her there with him. It was a new, odd feeling, strange in its impact on him. He turned off the cell phone and showered. When he had dressed, he used the apartment phone to make a reservation. The owner answered and was thrilled to have Butch and his lady friend be their guest this evening. Yes, they were operating. Yes, of course, they would have a very exclusive table where he could talk to his lover and not be bothered. Could they come in the rear door? Yes, of course, that would be smart to do. See you at seven-thirty.

When Cathy opened her apartment door, Butch was stunned with the gorgeous, radiant young woman who greeted him in a revealing cocktail dress that accentuated every positive aspect of her trim, athletic body. He stared.

"Do I look all right?" she asked. "You're staring at me in a funny way."

"No, no, you look great. It's just that I haven't seen you…ah…dressed up before."

"Is it better than naked?"

"Different, very different."

Butch parked in the alley behind Joie de Vivre. It was a tow away zone, but under the conditions everyone was operating, there would be no tow away. Butch could hear the sound of an electrical generating set running behind a fence and realized how Joie de Vivre was able to be open.

They went in the back door to the stares of the kitchen help and several of the waiters. Jeffrey Cousins, the owner met them at the door to the dining area. Video cameras had alerted him of their presence.

"Welcome to Joie de Vivre, we are delighted that such distinguished guests are with us tonight."

"Thanks," Butch said, "there might be a hassle with the press later on if they get a wiff we're here, but if that happens we'll get on the move. Here's my card. Send me the bill if that happens."

"No problem, Mr. Greiner. We'll take care of everything. I don't think the press will be a problem."

He showed them to a small table in a secluded section at the rear of the restaurant and they were seated.

"What can I get you to drink? Compliments of the house." He smiled at Butch. "You are a celebrity in case you did not know it."

"She told me." Butch nodded at Cathy.

"Vodka…rocks," Cathy ordered.

"Bohemia," Butch said. He wondered if they had it, but Cousins never flinched and went away to get their drinks.

Before Butch had a chance to ask Cathy about her day, she slid a crisp, new fifty dollar bill across the table to him. He chuckled, knowing full well the significance of the money.

"You were right," she said, "I underestimated myself."

"I did not."

"I know. Thank you."

Butch did not pick up the bill. She smiled at him. It was a new smile, one he had never seen before, but he knew what it meant. It was the smile of embarrassment, the smile that is forced, pushed from the inside to create an effect, pushed out to set the groundwork for saying something unpleasant, something she did not want to say, something she did not want to reveal, something she wished were not true.

Butch said nothing and just looked at her and her lips quivered and the smile faded away.

"You got Chet's job just like I said and just as Chet would have wanted. He trained you for this to happen."

"Yes. Mr. Dawson said I have done a terrific job and they want me to carry on."

"The way it should be."

"Not the way I thought things would work out…"

"What…?"

"They want you gone. Don't give interviews, don't talk to the press, just leave town. Tomorrow."

"Ah…okay, but why?"

"He didn't say why. It's the way Gladstone wants it. I do the interviews, I am their face, and…"

"…and you are their heroine," Butch smiled.

"Yes."

"Makes for good copy. Gladstone lady solves crime."

"I know this is sudden…"

"Not to worry, I know how these things work. Great, no problem." Butch smiled.

"There is a problem…"

"Us? It's the delicate question. Is that the problem?" His smile was gone.

"I think this is the place it ends."

"Our relationship…"

She didn't look back at him at first, but then she raised her head and gazed directly into his eyes.

"Sorry."

She slid an envelope toward him that contained a ticket for his flight back to Detroit. He knew what it was without opening it. Bingo! Double whammy. Fired from the job and given the brush off with one easy gesture.

"Send your invoice to me," Cathy said quietly, almost apologetically, but with that edge of professionalism that let him know she was comfortable with her new position.

Ah yes, written out of the scene as calmly as any needless character in a movie script. And he had agonized over how he would tell her their relationship could not continue. What a sap he was. The ending was written for him and the issue kept unemotional. If she cared that their relationship was over she did not reveal it at this point. The casual observer could never have guessed that a few hours earlier they were making love in naked ecstasy. So it goes.

"I will." He wasn't sure what else to say, maybe some monumental departing line that would stab her in the heart. He wasn't sure she had a heart. Perhaps. "Maybe our paths will cross again, sometime." It was the best he could do.

She did not respond verbally, but she smiled at him and cocked her head to one side and gave him a look as if to say, "I don't think so, but you can dream on."

He picked up the fifty dollar bill and the envelope and headed for the kitchen. Jeffrey waylaid him before he could get there.

"You're not staying? What is the matter? Is it something we did?"

"No, no, everything was fine and you were just great, but the lady just fired me and I don't think I want to stay. Give her the check for any expense you've got. She'll make it good."

Butch exited through the back door. He drove back to the apartment knowing full well she could get home without his help. She didn't want his help. Word had gotten out to the media that they were inside and the front of the restaurant was packed with reporters. Minutes later she held an impromptu news conference on the front sidewalk of Joie de Vivre. She was engaging, a media pixie that Gladstone wanted, and fully able to deal with the best that was thrown at her.

The power was off when he got back to the apartment. In the fading light of evening, Butch packed listlessly, half-heartedly, knowing full well that he was out of his element here. Southern California was complex and demanding. The strain of going to the super market around here was more than he wanted to endure, let alone dealing with the reporters and the rest of the press.

He called Donna and some friend of the family answered. Donna did not want to come to the phone. Butch offered his condolences for Chet, explained the connection he had with the man, and asked the friend to have Donna give him a call.

The power was on again when he got up and he watched the morning news as he dressed. There was Cathy explaining how she had worked to capture Kyle Dixon. She was standing next to Toby Grant and other officials of every stripe. She was outstanding, he conceded, a real face to have before the media. He was glad he did not have that chore.

Butch drove to LAX. He finally found a parking spot deep inside the garage across from Terminal Two. He pocketed the keys and figured he could mail them to Cathy with his invoice

As Butch's plane lifted off from LAX out over the Pacific, advancing into blue sky and away from the gray murkiness of smoggy LA and the fog-bound coastline, he relaxed for the first time since he had arrived. His relief was in place and he was headed home to sanity, normalcy, and verdant surroundings. Damn glad to be out of here.

What is it, he wondered, that I just simply can't stand certain cities, certain locales? Los Angeles is one of them. He tried not to think about Cathy, but that was nearly impossible. She was smart, sexy, fun, and gorgeous. She was an LA phenomenon and she was out of his life. Chet was gone without ever having another conversation with Butch, and Donna had escaped into the bosom of her family. It was best he was heading home. He didn't belong here.

Funny how things work out, Butch thought, but for other conditions, this city might have been my home. He was loathe to be circumspect about his life at this point. What is…is. Not with a bang, but a whimper, Butch said to himself and settled back for the flight to Detroit. At least Cathy got him a seat in first class.

Epilog

Butch was glad to be home and within ten days competed in a triathlon in Cincinnati. He won first place in his age group. This helped him feel somewhat better, but the shock of being summarily dismissed still grabbed at him. He kept track of the aftermath in California from news reports and an occasional E-mail from Cathy. She described in detail how she accompanied the Marwood family to Wisconsin in the Gladstone jet that carried Chet's body and how beautiful the funeral service was. She said she was sorry he was not there with them. Butch struggled with reconciling why he was not included, but let it go. He knew there would never be an adequate answer; evidently it was something he had once said or done that struck Donna the wrong way.

Southern California suffered for months from the practical impact of the destruction Kyle brought to the area. This included power and water problems, reconstruction of damaged infrastructure and buildings, and the suffering imposed on so many families by the loss of lives. But the effects would linger for years in terms of the many intangible aspects from what had occurred. In both a political and social perspective, there was grappling with responsibilities and resolutions for dealing with the ominous implications of vulnerability that Kyle's attacks starkly highlighted.

Kyle's mother, Doris Taylor Dixon Krause, had watched television news intently as the arrest, indictment, and prosecution of her son unfolded. She wanted desperately to visit him in jail and then in prison, but her health dictated otherwise. Still bed ridden in the hospital, she was panic stricken with the potentially awful possibilities for her son and for her. Sol Jacobs also watched. Neither of them, at that point, knew how many law suits would involve them and consume their lives for years. For Doris, maybe that was an adequate punishment for her support of her son's exploits. Each of them had their own lawyer and over a period of time, harassed and condemned, they went their separate ways. Sol Jacobs was hit by a sports car as he walked from the Santa Monica Farmers Market one day and died at the scene. His estate settled all claims relating to the use of his house by Kyle and his cohorts. Sol was not there to defend himself and assert that he had no knowledge of Kyle's plans. He also had no chance to explain that he thought Kyle was nuts.

Doris, on the other hand, was rightfully connected to Lyle and the mountain of law suits which ensued. She never fully recovered from the shooting and battled her antagonizers and plaintiff litigants as best she could. Still trying to defend her position, she suffered a massive stroke and was left in an almost vegetative state of coma and paralysis. She would live several weeks in this condition before eventually dying in her sleep.

Ellis Wilson's wife sued Doris and Kyle and Sol and Kyle's sister Kellie Rothstein and all of the holding companies and non-profits that were connected with these folks. Kevin Rothstein wrote her a check for a hundred thousand dollars and she signed the necessary papers and was never heard from again.

Following these suits was a conflagration of legal action from the public that proved to be an almost overwhelming matter for the local, state, and Federal courts, and the cases did not go away simply and easily. Lawyers and law firms would be working full time for many years as plaintiffs and defendants wrangled over the complex and unusual set of issues that arose from what had happened because of Kyle's bombings.

The deluge of litigation was highlighted by Myron Kallman who had lived across the street from the Brentwood Pumping Station. His suit named dozens of individuals, governmental organizations, and companies with a blanket approach that was sure to tag someone, some entity, with blame for what happened to him. Myron eventually died from his injuries before the case could get to court and his daughter, the executrix of his estate, carried on the battle.

Barry Walker never returned to his job with the LA Times. He moved to Jacksonville, Oregon, rented a small house, and started writing a book about his experience with Kyle. To this date it has not been published.

Four months after the bombings, an FBI task force raided a small truck farm outside of Yakima, Washington, and arrested Connie and Leon Herrons without much fuss. They cut a deal with Federal prosecutors and testified against Kyle. Connie spent minimal time in the Female Section of the Federal Correctional Institution at Tucson, Arizona. Leon spent three months longer in the Victorville, California, Federal facility. After Connie waited for him at her sister's in Pendleton, they moved near a friend of Leon's in Orting, Washington, where Leon worked odd jobs and Connie was again a waitress.

Alan Simmons sold his blood-splattered Newport Beach house at a terrific loss, which, as it turned out, did not matter much. He moved onto the *Paprika*, got dock space at a marina across the bay, and welcomed the new environment and renewed opportunity for meeting female neighbors. His notoriety put tremendous good and bad pressure on his practice, but the net-net result was an upswing in patient load at higher fees and a seven-figure publishing advance. He was, of course, part of Kyle's legal defense team and was therefore in front of the TV cameras as much as he could have possibly wished. High profile meant higher income. He loved it. He was with Kyle from the beginning of the legal process until the end and he reveled in his position.

Kyle Dixon suffered every indignity that the legal system could create for him, although that was not the intent of Federal prosecutors. His humiliation came merely from the circumstances in which he found himself and the way he thought and felt about them, and consequently reacted. He was able to see Alan Simmons on a regular basis. This contact helped to ease his angst and his overwhelming rage, although it did not lessen his never-ending flush of self-righteousness. The biggest blow, what made him bitter and frustrated to despair, was that he never again saw or talked to his mother. This was a loss he could not overcome and it broke his spirit and eventually rendered him nearly uncommunicative. The mental heath angle that Alan helped the defense team concoct for him was brushed aside by the court and he stood before a jury who heard the facts in a litany that directed their decision of guilt on the numerous charges Kyle faced. Change of venue was deemed appropriate, so the trial was held in the Federal Court in St. Louis. He was put to death by lethal injection in an anticlimactic resolution for the destruction and loss of life he caused. Cathy Simon was a witness to the execution as was Kyle's sister. They never spoke to each other.

Over time, Butch stopped getting E-mails from Cathy. He decided that was a good thing. He vowed to himself never to go to California again. He wondered if he could make it stick. He hoped so.

www.ingramcontent.com/pod-product-compliance
Ingram Content Group UK Ltd.
Pitfield, Milton Keynes, MK11 3LW, UK
UKHW021301180426
11947UKWH00015B/959